YOURS
FOREVER AFTER

BETH BOLDEN

Beth Bolden Books

www.bethbolden.com

beth@bethbolden.com

Publisher's Note: This is a work of fiction. Names, characters, places, and incidents are a product of the author's imagination. Locales and public names are sometimes used for atmospheric purposes. Any resemblance to actual people, living or dead, or to businesses, companies, events, institutions, or locales is completely coincidental.

Book Layout © 2022 Beth Bolden

Book Cover © 2020 Sleepy Fox Studio

The people in the images are models and should not be connected to the characters in the book. Any resemblance is incidental.

Ordering Information:

Quantity sales. Special discounts are available on quantity purchases by corporations, associations, and others. For details, contact Beth Bolden at the address above.

Yours, Forever After/ Beth Bolden. -- 2nd ed.

PART I

CHAPTER ONE

SHE CAME FOR HIM in the middle of the night.

Prince Graham of the kingdom of Ardglass woke suddenly, and despite being only eleven years old, knew something was not right.

The castle fortress of Tullamore bustled with noise during the days—servants, visitors, and diplomats from the thirteen clans that comprised Ardglass talking and laughing and drinking. Led always by his father, King Gideon. But during the nights? Tullamore quieted, only the occasional creak of wood and stone as the castle shifted with the occasional servants' preparations for the next day.

But tonight, sound vibrated in the walls, the rhythmic echo of booted feet wrapped to dull the noise, pounding in harmony with the fierce beating of Graham's heart. Something was definitely not right. Had the clans laid down an ultimatum that his father hadn't told him about? Graham knew they were unhappy with his advisor and the King's own increasingly dissolute and drunken ways. Sabrina, the King's advisor, was noted throughout the kingdom as a powerful and intelligent woman. But some whispered she was a witch and a sorceress and that her magics had enslaved the King until he did not know what he did or why. But Graham believed it wasn't entirely Sabrina's fault that chaos was rising in Ardglass. His father, who was the tenth of his line, had, at the beginning of his reign, been a strong and steadfast ruler, but as time had gone on, power had corrupted him. He now spent most of his days drinking and his nights with a revolving group of girls that seemingly materialized from thin air.

Graham had asked his tutor, Rhys, about these women, and Rhys had simply affixed a bland expression on his face and told Graham that with his mother long dead, his father was lonely and desired company.

Graham had not replied that, if his father was lonely, there were many in Tullamore he could pass the time with—namely his only son, and in addition, all the many clan representatives who had begun to arrive in larger and larger numbers. But Graham did not particularly care to spend time with his father lately, so he said nothing.

Tonight everything felt different, and his apathy over his father evaporated as Graham was gripped by the real fear that something terrible had happened while he'd been sleeping.

His door opened, a wedge of dull candlelight spilling into his tower room. Graham fumbled for the little dagger his father had gifted to him on his last name-day, but even he was not naive enough to believe it would make any difference against a broadsword.

"Graham." The voice of his tutor, Rhys, was harsh. "Graham, you must wake quickly."

The one person in Tullamore, and truly in all Ardglass, that Graham trusted was Rhys. He made sure he was fed and clothed and educated—both from texts and from the members of the guard. Often it felt like the only one in all of Tullamore who gave more than a passing thought to Graham was his tutor.

Graham climbed out of bed and stared at Rhys, who was illuminated by a single candle. His face was white and drawn, as if all the blood had leaked out of it.

"Quick," Rhys repeated, his voice frantic, "put your boots on, lad. Yes, good, you have your dagger." Rhys glanced behind him, as if he expected someone to suddenly emerge from the dark shadows. "There is no time to lose."

Graham did what he was told, and even grabbed his cloak from the chair by the desk, where he had carelessly tossed it earlier in the evening.

Rhys' expression as he looked at him was frozen, and it nearly stopped Graham's heart in his chest. Something indeed was wrong, and though he wished to ask what it was, the cold look on Rhys' face trapped Graham's words in his mouth.

"There is a rope outside your window," Rhys said. "You must use it to climb down. At the bottom is a horse, with several saddlebags of supplies. You must take it and ride as far away from here as you can."

He could not help it; Graham gaped at his tutor. "I must what," he repeated, panic lancing through him.

If it was even possible, Rhys' face grew even colder, until it looked to be carved from the marble that lined the walls of the great throne room of Tullamore.

"You must go, they will be here any minute, and . . ." Rhys paused, and suddenly, there was fear in his eyes. "I promise that if they catch you, you will not survive her."

Rhys had long been the only constant companion that Graham had had. Rhys' face came more easily to him than his dead mother's. He had always been there—firm and much enamored of enforcing discipline on Graham's behavior—but always there. Did he mean that Graham should leave without him?

"What about you?" The words tumbled out of Graham, even as he tried to hold them back. He did not want to go into the forest surrounding Tullamore at night. He did not want to leave. He especially did not want to leave without Rhys. His father surely would have frowned and chastised him for his lack of bravery, but at that moment, Graham simply didn't care.

Rhys bent down, his head level with Graham's own. "I must stay, my prince. I will delay them, if I can. But you must be very brave for me now, and go."

Swallowing back tears, Graham nodded. "When may I return?"

Solemnly, Rhys just shook his head, and Graham could not hold back his choked sob. "Why?" he asked plaintively.

"It is your blood she wants," Rhys said, "and he has finally agreed to give it to her."

Graham had an idea of who "she" was, but did not ask the identity of the man who had acquiesced. He did not ask, because deep down, he knew the truth, and he did not want to see the look on Rhys' face as he told Graham that his father had agreed to sacrifice him.

He wiped his eyes. Fear still clogged his throat and held his lungs in a vise, but Rhys would not lie to him. If he needed to go, he would do as he was told, and go.

Rhys reached out and laid a reassuring hand on his shoulder. "You are brave and strong and loyal," he said to Graham. "Someday, you will need to remember that."

Graham did not ask what he meant, just nodded, and then turned towards the window.

He fumbled for the latch, and after pushing the heavy leaded glass panel, it swung open. There, just as Rhys said, was the rope, dangling right in front of the open window.

But when he glanced back, Rhys was gone, the candlelight disappearing down the darkening hallway.

Taking a breath, Graham faced the window and the rope again. It was not so much different than the exercises that the guard had set for him. Of course those exercises had been only a few feet over the dust of Tullamore's training grounds, and now there were several stories between him and the ground below.

Not that different, he told himself as he sat on the ledge and gripped the rope carefully in his hands. It was too dark to see from where it came, but it seemed solid as Graham gave it a hard tug. Still, his heart pounded as he gripped it hard, and swung his body out the window.

For eleven, he was tall and, as his father had crowed about on more than one occasion, he had inherited the hardy, muscular build of the Ardglassian line. His palms slid a little as he positioned his feet against the hard stone of the tower, and he began to carefully shimmy down the rope.

There were more windows in the tower aglow than normal at night, and each time he passed one, Graham's breath caught in his chest. His dagger was tucked in his cloak, and he could not easily draw it to defend himself if one of the windows suddenly and unexpectedly swung open.

But all the windows remained closed, though more than once, Graham saw dark-cloaked shadows pass across them.

He reached the ground, and as Rhys had promised, the horse was saddled and waiting, tied up by its reins.

"Hello, boy," Graham whispered to the horse, who dipped his head, and let Graham rub its nose. He was just about to grip the pommel of the saddle and swing up to mount when a rustling noise stopped him in his tracks.

A tall woman with long dark waving hair and a single emerald set into her gold circlet emerged from the thicket of trees surrounding the tower. Graham mounted before she could stop him, but when he dug his heels into the side of the horse, nothing happened.

"My prince." The woman's voice was dark and rich, like the honeyed wine that had so enslaved his father recently. Graham did not believe that was a coincidence.

"Lady Sabrina," Graham said, his voice calm even though he did not feel calm. He had heard much talk about how difficult she was to have as a friend, nevermind an enemy, and even though Graham did not believe he could convince her to change her mind, it was wise to proceed with caution. "Please release my horse."

"Why?" She laughed melodiously. "So you can escape?"

Graham had trusted Rhys. He had not believed Rhys would lie to him, but hearing the Lady confirm his suspicions was painful. He swallowed hard. "Gideon, the King and my father, would not stand for this," Graham insisted, because if he was not mistaken, he had few choices left and one of them was to appeal to his royal blood.

But then he remembered, with a horrifying chill, what Rhys had told him. It is your blood she wants.

She laughed again. "Here he comes." She beckoned to the trees, where a cadre of guards emerged, led by his father on his great black war destrier. "He may tell you himself."

Graham did not want to listen to his father, but even as he dug his heels into the horse's side repeatedly, the horse remained still and unbothered, like Graham was not even on its back.

Some terrible enchantment, Graham thought, but did not know how to possibly break it.

If the situation had been slightly less dire, Graham would have dismounted, come to the King's side and begged to be spared. But despite the inactivity of his horse, Graham still knew the safest place for him to be was on its back. If somehow Sabrina's enchantment could be broken, he was a good rider, and he had a chance at escaping the guard.

But before he could phrase his request, Sabrina's face shifted, like water under glass, and suddenly she was terrible and unrelenting. "My king," she said to Gideon, even as his gaze barely shifted to her. He was either heavily in his drink, or ensorcelled by Sabrina's powers.

"What is the meaning of this?" Gideon asked, words slurring together. "Graham, you have left the safety of your room."

Graham was speechless, and for a split second, he was not sure who he should trust. Had Rhys betrayed him? Had he indeed been safe in his room? It hurt to believe it, but it hurt less than believing that his father had agreed to give him to Sabrina.

"Father, I . . ." Graham stuttered. He'd meant to ask for safe passage, but the words stuck in his suddenly uncooperative mouth. He did not know whether this was another dark trick of the sorceress' or if fear and anxiety had suddenly overcome him.

"Graham," Gideon said, "you will go with the Lady Sabrina, at once."

"Where will she be taking me?" At the same moment the words tumbled out, Graham felt the horse stir beneath him for the first time since Sabrina had come into the clearing. Was her spell lifting?

"That is none of your concern," Sabrina insisted. Her dark eyes grew somehow darker in her beautiful face, and it morphed again, frustration marking it, before her features smoothed out again.

Graham's heart leapt in his chest. Something was preventing her from continuing the enchantment, and whatever it was, it wouldn't last long. He needed to make a choice, once and for all.

"Father," Graham repeated. "Where is she taking me?"

Instead of answering, the King turned his horse away, his face fading into the shadow.

Graham felt sick to his stomach, but he couldn't waste even a second, because he now knew, unequivocally, that his father had betrayed him. He dug his heels hard and fast into the horse's sides, and held tight to the reins as the horse reared and took off. Luckily, the guard had not surrounded him, probably because they hadn't wanted to frighten him, but it gave him the necessary gap between Sabrina and the guards' horses to squeeze through. Graham leaned over the horse's neck and urged it faster and faster, dodging trees and upturned roots. He knew the forest around Tullamore like the back of his hand, and he used every bit of his knowledge to wind his way through the trees, jumping over a stream as he heard the pounding echo of the guard chasing him. Sabrina's voice carrying through the dark leaves, threatening and cursing and angry. If her true colors hadn't been exposed before, they were laid bare now. Graham had no doubt that if she got her hands on him, he would be immobilized and taken someplace where he'd never see the light of day again. He did not really understand why she wanted him or his blood so fiercely, but he did know she wouldn't risk him getting away again. He'd be locked up, and not even his princely status would save him.

Graham's heart pounded in rhythm with his horse's hooves as they galloped through the forest, towards the main gate and freedom. It was the middle of the night, and Graham was counting on the fact that Sabrina, despite all her magical power, could not have raised the guard at the gate so quickly, and the way through would be open.

More shouts sounded from behind, and he heard Sabrina yell, "He's headed for the gate."

Risking a look, Graham saw that two of the guard were chasing him, but their horses weren't bred for quickness or speed, as his clearly had been. They were loaded with a lot of fancy armor, worked with gold and brass, and glinting with silver, and with those ridiculous velvet tassels that his father had once found dashing. All that extra weight meant that they might be excellent riders, but they could not overtake Graham and his light, sure-footed horse.

"Good boy, faster, faster," Graham breathed out and the horse leapt ahead, the wind streaming through Graham's hair, his cloak billowing as they gained more speed. The horses behind may not have had a chance, but he would be a fool to think that Sabrina had made no precautions at the front gate. She couldn't have raised the guard, not so quickly, but she was a woman of unusually keen intelligence, and he would be stupid to underestimate her.

They made the final turn towards the gate, hooves skittering across the cobblestones as they raced through the village. The light was better here, and he could see signs of people stirring in their beds, awoken with the noises of the chase. Please don't let her have raised the guard at the keep, Graham prayed as they approached. They were good men—loyal and obedient—and they would take him with only a word from her, and he would have no chance of evading her capture.

But it was not the keep's guard that met him at the gate.

Sabrina stood in the middle of the archway, eyes closed, murmuring a long string of words, flames spitting from her fingertips. He might have kicked his horse's heaving sides and tried to make it past without stopping, but just as he approached, her eyes shot open. Instead of their normal darkness, they glowed bright gold.

"You will not escape me," she said, her voice unearthly, and echoing with the power flowing through her veins.

He pulled up abruptly on the reins and watched in horror as her long golden cloak fell away in flaming strips, and her body began to bulge and shift into something out of a nightmare.

Graham set a reassuring hand on his horse as it bucked and skittered away from the creature Sabrina had become— head like a lion, attached to an oversized body, with a long, whip-like tail. Heart in his throat, Graham shrank as he realized the end of the tail was actually a spitting serpent.

"A chimera," he whispered out loud, remembering all of Rhys' lessons on creatures that had long ago tormented Ardglass and its neighboring kingdoms. A chimera had not been seen in many, many hundreds of years, but Graham couldn't doubt what he saw in front of him. He did not know how he could possibly evade such a creature and make it through the gate, but he would not cower in the dark and let her corral him into captivity. He would face this thing head-on, as the Prince of Ardglass, or he would die trying.

Then it occurred to him. She wanted him alive. She needed something from him, from his blood, and though he did not know what it was, it might stop her from fully attacking him if he approached.

The chimera growled and flames spit from its jaws as it paced in front of the gate, its tail whipping back and forth rhythmically.

It was expecting its very presence to cow Graham, to push him back, but he could not let that happen. Whatever occurred, Graham knew he could not stay here. His fingers trembled on the reins, but he gripped them tightly, his knuckles glowing dull white in the graying darkness.

The horse underneath him seemed to understand his purpose, and even though it shied a little under his hands, clearly terrified of the chimera, Graham knew—the way he knew he couldn't stay—that it would follow any directions he gave it. This horse had been bred for the royalty of Ardglass, and it recognized the Crown Prince on its back, and would follow Graham unto death, if that was what Graham asked of it.

But Graham hoped, fear making the edges of his vision fuzzy, that neither of them would be dying tonight.

"With me," Graham whispered to his horse, and it sprang suddenly, moving forward like a ghost in the night, weaving and dodging the chimera's flickering, hissing tail, and its spouts of flame. It screeched, the sound grating and unholy, but somehow still feminine. Graham ducked as the serpent-tail lunged for him, narrowly missing his shoulder, its teeth clacking uselessly against the heavy wool of his cloak. He reached up, blindly slashing with his dagger, disorienting the tail, and before the lion could turn and sear Graham and his horse onto the paving stones, they were gone, racing off into the darkness outside the gate.

They rode for what felt like hours, even though there had been no sound behind them and no obvious pursuers. It seemed impossible that he could have escaped so easily, even though battling a chimera could hardly be called easy. Still, he rode on, despite his horse's increasingly panting sides. They rode deeper into the forest surrounding Tullamore, and then deeper still, until between the darkness and the strange territory, Graham did not know where they had gone. They were away; that was all that mattered in the moment.

Finally, abruptly, the horse slowed, and then veered to the right, and then stopped in front of a small, bubbling stream. Light was beginning to seep through the trees, and Graham supposed dawn was only a few minutes away.

Graham dismounted on wobbly legs, still feeling like he might vomit. Between his father's betrayal and then Sabrina's enchantments, he felt unmoored and lost—and not just because he had never been to this part of the woods before. He could not easily hide, not in Ardglass. He would almost certainly be recognized instantly as the Crown Prince, and easily captured by Sabrina. Perhaps, Graham thought moodily as he watched the horse dip its head to drink in the clear water, that was why he had gotten away. Because she knew it was only a matter of time before she or the guard caught up to him. After all, he was young, and he was alone.

Not for the first time, Graham wished that Rhys had been able to come with him, to guide him, to show him what he should do. To explain what had just occurred. Why did Sabrina want his blood?

He decided that her reasons did not matter—only her purpose, and that certainly seemed terrifying enough.

"What should I do?" he asked the forest, even though he knew quite well that the forest could not answer back.

Yet, it did.

"You will come with me," a deeply resonant voice answered. Graham jumped and nearly reached for his horse's reins, but it moved away, giving him a bored, lazy look as it continued to drink from the stream.

At first, the source of the voice was not immediately apparent, and then before Graham could get his bearings or decide to wade into the stream to capture his horse's reins, a bewildering mirage appeared between the trees.

Graham shouldn't have been so astonished. After all, just tonight, he'd been betrayed by his father, then chased by a sorceress turned chimera, and now he was in the deep woods and alone for the very first time in his life. A unicorn shouldn't have felt like such a surprise, but Graham stared openmouthed and wide-eyed as it picked its way through the underbrush both elegantly and snootily. A little like all those bits of pine needle and bark were not quite good enough for it to walk across.

The unicorn shimmered—there was no other way to describe the brilliant white shine of its coat, or its single, silvery horn. Its flowing mane and tail were so ethereally pure white, they nearly gleamed blue in the muted dawn light of the forest.

Graham blinked, and then blinked again. Each time, he expected the vision in front of him to pass. Maybe he had hit his head? Maybe the chimera's serpent-tail had gotten him after all and injected him with some form of hallucinatory poison. Otherwise, what he was seeing simply did not make sense. Unicorns had not been seen in Ardglass for hundreds of thousands of years, if they had ever even existed at all. They had long since passed from history into legends whispered over the fire and a good tankard of mead. Emphasis on the mead, as most rational and reasonable men did not believe they had ever even existed.

But the unicorn remained present, as it gracefully stepped towards Graham. Then, stopping in front of him, it unexpectedly—Graham knew if he ever looked that word up in the large, leather-bound dictionary housed in the library of Tullamore, there would be a description of this night inscribed as the definition of "unexpected"—bent one knee and bowed to him, its long white mane rippling in waves to the forest floor as its head tipped towards Graham.

"My prince," the unicorn said again, in that deep, sonorous voice. "I am at your command."

Rhys had been carefully preparing him for a distant future in which he would be King, but he had never covered what one should do in the event of a talking unicorn pledging itself to Graham.

"Um," he said, because words had failed—and were still —failing him.

The unicorn raised its head and affixed Graham with a stern look. "Your Highness," it said, the two words it uttered an undeniable reprimand.

Graham flushed, embarrassed and flustered, but still not at all sure how he should proceed.

"It is very nice to meet you," he finally said. "You can call me Graham."

The unicorn huffed in surprise. "I certainly will not," it said. "But you may call me Evrard, Your Highness."

"Evrard," Graham said, testing out the name. "I have never met a unicorn before."

Evrard's face turned haughty. "I am not just any unicorn," he said, "I am King of the Unicorns." His attention flicked suddenly to Graham's horse, who had lifted its head from the stream to observe the newcomer.

"Goodness, there is no need to stare," Evrard continued, directing his comments towards Graham's horse. "How rude."

"He's not being rude. He just got ridden half to death, saving my life." Graham felt somewhat duty-bound to defend the creature who had protected him, while bravely and selflessly facing off against a sorceress-turned-chimera. For all his formality, Graham had difficulty imagining Evrard throwing himself into a fight with such reckless abandon. He'd probably want to negotiate with the chimera first, and then find a pair of seconds, and then set off at fifty paces, and make some sort of ridiculous honor-bound production out of a fight.

"Excuse me, he did not save your life," Evrard corrected him. "He prevented your untimely death. I intend to save you. That is why I have come to Ardglass."

"I'm why you're here?" Graham questioned in awe. The King of the Unicorns had come to Ardglass for him?

"I told you that you should come with me, and you will. We shall journey to the Valley of the Lost Things, and you will be safe from the sorceress who intends to take over your father's kingdom and drain you of your innocent royal blood in order to further her own filthy life."

Graham stared at the unicorn, another shock invading a system that was already over-full of them. "That's why she wanted my blood?" He shuddered, imagining her treacherous face looming over him, a silver knife flashing in her delicate, graceful hands.

Evrard dipped his head, sorrow in his voice. "Your blood is valuable for the power it contains, Your Highness," he said. "You are of the royal house of Ardglass, historically known to possess powerful magic, and you are on the cusp of adulthood, yet still innocent. It is that which the Sorceress Sabrina wishes to utilize for a spell that will extend her own life. Immortality is a powerful motivation." Evrard hesitated, the first time since he had appeared that he did not seem fully certain of everything he said and did. "That is why I believe your father agreed. Power works viciously on a weak mind."

It was one thing to have witnessed his own father's betrayal; it was entirely another to hear Evrard speak of it in that careful, sympathetic voice. Graham's throat closed and he pushed back the angry, hurt tears and wiped his eyes with hard, quick movements. He did not want anyone to see, especially Evrard. Some pain felt too great to expose to the light, and there was nothing in the world Graham had seen that was as light as Evrard. He glowed. "He was weak," Graham agreed quietly.

Evrard's eyes stared deeply into Graham's own. "He was weak because she wished him to be weak. It was not entirely of his own making. She saw the seed in him, and she exploited it. It is one of her great talents."

"How do you know all this?" Graham questioned. Evrard seemed exceptionally well-informed considering he was a unicorn. A royal and talkative unicorn, but still, a unicorn nonetheless.

"I was called here because, in the world of magic, there must be balance," Evrard said.

"Who called you here?"

"I think you know," Evrard offered. "He who was always loyal to you, and was loyal to you to the very last breath he took this night."

It was just as Graham had feared. Rhys must be dead, but his actions had also prevented Sabrina from obtaining what she wanted most—him. And even though he could not accompany him, Rhys had made sure that he was not alone. Somehow, he had summoned Evrard to help him.

Graham felt undone. Too many emotions he could not control swirled inside him like a storm cloud. Abruptly he stomped away, choosing a fallen log some distance away and sitting down upon it heavily. He had been afraid that Evrard would follow him, but he did not, and let the Prince sit there in quiet contemplation for several minutes.

The tears he'd barely held back before began to fall. He had lost his home, his loyal tutor, his safety, and his father in one single moment. Nothing would ever be the same again. Never again would he spar in the courtyard of Tullamore, or sneak honey cakes from its kitchens. Never again would his father swat at him good-naturedly when Graham made an impertinent remark. Rhys would never again tuck him into sleep or set for him too many mathematical problems or texts to be read. Life as he had known it, Graham thought dully, was over. He could not go riding back to the keep and pretend that what he had seen and heard had not occurred, even though there was nothing he wanted more.

There was nothing left to be done except move forward, one foot in front of the other.

He stood and walked back over to where Evrard and his other horse stood. "When shall we leave?" Graham asked.

Evrard gave a sharp, decisive nod. "It becomes light. We will leave immediately. Fetch the supplies and I will deign to carry them." Graham went over to his other horse, and then hesitated, his hands on the saddlebags.

"But what about this horse?" Graham asked.

"He will find his way back to the keep eventually," Evrard said dismissively.

Graham had always been a quiet boy, an observer more than an active participant, which was probably because he had grown up in a castle full of adults who usually did not wish to be bothered by a child or a child's questions. He'd long since learned to watch, and to form conclusions based on his observations. Even though he had spent less than an hour with Evrard, he could already tell that the unicorn was a snob who looked down on any creatures that could not speak as he could.

Clearly, Graham's horse had been relegated to this view by Evrard, no matter its bravery or tenacity in helping Graham ride to safety.

Rhys had always told Graham that loyalty was the most important currency he could gain as a king. And even though now, Graham had no reason to believe that he ever would be a king, those lessons still felt important.

"No," Graham said firmly. "He will come with us."

"That creature cannot speak," Evrard said, cruelty edging his voice. "Why would we need it?"

Graham shot the unicorn a chastising look not unlike the one Evrard had given him earlier. He was also a very quick learner. "We will not leave it behind because it has earned the right to come with us," he said.

"Well, I suppose we can hook his reins to your person, and he can carry the supplies. He may be useful, yet," Evrard said with resignation.

The horse gave a little whinny of agreement, and turned kind, warm eyes onto Graham, as if it knew what Graham's intervention had saved him from.

"I pay my debts," Graham murmured to the horse, and went to make sure all the saddlebags were properly secure, before looping the reins across his arm and leading the horse out of the stream and towards Evrard.

"What about the saddle and the bridle?" Graham asked, when he stopped next to Evrard. "How shall I ride without them?"

The look on Evrard's face was worth a million gold pieces. "You shall ride me like men have always ridden unicorns. Carefully and with respect," Evrard said in a haughty tone. "You may use my mane, carefully, as means to keep yourself secure."

To Graham, it seemed the utmost disrespect for him to even touch that pure white hair that cascaded from Evrard's brow, but in his hands it felt much as any regular horsehair did. He tied the reins to his cloak, and the horse trotted carefully behind as Evrard began to pick his way through the forest. There was no trail, which was a blessing, because on a trail there might be other people, and a unicorn would surely raise questions that Graham couldn't answer.

As they traveled a direction that Evrard seemed very certain of, Graham asked additional questions.

"Where are you from?"

"A place very far from here," Evrard answered patiently.

"What's it called?"

Rhys had always told Graham that one day his curiosity might get him into trouble, and Graham felt it must be true when Evrard paused in his normally very steady gait, and then continued without answering. Some questions then, Graham realized, were off-limits.

But that did not stop him from asking.

They stopped when the sun was very high in the sky by another bubbling brook. Graham chewed on a few pieces of dried meat, while Evrard and the horse drank deeply from the cool water.

"How do you know where we're going?" Graham asked before climbing back onto Evrard's back.

"I know because the valley we are headed to is one of ancient magic. Protective magic. It calls to the magic in me."

"Is it far?"

Evrard took off at a slighter faster canter than before, the horse moving behind them like it had always followed Evrard.

"It is several days' journey," Evrard said, "since we must keep to the forest, and off any known trail. For your safety, of course."

"But what if someone spots you?" Graham asked. "How am I to explain what you are?"

Evrard glanced back at his passenger. "People see what they choose to see. I do not think you will have any questions about me, Your Highness."

They slept that night in a well-hidden cave that Graham further camouflaged with several large leafy branches he had cut from neighboring trees with his dagger. There was a small ax in one of the saddlebags and a tinderbox kit, and Graham kindled a small fire with twigs to take away the chill of the night. The cave was large enough for both Evrard and the horse, though Graham knew that Evrard was not altogether pleased about sharing even a temporary domicile with the horse.

They set out bright and early the next morning, continuing to journey into the thick of the forest. By midday, there was a fine sheen of sweat on Evrard's back and Graham realized that as he'd been daydreaming, staring up at the leafy canopy of the trees, they had been steadily climbing uphill. After stopping for a rest, they continued on, and once Graham offered to help conserve Evrard's energy by walking, and leading the horse himself, but Evrard's complete silence as a response told Graham exactly what he thought of that particular idea.

By later in the evening, when the shadows were beginning to grow longer, the trees had thinned out, and the ground had gone from densely packed dirt to a much rockier, harder surface.

When they stopped, Evrard's voice finally reflected his own exhaustion. "Tomorrow, we will climb," he said, "and then we will be in the valley."

As Graham gathered branches for their fire, he asked, "What is in this valley?"

"A farm, though I do not know how inhabitable it will be. It may need repairs. It has been abandoned for many, many years." Evrard paused. "But no matter, it will be safe there."

Graham realized then that ever since Evrard had appeared in all his majestic glory, he had not felt particularly unsafe. He had been sad, mourning a life lost to him, along with Rhys and his father's loyalty and affection, but he had not once felt like they were in any particular danger. When he said so, Evrard shook his head gravely.

"We have always been in danger, Your Highness. Sabrina searches for us in many forms. Our magic has shielded us from her view, though with the taxing climb tomorrow, I may not be able to shield us for much longer." Evrard sounded reluctant to share this information, but Graham was glad he had.

"What can I do to protect us?" he asked.

The unicorn's eyes seemed to bore into his very soul. "Be brave a little while longer, my prince."

The next day was the most grueling day that Graham had ever experienced. Nothing, not even training with Tullamore's guard or the night he had escaped from Sabrina's clutches, had prepared him for the grueling climb to the top of the mountain peak. The air grew thinner, and the ground much tougher for Evrard and the horse to pick their way across. Graham descended from Evrard mid-morning, and was glad he had, because only a few hundred yards further, a hissing viper slithered out from around a rock and stood right in their way, spitting poison onto the ground, where it sizzled and bubbled.

"Graham," Evrard said sharply as Graham pulled his dagger, which he had kept much closer to hand since the unicorn's warning the night before.

He knew why Evrard had not told him of the danger previously; he still thought of Graham as a somewhat helpless child, but Graham knew he had not been a child since the night he'd escaped Tullamore. It was the same reason why Evrard warned him back now, but still Graham approached, soft footfalls on the ground as the viper eyed him with gold, flashing eyes that somehow brought to mind a woman's.

"It is her," Evrard said steadily from somewhere behind him. "She means to stop us while she still can, because once we are in the valley, you are lost to her."

Graham weighed the dagger in his right hand. If he misjudged even the tiniest bit, or worst of all, missed completely, the viper would be on them instantly, and Graham did not think their chances of survival would be very good.

"Graham," Evrard said again, and that was all the motivation that he needed to throw the dagger.

It flipped perfectly, just as Graham had practiced thousands and thousands of times, and though the dagger did not land quite as precisely as he'd hoped, it did hit the viper in its soft, meaty underbelly. It hissed loudly and angrily and then fell deathly still, its head lolling across the rocky ground.

"Is it . . ." Graham hesitated. "Is it dead?" He did not think he'd dealt the viper a mortal blow—an injurious one certainly, and one that he'd hoped would at least stop it from attacking them—but Evrard nodded slowly.

"Sabrina has many powers. One of them allows her to transport her soul into various creatures at a significant distance." Evrard looked at the dead viper with distaste. "It was once a stupendous skill, born of beautiful and good magic, but she has twisted it, like she twists all things. The viper died not just because of your blade, but because most creatures cannot survive her abrupt departure."

"What would have happened if she had been inhabiting the snake when it died?" Graham asked. If they managed to reach the valley in one piece, he had no intention of tangling with Sabrina ever again, but it wouldn't be bad information to know, just in case.

"She would also die," Evrard said. "But you are not to attempt such a stunt again. I could have dealt with the viper."

Graham walked over to where the dead snake lay, and carefully, using a corner of his cloak, retrieved his dagger, cleaning it thoroughly before returning it to the makeshift sheath he'd made. "You are struggling with the climb," he pointed out, "and I could handle this, so I did."

"My prince," Evrard said, somehow his voice becoming even more formal, "you are irreplaceable. I beg you to remember that."

"I'm also no longer a prince," Graham said bitterly. "Let's head for the peak. I don't want to risk her sending anything else."

The remainder of the climb felt strangely anticlimactic after the thrilling, heart-stopping episode with the viper. They reached the summit, and then carefully began to pick their way down. Slowly, more trees appeared, and the air grew sweet and clear. Graham leaned against a trunk as they stopped at the first stream they encountered.

"When will we reach the valley?" he asked.

Evrard lifted his head from the water. "We are nearly there," he said. "We will reach it by nightfall. But even now, I feel my magic is rejuvenated. We should be safe here."

"Should be safe," Graham muttered, and went to grab some jerky from one of the saddlebags. It wasn't that he didn't trust Evrard—after all, the unicorn had given him both imperative information about his situation and protected him from Sabrina. He had come to save Graham's life, and he was grateful, but he always felt like there was something Evrard was holding back. Important details or vital pieces of information that he kept silent on. Graham did not know what held him back. Was it that he thought Graham was too young? Too inexperienced? Too stupid? Graham wasn't sure what the reasoning was, but he didn't particularly like it.

The sun was setting across the faraway peaks on the other side when they finally climbed the rest of the way down into the meadow that carpeted much of the valley floor. From a distance, Graham could see a cluster of buildings, low and squat, and as they traveled closer, he could see that Evrard had been honest—they were not in the greatest of repair. The roof was nearly collapsed on one, and what had once been a large garden had been nearly taken over by weeds.

"So this is the Valley of the Lost Things?" Graham asked as they approached the buildings. "Why is it so empty? I'm certainly not the only lost thing in this world."

"No, but you are the most important," Evrard said, with that maddening superiority that made Graham want to gnash his teeth and demand the whole damn truth. But there was no point, because Evrard clearly did not do or share anything that he didn't want to.

When Graham wrenched open the main building's door, a whoosh of dust settled over him. The whole interior could

29

use an intense cleaning—it was full of dust and cobwebs, but it did contain several rooms, as well as a full complement of sturdy, hand-built wooden furniture. Two fireplaces constructed of river stone stood cold and empty. The building with the mostly collapsed roof turned out to be the stable. Luckily, there were still a few bales of only slightly rotted hay. And even though Evrard turned up his nose at the meal, Graham's horse leaned down and munched away happily.

"Tomorrow, the roof will need to be repaired," Evrard said practically, clearly dictating this request towards Graham, even though he had no experience at all repairing roofs.

Graham considered saying so, but already knew his concern would be brushed aside. He would have to learn. He would have to learn to take care of all of this. This place, unceremonious and humble, was his new home, and if anything was to come of it, there was only him to do the work.

"Of course," Graham said.

"And one more thing," Evrard said, as Graham went to find a less dusty room to spend the night in, "you are lost here. Safe and lost. But perhaps a subterfuge to confuse anyone that might come upon us? As you say, you are not the only lost thing in the world."

"A subterfuge?" Graham asked tiredly.

Evrard glanced down at the heavy cloak he wore. "From now on, you shall be known as Gray."

Graham had thought he had nothing left to lose, but as Evrard walked away to the stable, he realized he'd just lost the last part of who he'd been before.

The next morning, Gray, as he was now known, tackled the stable roof, and then the dusty interior of the main house. Then, over a long, hot, arduous summer, began to clear the vegetable garden. Evrard made suggestions, but besides his own stable, he cared little of what Gray's living conditions were. As long as Evrard had sweet grass or hay to eat, cool, clean water, and a roof over his head for the occasional rainy day, he was not particular about the state of the farm. But Gray, who had been raised to rule Ardglass, felt the sting of his pointless life a little less if he kept busy. Each night he lay in his cot and thought of what he could do the next day to keep his mind and body occupied—and silent.

Being lost had its advantages. There was nobody to tell him what to do except for Evrard, and mostly Evrard left him alone, except in the evenings, when they would talk of legend and history and magic.

Gray was eventually forced out of the Valley of the Lost Things to buy supplies that could not be taken from the meadow or the woods or the valley itself. But he had grown in the two years since coming to the valley and was unrecognizable to himself in the creek as he hacked off big chunks of his dark, wavy hair with the same dagger he'd been carrying during his flight from Tullamore.

The village where Evrard directed him was exactly as he'd described, and as long as Gray kept his head down, nobody seemed to care who he was. He traded for supplies, and returned a year later, and a year after that.

Slowly, he eked out a profitable farm from the fertile ground of the valley. He built a hen house, dug a well, and began to keep sheep and cows. His garden expanded, and the next summer, he planted a whole field of hay for Evrard and his old horse.

Time both crawled and flew. Years passed, but with each successive birthday, the only marker of the passage of time were the inches Gray continued to grow. He continued to stay as busy as he could, and most nights he fell into his bed exhausted from the day's work. And that, he learned during the years, was better than lying awake and wondering what had happened to the keep of Tullamore, the kingdom of Ardglass, and his father. He heard bits and snippets on his annual trips to the village, but mostly he blocked out any talk of politics. He had no interest in the goings-on of the nobility. He was no longer a member; he was lost, and he intended to stay lost.

And so, many years passed. Occasionally, a visitor would make their way into the valley. They too would be lost, in some fashion, and they would stay for a night or a week, and then move on, but Gray stayed. He had nowhere else to go.

On the morning of his twenty-sixth year, Gray woke and did not even start at the realization that flickered across his consciousness. He would never leave this place; he would die here, lost.

Of course, the year he came to terms with the course of his life, that was when it changed irrevocably.

CHAPTER TWO

HIS ROYAL HIGHNESS, PRINCE Emory of Fontaine, looked up from the manuscript he was studying, and pasted on an agreeable smile.

It was much harder than it should have been—Rory knew that, but the knowing did not make it any easier to accomplish the pleasantries required when facing the Regent Queen, his aunt Sabrina. She did not bother him often, which he appreciated, as he always felt vaguely uncomfortable after her visits. Like her presence was a disagreeable reminder of everything she did that he did not.

She herself would never say anything of the kind. In fact, he was always grateful at how little pressure she put on him as the Crown Prince of the country of Fontaine. At his age, a deep, hidden voice inside told him, he should be sitting next to her at council meetings, and alongside her during the weekly audience with Fontaine's subjects. That ugly reminder that he wasn't doing enough—wasn't doing much of anything at all, except for studying his books and his languages and his ancient manuscripts—was always louder right after one of her visits.

Thankfully then, they did not occur very often.

Rory stood, and held out his hand. His aunt was still young and still stunningly beautiful, with lustrous dark hair and a pair of shining dark eyes that kindly turned down every proposal that was made to her, all under the auspices that she was far too occupied caring for her nephew's future throne and for the people of Fontaine.

She was beautiful and majestic, and therefore Rory could not fault her for being somewhat distant as well. After all, she was occupied with the business of the Crown, and he himself always seemed to be neck-deep in some important discussion or analysis or translation. Often, before he was even finished with one, another would appear, and so he passed his time as he had since he was in his early teens, in the library, situated in the tall round tower of Beaulieu.

"Your Highness," his aunt said respectfully, dipping into a graceful curtsy. After the formalities were observed, she took the chair opposite his, demurely folding her hands in her lap, even though in his personal experience, she was not exactly the demure type. She rode as well as any of their guards, and often took morning training in the yard with some of her most loyal attendants. Still, her act was excellent, and his was not—thus, another reason why neither of them had made any push to change the status quo since Rory had turned eighteen. Two years later, and there had still been zero discussion of transferring power; a situation Rory was perfectly fine with.

"What can I do for you?" Rory asked, that awkward feeling in his stomach intensifying. She never came to see him unless she needed something that only he could provide.

"You recall the terrible northern brigands who have been devastating our supply trains?" his aunt asked. Occasionally, she would provide a single parchment inscribed with some of the highlights of realm business. Rory usually read it, assuming that his aunt did not want him to be caught unawares at one of the few royal banquets he attended. The brigands looting the supply trains had been a large portion of the last installment. Rory nodded, even though he knew very little detail other than the basic facts of the case. It was not ancient, it was not in another language, and it was not a mystery to be unraveled. It needed a practical, experienced military hand to guide the problem to a solution, and therefore Rory had left it alone. He was neither particularly practical nor experienced in any military maneuvers except for archaic ones.

"We recently received intelligence that suggests they have retreated to the far north, right on the edge of our borders, to a valley lying between two mountain ranges."

Rory had no idea what this could possibly have to do with him. "Excellent," he said uselessly. This was why he never involved himself; his aunt was a paragon of efficiency.

"I would like you to travel with a squad of the guard to this valley and fetch them back to Beaulieu to see justice," the Regent Queen said primly, as if she was asking him for another translation of Gawain, and not to undertake a dangerous, active journey with the intent of capturing criminals.

Rory had very little experience concealing his feelings, even in the royal court, since he was called to participate in it so infrequently. He couldn't help his reaction; his jaw fell open. "You would like me to do what?" he asked slowly.

Occasionally, Rory wondered, since he had little occasion to witness it personally, how his aunt had achieved all that efficiency she was so famous for. He saw a little of it now, in the hardening of her jaw and the sudden ferocity flashing in her eyes. This was a woman, he realized suddenly and unexpectedly, whom you would not want to cross. He had never had any opportunity to do so, but he knew now that if he ever did, treading carefully would be of utmost importance.

The Regent Queen rose, as elegantly as she did everything, and walked to the large leaded window that overlooked the courtyard of Beaulieu, her fingertips tapping alongside the spines of the books casually piled everywhere. "I ask for so little," she said sweetly. "I assumed you would be eager to assist me with this task. Was I incorrect in my thinking?"

Rory steeled himself. "No, you were not. You know I would be honored to help you with this, but we both know I am the wrong man for the task."

She turned, and suddenly he was a bug, crawling pathetically under her gaze. Another unexpected revelation: Rory understood what it was like for those men she had rejected. Even knowing she was kind did not prevent the sting of humiliation, not when she applied it so expertly. "A man," she said. "Yes, that is what I expected to find when I ventured here. Not a boy, still enamored with his little mysteries and his picture books."

There was a very loud part of Rory that wanted to ask if she had always been this vindictive, and she had hidden it from him on purpose, but it was impossible to do so when she was staring at him like that. Rory spoke ten languages, and they all dried up under the onslaught of that hostile gaze.

"So," she continued, "you shall travel to this valley in the far north, and you will capture the criminals and brigands who live there, and you will bring them back to Beaulieu. Thus, justice shall be served."

Rory swallowed hard. He did ride well, usually when he wanted to clear his head, or examine a problem from a different angle, but he had only the most basic of defense training, and could barely use Lion's Breath, the ancestral sword of Fontaine, at all. It wasn't quite right to say that she was sending him to his death—because surely, that was impossible. But then it had been impossible to imagine her ever speaking to him with that particular tone in her voice before. Today, the impossible had become possible.

"I assume we leave at first light tomorrow," Rory said, "and I assume my guard shall accompany me."

Her face was so cold, it was etched in ice. Clearly she had not intended for him to take his guard, only the guard she had picked. Rory, who had read dozens of epic tales of bravery and disloyalty and of thrones and kingdoms changing hands, had somehow never once imagined that he would find himself in such a precarious position. After his parents had died in the carriage accident, and Sabrina had come, pale with grief but also determined to rule wisely in her five-year-old nephew's stead, he had never conceived that she would attempt to dispose of him, and keep Fontaine for herself.

And yet, it was as if a curtain had risen and Rory saw all her actions in a totally different light. Never encouraging him to learn to rule. Letting him lose himself in his studies and his books. Never once ordering him to learn to defend himself. He had no practical knowledge of which to speak, and he could not even blame that choice on her—it had been entirely his own. Her absence in his life had made it possible, but he had crafted the noose himself that would eventually be his doom.

If he let it.

"Your guard?" the Regent Queen questioned.

"I shall prefer to take my own guard," Rory said firmly. He was still the Crown Prince of Fontaine, at least until he left the walls of Beaulieu behind. He would exercise his rights—they were all that was no doubt between him and a mysterious "accident" during this dangerous journey.

"So be it," she said, smugness edging her voice. She clearly believed that his fate was in her hands, regardless of the guard.

He would just need to ensure that all was not what it seemed, at least to her eyes.

Once the Regent Queen departed, Rory hastily packed a few thin manuscripts that he believed might serve him well on this trip, and then made for the guard's quarters on the other side of the courtyard.

His guard was famously comprised of the best female warriors in the kingdom, though they saw little to no action. It occurred to Rory as he approached their barracks that Sabrina might think so little of her own sex that she had appointed his guard hoping they would be less competent, but if that was the case, then the joke was on her. Marthe, who headed the Prince's guard, was the most terrifying fighter that Rory knew, and the rest of the guard, handpicked by Marthe, had spent their lives being undervalued and underappreciated, and worked twice as hard as a result.

Rory found Marthe sharpening her longsword just inside the barracks, in the common room. He had no idea how circumspect he needed to be, because if his aunt was half as disloyal as he imagined, she would certainly have spies planted all over Beaulieu.

Marthe shot him a look over her whetstone. "Lost, are you, my prince?" she asked.

It was true, he rarely came down to the courtyard, and almost never into the barracks. A point Marthe had made many times over, but which Rory had never deigned sufficiently important to listen to. He was listening now.

"We are to leave first thing in the morning," Rory said, tempering the order with an apologetic tone. It was hardly enough time to mount a fully armed guard, which no doubt was something the Regent Queen was counting on.

Marthe raised an eyebrow questioningly. "A journey? To where?"

Certainly, she was likely expecting that Rory wanted to visit a neighboring castle with some particular tome in its library. They had done that before, on more than one occasion.

"We are tasked by the Regent Queen to travel to a valley in the far north and apprehend brigands who have set upon some of our supply trains." Rory managed to get most of it out without flinching, but his voice wavered at the end. Not enough that many might notice, but Marthe was exceedingly observant.

She sighed, a long, terrible gust. "I see," she said, and Rory suddenly had an inclination that she did. That maybe Marthe had been watching and waiting for something like this sudden journey to come to pass. Hopefully, Rory thought, she was more prepared than he was.

When she stood, Marthe was several handspans taller than Rory himself. She put a reassuring hand on his shoulder. "We will be ready," she said, confidence ringing out from every syllable. "I will gather the guard immediately and set preparations in motion." She gave him a single, knowing look, and went out the door to the courtyard.

Rory could not be entirely certain, but it did seem as though Marthe understood the potential treachery of the journey and what must be undertaken to prevent it.

At least he hoped so, because he himself was woefully and painfully unprepared to face whatever they encountered.

Dawn was a gray smudge on the horizon when Rory walked into the courtyard to meet his guard. There were five of them, led by Marthe, their heavy armor shining dully in the early morning light. Marthe's expression was grim but determined, much like Rory expected his own was.

The Regent Queen had not awoken early to see them off, but Rory was not surprised by this, as he might have been once. He had lain awake the night before and gone over in his mind so many incidents over the last fifteen years. Small, insignificant events now took on greater meaning once examined with an understanding of Sabrina's clear purpose. Rory saw just how effortlessly she had manipulated him, and in fact, much of the court of Beaulieu. Even though he was hardly alone, the thought undeniably stung. He was the Crown Prince, Fontaine was his country to rule, and he had stood aside and let her do whatever she wished to it. The land seemed to be thriving, but it was impossible to say if that was actually true, or just another of his aunt's subterfuges.

"Prince Emory," Marthe said respectfully, nodding towards a page who had appeared in the doorway from the castle proper. He carried a scroll, which was no doubt a signed declaration of their purpose, signed by his aunt. He was the Crown Prince, he should not need permission to be riding with armed guards or to apprehend criminals, but Rory realized that this act took away any agency he'd grasped when he'd requested his own guards. She was reminding him, in that cruelly subtle way of hers, that he was on her business. That he lived and breathed by her grace.

He took the scroll from the page with clenched teeth and a sharp nod. He could not thwart protocol, not so publicly, but he did not have to like it either.

They rode out in a loose triangle formation, Marthe at the front, Rory in the middle, and the rest of the guard surrounding him. Protecting him, Rory realized as they stopped for a midday break.

Deep in the forest, it was difficult to imagine there were any spies, and for the first time, he and Marthe were able to speak freely.

"I knew she would make her move eventually," Marthe said, chewing her portion of bread and cheese carefully. "I knew it would be coming, and I was still surprised when it happened. Do not feel ashamed that it surprised you, my prince."

"How far is it to the valley?" he asked. He did not want to address how stupid he had been. It was hard enough to face his own idiocy; he did not want Marthe's sympathy, as kindly as it was meant.

"Several days' ride. Perhaps a week if we take our time," Diana, one of the guards, spoke up. "And we should. No good reason to get to the valley exhausted, with tired horses."

Rowen, another guard, gave Rory a contemplative look. "A week would even be enough time to give you some rudimentary training, Your Highness." She glanced down at the sword at his belt. "Perhaps not enough to truly use Lion's

Breath, but enough to make sure you can defend yourself with a dagger, if need be."

"Yes," Marthe agreed. "We will stop early every evening, and spend that time working with the Prince. He has our protection, but he must also learn to protect himself."

Rory couldn't stop himself from making a face. He knew it needed to be done; in fact, it should have been done long ago, and no doubt, would have, but his aunt had clearly wanted him to be helpless and completely indebted to his guard.

"Prince Emory," Anya laughed. "Truly, it will not be so bad. After all, don't you enjoy reading books about weapons? Skirmishes and battles? Military strategy?"

He did, but the idea of practical application made his stomach clench and then roll unpleasantly.

Marthe smiled at him. "It's quite a lot of adjustment to make at one time. You'll get used to it."

Rory had no doubt that he would eventually—he just did not particularly want to.

Later that afternoon they stopped just as the sun was just beginning to sink, and as Rowen and Acadia set up camp, Marthe, Diana and Anya worked with Rory to master using one of the small-handled sharp daggers they all carried. To Rory's surprise, Marthe even pulled a wickedly sharp version out of one of the packs, and gifted it to him, handle first.

"Is this mine?" Rory asked.

Marthe nodded. "Very useful at close range, and if you can learn to throw it, useful even at a longer range.

Unfortunately, a week is not really enough time to teach the latter."

"In my country," Anya said, "we learn to throw these when we're practically in the cradle."

Rory had forgotten that Anya was not originally from Fontaine—but when you looked closer at her dark braided hair and steely gray eyes, the hint of wildness in her expression gave her away. "You come from Ardglass, right?" Rory asked.

Of all the countries bordering Fontaine, he knew the least about Ardglass. Of the Ardglass of old, he knew much, but thousand-year-old history could not help him much now. If by some miracle, he survived this journey, going back to Beaulieu might not be possible; he might need to seek asylum in another country. Ardglass was the closest, and also currently in the direction they were headed.

"I do, Your Highness," Anya said as she adjusted his grip on the dagger. "My father started teaching me to fight when I was very small, and I had hoped to wield a sword in the garrison there, but . . ." She hesitated. "After the Crown Prince disappeared, nothing was the same. The King withdrew from court, the garrisons were mostly disbanded. The kingdom is a shadow of what it once was."

Rory knew Prince Graham of Ardglass had disappeared shortly before his own parents were killed, fifteen years earlier, but he did not know the details of the situation. Many believed he was dead and would never be found. Anya looked upset enough by divulging just that much information that he did not want to press her.

"Focus," Marthe barked at him as he practiced shoving the dagger into an old rotten log that Diana and Rowen had found and hauled upright to replace the sandbags they usually practiced on. "Put all your force behind your strike."

Next, they began to teach him defensive maneuvers with the dagger, and an hour later, he collapsed next to the fire, damp with sweat and utterly exhausted.

And the next night, Rory thought miserably, it would start all over again.

The trip to the valley took, as Diana had predicted, just over a week. The last day was a difficult climb on the horses, and on Rory himself. He was sore from a week straight of riding from dawn to late afternoon, and then hours after of swordplay and sparring. He had finally graduated, with grudging acceptance from Marthe, from the dagger to his ancestral sword, and hefting the heavy weight had left his arms weak and tired. Another man might be ashamed that he was far less proficient or seasoned than any of his guards, but then they did not speak ten languages. Rory had spent his lifetime indulging in the pursuits that he enjoyed. They might have even borne fruit, if he had truly been expected to succeed the Regent Queen and take over the throne of Fontaine. But finally, he understood that she had never had any plans to abdicate in his favor. And now that he was twenty, and of perfectly suitable age to rule, she had clearly felt the need to remove him completely.

At night when he lay in his bedroll, he should have been tired enough to sleep, but he lay awake instead, turning his aunt's actions and motives over and over and over again in his head. How could she have hated him so much? He had tried never to be much trouble, and there had always been so many servants to make sure that she was never truly bothered by his presence. She had never needed to be a mother to him; if he'd wanted one, he'd understood very quickly that that was not a position she wished to hold, and he'd lost himself in his books instead. He realized she'd undoubtedly seen the advantages of his scholarly interests and had encouraged him to cultivate them.

It was on the third night that Rory realized that it wasn't that his aunt loathed him or wished him dead. It was not about him at all. Instead, it was power that drew her and controlled her. She would do anything in search of more, and if he stood in the way, then he must be eliminated. She could not risk the chance of anyone suggesting, especially himself, that he take the throne.

Rory resolved that he would not be disposed of quite so easily.

On the eighth morning, Rory and his guard stood on the edge of the valley, their horses impatiently shifting their hooves, ready to make the descent down to the lush land below.

"If I'd known this place existed, I'd run and hide here too," Acadia said.

Rory nodded, agreeing with her assessment. Trees ringed the edges of the valley, fringed with bright green leaves and sharp sweet-smelling needles. As the ground sloped downward, the pockets of trees gave way to meadow land, plush, waving grass as soft and luxurious as velvet. Wildflowers bloomed intermittently across their view— purples and yellows and blues and reds almost blinding in their intensity. A stream meandered through the very center of the valley, far enough away to look like a lazy silver snake. And as far as the eye could see, only one set of dwellings.

"That is where the criminals must be hiding," Marthe said, extending her hand to point towards the small grouping of buildings. It was far enough into the heart of the valley it was nearly impossible to see if any people were wandering about, but even from this distance, Rory could see the farm was well-kept, with several large fields beyond its walls and a large garden on the other side, the pattern of the broken ground much different from the undisturbed land.

It did not look like a hideout populated by bandits, but Rory knew enough to understand that sometimes appearances were deceiving.

"Your Highness," Marthe said, her voice taking on the taint of deference that he rarely heard from her—and had truthfully never wanted. In this realm, away from the library and his books, he was out of his element. "Your Highness," she repeated when he did not respond, "it may be better for you to lead the way."

He shot his captain a disbelieving look. His guard may have been training him every day on this journey, but seven days of training could not possibly make up for a lifetime of skipping it. Marthe knew that as well as Rory did.

"The appearance of you leading the way, then," Marthe corrected, the corner of her lips tilting into an amused smile. "These are your lands, after all."

But Rory, who had made a considered study of his own lands, shook his head. "If they are mine, they have been on no map that I have ever seen."

"Regardless," Marthe insisted, and finally, Rory inclined his head, agreeing with her assessment.

He led the way down the incline towards the valley floor, marveling the whole way at the undisturbed and spectacular greenery surrounding them.

"It's as if someone planted a garden and then left it to grow for a very long time," Anya murmured to Rowen, her voice pitched low, as if words did not belong in such a beautiful place.

"It gives every appearance of being empty except for the farm," Marthe warned him a few minutes later, "but I would be very surprised if there were not invisible guards or booby traps, all planned to warn the inhabitants of strangers coming upon this place."

Rory couldn't help but agree with Marthe; it seemed impossible the valley could exist, and yet be so unguarded. Yet as they ventured further into the valley, they saw no evidence of any human presence. Birds chattered in the trees, their song lighthearted and free, and from a distance they caught sight of squirrels and other small animals frolicking through the tall grasses. But they were completely undisturbed.

As they grew closer to the farm itself, Rory found himself growing tenser and tenser, battling the sense of relaxation and peace the valley seemed determined to lend him. Such an unmapped, undiscovered, perfect place could not exist. It must be some kind of trap, and Sabrina was just waiting to spring it, capturing Rory and his guards in her deathly grip.

"Carefully, my prince," Marthe warned quietly as they approached the farm. It contained four well-maintained outbuildings, as well as the central farmhouse. A large garden spread out like a flawless coverlet across the front of the farm, and at the back, corn grew tall and thick as far as Rory could see. But as much as his eyes scanned the grounds, he could not see any of the people who had clearly worked very hard to make it a haven.

"It looks . . ." Diana hesitated, like she did not even want to voice the sentiment they were all thinking.

"Abandoned," Marthe finished briskly. "And yet it cannot be. This place is impeccably kept. There are clearly people about, they just do not want to be found. It is our job to find them."

Rory didn't want to dismount and leave his horse behind. He felt like he was abandoning the one advantage he had, which was his excellent horsemanship. However, Rory wasn't dumb enough to think he could properly join in the search while on horseback. So he tied up Chestnut, his fine brown stallion, and watched as the rest of his guard did the same.

"Pairs," Marthe ordered, and as the rest of the guard paired off, she walked over to Rory's side, hand on her sword pommel. "Shall we?" she asked him as they watched the rest of the pairs begin to walk cautiously around the seemingly deserted farm.

Rory nodded, and they started together towards the garden. He knew very little of such things, except in theory, but the garden looked extremely well-tended, with neat, orderly rows of vegetables, the ground around the plants entirely cleared of weeds. He reached over and plucked a small tomato from a nearby plant.

"Hey, watch yourself," a voice said, and Rory looked, and then kept looking as a very tall man, shirtless, his face and muscular chest smeared with dirt, rose from the middle of a patch of squash.

Marthe was instantly by his side, sword out of her belt, but the man simply looked at her, expression blank and bored. He spread his empty hands in front of him. "If you're hungry," he said, "take what you like. If you are lost, you may stay."

The man's hair was long and dark, nearly shaggy, but did not obscure the bright blue eyes that gazed out at him. A bead of sweat trickled down his bare and undeniably dirty pectoral muscle. Rory swallowed hard. He had never met anyone like this man before—someone rough and uncouth and utterly, completely compelling. Rory felt his blood sizzle, like a drop of water on a stove that had been stoked with firewood all day. He stared, mesmerized, by the man.

Was he a bandit? He certainly did not seem like one, if his offer of food and shelter was any indication.

"Sir," Rory said, trying to find his voice under Marthe's accusing stare, "we are in search of some dangerous criminals who have been looting the supply wagons from Fontaine."

The man gave him a disbelieving look. "Does it look like we're harboring bandits here?"

Truthfully, it did not. It looked to Rory that all the man was harboring was an excellent crop of vegetables. As well as a physique that made Rory desperate to reach out and place a palm on that firm chest, even though it was smeared with dirt and sweat. Somehow, that made it even more attractive, though Rory did not think that thought could possibly be logical.

But Marthe was clearly not as distracted by such a fine chest as Rory was. Her glare was still fierce. "You will not mind if I do not take your word for it," she said. "I would like to search the grounds and buildings of your farm."

The man threw his head back and laughed. Rory did not know what was so amusing, but he discovered that he was desperate to know.

"There is nothing here but my farming implements, the animals I keep here, and the store of food to last us through the winter," he admitted. "But feel free to search all you like."

"Do you have any weapons here?" Marthe asked, her hard voice making it clear she did not believe the act. If it was even an act. Rory was strangely inclined to believe his words, but that might have been because of his beautiful eyes.

"A dagger or two," the man said, leaning against his shovel. "We have no need of weapons here."

Marthe sniffed. "We will be the judge of that." After throwing Rory another reprimanding look, she marched away, clearly intending to find the rest of the guard and do a thorough search of the farm. Rory thought she must not have thought the man was a threat, or else she never would've left him alone.

The man stared at Rory, who stared back. "Do you always travel with a full complement of lady warriors?" he asked offhandedly.

Rory blushed. It was impossible to admit to this man, who looked eminently capable of dispatching any threat, weapons or no, that Rory had to, because he could not defend himself. "It was very rude of me not to introduce myself," Rory said, extending a hand, "I am Prince Emory of the kingdom of Fontaine, but you may call me Rory."

It was as if his words changed everything. The man's eyes went blank, his face cold and hard, and he turned away, leaving Rory awkwardly standing with his hand out. "Gray," he said shortly. "Welcome to the valley."

One of the reasons Rory had always loved reading was that he felt an inescapable compulsion to know things. His curiosity was legendary, and faced with a man such as Gray, couldn't have been more engaged even if he'd tried.

"How long have you lived here?" Rory asked, as Gray returned to his squash, carefully digging around a plant.

"How did you come to be here? I have never seen this valley on a map before."

Gray did not bother to meet his eyes as he responded, his tone short and hard. "I have been here many years. It's a haven for those who are lost, a magical place not found on any maps."

It did not make any sense at all for Sabrina to believe that the bandits stealing their supplies would hide in a magical valley for the lost. They might have little in the way of a moral compass, but they could hardly be lost.

"Are you lost then?" Rory asked.

Gray looked up then, eyes boring into Rory's own. He said nothing for a long moment. "Aren't we all lost?" he asked. "In our own ways?"

CHAPTER THREE

GRAY KNEW WHO PRINCE Emory was. He'd heard them talking of him in the village, last time he was there. How the Regent Queen seemed to grip the throne of Fontaine tighter and tighter, and the Autumn Prince, as they called Prince Emory, was still seemingly unaware because his head was always in a book. Gray had turned away when the shopkeeper continued speaking of the Autumn Prince, because he'd not wanted to hear anything about any of the kingdoms surrounding his valley. But Fontaine was at least not Ardglass, and it was hardly like he could storm out without his supplies or close his ears completely.

He'd wondered why they called him the Autumn Prince, but face to face with Rory now, he understood. He looked like a particularly beautiful autumn day in the valley with his wavy auburn hair, tawny eyes, and fair skin. Delicate, Gray would have called him. He definitely had the look of someone who buried his nose in a book and couldn't see what was going on around him. Naive, that was another term Gray might have used.

Rory seemed to be a particularly terrible choice to go after a pack of criminals and apprehend them, though his guard seemed both appropriately suspicious and also eminently capable of capturing whomever they wished. Probably, Gray thought, they'd just brought him along as a particularly useless figurehead. Gray couldn't see any other possible practical use for the pretty prince.

He'd been mildly intrigued by Rory's attractive looks, but once he'd revealed who he was, any curiosity Gray had held about the younger man had died. Royalty, Gray thought with an annoyed sneer, was all the same. A complete waste of air.

Gray did not care that Prince Emory's guard was currently searching the farm; they would not find anything of value to them. He just wanted them to complete their search, confirm what he'd told them was the truth, perhaps stay the night, and then be on their way. He had no use and no time for inept princelings, even ones who stared at him like he was the most compelling thing they'd ever seen.

He knew he'd grown tall and strong, like his father had always predicted. The bloodline of Ardglass always throws true, he'd say. Gray shook his head. He did not want to think of his father, ever, but especially not today, when faced with the mirror image of what could have been. If Sabrina hadn't needed his blood, if his father hadn't been so weak, and if he hadn't been forced to run from Tullamore, he and Prince Emory would likely have met across a banquet table, or in the marble-walled throne room. They would have exchanged useless pleasantries, and maybe even eventually found their way to each other's beds for a night or two of pleasure, but they certainly never would have met in a patch of squash.

But that was what could have been, and circumstances being what they were, could never be. Prince Emory would leave in the morning, none the wiser that he had met the lost Prince of Ardglass in a mysterious valley not found on any maps.

Maybe next time Gray ventured into the village, he would hear of Rory's exile, and the Regent Queen taking over the throne of Fontaine permanently. He had never met her, but based on Rory's appearance, perhaps she would be better suited to ruling.

"Do people often come here?" Rory asked, as Gray continued to tend his squash. Rory, probably accustomed to a castle full of courtiers honor-bound to answer, didn't seem to understand that he had no interest in actually continuing their conversation.

"We're all lost, a little," Gray repeated between clenched teeth. "Or do you disagree?"

Rory smiled, the sun streaming onto his porcelain-pure features as he tipped his head back to soak in the light. "Actually, I believe you, but you also didn't answer the question."

He was intelligent then, and definitely quick, and Gray found it harder to believe that his aunt had managed to essentially usurp him without him noticing.

"After all, there is nobody here in this valley except you," Rory continued, still smiling. Gray grimaced.

"And you, and your guard," Gray added.

"But we're not lost."

Gray gave a particularly vicious shove to his spade, thought of what he'd heard in the village, but decided it wasn't worth it. If Prince Emory thought all was fine in his kingdom, then who was Gray to enlighten him? The noble game of politics and royalty and all that blasted honor that ultimately meant less than nothing was one that he had washed his hands of a long time ago. Even if Rory died at the hands of his aunt—and it wouldn't be the first time a relative bloodied their hands to gain a throne—it wasn't any of Gray's concern.

"Is this what you do here?" Rory asked, another question after a blessed moment of silence.

"What I do here?" Gray knew he should turn and walk away, find shelter and quiet in the stables or in the far-reaching hay fields. There was undoubtedly work he could do in either of those places, but then again, it had been a long time since they'd had any visitors to the valley, and even longer since he'd been to the village. Conversing with someone, even this prince, was actually kind of nice.

He could always talk to Evrard, but sometimes it was easier not to talk to Evrard.

Rory gestured towards the earth he was turning with his spade. "Work in the garden, move dirt around, that sort of thing," he said awkwardly. It was clear that the excessively clean and relatively callus-free hands of Rory's weren't a mirage; he did spend all his time with books, never working with the golden sword he carried at his hip or ever in anything resembling dirt.

"I'm mixing manure into the soil," Gray explained, and couldn't help but smile at the way Rory flinched. "But yes, this is what I do. Do you see anyone else here?" When Rory shook his head, Gray gave a short bark of laughter. "Then there is nobody else here to do what needs to be done," he said. "Only me."

"You take care of all of this?" Rory asked wonderingly, gazing around at the farm.

Gray couldn't help but be proud of what he'd built, nearly from nothing. Everything had come from sweat and blood, and was learned the hard way, which was usually doing it wrong once or twice or many times first. Others in his place might have been afraid of so much hard work, but idleness terrified Gray. Boredom brought thinking, and thinking brought a bone- and soul-deep fury that he didn't always know how to contain. Sometimes exhausting himself was all that had kept him from saddling his horse and riding back to Tullamore and demanding satisfaction for the merciless, ruinous way he'd been treated.

He did not know if Sabrina still resided in Tullamore, or if she still advised his father. It would likely be a death sentence for him to return, and ultimately, likely advantageous for her. It was the latter more than the former that usually stopped him.

After all, what use was his life? What use was his strong pair of hands? He'd created this farm, and he helped those lost souls who happened to wander by, but nobody stayed. Evrard and he kept their company, and he swam occasionally in the stream that rippled by the farmhouse. He rode his old horse through the meadows. He tended the hay and the garden and cleaned the little farmhouse. Cared for the cows and sheep and chickens. Always put away far more food than he could ever eat for their mild winters.

It was a little like being King of this valley, but Gray wasn't dumb enough to truly believe that. If he'd become a king, he'd be doing more; he'd be useful.

He wasn't even a prince anymore, and even he knew just how stupid it was to keep thinking that way.

This was his situation now, and nothing could change that. Raging against circumstances out of his control was pointless. Just as pointless as expecting Rory to do something with the position he'd been graced with—or dirty those delicate, pale fingers.

"I do care for all of this," Gray finally said, turning towards the Prince. "There is nobody else to do it, and it keeps me occupied."

"My occupation is . . ." Rory hesitated. "Not as useful as yours."

That much Gray believed completely. He had to remind himself again that when he had come to the valley, he'd been as green as Rory. Not perhaps quite as soft, or as pampered, and definitely not as naive, but then Rory was also much older than he'd been. Rory had had the opportunity that Gray never did: to grow up in the secure enclave of the court, shielded and protected. If he'd been honest with himself, part of Gray was jealous.

But the other part of him, knowledgeable and world-wise, preferred the reality of what he'd lived through. He would never again be subject to the whims of someone else. It might be a very little kingdom, but it was still his.

"What is your occupation?" Gray asked, even though he already had an idea.

"I study," Rory explained quietly, his fingers rolling up a corner of his glove again and again, until the leather creased. "I speak ten languages and can read others. I translate important manuscripts and analyze them."

Gray made sure his voice was neutral when he said, "That sounds fairly useful."

But Rory's own was scornful as he answered back. "How can you say that? You manage this entire farm. You grow the food you eat, you repair the roof over your head. You and you alone are responsible."

"And you are subject to the whims of others?" Gray observed quietly. Maybe Rory was not quite as naive as he'd believed. Maybe he understood exactly what his aunt intended. "I understand that all too well."

"So you came here from someplace else, then?" Rory asked. "Where were your parents from?"

Evrard had cautioned Gray never to give a hint to any of the people who passed through the valley what his origin was, or his real name, or anything of value. He said Sabrina's spies were everywhere, and they were still constantly hunting for even the tiniest hint that he was alive.

Prince Emory did not look much like a spy of Sabrina's, but then he had also come here on a foolish, impossible errand. There were no brigands in the valley, or in the woods, or in the village beyond. And sending someone like

Rory to dispose of them was even more of a fool's errand. No, someone had sent him here, had lured him here, specifically. Gray, who had let himself get carried away with talking to someone who wasn't just here for the night or a snob, like Evrard, went still. In the years since his escape, he'd clearly grown soft and lacking the suspicious instinct that had ruled the beginning of his time in the valley. One look at the pretty prince and he'd been so distracted that he'd let Rory and his five guardswomen—capable and deadly guardswomen—essentially invade his property and his valley.

"Nowhere you need be concerned with," Gray said in a hard, resolute voice. He picked up his spade and decided that it wasn't enough that Rory's guard wouldn't find anything here. They needed to be gone. They were all armed to the teeth, and while he had not gotten the impression from any of them that they wished to harm him, Gray knew he could not take on all five at once.

He'd tried to keep up with his sword forms and practiced occasionally on a straw dummy he'd set up in the back of the stables but finding ready and willing partners to spar with was difficult. Once in awhile someone with training would pass through and Gray would challenge them to a practice bout. But otherwise, like with all things, he was on his own.

It would not be enough to handle more than one or two of Rory's clearly well-trained guards.

Definitely not all five, and absolutely not all at once.

Gray leaned down and rested his hand against the leather holder he'd fashioned for his dagger, kept strapped around his calf. He never went without it, though these days he used it more to cut stalks of wheat or to pick squash for dinner. Still, it could kill if he needed it to. He kept it clean and sharp, cautioned always by Evrard that out beyond the valley, danger still lurked.

Now it was possible that danger had actually come to the valley.

"What's the matter?" Rory asked as Gray stalked off towards the stables. He needed to check on Evrard, preferably without his annoying—and attractive—companion. Because he couldn't exactly converse with Evrard, not in front of Rory anyway.

Evrard had been correct—nobody who expected to see a horse ever saw anything other than a horse, but as soon as Evrard opened his mouth, it would be obvious he wasn't just a horse.

"You should find your guard," he told Rory as they approached the stables.

"I'm sure they're fine," Rory said, clearly unconcerned. Gray supposed it made some sort of sense; after all, the only one with very little training, except in ancient languages, was Rory himself. Everyone else on this farm could handle themselves in a fight. The guard had obviously decided that Gray wasn't a threat either, as they'd been left alone together for the last ten minutes.

"Were you really sent here to capture criminals?" Gray asked. If there was a plan to capture or kill Gray, Rory was almost certainly not aware of it.

"Yes, yes, of course we were," Rory insisted, "though it does seem like this couldn't possibly be their hideout. Unless . . ." He hesitated and his face was so open, the thoughts easily read there, Gray knew exactly what he was thinking. Unless you are lying.

"There's nobody here but me," Gray ground out. "We've established that."

"True," Rory admitted.

"So why are you really here?" Gray demanded, and took a step closer to Rory, crowding him against the side of the stables. Was he hoping to scare him a little? Certainly. Rory seemed a much easier nut to crack than some of the women on his guard. They would never tell him the truth of their journey here, but Rory? If he knew, he'd spit it right out. "Tell me what your purpose is."

"I told you already," Rory spluttered, likely flustered by the fact that Gray's bare, dirty chest was pressed right up against his own butter yellow silk doublet and fine turquoise traveling cloak. He'd probably never seen a dirty man in his entire life.

Rory felt as small and lean as he looked, but he also didn't fold the way Gray was expecting him to. Instead, he stared defiantly into Gray's eyes with his unearthly pale gaze. A thousand colors in those eyes, Gray thought, in a daze. Gold and amber and citrine. How had this backfired so spectacularly?

Occasionally he slept with men and women who passed through the valley, and once or twice on trips to the village. But they were only momentary pleasure, a moment of respite in an otherwise somewhat drab existence full to the brim with backbreaking work. But he had never wanted anyone the way he found himself wanting Prince Emory of Fontaine.

Firstly, it was terrible timing, and secondly, Rory was absolutely the last person that Gray should be wanting. But Rory's soft, pink lips were right there, and his slim body was pressed tightly against his own. It would take but a moment to tip his head down and thread his dirty fingers through the silky, fiery strands of Rory's incredible hair. Then he might know if it would be hot to the touch, flaming like its vibrant shade, or cool and soft against his fingers. Maybe he'd even end up with a knife in his back for his trouble. But before that moment, the trouble would be dizzying and rapturous.

"What's wrong?" Rory asked in a soft voice. "Why are you worried?"

Gray took a step back and tried to clear his head. It was nearly impossible to do so when Rory kept staring at him, that hopeful, somewhat quizzical expression in his eyes, like he hadn't quite understood why Gray hadn't leaned down and closed the distance between their lips.

Gray was still trying to understand it himself.

"Why am I worried?" Gray repeated, annoyed. "You've shown up here looking for something that doesn't exist. And anyone with a shred of information would have known that. Your presence here . . ."

"Could be a trap," Rory interrupted him, proving his sharp-edged intelligence yet again. How had his aunt maneuvered him into such a terrible position? Gray still did not understand it. "I . . ." Rory hesitated. "It's likely that's a correct assumption."

Gray tensed. Rory's assessment and his own were strangely similar. "Your guard," Gray said, not sure how to phrase the question.

Where was his guard? Were they lying in wait for him? Planning to kill him? Capture him? Return him to Sabrina after all these years of evading her powerful magic? He would kill himself first—simply slit his wrists with his sharp dagger. She could not be trusted with him. He did not understand entirely how she planned to use him, but it was clear that his usefulness would end with his death. And after all, Gray thought bitterly, who was even left to mourn him? Certainly not his father, who had betrayed him. Perhaps Evrard, but then, Gray had always felt like he represented more of an idea than an actual person to Evrard. A pawn, in the battle between him and Sabrina. Between good and evil.

Evrard would return to the place he had come from, and dismiss the whole time from his mind as an unpleasant experience during which he'd been forced to share a stable with Gray's stupid horse.

"What about my guard?" Rory asked, a confused wrinkle appearing between his auburn brows.

Gray took a step closer, even though there was something about Rory that was even more terrifying than the prospect of death. He leaned down, and caught the anticipation on Rory's face, even as he shifted towards his ear, not his mouth. "Can they be trusted?" he murmured.

He kept underestimating Rory. It was easy, with his soft hands and innocent eyes and stunning face. It was so easy to forget that under all that gorgeously waving hair, he had a clever, astute mind. Gray had expected an automatic affirmative, without much thought put behind it. He knew what it was like—royalty always assumed they were unassailable. Gray himself had believed that, once upon a time. But instead of what he expected, Rory furrowed his brow and gave the question serious consideration.

"Marthe is not particularly ambitious," Rory said. "She has been in my guard almost since my birth, and captain for the last ten years. Also, she was originally appointed not by my aunt, but by my father, before his death."

It was the first evidence that Rory had some inkling that his aunt was not to be trusted.

"And the rest?" Gray asked, very aware his questioning seemed relentless, but not willing to sacrifice politeness for safety.

Rory frowned. "Anya has been with me almost as long as Marthe has been captain. She's from Ardglass, but I do think she can be trusted." Gray's heart skipped a beat at Rory's admission. Would this Anya recognize him as the lost prince? It was doubtful; the last fifteen years had wrought many changes in him, but the chance still remained. "As for Acadia, Rowen, and Diana, I picked them myself after extensive interviews, and all were desperate for a chance to serve, a chance they would not have been given otherwise. I do not trust them as much as Marthe or Anya, but I would still trust them with my life."

It was enough. Still, they needed to locate the five guardswomen. Gray no longer wanted them roaming his farm unaccompanied. At least not until he could trust them as much as Rory did. His conversation with Evrard would have to wait.

Gray found them grouped together outside the farmhouse, talking in low voices as he and Rory approached.

"My prince," Marthe said, separating from the group. "Something here is . . . not right."

From the way she spoke in front of Gray, he knew the problem did not lie with him personally or with the farm, but rather the complete lack of criminal activity. They had come here expecting to find one thing and had found something entirely different. Obviously a cause for serious concern.

Rory nodded, and Marthe continued, after giving him a long, searching look. "Perhaps we should discuss this privately," she said.

Ahhhh, Gray thought, there is the strategy I would assume from a captain of the Prince's guard. She doesn't quite trust me either.

But Rory's chin stuck out stubbornly as he shook his head. "No," he said emphatically. "I believe we can trust Gray. After all, this is his farm. He has a right to know our plans."

Marthe's expression made it clear she did not agree, but she did reluctantly speak anyway. Whether that was blind obedience to her prince, or a grudging acceptance of the point he'd made, Gray wasn't sure. "I think we need to stay here," she said. "I considered seeking out the next village, and potentially evading the trap that was set for us here, but I believe we can protect you here, and we could possibly learn something useful by letting the intended action come to pass."

It was a gutsy call, but Gray didn't disagree with it.

Marthe then turned her attention to him, asking many of the same questions Rory had, except she had a different purpose. "How often do strangers come here?"

"One a month? Perhaps less?" Gray answered. Understanding where she was going with her questioning, he continued. "But it would be difficult for a soldier or a fighter to disguise themselves as one of them. They are often running away from a bad situation, wanting not to be found. An unwanted betrothal, or a father with heavy fists. They find the valley because they need it, they never expect it to be here."

"Then how were we able to find it?" Rory asked. A question that Gray had been asking himself since they had appeared outside his garden.

"I'm not sure," Gray admitted. Evrard would know, but he could not exactly excuse himself to go discuss the problem with the King of the Unicorns.

"Perhaps because we knew it was here," Anya volunteered.

"Perhaps," Gray agreed. It did seem like the most likely of explanations.

"We will set a guard," Marthe said. "Two per shift."

She did not glance in Gray's direction, so he knew she did not intend him to be part of it, but even then, he very much doubted he would rest tonight. He would lie awake, as he did many nights, and wonder who was going to come for him.

Maybe tonight the unknown threat would be coming for Prince Emory, instead. Gray had believed earlier he wouldn't care if Rory paid for his own ignorant mistakes, but to his surprise, now this thought did not bring any particular relief.

"You may rest in the bunkhouse," Gray offered. "I keep it clean for the occasional visitors. There is a separate stable, as well, stocked with hay." He had built the additional stable, even though newcomers to the valley rarely came with horses, because despite Evrard's confidence that no one could ever identify him as a unicorn, Gray still worried. Also, it alleviated the occasional awkward question, about why he would spend any amount of time in the stables, seemingly conversing with silent animals.

Marthe nodded, and one of the guards walked off with their horses, to water and feed them.

Rory did not follow them, but instead continued to stare at Gray.

"Would you give me a tour of your farm?" he asked.

Gray had hoped to slip away, to visit Evrard, and get his impression of the situation, and perhaps clean himself, maybe even find a threadbare shirt to throw on. Rory hadn't seemed offended by his lack of dress—more like the opposite, in fact—but some rules went deep. He could hear Rhys still, yelling in his mind, that meeting another prince with only a pair of loose breeches on was not done. You're from Ardglass, not a barbarian, Rhys would have insisted. And even though Rhys had been dead all these years, and his guidelines regarding attire, etiquette, and polite behavior should have died with him, Gray found himself squirming in a place he'd believed long forgotten.

"I have work to do," Gray said awkwardly, definitely not used to making polite excuses. He tried to ignore Rory's disappointed look, but it was much harder than it should have been. "Perhaps afterwards," he tacked on. He doubted Marthe would let the Prince out of her sight, but then she had done so earlier, so she must not find him too much of a threat. Gray didn't know whether to be pleased or insulted.

Gray entered the stables, his eyes adjusting to the dimmer light. He'd installed two larger windows, filling the panes with precious sheets of glass he'd bought in the village. Evrard hadn't expressed any particular gratitude, but then that was Evrard's way; expectation and then very little to follow in the way of appreciation. Still, Gray knew he enjoyed the windows, as he often found Evrard looking out them into the valley.

He found Evrard in front of one now, his expression the unicorn equivalent of discontent. "There are visitors," he said.

Evrard's great jeweled eyes swung his direction. "I saw myself," he said, "and not the usual kind."

"No," Gray said, sitting down on a stool he'd placed in Evrard's stall expressly for their chats. "A prince, and his guard."

Evrard did not seem surprised. "From Fontaine, then?" he asked.

"How did you know?" Gray did not really expect an answer; there was still much about Evrard's knowledge and his magic that he liked to keep close. Gray was never sure if it was because his methods were truly secret, or if he just enjoyed the mystery.

Evrard, unsurprisingly, ignored that particular question, and asked another. "What is your impression of Prince Emory?"

He thought for a long moment. What did he think of Rory? "He's soft, but strong," Gray finally said. "He isn't particularly experienced or skillful in the real world, but he's intelligent, and he isn't easily intimidated, even in stressful situations."

"He has potential then." Evrard sounded very pleased with himself, as if he'd predicted this result.

"Potential for what?"

Evrard just stared at him, one of those inscrutable looks on his elegant features. "Potential to be someone you could . . . trust."

Gray didn't know what Evrard had been about to say but had thought better of it at the last minute. He almost asked, but again, that was useless. If Evrard had wanted to tell him, he would have. Another mystery in a long line of infuriating mysteries.

"What does Fontaine have to do with us?" Gray asked instead.

"Much more than you realize."

"Prince Emory and his guard were likely lured here, but for what purpose, I don't know," Gray pointed out.

"They are strong and capable of protecting him," Evrard replied, "but ultimately, that job will come to you."

"So he will stay here? Is it his aunt?"

Again, instead of answering, Evrard turned his head and looked out the window. When Gray glanced in the same direction, he saw Rory practicing against a bale of hay with the sword that had sat at his waist. Anya was directing him, and Rory was just about as bad with the weapon as Gray would have guessed. Still, Evrard was right, he showed potential. Only glimpses of it occasionally, but it was there all the same. It was useless to imagine what Rory would have been like if he'd grown up like Gray, on his own, paranoid and a little desperate, but Gray imagined it anyway. He'd have been a force to be reckoned with, Gray realized. Just as strong as himself, maybe even stronger. Smarter, for sure.

"Yes, his aunt," Evrard agreed. "She is not to be trusted."

A problem Gray understood all too well.

CHAPTER FOUR

IT WAS SO PEACEFUL on the farm, Rory could scarcely believe that danger could be imminent. After a training session with Anya, Rory sat down against the small, squat house that Gray had specified for their use. Inside it wasn't particularly fancy or luxurious. Simple wood interior, filled with basic but well-made wooden furniture. Trundle beds with mattresses filled with clean straw stood against the walls. The stable was equally simplistic, but also very clean and well cared for. Rowen, who tended their horses, hadn't had any complaints, and she could be particular about stables.

Rory watched the main house and wondered where Gray had gone. He'd been so abrupt in his refusal to give Rory a tour of the farm—then had unexpectedly softened his stance, instead claiming they could do it later. He couldn't help but wonder if later could possibly be now. Gray had been, at turns, both standoffish and clearly intrigued by Rory. And Rory, who had met plenty of men before in the castle of Beaulieu and elsewhere, had somehow never met a man quite like Gray before. He'd kissed a few boys—because now, after meeting Gray, it was undeniable that they had been boys, not men—but there had never been anyone as guarded and mysterious and exceptionally intriguing as Gray. His secrets seemed to have secrets, and Rory was just stupid enough to want him to share, even if such a possibility seemed ludicrous.

He stood, and decided that if he wanted a tour, then he would have to be the one to request one, again. Walking around the side of the main house, Rory stopped dead in his tracks.

Really, he didn't know how Gray kept stealing his breath and his words from his mouth, because he'd done it the first time they'd met, and now he'd done it again.

He was still stripped to the waist, but now he was washing, big handfuls of water cascading down his much-cleaner chest, the muscles even better defined as they shone wetly in the late afternoon sun. Reaching down, Gray groaned as he took a small wooden bowl and filled it, pouring it over his head and slicking his dark, wavy hair back. Clean, with no hair to obscure his features, his face was even more arresting, as if it had been carved by a master in one of Rory's art history texts. Rory's heart pounded and his skin felt too tight. Should he stop watching? It felt wrong to stare when Gray didn't know he was being observed, but Rory wasn't quite sure he could tear his eyes away.

He wondered if Gray was like many of Fontaine, who enjoyed the company of both women and men, and if he did, if he would ever be interested in someone like Rory. It was a wildly insane thought, as Rory was a prince, and the entire court of Beaulieu would have been aghast at the thought of Rory entertaining someone who was essentially a farmhand, but Rory simply couldn't help it. It was impossible to be faced with a man like that, with that face, and that chest, and apparently those legs, as the dripping water molded his baggy breeches to a pair of exceedingly fine legs, and not wonder. Gray was the kind of man that you saw once and thought about for a very long time afterward. And Rory, who couldn't deny he was used to getting nearly everything he wanted, wondered if he might have the opportunity to do more than just look.

"Are you done staring?" Gray asked, not even glancing in Rory's direction.

Oh, he'd been caught red-handed. Rory tried to paste on a contrite expression on his face, but he couldn't quite manage it. He did feel a bit guilty, but he didn't regret one moment of what he'd seen. Gray was too beautiful for that.

Rory had observed the behavior of some of the more romantically inclined courtiers in Beaulieu, and had long since noticed what set them apart from the other, less successful courtiers, was a brash sort of confidence. Not quite sure he could emulate that, Rory smiled and walked over, hoping a poised but purposeful saunter would do the trick.

It didn't, but that might have been the unexpected root he tripped over on his way to where Gray was wiping his face and hands with a clean, rough cloth.

"Are you alright?" Gray asked with amusement.

Rory inwardly cursed his prodigious mental abilities—because they always seemed to preclude any sort of physical grace. "Yes, of course," he said. "Is it later? I'd like my tour now."

Gray looked at him thoughtfully. "You can see all of the farm from this spot," he said. "What is it that interests you?"

You, Rory thought before he could stop the word from popping into his uncooperative brain. Always you.

But he did not quite have the confidence to say it, so he just gestured wildly to the surrounding areas. "Anywhere you like to go, particularly. Even with all the work you do to maintain the farm, you must have some time to yourself," he said. Certainly not his best effort, but not his worst either.

Gray smiled, and this time it reached his eyes, warming the blue until it reflected the sky high above. "There's a place I like that you might also enjoy," he said.

Your bed? Rory thought, but didn't say out loud, because even as a jest, he didn't know how it would be received.

He knew he was attractive, but he also remembered the way Gray's expression had shuttered when he'd introduced himself as Prince Emory. Maybe Gray didn't like members of the nobility. Maybe he'd had a bad experience, and that was why he was hiding out in this valley. Rory didn't anticipate successfully persuading Gray to tell him about his past, but he still intended to try.

"I'd love to see it," Rory said.

Gray laid the cloth he'd used to dry on a length of fence and pulled on a threadbare shirt that had been hanging from the post. Rory ordered himself not to be disappointed that

Gray was covering up, and at the same time, wondered if it was because of him. Was it because Gray didn't want him to get any untoward ideas? Men didn't usually look at Rory and attempt to push him away, even if Rory rarely gazed back. They never seemed as interesting as his books did, though Gray put them all to shame.

Gray took them past the farmhouse, around the bend of the river, to a makeshift bridge, and walking over the rickety structure, he pointed out towards a meadow blanketed with flowers in a thousand different shades of purple. It gave the look of an endless, meticulously crafted coverlet, spread out across the ground, even though it was only Nature's random work. "Here," he said. "Sometimes I come here to think."

Rory knew that the man who had sat in the library tower in Beaulieu would have heard that and scoffed, imagining that a man such as Gray didn't do any thinking. At least any that was as intricate and important as the thinking Rory did. But something had shifted since he'd started this journey, and he was looking at the world and the people who inhabited it in a slightly different way now. He'd been so closed off in that tower, at first out of his own misplaced desire, and then because he suspected his aunt had never wanted him to look anywhere but at the book right in front of him. Now he was truly seeing, maybe for the first time, and he wondered at the risk she had taken to send him here, knowing that his world view might alter. Truthfully, the thought left Rory chilled to the core. Whatever was here, hidden in this valley, was important enough to be worth the risk, and he dreaded whatever consequences had followed him to Gray's farm.

"It's a beautiful place. Serene," Rory said, trying to shake his increasingly despondent thoughts from his head. He sat down, Gray following suit a few feet away. "What do you think about here?"

Gray tipped his head back and stared at the sky, an inky lock of wet hair sliding invitingly along his neck and exposed collarbone. Swallowing hard, Rory tried to follow suit and direct his attention to the sky above, but it was hard to turn away from someone so compelling.

He was silent so long that Rory was almost afraid he'd scared him away with the rather direct question. "Life," Gray finally said quietly. "Where it started, and how I ended up here."

"Was it your choice to come to the valley?"

"Choice? An interesting word and an even more interesting concept," Gray replied bitterly.

Much like some of Rory's tougher translations, he was discovering that Gray could be coaxed with space and plenty of time. Gray was suspicious and naturally cautious, and that, Rory realized, was because Gray didn't trust him.

Yet, he added to the end of the thought. Gray doesn't trust me yet.

But it was impossible to say if they would ever get a real chance to trust each other. In any other circumstances, Rory and his guard would've been on the road out of the valley first thing in the morning. The only reason they had decided to remain here was the uncertainty that awaited them. He and

Gray could be separated tonight or tomorrow or any day in the near future, and an opportunity to learn and know and trust each other would never exist.

Gray plucked a deep violet flower and twirled it between his fingers. They looked thick with calluses from where Rory was sitting, but he was gentle with the flower, nearly delicate. "That is much of what I dwell on," he continued, his voice nearly as rough as his fingertips. "Choice. There is much in this life I never had the opportunity to choose, but in the end, it's not a bad life."

"I chose all of mine," Rory said, and to his own surprise, his voice was nearly as bitter as Gray's. Yes, he'd made every choice himself, and every one of them wrong.

"Doesn't sound like the choices were good ones," Gray pointed out. His hair, drying in the warm afternoon sunlight, was growing waves, and Rory itched to smooth it back, to feel those rich locks between his fingers. Unlike Gray, his fingers were still untouched and smooth, despite the week of practice, and he'd feel every single strand.

"They were selfish, and a little stupid," Rory admitted. "I'm sure you don't know what that's like. You give everything of yourself, every single day. I can see it in the way you take care of this place."

"It's a little selfish." Gray hesitated. "Working hard is a good way to avoid thinking about anything in particular."

Rory laughed, and unexpectedly, Gray smiled, his quiet happiness lighting up his blue eyes. "Don't tell Marthe that," Rory said conspiratorially, "she'd never let me forget it."

Reaching out, Gray lightly cupped his shoulder. "You look like you could use some hard work," he said, then as suddenly as he'd touched Rory, his hand dropped away. But Rory, shocked, felt the pressure radiating through his skin and muscle and bone, the heat of the single touch permeating him to his core.

It was hard to say with the sunlight and Gray's skin, tanned from working so many hours outdoors, but he might have flushed. "Sorry," he added quietly.

At first, Rory thought the apology was because you weren't supposed to touch royalty unless they invited it first. A lonely way to live, Rory had discovered. But then he realized that wasn't it at all. Gray lived here alone, with only the occasional visitor. He was likely unused to touching and being touched.

"You're not wrong," Rory said, refusing to acknowledge the apology, because Gray hadn't done anything worth apologizing for, "I could."

Gray stared at him, his eyes a penetrating and impossible shade of blue. Rory had never seen anyone with eyes like that, eyes that could bore into your very soul. He hesitated, wanting to shift closer, to be closer, but before he could, a voice interrupted them.

"There you are," Marthe said, striding into the field and ruining both the moment and the serenity. "I've been looking for you everywhere, Prince Emory."

Rory rolled his eyes.

"You should stay closer," she continued, "it's our job to protect you and we can't do that if you aren't close by."

She reached down and helped Rory to his feet, shooting Gray a look as she did so.

When they were across the bridge, Rory turned to her. "What did you do that for?" he hissed.

Marthe looked unimpressed by Rory's insistence. "Do what? Interrupt you? You should be close by. Also, that man is a stranger."

"A handsome stranger," Rory sighed.

Marthe laughed. "He may be, but he still is not to be trusted. He has yet to prove himself or his loyalty. His motives may appear pure, but anyone can hide behind an innocent mask." Her knowing gaze told Rory exactly who she was referring to: the Regent Queen.

"Fine," Rory agreed with a grumble.

"Besides," Marthe added, "Acadia is putting together a rather delightful-looking stew with vegetables from the garden, and I thought you might want to assist her."

"I don't know . . ." Rory started to say, but Marthe's single quelling look shut him right up.

"But you should learn," Marthe insisted flatly.

The sun set in a glorious wash of golds and reds and oranges. Rory stood outside the bunkhouse and watched it as it finally sank behind the trees rimming the valley, curtaining the meadow below in darkness.

"Come inside," Diana urged him, hand out, ready to corral him back into the shelter. She didn't know that what Rory most wanted was to go find Gray again and continue their conversation from earlier. He'd sat with them for the evening meal, mostly silent, and only answering questions put to him directly. He'd barely met Rory's eyes, and as soon as the food was gone, he'd ducked out, quietly murmuring that he had work to do securing the farm for the night.

"I want some air," Rory argued, and Diana shot him a fond look.

"Remember at Beaulieu, when we would have to physically drag you out of the library?" she asked. "What happened to those days?"

Rory wasn't entirely sure; only that he wasn't sure he would ever be the same after these weeks on the road. Even if, against all odds, he could return to Beaulieu and resume his life as it had been, he didn't think it would fit him as well as it had before.

"Oh," she added with a quick blush. "You want to find that farm boy, don't you?"

Diana was the nurturer of the guard, and also the romantic. She was always falling in love here and there. After a few weeks, the fairy dust would fade from her eyes, and then a month later, another girl would catch her eye. Rory knew he was not the only one who hoped that someday she might discover love a little closer to home and melt Marthe's grumpy heart.

"His name is Gray," Rory said. "And he's . . . well . . . you've seen him."

Crossing her arms across her chest, Diana's dark eyes grew bright with excitement. "But it's more than that, you like him."

"I don't even know him," Rory admitted.

"But you want to," Diana said slyly.

At Rory's nod, Diana clapped her hands happily and leaned closer. "If I distract Marthe, you could steal away for a little while," she said.

Rory raised an eyebrow and Diana blushed again, more fiercely this time. "Not like that," she insisted while Rory ducked out the front door and gave her a little wave. "If I'm not back," he said, and then thought better of his suggestion, because the last thing he wanted was, if something actually did happen, for one of his guardswomen to ruin the moment again. He shook his head briefly, and Diana gave him another grin and a happy little wave of encouragement.

First he checked the stables, but other than two horses, one occupying a stall with a large window, its face haughty and somehow familiar, the other plain and brown and steady, it was empty.

There were no lights on yet in the farmhouse Gray slept in, and even though the light was still peeping through the trees, dusk had fallen. Rory realized belatedly that he should have taken a lamp or even a candlestick if he was going to go wandering about a strange place at night. When he returned, Marthe would likely skin him. But then maybe tonight was the night that Diana and Marthe finally opened their eyes and truly saw each other for the first time. If that happened, then it wouldn't matter how late the hour it was when Rory returned to the bunkhouse.

Still, Rory remained undaunted, and headed towards the makeshift bridge and the meadow Gray had shown him earlier. It didn't make much sense to come here in the dark, but Rory was determined to leave no stone unturned. But after wandering around half-blind in a quickly darkening meadow, he finally hurried back over the bridge. Gray hadn't returned to the scene of their earlier moment. He was still nowhere to be found.

Marthe's voice whispered in his ear, maybe he has betrayed you after all. I told you not to trust him. But he shook his head, refusing to believe that someone with Gray's quiet, wry reserve, with all that kindness and determination in his eyes, could truly be bad.

He checked the stables again, heartbeat racing as he hurried from building to building, and then back to the garden, where they'd first met. But this time, the patch of squash was disappointingly empty. Where has he gone? Rory thought worriedly. Had he truly abandoned them?

It didn't seem possible, but then that was when Rory realized the pounding he was hearing wasn't just the beating of his own heart in the darkness. It was the pounding of horse hooves against the valley floor, and far more of them together than his guardswomen. There were visitors in the valley, and by the way they were riding at such a speed, they hadn't come for a friendly chat.

This was the trap that Marthe was so certain would be set for them here, and now it had been sprung, and where was Rory? Separated from his guard and hiding in a squash patch. He ducked behind a particularly tall plant and hoped he could make himself small and unobtrusive enough that he wouldn't be noticed in the dark.

He crouched down, reaching up to pull his cloak around him, hoping the bright blue which had seemed so eye-catching and flattering in Beaulieu wouldn't be the thing that gave him away to the intruders. Perhaps these were finally the brigands they had been warned of? Maybe he'd been wrong about his aunt all along, and she wasn't trying to kill him. The hope had just begun to bloom inside him—a perfectly peaceful resolution to a problem that hadn't actually been a problem at all—when he heard a female shout and then another, and he realized with lead sinking in his stomach that it was his guards, yelling at each other as they fought. He heard the first clang of metal on metal and grabbed the little dagger that Marthe had thankfully insisted he carry with him at all times, his trembling fingers closing tightly around the metal, his damp palm slippery on the handle. It was nothing, not compared to a sword or an ax or a war hammer, and he hadn't even been properly trained to wield it. A week's worth of lessons wasn't nearly enough to take on a fully grown soldier who had trained their entire life to kill silly little princes like Rory.

He could have grabbed Lion's Breath, still sitting ornamentally in its jeweled scabbard on his hip, but he was even more out of his depth with the sword than he was with the dagger, so he stuck to what he knew.

How had he come to this, hiding in a patch of dirt, trying desperately not to cry as his friends fought an unknown enemy? Rory knew one thing for certain; he was not proud of the decisions that had led him to this moment.

If I get out of this, he bargained with fate and the gods and whoever was listening, *if I get out of this, and Marthe and Diana and Rowen and Anya and Acadia don't die, I will make different choices, I swear to you. I'll put others first. I'll stop being so selfish and self-centered. I'll figure out a way to take the throne and I'll rule my kingdom. Or at least figure out how to rule my kingdom. I won't hide in my books, not anymore. I'll face my aunt, and maybe I won't best her, but I won't let her win without a real fight.*

He repeated it over and over again in his mind, eyes straining as he watched shadowy figures, with the occasional glint of armor, fight across the farm. *If I get out of this, I will make different choices.* Several of the male-shaped figures fell, and Rory prayed he had seen correctly—that it wasn't Marthe or Diana or Anya. He'd taken them for granted; their loyalty and their unyielding friendship. And then he'd selfishly made their job harder by sneaking out alone, in search of the man who had probably been the one to betray them to his friends.

Rory swallowed hard, pushing back the tears as the sound of battle echoed in his ears. *If I get out of this, I will make different choices.*

Hooves, walking, not riding, the sound cautious on the ground, like someone was trying to sneak towards the garden, caught his attention. Rory tensed, and tried to crouch down even lower. He wished he'd discarded the bright blue cloak; it would probably be his undoing in the end. God, what an idiot I have been. If I get out of this, I will make different choices.

More rustling, like a man was wading through the garden, but trying to be quiet about it. Rory considered giving up his hiding place and running. He also considered rising and attacking, which surely this soldier, come to kill him, wouldn't expect from useless Prince Emory.

He'd made all the wrong choices leading up to this moment, but it was surprisingly easy to choose one now. Rory didn't know if it was the right one or not, but he sprang out of the squash, brandishing his dagger, and froze at the figure in front of him.

Bright blue eyes shone even in the darkness, and even though the man wore a dark cloak, his face was unmistakable.

"Gray," Rory whispered, his heart thudding painfully. Gray had betrayed them after all. He'd been part of the conspiracy all along, probably sent here by his aunt to lie in wait for stupid, silly Prince Rory and his tiny guard, and to dispatch them to their deaths once darkness fell. And Rory, blinded by Gray's handsome face and impressive set of muscles, had pounced at the bait just as she'd intended.

It hurt, and it stung, somewhere deep inside, where he'd always been so proud of his intelligence, of how many languages he'd spoken. All pointless now, Rory thought bitterly. Anger swelled inside as they stared at each other in this dark vegetable garden, and he gripped the dagger harder and decided that if death was calling to him, then he would try his hardest to take Gray along.

A second before he sprang at Gray, fully intending to bury his dagger in his chest, Gray hissed at him. "We need to go."

"What?" Rory couldn't believe it. Was he truly going to continue this play act, like Rory hadn't seen right through it? Did he truly believe him that stupid?

"There's soldiers, assassins, I think. Your guard is holding them back but we must go," Gray begged. "They can't keep you safe. There aren't enough of them. If we can sneak out of this valley, we can find a place to be safe."

Rory stared at him. "You really think I would go with you? After you betrayed me?"

"I didn't betray you," Gray muttered. "But someone did."

There was no logical reason Rory could ascertain that he should trust Gray. It did seem extremely likely that Gray had been the instrument of his betrayal, but his heart must have been more constant than Diana's, because Rory yearned to trust him.

The sword fighting grew in intensity. He heard a heartrending yell, and his own heart turned over. One of his guards must have fallen. He did not know which, but if he was going to depend on logic, then it was clear Gray was right and they could not hold their attackers off forever. And, that quiet, annoyingly logical voice added, if Gray truly intended to kill him, he could kill him now, where they stood. He did not have to spirit him away to take his life.

Gray held out his hand. "We must go," he begged. "You must trust me."

"I suppose I must," Rory said and took his hand.

Gray took them outside of the garden, to where a horse was standing, heavy saddlebags loaded on its rump, but lacking a saddle. "We will ride," Gray said, and gave him a quick boost up to the horse, who glanced back at him, the intensity of his expression nearly matching Gray's.

You must be imagining things, Rory thought hysterically. But then Gray launched himself behind Rory, kicked at the horse's side and they were galloping away.

Unlike the soldiers, they were riding a horse who knew the land, and could also be astonishingly quick and quiet. Rory couldn't believe how little noise it made as they rode away towards the other side of the valley. Gray did not say a word to either the horse or to Rory, just clutched his back and Rory, burying his hands into the horse's mane, held on tight and fast.

The horse did not break pace until they reached the first cluster of trees on the other side of the valley, and then it began to slow.

"Nobody is following us," a voice said, almost eerie in the darkness. It was a completely different tone than Gray's voice, and yet it had to be Gray because Rory could not see anyone ahead of them, and the voice had come from very close.

"They could follow our tracks," Gray replied and his own voice was grim.

"I obscured them. It would take a very skillful tracker to follow," the other voice promised. A little smugly, if Rory had anything to say about it.

"Excuse me," Rory finally said. "Who goes there?"

Gray gave a short, unamused laugh and suddenly the horse slowed, and he dismounted. He held out his hand again for Rory to take, but Rory, suspicious and acutely aware of how alone they were in the forest, slid off the horse without his assistance.

"You said those who cannot see, do not see," Gray said, and Rory froze. His comment, unless Rory was more rattled than he'd believed, was clearly directed at the horse. "How do we open his eyes?"

"Whose eyes?" Rory demanded. "And what are they supposed to see?"

"Trust your instincts, they have yet to fail you," the voice said again, and even though the light was extremely dim, Rory swore it was the horse who was speaking. But that was completely, entirely impossible.

Gray sighed, and turned towards Rory, a wry smile on his face. "I would like to introduce you to Evrard, King of the Unicorns."

He had seen this horse twice before. Once, while searching for Gray earlier this evening, when he had walked into the stables, and again right before they took flight out of the valley. It had only ever looked like a horse to Rory, plain gray sides, normal musculature—a completely unassuming creature. But now, Rory looked closer, and suddenly, the horse's coat was not gray at all, but blinding, perfect white, like the first unadulterated snowfall. It had a horn, also white and shimmering vaguely in the moonlight.

Rory's jaw fell open as the horse—no, the unicorn—bowed to him. "Prince Emory of Fontaine," it said in its deep sonorous voice, "it is very good to meet you, though I do wish the circumstances were better."

"You always do," Gray muttered.

The unicorn—Evrard, Rory corrected, still stunned by the sudden turn of events—shifted his hooves impatiently, his long mane rippling. "Then I shall have to stop saving you and Prince Emory both from certain death," he retorted sharply.

"It's . . ." Rory found his etiquette rules falling short at being introduced to a unicorn, though Evrard was a king, so maybe that was where he should start. "It's a pleasure to meet you, Your Highness," Rory said, and bowed deeply.

"Ah, Prince Emory, the pleasure is entirely mine," Evrard claimed as Rory met his deep, jeweled eyes once more. "Your elegant manners are such a balm after spending years with this one."

This one clearly referred to Gray, who had a curious mixture of affection and annoyance on his face as he looked upon Evrard.

"Neither of us is very easy to live with," Gray offered wryly by way of explanation.

"How did such a creature come to live at your farm?" Rory wondered.

He fully expected to receive an evasive answer from Gray, and a smug one from Evrard, who clearly had not met an etiquette manual he didn't enjoy.

"I rescued him, much as I have rescued you tonight," Evrard pronounced.

"He did," Gray agreed, "and he took me to live in the Valley of the Lost Things."

"Valley of the Lost Things?" Rory puzzled. "Is that the official name of it?"

"It has always been a haven for those who have need of it," Evrard said.

"But not tonight." Gray's voice was stark and his face was full of concern. "Tonight, it was found."

Sudden guilt swamped Rory. It was his fault that Gray had temporarily lost the home he had built. Rory and his guard had led the soldiers there, which must have been his aunt's purpose in sending him in the first place.

"I'm sorry," he said, genuinely meaning it.

Evrard impatiently shook his mane. "Do not apologize for actions that were not your fault. It was inevitable the magical barriers would be breached; she has been trying for many years to find a way around them. You were a convenient pawn in her plan."

Rory straightened his cloak, brushing off some of the dirt remaining from the squash patch. "Then the soldiers were not looking for me?"

"They were," Evrard said. "But not only you."

"You should start at the beginning, you are only confusing him. Considering his reputation as one of the most intelligent in the realms, it can't be too difficult to explain," Gray said.

Evrard inclined his head. "My apologies, Prince Emory," he said.

"Rory," he insisted. "Please call me Rory."

"He won't like that," Gray inserted, "but make sure he doesn't choose to give you another name in its stead."

Rory glanced over at the other man. "Is that what he did with you? Is Gray not your given name?"

"It's his name now," Evrard said firmly, making it abundantly clear that part of the conversation was over. "We will start, but not at the beginning. There is no time for such a detailed story. Are you aware, Prince Emory, that your aunt has been making plans to usurp your throne?"

It was embarrassing that he had only just realized it, but at least he did not have to stand in front of the King of Unicorns and be surprised by that information. Rory nodded.

"Fontaine must not fall into her hands," Evrard said.

"How can I possibly prevent that? I have no army, no guard, no followers, no courtiers who would possibly be on my side." Rory had known the difficulty of his situation before, but was newly faced with it now, and the impossibility of it made his throat tight. But he'd made himself promises when he'd been hiding in the garden, and the most important had been that he would make different choices. Harder choices, Rory realized. That was what he'd really meant; that he would stop taking the easiest road, the road of least resistance.

It would not be easy to leave the throne to his aunt, most likely because she wouldn't want any loose ends, but it was certainly much harder to actually challenge her.

Add to that fact how few resources Rory actually possessed, and it took on shades of the impossible.

But Evrard did not seem much deterred. "You have more than you realize. You have me, and you have Gray," he boasted arrogantly.

Rory did not want to discount Gray—after all, he was rather in thrall to the man—but what use was a farmhand in taking back his kingdom from someone who had spent many years solidifying her position to prevent any opposition?

He was about to delicately broach this subject, when Gray entered the conversation abruptly, bluntly. "What," he declared harshly. "No."

"No?" Evrard asked.

"No," Gray said, his voice as resolutely hard as Rory had ever heard it. "No, I will not assist this silly princeling who let his aunt take over his throne." He turned and stomped off, headed into the darkest part of the woods.

Rory was left staring after him, completely lost as to his sudden change of mood. Also, silly princeling . . . that hurt more than he'd anticipated. And it hurt even more because it wasn't entirely untrue.

CHAPTER FIVE

GRAY SHOULD'VE KNOWN IT was inevitable that this whole time, Evrard had just wanted something from him—and not even to help him return to his own kingdom, but to assist some pretty little prince to pull off the impossible and defeat his shrewd, clever aunt. When it came to Evrard, there'd been a lot of things Gray had been pissed off about over the years. The unicorn's unbearable smugness was definitely one, and his high-handedness in believing he knew better than anyone or anything else was another. This was the worst of those two poor character traits combined into one singularly offensive assumption that of course Gray would be thrilled to leave the safety and peace of the valley to help another prince take back a throne that Gray wasn't sure he deserved anyway.

Initially, he'd headed towards the very edge of the valley, to the rim of trees that hid it from the world, which also happened to be the direction of the village. He could get a weapon there and come back to his farm. If the soldiers were still there, he'd kill them all and take his land back by force, if need be.

The last thing he intended to do was fall in line with Evrard's machinations and help Rory out. And there was absolutely no doubt in Gray's mind that Evrard was right in this scenario: Rory needed all the help he could get.

The closer he got to the ring of trees, the cooler Gray's temper grew. He still had no intention of leaving the safety of this valley, and he had no intention of going anywhere to help anyone, but despite Evrard's boasts to the contrary, Gray thought it was very possible their tracks could be followed. And for all Evrard's confidence, he was hardly a fighter, and Rory was even less capable. That little dagger might do a little superficial damage, and that was if—a very big if, Gray believed—Rory actually knew how to properly use it.

It was such an acute contrast to his own upbringing in Ardglass, when he'd been taught to throw a dagger with force and accuracy practically from the cradle. He could've used that dagger to stop someone in their tracks; Rory might leave a minor scratch.

"Silly princeling," Gray muttered under his breath, and turned around, doubling back on his own tracks, looping back around behind where Evrard and Rory were still speaking, making no attempts to quiet their voices or hide their location.

Typical, Gray thought as he leaned back against a conveniently placed tree. He could hear them talking as clearly as if he were still standing with them.

"What should I do?" Rory asked plaintively, and he sounded so like Gray had felt when he'd asked Evrard the same question. But Gray had been a child then, a mere eleven years old, and Rory was supposedly past the age when he normally would have taken the throne of Fontaine. He was supposed to be an adult, but he was so soft and sheltered, it was difficult to see him as a particularly competent one.

"You will need to convince him," Evrard insisted.

From his hiding place, Gray scoffed. Sure, the Prince was attractive. Sure, he'd been tempted at least twice to kiss him, but that was just a momentary pleasure. That didn't mean anything. It wasn't like Gray had ever intended to pledge his life to the other man. Evrard was a remnant of a different time, when things like nobility and honor might have meant something. And to someone like Rory, they probably still did, but then Rory was still grappling with the fact he'd been betrayed.

Gray had spent the last fifteen years living in the aftermath of betrayal, and that life had shaped his belief that honor and nobility meant very little indeed. They were just pretty words people used to control others, and Gray had no intention of ever falling into that trap ever again.

"How will I do that?" Rory asked.

"You must appeal to his greater nature," Evrard explained, and Gray made a face. He wasn't sure he had one, and surely Evrard would suspect that. "He wants to pretend it doesn't exist, but it's a part of who he is."

"Are you sure?" Rory didn't sound very sure, but then Evrard always contained enough certainty for himself and everyone else.

"Of course I am sure." Evrard's haughty voice made Gray smile, even though he wasn't looking forward to Rory's clumsy attempts to appeal to a part of him that no longer existed.

"I guess I should go find him," Rory said.

"He'll be headed towards the village, with the misguided notion that he will find weapons to help drive the soldiers out of his valley. I brought him there to save his life, and while I am pleased he's found peace there, he's grown complacent."

Gray gnashed his teeth, certain that Evrard must know he was listening in, and that was why his words were so cruelly pointed. Hadn't Evrard insisted for so many years that Gray needed to be cautious and always on alert for those who might betray him? Wanting to return to his valley wasn't complacency; it was necessity, because Evrard himself had emphasized its importance in their lives dozens of times, hundreds of times.

"There is no need to bother," Gray said, emerging from his position from behind the tree. "And," he added tightly, "I have done always as you asked. Stayed in the safety of that place, because that was the only safe place, or so you always said."

Rory looked astonished to see him; Evrard, not surprisingly, did not.

"Our circumstances have changed," Evrard pointed out, "and there is no safe place for you or for the Prince, not anymore. The valley is overrun. The Prince's guards are likely dead. We need to go to the Karloff Mountains. There is an important magical heirloom there that will be instrumental in assisting Prince Emory in gaining his throne."

"A fool's errand," Gray muttered. To reach the Karloff Mountains, they'd have to skirt Ardglass to one side, and make an arduous week-long journey. Gray believed Rory would never make it, and Evrard himself, while still in possession of his magical skill, had grown soft during their sojourn in the valley. If anyone was complacent, it was him.

"Perhaps, but it must be done," Evrard said.

"And you will do it without me, though I doubt, even if I assisted, that you would be successful."

Silence fell over the group. Gray could tell Rory was working on a plea, turning over various methods and words in his head, trying to find a serendipitous solution to Gray's adamant refusal.

Finally, he spoke, quietly and with a surprising authority. "I know you wish to return to your former life," Rory pointed out. "Before tonight, I wanted the same thing. I wanted to go back to my comfortable life that I understood, that understood me in return. I have no battle training, almost no weapons training, my guard is likely . . ." Rory paused, trying to collect himself. "They are likely dead. I am at the mercy of my aunt, who has been carefully and systematically ensuring that I am not capable of taking my own throne. I could take the easy path, and leave, and never return. I could hide. But even though victory seems uncertain, I can no longer pretend that avoiding a fight would be the right thing to do."

"You can forget about appealing to my honor," Gray said dryly. "Because I don't have any."

"I'm not trying to appeal to your honor," Rory promised. "I'm telling you that your comfortable life is gone until I can guarantee it again. And that will only happen when I have regained control of Fontaine. I can guarantee this place is erased from every map it is mentioned in. You will be left alone, entirely, if that is your wish. But I cannot achieve anything if I don't have your help."

Gray was silent for a long moment. "Logic," he finally said. "I'm surprised that's the angle you took."

"I know what you want," Rory said, "and it occurred to me that I should remind you that we actually want the same things."

"No, you want to go on some ridiculous quest to find a magical bauble in the Karloff Mountains, and I want to go back to my farm and be left alone," Gray insisted.

"Except," Rory reminded him, "that you can't go back to your farm and be left alone, not until I achieve my purpose. So you either must make do outside of the valley and leave your farm to the soldiers who are no doubt currently forming an encampment there, or you will come with Evrard and me and assist us in ejecting my aunt from Fontaine."

Evrard gave Rory an admiring, appraising glance. It annoyed Gray even more. Probably because he had never been the recipient of one of those looks, and also because no matter how much Gray wanted to deny it, Rory was actually right.

"Fine," Gray said, "but my assistance ends the moment we actually get this thing that Evrard thinks we need. And you'd better hold to your promise about the valley."

"You have my word. Shall we shake on it?" Rory asked.

"Well," Gray said sarcastically, "it's not like we have a scroll and a quill here so we can sign a proper contract." He extended his hand, and even though Rory wore a pair of those ridiculously buttery soft, pale yellow gloves, Gray felt the heat of his skin through the leather as they shook hands briefly.

"Excellent," Evrard said. "I knew you would see reason, Gray."

Gray glared at him. "Did you now?"

"And you, Prince Emory," Evrard said, simpering, "I wasn't sure whether to believe your vow, but you kept to it admirably."

"What vow?" Rory said, brows creased with confusion.

"You swore that if you got out of the valley alive, you would make different choices. Better choices. I believe that is what you truly meant, though I suppose you can be excused for being nonspecific as you were currently being hunted by several assassins sent by your aunt." Evrard paused, eyeing Rory sternly. "Or did I get it wrong after all?"

"No, no, no, that was it." Gray wasn't sure Rory was going to be able to speak at all, his eyes were so huge in his pale face, and his jaw seemed to have permanently dislodged as he gaped at the unicorn in front of him.

"Make a note," Gray murmured to him under his breath, "don't make a vow to anything unless you want Evrard to know all about it."

Rory looked like he was only a few moments from running away into the forest, despite all the inherent danger.

"How did you know that?" Rory asked Evrard. "I didn't even say it out loud."

As Gray expected, Evrard didn't answer. "Don't bother asking," Gray finally told Rory. "The best explanation I ever got out of him was, magic was intended to be mysterious, whatever that's supposed to mean."

"It was a perfectly reasonable answer," Evrard said with a sniff.

Leaning closer, Rory looked up at Gray. The only outward evidence of their sudden and rash departure and gallop across the valley was a few slightly mussed curls. This partnership would have been easier, Gray thought, if the Prince was a little less attractive. "You lived with him for years?" Rory questioned in a murmur, the edges of his lips quirking into a smile. "How?"

"Carefully," Gray retorted.

"He was a most attentive pupil, when he wasn't digging around in the dirt or fixing the stables," Evrard granted him somewhat graciously.

But Rory was still stuck on the particularly annoying vein that ran through Evrard's personality. One, that he was a king, and therefore believed himself to be infallible and two, he was a unicorn, and therefore knew himself to be unique. "I think you're right but you're also wrong. Gray didn't just dig around in some dirt or fix the stables, he created the farm out of practically nothing, and it's an accomplishment to be celebrated, not a punchline to your ego," Rory said hotly.

Gray stared at him. He knew Evrard appreciated the work he'd done over the years; perhaps he'd not always understood the drive that had kept Gray working as hard as he had, but of course it was better for Gray to be a diligent worker than a lazy ass. What he had never expected was for Rory to defend him.

"Ah," Evrard said knowingly, "you admire Gray. As well you should. You must be partners, and admiration is a good stepping-stone to trust."

Rory blushed. "He's easy to admire."

Evrard's gaze swung towards Gray but he didn't say a word. Didn't really trust himself to speak. What could he possibly say? Other than his stunning looks, Gray had yet to find something in Rory that he truly admired. Maybe in time that would change, but for right now, he liked him even though he didn't particularly want to, and he definitely did not trust him yet.

"What is this object we are seeking in the Karloffs?" Gray said, because it was better to change the subject. Better to stick to the quest that Evrard had set for Rory and get it over with as quickly as possible. Gray was already itching to go back to his valley and be left alone again.

"It is a magical heirloom of significant importance to Prince Emory, if he is to take back his throne," Evrard said and Gray rolled his eyes.

"You've already said all that. Where is it? What is it? How do we get it? All things that you clearly don't want to disclose, but all-important facts we will need to actually obtain it," Gray pointed out.

"All in due time," Evrard said smoothly, clearly much less concerned than Gray himself. Which, Gray supposed, was par for the course with Evrard. Perhaps all magical creatures contained such confident aplomb. He couldn't be sure, since Evrard was the very first he'd ever met. He wasn't counting Sabrina, because she'd been a sorceress, in thrall to dark magics, who had merely transformed temporarily into a magical creature.

The hair at the back of his neck slowly rose. "Are we going to be encountering any opposition to our quest?" Gray asked quietly. He did not want to specify Sabrina by name, but he knew from the solemn look in Evrard's eyes that he knew exactly who Gray was referring to, and to Gray's great dismay, he nodded his head.

"Many dangers on the road, and perhaps even more once we reach our destination, deep in the Karloff Mountains," Evrard confirmed.

Such a pronouncement wasn't a surprise, but Gray could grimly acknowledge it was definitely not what he'd wanted to hear.

They spent the rest of the night tucked away in the shelter of several thick trees. Gray had insisted they wait for daylight before continuing. They would need supplies to make the trek to the Karloff Mountains, and Rory was too recognizable to take into the nearby village. They'd wait for daylight, Gray pronounced, and then he would get additional supplies, while Rory and Evrard waited in the forest at the edge of the village.

Rory curled up in an empty, rotted tree trunk that had long since fallen, pulling that ridiculously bright blue cloak around his shoulders. First thing, Gray thought, we find the Prince some new clothes. He was far too recognizable with all his beautiful fabrics and arresting looks, and the last thing they needed was for Rory's aunt to discover their whereabouts.

It was too close to dawn to light a fire, so Gray hunched down into his own gray cloak, leaning against Evrard's warm body. "It feels like old times," Gray said quietly as he watched Rory doze fitfully.

Gray could feel Evrard sigh mightily. "He is not as adaptable as you," Evrard murmured, "but he will need to learn, nonetheless."

"Not an easy thing, discovering your closest relative in the world wants you dead," Gray pointed out.

"Your father never wished you dead. Sabrina had discovered a particularly powerful immortality spell that required innocent, royal blood. Not a lot of it, but enough, and the potion would need to be re-consumed occasionally, to continue its efficacy. All Sabrina told your father was she needed a little of your blood, every once in a while. Of course, she had led him to believe that he would share in the spell with her. But he was too power-hungry, and his mind too influenced by her, to understand that she could never risk you running away or growing up. She would have drained you completely," Evrard said. "You would've been dead that night."

Gray took all this information in, wishing, despite what he'd already told Rory earlier, that some of this had been given to him long ago. But then would it have made any real difference? He knew, if he hadn't escaped Tullamore, she would have killed him, one way or another. And whether his father had expressly given permission for his death or not, the end result was still the same.

"It doesn't change anything," Gray said roughly.

Evrard shifted again, and he could feel the impatience of the motion. "Semantics always matters," he insisted. "I promise you; it matters. Someday, you will see that."

"And if she wanted royal, innocent blood," Gray asked, "why is it she still apparently hunts me?"

But Evrard, who had already shared more in the last five minutes than he had shared in the previous fifteen years, went quiet, much to Gray's frustration and complete lack of surprise.

It is enough, he told himself, but he wasn't entirely sure he was telling the truth.

As dawn crept across the ground, he stood slowly, shaking off the sluggishness of his muscles, and left Rory sleeping with Evrard.

The trip to the nearby village was quick, and he made good time. The men in the village knew him well, though they also understood he often kept to himself when visiting. They did not question his purchasing of several saddlebags' worth of dried meats and crackers baked specifically not to spoil, and several good waterskins. There were some curious looks when Gray stopped by a used clothes stall in the main village market and purchased plain brown breeches and doublet, and an even darker brown cloak—none of which would fit his much taller, much bulkier build—but he stopped all questions with a single, hard glare. It was nobody's business but his own what he was buying.

The sun had barely crested over the trees when Gray returned to the grove where he'd left Evrard and Rory. The latter was now awake, sitting on another log, speaking quietly to Evrard. Their conversation largely faded as Gray approached, and he wondered, idly curious, if they had been speaking of him, and what the topic had been. Likely Rory had been asking more questions, and Evrard had been largely ignoring them.

"Here," Gray said, tossing Rory a shapeless bundle. "Put those on. You can't go fluttering around like a butterfly in a spring garden when we get on the road."

Rory opened the leather thongs to find the clothes Gray had bought. Fingering the rough cloth, he glanced up. "These are for me?"

"Like I said," Gray ground out, "you can't be prancing down the roads like a beautiful butterfly. We'll be robbed blind a thousand times over."

Gray watched as Rory retreated to a denser part of the forest to change, and just before he averted his eyes, saw Rory finger the clasp on his fancy cloak one last time before discarding it.

"I have supplies for the journey. Should be enough to last us," Gray said, directing his words to Evrard. "The saddlebags will be heavy, though."

Evrard sniffed. "I am sure I am capable of carrying a few bags," he said. "I'm only surprised you were able to circumvent your need to bring a horse on every journey we take together."

"Fifteen years in, and you still resent poor old horse," Gray said with a smile. He hoped the soldiers had left him well enough alone. Before they'd escaped out of the stable, Gray had released him and urged him to head to the opposite end of the valley, where there were streams and large fields full of clover for him to snack on. At the very least, he would not be subject to the enemy soldiers' whims. While Evrard thought the horse was quite stupid, Gray had firsthand evidence of how smart and brave he was. He'd never let himself be captured.

"Everything . . . sort of fits, I suppose."

Gray glanced up from where he was strapping the saddlebags to Evrard's back to where Rory was standing, having returned to the clearing after changing his clothes.

It was true; unlike his brilliant yellow satin doublet, the brown hung on his smaller frame, but at least he looked like so many other young men who lived in the village and outside of it.

"The idea is not to attract any attention," Gray said. "And only rich men have their clothes tailored to fit."

What he didn't say was that even though Rory was swimming in extra fabric and was lacking the brightly colored wardrobe to set off his astonishing looks, he still looked . . . incredibly beautiful. Too beautiful, if Gray was being honest.

"Perhaps, Prince Emory," Evrard suggested, "you could dirty yourself up a bit. Slump your shoulders. You still look . . ."

"Princely," Gray finished for him, afraid of what Evrard would have said, and that it would've echoed Gray's own thoughts too closely. "You look like a rich boy, slumming it in his servant's clothes."

Rory frowned. "You want me to roll around in the mud?"

"I'm sure the hard travel to the Karloff Mountains will put some necessary travel dirt on him," Gray inserted hastily. "Just keep your head down and your cloak hood up, your hair is so distinctive."

"Your reputation as the Autumn Prince precedes you, I'm afraid," Evrard agreed.

"I could cut it off . . ." Rory suggested.

Gray hated the way his heart stopped at his words. He still remembered the way he'd felt when Evrard had changed his name all those years ago. Unlike a name, hair could grow back, but without it, Rory wouldn't be . . . Rory, and that seemed like too great a crime to bear.

"We're keeping off the main roads anyway," Gray said hastily. "There's no need for such a drastic action."

Gray finished strapping the saddlebags onto Evrard, and after a quick, hushed confrontation, beckoned Rory over to where the unicorn stood. "I know the way, so I'm going to ride in front," Gray said. "You'll have to hold on to me. It won't be as easy as before." He didn't add that, without any saddle, it would take a great deal more thigh strength to stay mounted when Gray was so much larger than Rory was. Truthfully, Gray didn't want to contemplate Rory's thighs, though they looked . . . fine.

Incredibly fine, his uncooperative mind supplied, taking in the breeches he'd changed into, which were thankfully quite a bit more fitted than his new doublet.

"It won't be an issue," Rory promised. "I'm a good rider."

Gray had gotten that impression already, which was one of the reasons he was suggesting this at all. The problem was that, since the Karloffs bordered Ardglass on one side, it turned out that Gray was much more familiar with their route than even Evrard. And unlike the valley, with its magical pull, the Karloffs—other than the magical item they were after—didn't particularly exude any special feeling that Evrard could track. They would have to rely on Gray's fifteen-year-old knowledge of the maps he'd studied as a boy.

Not an ideal situation, but they had no other choice.

Without ceremony, Gray mounted the unicorn, and gracefully, Rory followed suit, tucking his cloak around him and pulling up the hood, even though the sun was bright overhead. Gray nodded in approval, and then Evrard started to pick his way through the trees, searching for the road that would take them around the village rather than through it.

After a few minutes, Evrard came upon it, and thus began their journey.

CHAPTER SIX

EVRARD PULLED THEM OFF the little-traveled road only when the sun began to fall behind the trees. Rory's stomach was growling; he and Gray had each chewed a little dried beef and a small piece of hard cheese during the day, but he was ravenous for real food. Something fresh and hot; he already missed Acadia's ability to make a delicious meal out of just about anything. Rory dismounted on shaky legs, stretching his muscles as he glanced around. Evrard had pulled them quite a bit off the road, deeper into the forest, where travelers on the road might not see their fire.

Of course, it wasn't likely that anyone would even be traveling this road, because they'd only seen a handful of people during the entire day. Rory had kept his eyes averted and his head tucked into his cloak, and as far as he knew, none of the few farmers they'd passed had even glanced their direction. Rory wasn't used to being quite so invisible and he wasn't sure he liked it.

On the other hand, traveling by wrapping his arms around Gray's firmly muscled midsection was definitely a positive. His legs were sore and definitely stiff, but the journey from

Beaulieu to the valley had gone some distance to getting him used to long, tough days of riding.

"Shall I gather wood for the fire?" Rory asked. He wasn't much help setting up a campsite, as his guard had teasingly reminded him more than one evening on the road, but anyone could gather sticks and branches, and that was often the job he gave himself.

"What fire?" Gray asked blankly.

Rory was confused. "The fire. Aren't we stopping for the night? Having an evening meal?"

Gray dismounted, and reaching back into one of the saddlebags, rustled around for something, and then tossed it, without ceremony, in Rory's direction. He caught it, barely, and stared, more dismayed than he wanted to let on, at the piece of dried meat in his hands.

"We can't risk being seen," Gray said. "I'm sorry if your princely sensibilities can't live without a fire. Or a hot meal."

He was pathetic and spoiled. That was what Gray was truly saying, and Rory had to admit that he probably wasn't wrong.

"No," Rory stumbled, "it's fine. I was just . . ."

"Expecting something different," Gray finished, and while the words were sympathetic, his delivery was flat. "Expect it from now on. Your life is no longer as it was; it's changed." He turned and walked away, deeper into the forest, perhaps to relieve himself, or maybe just because after spending all day on Evrard with Rory, he needed some space.

Rory turned to Evrard. "Do you need anything?" he asked. After all, Evrard had been doing the lion's share of the work today. All Rory had had to do was hang on.

"Your Highness," Evrard said, "shouldn't it be I asking that question?"

"I really wish you would call me Rory," he pointed out. If Gray had been present, no doubt he would've said the request was pointless, but Evrard's constant deference was off-putting.

Perhaps because while he'd always known he was a prince; Rory had never seen himself as particularly prince-like. An impression no doubt encouraged by his perfidious aunt.

"Perhaps in time, when we get to know each other better," Evrard said. Rory had just spent the last twelve hours plastered over his backside, so he definitely felt like that statement could have been better phrased as never.

"Did you know those men who came to the valley?" Rory asked.

"Not personally, no," Evrard said, his voice careful, "but their purpose was well known to me. Her purpose has not changed since I rescued Gray fifteen years before."

"Why would someone want him?" Rory asked, resentment leaking into his voice.

Naturally, Gray would choose to re-emerge into the tiny clearing at the worst possible time. He was scowling, no doubt at Rory's words, and at the impression that he and Evrard had just been talking about him behind his back.

"There's a stream a little distance away," Gray said shortly. "You should drink some water."

"In time, yes, I will," Evrard said. Rory wished he could emulate the unicorn's abundant dignity—but perhaps without his smug condescension.

"It's a long journey to the Karloffs," Gray said, and Rory wasn't sure if the comment was directed at him or Evrard. "You should get some rest."

"Our young prince was asking important questions," Evrard said, much to Rory's surprise.

"He was?" Gray too seemed surprised, but Rory had a feeling that his astonishment had nothing to do with Evrard and everything to do with his seemingly unfavorable opinion of Rory.

"The woman you know as your aunt," Evrard said, looking at Rory, "who is currently the Regent Queen of Fontaine, is the same woman who sought to capture you many years ago, Gray."

Rory realized then that he had never seen Gray truly angry, he'd only ever been passingly annoyed. The expression on his face now was truly murderous—hard and taut, his features carved white in the setting sun. "Why didn't you tell me?" he demanded of Evrard.

Rory would have cowered if it had been him, but Evrard merely glanced up from the patch of clover he was chewing on. "It was not the right time."

"You let her take over another kingdom?" Gray challenged. "After what she did to Ardglass?"

Rory was shocked to discover that Gray was Ardglassian. Though in retrospect, he supposed he should have known. He had the big build, and the same dark hair that was so common in that country. Now that Rory was looking, he could see the similarities Gray shared with Anya, who had been a member of his guard.

Was still, he hoped, though he didn't have much faith that any of them had survived the soldiers who had descended upon the valley.

"I could not stop her," Evrard said. "It was not my responsibility and it was not the right time. But now Prince Emory, with your valuable aid, can begin to move against her."

"What did my aunt do to Ardglass?" Rory thought it safe to ask the question because Gray's face had softened, and he no longer looked like he wanted to choke the life out of Evrard.

"She was an advisor to the King," Gray said shortly. "And she conspired to control him by seducing him with power and drink."

"She is very good at getting what she wants," Rory said despondently.

"She needs to be stopped," Gray said. "I should slip into Beaulieu and gut her with my dagger."

"No," Evrard said firmly. "We will find the artifact that we seek in the Karloff Mountains and then, and only then, will we attempt to remove Sabrina from the throne of Fontaine. Things must be done a certain way. Now, I will find this stream and have a nice cool drink."

As Evrard departed into the woods, to Rory's astonishment, Gray shot him a commiserating glance. "There is no use asking why things must be done a certain way,"

Gray said with a sigh. "Because he will not tell you. It's infuriating."

"If you had known my aunt was behind the suffering in your country, would that have been enough to convince you to guide us?" Rory asked. It was one of the very first thoughts he'd had, when he'd realized the importance of what the unicorn had told them. Here was a perfect reason for Gray to agree—he would be able to enact his revenge on the woman who had conspired to destroy the kingdom of his birth.

But Gray shook his head slowly. "No," he finally said. "No, it wouldn't have been. In fact, I might have stayed further away. I might not have agreed at all."

Rory could not believe it. "But here was an opportunity to destroy the woman who tried to kill you!"

Gray only shrugged. "What's the point? There is always some noble who wants power and to control the people. What does it matter if it's Sabrina or some other bitch? It doesn't matter to me. All I wanted was my valley, and to be left alone in it. I don't want to be involved."

"And yet you're here," Rory said, mystified.

"I'm here because you convinced me with a logical argument," Gray said flatly. "That's all."

And Rory might have believed him before, but there was a flash of something in Gray's eyes when he talked of killing Sabrina, of marching into Beaulieu and gutting her. He might wish to be jaded and bitter and beyond thoughts of vengeance, but perhaps Evrard was right after all; there was still some unknown quantity left, hidden deep inside Gray.

"You should get some rest," Gray repeated again after a long silence.

And Rory supposed he was right; after all, even if some speck of honor remained in Gray, he could not possibly reach it tonight, and tomorrow would be another awfully long day. He sat down against a downed log and took his ugly brown cloak, wrapping it around himself. It might be hideous, but at least it was warm.

To Rory's surprise, he found his eyes growing heavy. Gray was right, their journey was long, and he would need all the sleep he could get, when he could get it. Rory closed his eyes and nodded off almost immediately.

He woke with a start, and even though the forest was quiet, the silence was eerie and wrong.

Rory's own breath was harsh in his ears, and he tried to muffle it against a fold of his cloak. He realized then that he couldn't hear even the rustling noises that Evrard generally made, or even Gray's short, compact breaths. Was he alone? Had they left him here, all by himself, in a strange, unknown forest?

A hand clamped down around his mouth before he could pant any louder, the fear and panic overtaking him. "Shhhh." Gray's voice was a harsh whisper in his ear as he struggled futilely against the much bigger, much stronger body holding him.

It was slightly less terrifying that it was Gray holding him, and Rory stilled. The night air continued to be motionless and tense, even as his heartbeat slowed back to normal.

"We're surrounded," Gray whispered so quietly that Rory barely heard him. "I don't know who it is. It might be the soldiers who attacked us in the valley."

If it was the soldiers from before, Rory knew they were dead. They'd been armed and mounted, and while he and Gray were currently accompanied by a magical unicorn, they had almost no weapons, or the experience to wield them. Gray was strong, but he'd spent his entire life on the farm. And Rory had stupidly eschewed the lessons that might have saved their lives tonight.

"Do you have your sword?" Gray asked, his voice impossibly dropping even lower. "I only have my dagger, and it'll be no use against fully armed soldiers."

Exactly the problem, Rory thought hopelessly. But he did have it, it was currently strapped to his waist and he nudged Gray's left arm. Rory felt him shift the position of his fingers, searching for the hilt. One moment, he was looking, and the next he'd clearly found exactly what he'd sought, because he was thrusting Rory away from him as he drew the sword, all in one smooth, coordinated movement. The sword glinted in the moonlight, silver shining along the blade. It was Marthe's job as captain of the Prince's guard to maintain the sword, with its two lion heads wrought in gold and their ruby and topaz eyes, and the blade looked impossibly sharp. Lion's Breath was the ancestral sword of Fontaine, and would no doubt announce Rory's presence to anyone who recognized it, but he knew Gray hadn't had a choice. He couldn't be expected to fight off multiple attackers with a little dagger.

Of course, it would be nearly impossible to fight off multiple attackers even with Lion's Breath, if Gray hadn't had any training in swordsmanship.

But to Rory's surprise, Gray held the blade confidently, with the assurance he knew how to use it, and called out, "Come out, and I will not kill you all."

A man, not dressed in the same unrelenting black as the soldiers from the valley, but instead in various patchwork fabrics—lush red velvet, bright green silk, and swirling orange and bright blue patterns—emerged from the trees beyond the clearing. He had long hair, even longer than Gray's, and it was almost as dark. "That sword," he said pointedly to Gray, "is not yours."

Gray swung it once, and then twice, the arcs graceful, his grip confident. Despite most of his brain occupied by frantically searching for a peaceful exit strategy, Rory had a stray thought. He cannot be just a farm boy. Not when he moves like that, not when he swings a sword like he was born to do it.

"It will kill just as easily as if it were mine," Gray said. "Tell your men to come out or I will return you to them in pieces."

It must have been an epic boast, a feint designed to possibly save their lives without having any of the skill to back up his words. Rory could come up with no other explanation. But, he supposed, he should participate as well, not just continue cowering next to a fallen log. He stood, pulling his own dagger, and wondered, not for the first time, where Evrard had disappeared to.

The man in front of Gray started to laugh. "You hold something of great value, my friend. Something we would like."

Gray took a single, menacing step closer. "The sword may not be mine, but it is not yours either."

"And the Autumn Prince? Is he yours as well?"

Panic closed off Rory's throat. They'd recognized him somehow. No doubt Lion's Breath had helped in his assessment of the situation, but somehow his hood had fallen, and his hair was embarrassingly distinctive. Maybe he should have ignored Gray and cut it off after all.

"This whore?" Gray said negligently, gesturing towards Rory with the sword. "You must not have seen the Autumn Prince up close if you think this cheap fake looks anything like the original."

Rory schooled his expression to take on the bored, indifferent look of someone who wouldn't care that he'd just been called a cheap fake. There was very little chance they could pull this off, but it was far better than any of the ideas Rory had come up with.

"You've seen the Autumn Prince?" The man took a step closer. Rory wished, belatedly, that he'd listened to Gray and rubbed some dirt on himself or something to obscure his features at least partially. There was nothing to be done about the hair, not now, but the rest? Rory knew he'd been too sure that nobody would ever recognize him.

"A real looker," Gray said. "Way more attractive than this one, for sure."

"And the sword?" A frown had appeared on the other man's face, like he was no longer quite sure. "That a fake too?"

"Real gold. Real silver. Real rubies, but," Gray swung the sword almost carelessly, "not the actual Lion's Breath. Like we'd have a priceless ancestral sword out here in the middle of nowhere." The last bit was muttered under Gray's breath, and Rory knew it was directed entirely at him.

"Still worth a pretty penny." The man crept forward half a step.

The sword stopped mid-swing, and suddenly pointed straight at the man's exposed throat. "That's close enough," Gray said, his voice growing hard.

"There's twenty of us and one of you. Two of you if you count your little prince for the night," the man said, and suddenly he was not smiling. Or laughing. Or joking. He was all seriousness, and Rory realized that they'd both been posturing, but the man had had the upper hand all along.

"This is his fake sword. He's a master," Gray tried bluffing, but the man shoved aside the words like he hadn't even said them.

"You're not unattractive," the man said, "and the 'prince' is exceedingly so, even if he's a fake. Good money there. And the sword? That can be melted down." He smiled again. "You're coming with us, either easily and quietly or with twenty arrows in your back."

The clearing grew brighter as the clouds covering the moon gradually moved away and gold glinted on the man's hands as he pushed his hair back with a clearly studied nonchalance.

Rings, Rory realized. He's wearing gold rings on every single finger.

It was a risk, but everything had felt like some form of a risk since he'd left Beaulieu. He knew if he didn't do something to diffuse the situation, they could be carted out of here with half a dozen arrows each. Rory took one careful step forward and then another, watching the lines of Gray's back tense as he heard the leaves crunch underfoot.

"Gray," Rory called out clearly, hoping he wouldn't get shot, "it's fine. We'll be fine. Put the sword down."

Gray risked a look over his shoulder, his glare washing over Rory. "Put the sword down," Rory repeated, and then remembering the story Gray had attempted to weave, affected an imperious whine. "You're creating a scene and it doesn't matter who pays me as long as I get paid."

The man leered. "You'll get paid all right," he said reassuringly, and Rory had a feeling payment wasn't all he was promising. And that was, Rory considered, not all bad. He'd need to figure out how to get the man alone, anyway. Or at least as alone as their culture generally permitted.

From the way Gray had yet to lower his sword, Rory did not think he'd guessed who the man was, or considering how he'd grown up, it was possible that Gray had never encountered this particular nomadic tribe before. Gray didn't know how to deal with them, Rory realized, and he did.

"Gray," Rory repeated insistently, "please trust me." His words didn't really fit in with their act, but without them, he didn't think Gray would ever give up his weapon.

Rory watched as he re-gripped the pommel and then, finally, lowered the edge of the sword to the ground. The man snapped his fingers, and suddenly, an arrowhead dug into the side of Rory's neck. He glanced to the side and around the clearing, men and women dressed similarly, all with rings decorating every single one of their fingers and marching up their ear lobes in graduated sizes, materialized with arrows drawn on Gray and Rory.

Of course, there were far more trained on Gray than on Rory. That wasn't much of a surprise. Rory knew he didn't look like much of a physical threat, but he could use that to their advantage.

"Rory," Gray hissed as the newcomers approached him and took away his sword and Rory's dagger, tying their hands together in front of them with rough ropes. Rory looked closer and realized they were made of woven-together scraps of colorful cloth, some with gold thread and other bits with embroidery, all rubbing uncomfortably against his wrists.

"Can you get your knot loose?" Gray hissed under his breath as they were forcibly put together and marched deeper into the forest, surrounded by so many bows there was no possible way to escape. I hope Gray realizes he'd be shot in seconds, Rory thought.

"No, and I'm not going to try," Rory hissed back.

Gray stared at him incredulously, but didn't immediately go back to wriggling, trying to loosen his bonds.

They walked for what felt like hours. They walked for so long that Rory had to wonder how the tribe had even known they'd been there—surely the clearing had been so far from their encampment, they couldn't have known. And yet, Rory knew he must be wrong, because he and Gray were currently in their hands.

"Where did Evrard go?" Rory asked under his breath, when the first rays of dawn were beginning to creep across the forest. "Was he hiding?"

Gray shot him a look that Rory didn't quite understand. "He went to get water and didn't come back," he finally admitted. "It wouldn't surprise me if he knew this was coming."

"And what," Rory asked, his voice rising despite trying to prevent it, "he wanted us to get kidnapped?"

Shrugging, Gray turned away.

Even though there were very few other options available to him, Rory—not for the first time—contemplated whether it had been the smartest choice to select a farm boy who clearly wasn't who he seemed and a snobby, elitist unicorn to help him take back his kingdom.

Unfortunately, considering his hands were currently tied, they were being marched god knew where, and Evrard was missing, there wasn't much to do about changing plans now. Rory straightened his shoulders and dove deeply into his memory, because their fates probably depended entirely on his ability to remember everything he'd ever read.

A few minutes later, they came into another clearing, this time full of tents, all constructed of the same brightly colored patchwork as their captors' clothing and the ropes that were currently binding their hands together. A few smoldering fires dotted the ground, and horses grazed off on the other side of the tents. It was exactly as Rory had expected, and he set into motion the first part of his plan.

They were taken to the largest tent, but instead of being ushered inside, the man holding Rory's hands stopped him directly in front. Rory took a breath and gathered himself for the challenge to come.

He could feel Gray right next to him, bristling with indignity, straining at his bonds, and he prayed this would work, because surely any moment now Gray would attempt to escape, and would no doubt be killed in the process.

He cast his eyes downward, and then fell to his knees, hands clasped in front of him, head bent, all adding to the subservient vibe he was attempting to communicate.

"What are you doing?" Gray demanded, as their captors murmured to themselves, no doubt astonished that a stranger would know even one of their customs.

"On your knees," Rory hissed at his companion. "Don't look and for god's sake, don't say anything."

There was a long, drawn-out moment where Rory's heart sat in his throat and Gray did not move. Rory didn't know if this would work if he followed the proper etiquette and Gray did not. Truthfully, he didn't want to find out the hard way.

Finally, Gray dropped to his knees beside him. "This better work," he muttered under his breath.

Rory couldn't speak, because everyone was watching him, and one of the books he'd read had stated very specifically that once the ceremony began, the Seeker could not utter a single word before the Giver did.

But he did think that maybe if he managed to get them out of this mess, Gray might begin to find him a little less useless.

Rustling sounds emanated from the tent, and after a few moments, an older woman with long, dark hair streaked with silver, and braided with tiny silver bells, emerged from between the flaps. She took in Rory's position, and then Gray's.

And then she too fell to her knees.

We're on, Rory thought with determination, and began to speak.

CHAPTER SEVEN

GRAY DIDN'T RECOGNIZE THE language Rory had haltingly begun to speak, but clearly everyone around him did, because they were fascinated, hanging on every single word he said.

He also had no idea who these people were, or their customs, or anything about them. And the truth was, he should have because while they weren't necessarily close to Ardglass, they were in the lands bordering Ardglass. Maybe Rhys hadn't gotten to this odd sort of tribe in his education when it had abruptly ended? But then Evrard had never mentioned them either.

Rory's head was still bent as he spoke, and when he finished, a reverent hush fell over the group.

Risking a look, Gray peeked up and to his utter astonishment, found the woman staring at Rory with tears in her eyes.

She finally spoke, but she did not use the same language as Rory. Instead she spoke in the common tongue Gray knew. "You must forgive us," she said, reaching up to wipe her eyes. "It has been many, many years since any of us have heard our language spoken out loud. For some of us, we have never heard it, only had it described. How is it you are able to speak it? I thought the teaching of it was lost to us, like many of our brothers and sisters have been lost to farms and towns and villages."

Rory looked up and settled back on his heels. He looked as shocked as she did. "I am sure I did not do it justice," he said. "I've never heard it spoken, I've only read it, and the pronunciation guide was very rudimentary."

She stared at him. "Merleen tells me that you are a prostitute, fashioned to look like the Autumn Prince. How is it you have been able to study our language?"

She did not say that whores generally didn't have access to a lot of books, especially to valuable ones containing virtually lost languages. Then a half-second before he did, Gray realized what Rory intended to do. He wanted to reach out and stop him, but then he remembered Rory's whispered words. Trust me. Gray wasn't sure he trusted him at all, not yet, but so far this entire encounter had left Gray feeling like he'd taken one look at the Prince next to him, seen a different side of him, and had come to entirely the wrong conclusions.

Yes, he was a prince. Yes, he was pretty. Yes, he did not exactly understand how to defend himself in the traditional ways, with weapons and with fists. But he was defending them now, wasn't he?

Instead of stopping Rory, Gray stayed silent and let him continue.

"I am not a prostitute, maj," Rory said. "I am indeed the Autumn Prince."

Gasps resonated from the surrounding audience, but the woman in front of them did not seem even the tiniest bit surprised by Rory's revelation. She leaned forward and took his chin in her hands. Strong, capable hands, used to hard work. Gray could see the evidence of it in the swollen knuckles and the calluses up and down her fingers. She held strong to Rory, and he didn't flinch as she stared into his eyes. Gray, on the other hand, was a total mess. Yes, Rory had caused a sensation and had made the woman sentimental and sad for times long gone, but they were still tied up and they still had no weapons. They still weren't free.

Trust me. Rory's words echoed in Gray's mind, and though he had to fight against the suspicion that had maintained such a stronghold on his mind since that desperate night fifteen years ago, he did. When the attackers had come to the valley, Rory had trusted him—even if maybe he shouldn't have. Gray took one deep breath, and then another. It was his turn to put his life into Rory's hands.

"You are very far from home," she finally said, releasing his chin. "You have come to me as a Seeker, hoping I will be a Giver. What is it that you need?"

"Freedom," Rory said, re-assuming his prior position, humbling himself before the woman. A Giver, Gray thought, this must be some ancient ritual that Rory knew because he'd read about it. Just like the language.

"You speak of something that seems of low cost to us, but in reality, is worth very much," she retorted tartly. "You are valuable prisoners. You carry expensive belongings, including a priceless ancestral sword of your country."

Gray had to force himself not to roll his eyes. Why had Rory brought Lion's Breath with him to the valley? He couldn't even truly use it, at least not the way it was meant to be used.

"Maj, I am currently a prince without a throne, without a country. I could not leave it behind to lose it to those who would use it ill."

The woman settled back on her heels. "Your aunt?" she asked, raising an eyebrow.

"A story as old as time," Rory said, and Gray was impressed at how tonelessly he could speak about the relative who had conspired to betray him.

Most of the time he attempted Rory's cool, but despite what he'd boasted about not caring, he did care. If Sabrina ever walked into his valley, he'd have killed her on the spot. Which was why, among other reasons, she'd never done it. Instead she'd sent her soft, pretty little prince, and tied them up in a nice bow for the assassins she'd sent to follow.

"If I give you this request," she said, voice thoughtful, "what would you promise me in return?"

They had nothing to give. No gold, no goods in trade, Rory had his sword—in theory only, since it was currently in the tribe's possession—but nothing much else of value. For the first time since leaving Tullamore, Gray wondered what knowledge of Prince Graham would be worth to someone like the woman in front of him.

It was his closest held secret, the one he anticipated taking to the grave, but what if he gave it up?

If you gave it up, he reminded himself, you'd lose everything. You'd lose your valley, your freedom, your independence. Probably your life.

While he wasn't against Rory taking his throne from Sabrina—as far as Gray was concerned, that bitch didn't belong anywhere near one—that seemed an especially steep price to pay. So he kept his mouth shut, and a moment later, he was very glad he did, because of course, Rory had known all about this ceremony, and had known he would be asked to give something.

And knowing this, he'd already prepared something to offer.

"Knowledge," Rory said confidently. "I would give you knowledge. Once I have deposed my aunt, and regained the throne, I would invite you to Beaulieu, and we would study your language together, and hopefully, be able to revive some of the lost parts of your culture."

"How would we know you would keep your bargain?" asked Merleen, the man who had originally captured them.

"I would give my word," Rory said. Gray almost laughed. If he was Merleen, he never would have believed Rory. But then Gray had gotten the rotten end of the whole nobility and honor thing. He could at least acknowledge that, and also acknowledge that those experiences made him never want to trust anyone of Rory's stature ever again. Others might not be nearly as suspicious.

Merleen also did not look particularly convinced, but then the woman spoke up. "Swear on your sword," she said softly.

Rory blanched, all the blood draining from his face. His reaction was so severe, Gray had a feeling that breaking a promise you'd sworn on Lion's Breath led to something extremely unpleasant.

"You know the story then," Rory said, his voice equally as soft.

"I know that your ancestor, King Francis, swore a promise to some peasants, and he swore it on Lion's Breath. And when he broke the promise, he died in an agony of fire and flame."

Rory cleared his throat. "The sword has no known magical qualities. The story of King Francis was no doubt embellished to frighten any ruler of Fontaine from lying to their subjects ever again."

The woman raised an eyebrow. "Then it has worked," she said. "You will swear on Lion's Breath, or there will be no Accord."

"And no freedom," Rory said flatly.

"And no freedom," she agreed.

For the first time since he'd opened his mouth and spoken in a language Gray had never heard before, Rory turned and looked Gray straight in the eyes. "What do you think?" he asked.

Gray stared back at him steadily. "Are you intending to lie?" he asked under his breath.

"No," Rory said, shaking his head vehemently, "but I have no guarantee that our quest will be successful. And I do not believe Lion's Breath quibbles over particular circumstances. If you break your promise, it will exact retribution in fire and blood."

"You really believe that?"

Rory looked like he did, in fact, really believe it. "I wasn't always sure," he hedged, "but then I read the original version of the story, written by a steward present at King Francis' death. The only obstacle to believing that the sword was magical was magic existing in this world." Rory glanced over to where they'd come from, where presumably Evrard was somewhere, waiting for them. "And now I believe that I was wrong, and it does exist in this world. So therefore, if I am to take the logical approach, I truly believe that if I break a promise made on Lion's Breath, I will die. Badly. Painfully."

"In a storm of fire and blood, yes," Gray said.

There was a long silence. Gray re-examined the possibilities of knocking out every guard in the vicinity before he was killed, and again came up about five guards too short. And smartly, they had kept Lion's Breath on the other side of the clearing, as far away from Gray's hands as possible.

"Is the sword particular about the person who swears the promise? Do they need to be of the Fontaine royal line?" Gray did not particularly want to swear on the sword and possibly risk his own terrible death, but somehow it seemed worse that Rory, who had so bravely tackled this, who knew ancient languages, who had studied cultures that were dying, should risk his life this way. Gray's was much less valuable. Besides, nothing had been said about regaining the throne of Ardglass, only of Fontaine. Presumably, Gray would die a farmhand, never revealing to anyone who he truly was. Rory, on the other hand, was destined for a much greater fate—if he got the chance.

Maybe Gray should give him that chance.

"It does not matter," Rory said, "because I would never permit you to do it. This is my throne, and I will make the promise." He looked up at the woman, who was watching them carefully. "Bring the sword."

But of course, they were not going to permit Gray anywhere near a weapon. Gray was a little flattered by this. Instead, they yanked Rory up by the shoulder, and marched him over to where a big, burly man was currently holding the sword. Rory rested his bound hands on the pommel, right over the lions' heads, and said, "I swear on the throne of Fontaine and all my royal ancestors that I will keep my promise to assist the Mecant tribe in regaining their original language and reviving their customs."

The woman nodded her head once, and suddenly there was a knife cutting Gray's bonds, and he was jerked upwards.

Gray met Rory's eyes across the clearing and was torn between wanting to thank him for saving their lives and berate him for risking his own so foolishly.

Didn't he see that he was impossibly precious? Irreplaceable?

Gray had not always felt that way, but the last twelve hours had forcibly opened his eyes. Without Rory, without his precious knowledge and the incredible intelligence he possessed, they would have been dead or sold into slavery. The quest would have been lost. Gray's valley would have been lost. Sabrina, through happenstance and fate, would have won without having ever been challenged.

"A horse," the woman said, in a voice that brokered no argument and one was led towards Gray. He laid a firm hand on its warm neck. It looked to be an excellent animal, and well-trained. Rory came over to where Gray stood, strapping on the sword again.

Gray's dagger was returned, and brief goodbyes were said, though they were none too friendly.

No doubt everyone had been expecting a nice big payout for capturing him and Rory, and instead, they were being let go, and being given one of their horses.

"You know the way back," Rory murmured to him, and Gray mounted, followed by Rory behind him.

With a single nudge in the right direction, the horse trotted off in the direction from whence they'd come.

Riding, the journey not only seemed much quicker, but passed by in a flash. Gray realized that in the dark, the tribe had been leading them in circles, presumably to ensure that Rory and Gray could never return to their encampment. They crossed the stream he'd directed Evrard to the night before, but Evrard was nowhere to be found.

They reached the clearing, the saddlebags still lying on the ground, and Evrard was still not present.

"What should we do?" Rory asked uncertainly after they dismounted. "What if Evrard was also captured?"

"Then we would have seen him in the camp," Gray said flatly. "And as of course, Evrard has given us almost no information on how to proceed to find this magical thing, other than it rests in the Karloff Mountains, we will stay here and wait for him to return."

Rory flopped down onto the ground, into much the same position he'd occupied the night before. "I really can't believe that worked," he said, grinning. "But as soon as I saw their rings, I knew who they were, and I knew they could be reasoned with."

"Reasoned with? Asking you to swear an oath on a sword that could bring you a fiery death?" Gray muttered.

"I had to do it," Rory said.

Except that he hadn't, and they both knew it.

"I could have done it," Gray said lowly. "You don't need my help. What you know is so much more valuable. I lived over this direction when I was a young child, and I'd never heard of that tribe before today."

Rory gaped at him. "Are you really claiming to be expendable? You?"

At Gray's refusal to answer, Rory stood up and started pacing back and forth in front of the log he'd slept against the night before. Had it only been the night before? It felt like an eternity had already passed since they'd escaped the valley, but it had been barely forty-eight hours.

"You built a farm from nothing. You're a fighter. You were going to fight those men off; I saw the way you held the sword. You know how to use it much better than I." Rory paused. "A pretty princeling. Useless. I believe that was your impression before today."

Gray couldn't deny it. He also couldn't deny that his mind had been forever altered by their encounter with the tribe.

"You're a prince," Gray said, because he couldn't quite wrap his thoughts around everything that had changed, so suddenly and so irrevocably. It was easy to condense down all his jumbled feelings into one single fact: Rory was a prince, and he was going to reclaim his throne.

Rory stared incredulously at him. "You don't think that matters."

It hadn't, but somehow, now it did.

Flushing, Gray turned away. "You barely slept before. You should get more sleep now."

"Stop changing the subject. Were you really going to swear my promise on my sword?" Rory demanded.

Rory's intelligence had already come in very handy, but now Gray wished he was a little less perceptive. Squaring his shoulders, Gray glanced over at Rory. "It was logical."

"No," Rory said with an unbearably attractive decisiveness, "it was all emotional." Closing the three steps between them, Rory reached out and put a hand on Gray's chest, right above where his heart beat faster than he'd ever admit. "Try to tell me it wasn't emotional. I can feel it. Right here."

Gray could feel it too; his heart, which had been numb and alone for so long, was waking up, the numbness receding. It felt like too much, too soon, but before he could stop Rory and say, that's plenty close enough, Rory rose up and pressed his lips to Gray's.

He wasn't just pretty; he was stunning, perfectly bringing his nickname to life, all smoldering heat with that cool thread of logic running through him. Gray reeled back, but he hadn't lied to Evrard back in the valley. Rory was strong; strong and determined. Instead of retreating, he followed, winding his arms around Gray's neck, and tugging him closer, his mouth opening under Gray's.

Almost immediately Gray lost his mind, and it sank into the warm lassitude of pleasure, growing warmer and then hotter as Rory's tongue slipped into his mouth. Gray could feel his slender frame pressed tightly against his own much larger body. He wanted to strip the ugly, ill-fitting clothes off, and glory in Rory's perfection. Because he would be perfect, Gray realized. He'd be the most beautiful creature he'd ever seen, and somehow, also the strongest.

Nothing like he'd ever imagined when Rory had first ridden into his valley.

"I leave you alone for a few hours, and you're already pawing at each other." The voice was understated and cool, and it doused the flames burning between them.

Rory froze, and removing his mouth from Gray's, glanced to where the voice had come from. Gray had to resist the urge to drag him back against him.

"Where have you been?" Rory demanded, and Gray was proud despite himself. Evrard always believed he was in charge, and sometimes you needed to remind him that nobody gave a damn who was in charge; they were supposed to be a team.

"I was down at the stream and heard the men coming," Evrard said, casually trotting into the clearing like Gray and Rory hadn't had to avoid death or slavery by sheer nerve. "I hid, naturally."

"Naturally," Gray retorted. He wasn't sure he trusted his mouth to say anything else. He wasn't sure he trusted his mouth not to simply claim Rory's sweet one again and again, and then again. He knew, without a doubt, that now that he'd had a taste, he'd always be hungry for it.

"Yes, we're fine," Rory said testily.

"I knew you would be," Evrard said, their obvious frustration seeming not to bother him much. "How did you manage to escape so quickly?"

Rory shot the unicorn a hard look. "I invoked the ancient power of the Accord."

If Gray had to guess, he'd say that Evrard looked pleased, like Rory had just eclipsed even his high expectations.

"Interesting," Evrard said, barely acknowledging Rory's quick cleverness, and already moving past it. "We must get on the road. We have lost valuable time."

Gray couldn't contain his glare. "I haven't slept," he said. He couldn't really remember the last time he slept. Exhaustion was making his boundaries blurry. Or maybe that was the kiss.

"The road is fairly straightforward for the next few days. Your Highness, you will ride in front, and Gray can rest against you," Evrard ordered.

Rory glanced over at where the horse they'd been sent back on was munching on a patch of clover. "We should take him," Rory said.

Gray was almost certain that unicorns were incapable of rolling their eyes, but he swore Evrard did. "Another useless animal you want to save," Evrard moaned. "I expected better out of you, Your Highness."

"He's a good horse," Rory insisted stubbornly. "We can even sell him later on or trade him for supplies."

Gray wasn't going to get involved in their argument. He'd never heard the end of it when he'd insisted on bringing the horse who'd saved his life all those years before.

But of course, Rory wasn't going to let him avoid it. "Gray," he begged, "tell him."

Sighing, Gray reached down and picked up their saddlebags of supplies. "You hate carrying these," he pointed out to Evrard. "We can use it as a pack horse. And Rory is right; we can trade him further down the road for additional supplies."

"Fine," Evrard sniffed, clearly annoyed that he'd been outnumbered, but all Gray felt was overwhelming gratitude that Evrard had dropped the tiny matter of finding them kissing earlier.

He didn't need Evrard to tell him that it was the height of stupidity to become involved, physically or especially emotionally, with someone like Rory. Prince Emory, Gray reminded himself. And while he himself had once been of equal stature, those days were long gone, with no hope of ever returning to them.

Gray slept on and off as they regained the old road, and each time he opened his eyes, he was pleased with the steady progress they'd made. He'd only traveled this road once or twice as a child, and the markers were faded from the elements, but they could still be deciphered.

They stopped to rest as the sun fell behind the trees, and again Gray nudged them off the main road, and they found another, even smaller clearing of trees, and there they set up a quick camp. Gray even relented, and allowed Rory a small fire. It wasn't like a lack of fire had saved them from being tracked or abducted before.

Gray sat on a downed log that he'd pulled closer to the fire, and watched the flames dance moodily. This morning, the kiss had ripped through his veins like the fiercest quicksilver, but tonight, after too many vivid, uncomfortable dreams, all the kiss made him feel was dread. He was going to grow close to Rory, and maybe even let him in further than anyone since Rhys, and he would likely lose him in this mad quest. Even if they both survived somehow, Rory's destiny was to rule his people and sit in the high tower of Beaulieu—noble and royal and far beyond Gray's grasping fingertips.

All you want is to go back to your valley and be left alone, he reminded himself, but the thought didn't provide the same reassurance that it always had before. The kiss had changed things, as he knew it would.

Kissing Rory wasn't like kissing any of the other men and women who had passed through the valley before and whom he'd taken momentary pleasure with. Kissing Rory was willingly and eagerly sticking your hand into the fire and hoping to be consumed by it.

Gray was not quite self-destructive enough to welcome that.

To his dismay, Rory hadn't spent the last twelve hours regretting the kiss. In fact, as he picked a spot on the log right next to Gray, he shot him a very hopeful look from under those sinful lashes.

Why did he have to be so beautiful, both in and out? Gray thought with frustration.

"Did you get enough rest today?" Rory asked.

"Yes," Gray said shortly. He didn't want to have to lay out the reasons why continuing to kiss—or more—was a bad idea. But he had a feeling Rory was going to make it impossible to avoid that conversation.

"Good," Rory said, and Gray hated that his voice had slid further into uncertainty. Seeing Rory in all his brave, strong, confident glory had been life changing. He didn't want to be responsible for the disappointed look growing in Rory's eyes, but what else could he do? He was a realist. This couldn't be a passionate love affair; it was only a stepping-stone to better things for Rory.

"I'll keep the watch tonight," Gray said. "Feel free to get some sleep."

He stood and was about to go off to make sure the horse was secure for the third time, when Rory reached out and touched his leg. "Are you angry with me?" Rory asked.

At least that was easy enough to answer. "No," Gray said, "I'm angry with myself."

Of course Rory looked mystified. "I thought we both liked it . . ."

"We did. I did. Too much. You're . . . you're a prince, Rory. The Autumn Prince and the heir to Fontaine. I need to remember that, and so do you."

Rory just gaped at him as Gray shook his hand loose and walked away, ostensibly to check the horse, but really to sulk. Nothing new; he'd been spending all those years since leaving Tullamore trying to find something to do so he could avoid sulking.

But even if he'd had the farm to lose himself in, Gray knew a multitude of tasks couldn't have distracted him. Not when it was Rory.

CHAPTER EIGHT

IT WAS IMPOSSIBLE OVER the next few days for Rory to
pretend that he wasn't deeply pissed. He had never imagined
that his princely status might actually prevent him from
kissing a man he cared about. Because that was the root of
the problem: he'd begun caring about Gray. The seed had
been there from the first moment, when Rory had come upon
him in all his dirty, shirtless glory, and then had begun to
sprout during their escape from the valley together. Getting
captured and then being forced to rely on only each other
had encouraged even more growth. The wide, approving
looks Gray had given him over the Accord nurtured it
further.

And that kiss?

If Rory had possessed any intention of steering clear of
feelings for Gray, the kiss had obliterated it completely.

And yes, it was incredibly vexing that the only thing Rory
could not fix was the very thing that pushed Gray away.
Rory spent the past three days as they traveled towards the
Karloffs stewing on the back of Evrard. There were more
people on the road now, as it wound closer to the mountains,

but Rory was less worried about being recognized these days. He'd definitely grown dirtier, face smudged to match his brown cloak, and the ugly patchy beard he'd always shaved had begun to grow in. Gray had chuckled under his breath when he'd first seen it one cold morning, but Rory hadn't been very amused.

How was he supposed to win Gray over when he was deliberately making himself less handsome?

The answer was, he wasn't. At least that was the gist of the cold shoulder that Gray kept giving him. Just enough clipped, shortened sentences to communicate the plans for the day, then complete and utterly annoying silence during the ride. At night, Rory might have been a tree stump for how much attention Gray paid to him.

Truthfully, after spending approximately half his time stewing over Gray's silence and the other half silent and bored, Rory would've been miserable except for Evrard's company. Evrard was certainly every bit the snob that Rory suspected, but he was also so much more. A streak of something resembling kindness unexpectedly wove its way through Evrard's conversation occasionally.

Rory had wondered how Gray could have tolerated growing up in the valley with only Evrard for company. At first Rory had been shocked that Gray was as well-adjusted as he was, considering the sole friend he'd had, and then as the hours progressed, he realized that while Gray and Evrard didn't always get along on the surface, the undercurrents between them went deep.

Midway through the second day of Gray's taciturn streak, Evrard unexpectedly brought up Rory's parents. "I met them once," he said, his voice wistful. "They were lovely, and they were kind. Too kind."

Rory, who wished he had more memories of them, asked, "How can you be too kind?"

"Sometimes an open heart can be wrenched open even further, and then something insidious worms its way in."

Rory wondered if that was his aunt, but didn't ask because he was sure that was one of those questions where Evrard would give him one of those strangely opaque looks from his beautiful eyes—and even though Rory objectively knew he was the furthest thing from stupid, Evrard would make him reconsider for a moment.

"They certainly never told me about meeting a unicorn, especially a unicorn that spoke," Rory pointed out. He'd only been five years old when they died, but he believed that a fact that extraordinary would have been one he'd have remembered.

"Naturally, I was not in this form," Evrard sniffed. Like it was unbelievably silly for Rory to have assumed that Evrard had met them in his natural form.

"You take other forms?" Rory asked, curious. Maybe when this was all over, and he was safely installed back in his library tower at Beaulieu, he would pen a manuscript on all the facts known about unicorns. Rory was mentally composing the introduction—"Unicorns are surprisingly full of themselves, even considering their elevated status as a prized, unique magical creature"—when Evrard answered.

"I was expecting more from you, Prince Emory," Evrard said. Pockets of trees flashed by as Evrard trotted along the road, but even Rory could tell the mountains were growing nearer and the air thinner. "I thought you were considered a scholar of some repute."

"Unfortunately, there is not much to be read about unicorns as a breed," Rory apologized. He could feel Gray stiffen in front of him, and not for the first time during their journey, desperately wanted to know if he was smiling as he and Evrard teased each other. His back was solid against Rory's hands, an undeniable presence, but it was hard to believe he was truly there, since he so rarely spoke these days.

On purpose, Rory reminded himself, that little pocket of frustration boiling hotter, he's not talking to you on purpose.

It was a very annoying state of affairs, and one that Rory was not at all resigned to. Occasionally—or about two or three times an hour—he had to resist the urge to beat his closed fists against that straight, rigid back, and demand to know what was so terrible about being a prince anyway.

"Of course there is nothing to be read about unicorns," Evrard said. "We are very secretive."

"And very enamored of that particular fact," Gray pointed out dryly.

Even though Rory was still annoyed—he had hardly stopped being annoyed in the last forty-eight hours—he smiled. Gray's sense of humor was dry and caustic, which was likely the result of spending far too much time with

Evrard, but it existed, and he was surprisingly funny when he decided to share his thoughts.

"But how could you expect me to know more if there is very little written about unicorns?" Rory asked, the logic gap appearing very obvious after his amusement at Gray's comment settled. "That does not make any sense."

If Evrard had possessed a hand, he would have waved it airily. "Magical creatures are all very similar. Your aunt, for example, has a habit of turning into a chimera."

Thankfully, Rory did know what a chimera was. "She does?" he asked, more than a little stupefied.

"Gray faced her as one," Evrard said, and this time there was that sly edge to his voice that Rory had figured out he always used when he was hoping to manipulate Gray or Rory, or both of them at the same time. No doubt he had picked up on Gray's sudden cold shoulder just as well as Rory, and then there was the matter of the kiss he'd interrupted. Altogether, Rory felt like Evrard knew far too much about his relationship—or lack of relationship—with Gray.

"What was it like?" Rory asked, hoping that Gray would answer, but knowing better.

There was a long drawn-out moment of silence. They passed a small cottage set back from the road, smoke curling from the rough stone chimney, bright white against the gray sky. Evrard had observed earlier in the day that he was sure it would rain. Rory assumed he would likely be right, and no doubt they would not only be miserable with the wet and the mud, but with Evrard's insufferable attitude that he'd been right.

But to Rory's astonishment, it was Gray that answered. "Terrifying," he said, "but I had a very brave horse. If I'd been any older, I probably couldn't have done it. When you're a child, you always believe you can do anything."

Rory remembered so little of his childhood before his parents' death, and what had come after had never felt particularly childlike, though he'd enjoyed the many tutors and the crates of books that had continuously shown up at Beaulieu. If he concentrated very hard, he could envision a few hazy memories where his mom had held him tightly, and his father had played with him. Maybe before their deaths, his life had been a little more balanced between the books he loved and everything else, but it was impossible to say for sure.

A few hours later when they stopped for the night, Gray repeated his actions of the previous evenings and retreated further into the woods—supposedly to check the surroundings to make sure they weren't kidnapped again, but really because he was avoiding Rory. Normally Gray's behavior would have sent Rory's frustration spiking, but tonight, he had more he wanted to ask Evrard, and he thought it might be easier to do it if Gray weren't present.

Rory went over to where Evrard was munching on some nice soft grass, and sat down, drawing up his knees against his chest.

"What were they like?" he asked quietly.

Evrard was quiet for a long moment. "They loved each other, and they loved you," he finally said. "Do you remember much of them?"

"A few images. Their faces probably only because of their formal portraits in Beaulieu. I remember them encouraging me to read, but they never let me read too much." Rory hesitated. There was still a hurt, betrayed part of him that made it difficult to admit just how easily his aunt had manipulated him. How simple it had been for her to take something he loved and wield it against him. "Unlike the Regent Queen," he admitted softly. "She let me read as much as I liked. There were always new tutors, new languages, new books, new analyses that other scholars had requested. I would barely finish one project, and then another would begin."

"And you believe that your aunt arranged it that way?" Evrard asked between dainty nibbles.

Rory frowned. "If she'd asked me not to get involved in the running of the kingdom, I never would have agreed. She manipulated the situation—and me—so she never had to ask. I was so busy, so lost in my own world, that I never looked up from my work and thought, maybe I should be more involved."

Glancing up at him from underneath his rippling forelock, Evrard said, "But you're saying it now."

Rory picked at the fraying hem of his ugly brown cloak. "What if it's too late? What if I can't stop her?"

"Your Highness, I have gone to not-inconsiderate trouble to rescue you and save your life," Evrard said with a huff.

"Would I do that if I believed the quest was hopeless?"

Leaning back against Evrard's legs, Rory thought for a long moment. No, he wouldn't have. The one thing Rory had learned, beyond all certainty, on this journey was that Evrard never wasted his time on anything he believed was beneath him. If he was here, and he was pushing Rory—and by extension, Gray—then he believed in what they were attempting to do. And really, Rory added, it had all been his idea, anyway.

"I am not infallible, as it turns out," Evrard continued with a sigh. "If I was, I would not have left Gray alone for so long. He's grown too used to being alone, and too intractable. Stuck in a rut of his own making, which I should have discouraged, and I did not."

"What do you mean?" Rory asked.

Evrard stared out into the darkening woods surrounding them. "I mean, Prince Emory, that he is sad, and he has been sad for a long time. I should have looked closer, and done more, but I did not. That is now on me, and unfortunately it is also now on you, because instead of pulling you closer, as his heart tells him to, he pushes you away."

Rory blushed. He wanted to ask more, but did not know which questions to ask, and there was also a part of him that wondered if they weren't better posed to Gray himself—at least when Gray was talking to him again.

Branches crackled underfoot, and Rory looked up to see Gray standing there, a load of wood in his arms. "It didn't rain," he said, "so I thought we'd celebrate with a fire."

Before he could stop himself, Rory laughed, and next to him, Evrard snorted, and pointedly did not answer.

An hour later, the fire was crackling, and Rory sat moodily watching it, lost in thought, wondering if his parents had survived the carriage accident, how much of his life might have been different. At least, he would have been a true crown prince of Fontaine, who wanted the throne and had worked for it. Who deserved it.

To Rory's shock, Gray actually did not retreat to the other side of the fire, but plopped down right next to Rory.

"I heard what you said earlier," he said, without preamble.

Rory and Evrard had said quite a lot of things today, so he could not immediately identify which of them Gray was referring to.

"The part about your aunt manipulating you," Gray said quietly, as he poked the fire with a long, sharp stick he'd whittled at the end with his dagger.

"Oh."

"It's not your fault. Not your fault that you didn't see it and not your fault that you didn't prevent it." Gray nudged his leg with his own. "She's made a career out of manipulating far more worldly and experienced men than you, Rory."

"Is that why you left Ardglass?" Rory asked before he could stop himself.

"Yes."

At first, that was all Rory believed he would get. Already Gray had said more words to him tonight than he'd said for days. But then he spoke again. "My father . . . he is intelligent and wise, or at least he was. I remember a time before Sabrina came to Tullamore, when things were different. When he was different. But after she came, everything changed, and he changed most of all. I was eleven when I escaped, with Evrard's help. By then, she had twisted his mind so thoroughly that he was willing to sacrifice me to serve her own ends."

Rory stared into the fire. He did not know what to say. Gray's father had agreed to hand him over to Sabrina? It made Sabrina's petty machinations towards Rory feel small and so insignificant. And it helped bring clarity to why Evrard had said Gray was sad, and had been sad for a long time.

"I tell you this," Gray continued, "because it's not right for you to blame yourself. You were a child, and she is both a master at this game and extraordinarily dangerous. She will no doubt try to manipulate you again, but I believe you're smarter than she is. You'll see right through it if it happens again."

Rory hoped so. "I hope you're right," he said. He did not feel quite as confident as Gray sounded, but that he thought so much of him did help to boost Rory's belief.

"I know I am."

"I'm sorry for what happened to you," Rory added softly after a long, quiet moment.

Gray cleared his throat. "And I'm sorry for what's happened to you." To Rory's complete surprise, Gray reached out and laid his hand on Rory's knee. Nothing more, but nothing less either. A peace offering, perhaps? But something, and Rory felt the anger that he'd held on to for days begin to dissipate. It was difficult to stay angry with someone who went out of their way to stop you from blaming yourself for so many terrible things.

On the fifth day of their journey, the mountains were no longer a closer promise; they were there. The road had been climbing steadily, the trees changing and thinning. They'd traded the horse in for some much-needed gold coins at the last village, as managing Evrard was difficult enough. At night there were barely any trees to take cover under, and Gray spent a lot of his time muttering under his breath about bandits on the road. Fires were a thing of the past, and it was definitely, undeniably, growing colder. Rory spent the nights huddled under his cloak, trying not to shiver and trying not to think of sharing Gray's body warmth.

They had reached a shaky truce, but there was no indication that Gray intended to touch him again, never mind kiss him. Rory, his anger gone, only had to wrestle with his own disappointment.

Today, the sun was shining more brightly, no longer covered by grayish blankets of clouds, and Rory tipped his head back, letting the sunshine and warmth fall across his face. The road curved and bent around and Rory caught a glance of something sparkling and silver out of the corner of his eye as Evrard trotted around the bend.

"What's that?" Rory asked, pointing to the flashes shining in the midday sun.

"Water? A river? Maybe a lake?" Gray answered. He had been less taciturn, but Rory also discovered that didn't mean he wanted to chat incessantly. He was still a quiet, introspective man. And Rory, who'd always believed he wanted a mate as everlastingly talkative as himself, discovered there was an unexpected peace to be found in a comfortable silence.

"We should go see," Rory said, because he was a little bored. Too many long days and quiet nights, with nothing to see or do, until he was actively fighting against the impulse to create some sort of entertaining diversion. He had a feeling that wouldn't be very well-received by either Gray or Evrard.

"Go see a river?" Gray questioned. "Why?"

"It's an excellent idea," Evrard said with an annoyed sniff. "My nose is exceptionally sensitive and you both could use an application of water everywhere."

Rory blushed. Maybe that was why Gray hadn't moved to kiss him again. But then he thought better of it, because surely Gray smelled just as bad as he did.

Gray contemplated this suggestion for a long moment. Finally, he capitulated. "It's warmer today too, which means we won't freeze to death trying to get clean for Evrard's overly touchy nose," Gray said, directing his comment towards Rory.

Without prompting from Gray, Evrard turned off the road, and after picking their way through the forest and the downed trees, emerged on the shores of a small mountain lake sparkling in the bright sunshine.

Rory dismounted, followed by Gray, and approached the water. Dipping a finger in, he found it cold, but not unbearably so. They had extra blankets they had picked up in one of the last villages, to protect against the colder nights at a higher altitude, so they'd be able to dry off properly.

To Rory's surprise, Gray didn't even bother testing the water. Just stripped off his stained shirt, yanking it out of his breeches, and then leaned over to begin unlacing his boots.

In Rory's fantasies, the first time he saw Gray completely naked hadn't been at a relatively chilly lake with Evrard as an unwelcome supervisor. The romantic streak in him protested strongly, but Rory decided that in this particular situation, practicalities outweighed silly fancies. He pulled his cloak off, setting it on a nearby rock, and then turned his attention to the rest of the clothing he was wearing. But it turned out it wasn't only romantic illusions, but an unforeseen shyness that was preventing him from simply stripping himself bare. He unlaced his boots, but after pulling them off, made no other movements to undress.

"Don't worry," Gray's deep voice rumbled out. "There's nobody else around."

But you're around, Rory thought helplessly. You're who I'm agonizing over.

"I shall go provide a lookout," Evrard said, trotting back from where they'd come. Rory couldn't help but think that Evrard, despite all his many flaws, was actually attempting to generously leave them alone for a short time.

Alone and naked.

"Right, of course. There's nobody around." Rory glanced up and wished that Gray would stop watching him. But while he wasn't staring necessarily, Gray's gaze kept straying to where Rory was toying with the ties on the oversized tunic he'd been wearing.

As for Gray himself, he'd stripped down to his smallclothes, which looked very small indeed, cupping a pair of muscular buttocks and . . . Rory blushed again. Had Gray's cock grown hard at just the thought of Rory undressing? If that was the case, then maybe there was less to be worried about than Rory had previously assumed.

Gray tucked a finger under the waistband of his smallclothes and shot Rory a hot look. "Do I need to get naked alone?" he asked.

Rory gulped, and pulled off his tunic, the cool air rushing across his suddenly heated skin.

"Better," Gray said in a teasing tone and then turned towards the lake, pulling his smallclothes down, leaving them in a puddle on the ground with the rest of his clothes, and leaving Rory with an excellent view of a very excellent butt. Rory stared, because he could not help himself. Gray was magnificent; broad-shouldered with ridges of muscles on his back leading to narrow hips and that marvelously sculpted ass. He didn't want to just look, he wanted to touch, but before he could work up the nerve to say any of that, Gray took off at a run, launching himself into the lake at nearly full speed. He came up from the water dripping, his hair sleek against his skull, and so beautiful that Rory's throat went dry.

"You coming?" Gray teased again.

God, he wanted to. More than anything.

Maybe if Gray hadn't been staring at him so intently, his gaze burning across his skin, he would have felt the chill as he stripped down the rest of the way, but Rory couldn't feel anything but heat.

"Come, jump in, it's too cold to do it gradually," Gray encouraged as Rory approached the lake, his cock bobbing with each step he took. Don't be embarrassed, he told himself firmly, Gray was hard too. You're attracted to each other. It's normal.

But it wasn't all that normal for Rory. He'd kissed a few cute boys at the court of Beaulieu, but none of them had interested him particularly. He'd definitely never been interested in going further, in touching them the way he touched himself at night.

Now, Rory wanted everything—and he wanted it so much, even though he didn't have any idea how to go about getting it. He'd read plenty of erotic texts, of course, but none of them had ever described bathing together with the man you longed for in a cold mountain lake, with the King of the Unicorns standing watch only a few feet away.

"Rory," Gray said again, and Rory didn't think he'd imagined the pleading note in his tone.

Making the choice in a split second, Rory didn't let himself hold back as he matched the speed and path that

Gray had taken, the cold water hitting him in a breathless rush.

He was sure he looked far less attractive than Gray had when he came up, spluttering and cursing in every language he knew at how bitterly freezing the water truly was.

"You'll get used to it," Gray told him with a grin, as he floated onto his back and started to swim, his arms cutting powerfully through the water.

"I don't think so," Rory said, his teeth chattering.

In the water, with his hair wet and dark, Gray's eyes were an otherworldly blue, and as he swam closer, Rory was transfixed by them. "I think so," Gray retorted softly. And somehow, he wasn't wrong, because the closer Gray came, the warmer Rory felt, like the heat between them was impossibly raising the temperature of the water.

"See?" Gray said. "It's better."

It was, but Rory was desperate to be even warmer still. He reached out and braced a hand against Gray's shoulder. His wet skin was slick and smooth under his fingertips, the muscle sliding easily under all that softness. "You're . . ." For someone who spoke so many languages, finding the words to describe how stunning Gray was like this—wet and naked and kind—was surprisingly difficult.

"Believe me," Gray said dryly, "the feeling is mutual."

Rory glanced down at his pale skin, gleaming white in the sun, and at his much scrawnier arms and chest. It seemed impossible that Gray might be as transfixed by him as Rory was by Gray. But then, Gray couldn't seem to tear his eyes away. He reached out and tucked a stray, wet curl behind

Rory's ear. "They talk of your beauty for several kingdoms in every direction," Gray said softly, "and before, I never understood why, but I do now."

Even though the water was freezing, there was nothing Rory wanted more than to lean in and kiss Gray, but after how the last kiss had gone, the next one was going to have to be Gray's choice.

Digging his fingertips into Gray's shoulder, Rory floated closer, and hoped that was the last bit of encouragement Gray needed. It should be Gray's decision, yes, but that didn't mean Rory couldn't make any attempts to convince him. "Thank you," he said softly, his gaze falling again to Gray's lips.

"I keep trying to remember you're a prince," Gray finally said, the last inches closing between them, his eyes growing ridiculously bluer, "but to me, you're always just Rory."

Gray leaned in and kissed him then, gently and softly, like he wasn't quite sure Rory wouldn't turn him down after all. Rory's heart was thumping painfully, his skin prickling with heat, and now that Gray had given in, Rory could indulge in all the fantasies he'd considered from the first moment he'd seen the lake.

He pulled Gray closer, one hand reaching out to meet the other behind Gray's neck, his fingers sliding wetly across his skin. Tilting his head, Rory deepened the kiss, and as Gray's heartbeat accelerated against his chest, Rory wrapped his legs around Gray's much sturdier frame. Rory's cock, which had softened in the cool water, hardened almost instantly when it felt the brush of Gray's own.

Gray wrenched his mouth from Rory's. He was breathing hard, his pupils dilated with arousal, but he didn't push Rory away, he just stared at him. "You really want this," he said, like he couldn't quite believe it.

It was insanity because Rory had wanted Gray desperately from the very first moment he'd ever seen him—sweaty and dirty and with his hair falling in his eyes. He couldn't really understand it, but the poets had always spoken of attraction and desire and love as undefinable and illogical, and so Rory, experiencing these emotions for nearly the first time, wanted nothing more than to throw himself straight into the deep end.

"I've always wanted this, I just didn't know it," Rory confessed.

It was all the motivation Gray needed to kiss him again, and this time when Rory moved against him, hesitatingly at first, and then with growing confidence, Gray moved with him. It wasn't perfect, the slide of wet cock against wet cock, the lubrication of the lake water somewhat lacking, but it felt so good that Rory could hardly care. He'd never done this before, had never done anything more than touch himself, and he'd always believed the rapturous descriptions in the texts he'd read must be exaggerations, because nothing could ever feel that good, but this did. It felt so good, so right, so flawlessly perfect that Rory now understood why people would kill for it, would conquer kingdoms for it, would betray their own honor for it. He'd do anything right now, in this moment, for Gray to keep kissing him and touching him, and making those infuriatingly little gasps into his mouth as the pleasure began to overtake him.

Rory didn't even try to make it last, he hurtled headfirst as fast as he could, greedy and desperate, and Gray followed right behind, exploding with a deep, life-altering groan right after Rory's brain went bright and blinding with his own orgasm.

As his heartbeat slowly returned to its normal state, Rory still didn't let go of Gray. He pressed a single kiss to Gray's collarbone and opened his eyes to a world that was exactly the same, but somehow felt brand new.

"So that's what it's like," Rory said wonderingly.

Gray tensed. "You . . . you hadn't . . . with anybody?" he asked with trepidation.

"I hadn't really wanted to before," Rory confessed. "Is that okay?" He was suddenly worried, even though nothing he'd ever read stated you were supposed to make that fact explicitly clear. Maybe he had somehow made a mistake, and Gray wished he'd known. Would he have pushed Rory away? Was it unattractive to not have any experience? Inexperience was always a challenge, but he'd read the texts, hadn't he? Rory knew all the mechanics; he'd hardly consider himself ignorant.

"It's . . ." Gray hesitated again.

"I'm sorry," Rory said impulsively. "But truthfully I'm not very sorry at all."

Suddenly, a grin broke out over Gray's face, and it changed him. Made him brighter, softer, somehow. And Rory was captivated all over again.

"I'm not very sorry at all, either," Gray finally said. "I didn't mean to, and then I did. It's hard to keep looking at you, and riding with you and talking to you, and stay away. I couldn't do it."

Rory nuzzled against the damp skin at his neck. He smelled like Gray—like pine forests and warm earth and herbs.

"I didn't even try," Rory confessed, and Gray laughed again.

"We should really wash up," Gray said. "Evrard can't possibly be expected to stand guard forever."

Rory nodded, even though the last thing he wanted was to let go. But it wasn't really letting go, Rory reasoned, because he'd already decided that nothing, even Gray's own frustrating tendencies, could make him do that.

CHAPTER NINE

THEY DRESSED AFTER A quick wash, shivering despite the warmer air and the sun shining overhead. Remembered pleasure made Gray's thoughts sticky-slow, but one stuck out further than the rest. This was the worst time to be allowing personal indulgences to matter, but fighting against Rory's indefinable charm felt more distracting than giving in. It was easier, Gray reasoned, to give in a little bit—and there was the added bonus that it brought a smile to Rory's face that warmed his eyes for the first time since Gray had met him. Gold, Gray thought dazedly, his eyes are gold. Other men wanted strongboxes full of riches and treasure, but all Gray desired was his valley, and those eyes, gazing at him like he was the only man Rory could ever want.

But, Gray shook himself as Evrard emerged over the crest of the trees, reality made that dream impossible. Rory was meant for the throne of Fontaine, and Gray was meant for something else. A smaller, humbler life. Until Rory had started batting his eyelashes in Gray's direction, that was all Gray had really wanted. But now things were complicated and complicating them even further was the secret of Gray's birth.

He can never know, Gray thought as they silently climbed onto Evrard's back again.

"Your odor is much improved," Evrard pointed out as he briskly trotted back to the road, "and your moods as well."

Gray could feel Rory's blush even though he couldn't see it. Evrard had known the events he was setting into motion when he had retreated as a lookout. Part of Gray wanted to be annoyed that Evrard was matchmaking, because he undeniably was, but his time alone with Rory had been so pleasurable it was hopeless to regret it.

"We are reaching the end of my knowledge of the area," Gray admitted a few hours later as he and Rory gnawed at the last of their dried meat stores. "But there is a village at the base of the mountains. Nargash. We should reach it by nightfall."

"A village?" Gray tried to ignore the hopeful note in Rory's voice, but it was difficult.

Ignoring anything about Rory was difficult.

And there was also that matter of the small pouch of gold coins tucked in the pocket of his breeches. They could afford a night in a proper inn, with a hot meal, before the long, arduous climb the next day. It would be good for Evrard to be sheltered in a stable, especially with the exertion of the next few days.

"If there's an inn," Gray said grudgingly, "we will inquire and see if they have any rooms available."

"Hopefully a private room," Rory said softly, leaning closer and plastering himself along Gray's back, until his voice was a whisper of a promise in Gray's ear.

His blood heating was unavoidable and his reaction undeniable. Gray must want Rory as much as Rory wanted him, and it seemed foolish not to take this chance to indulge, if they indeed had a chance.

"We'll see," Gray said, trying to make his voice gruff, but instead it came out soft and tender and anticipatory. Like he could not wait to get Rory alone and kiss him and touch him again, this time on a decent bed, behind a door that locked.

"You sound eager," Rory said slyly, and for his professed inexperience with men, he was far better at teasingly flirtatious comments than Gray would have anticipated.

Gray's fingers tightened on Evrard's mane.

"I know you are very eager," Evrard pointed out, tone annoyed, "but please do not pull out my mane in your eagerness to reach the village."

It was Gray's turn to blush. "Sorry," he mumbled.

"Before we reach the village, we have much to discuss. Our further path, and the object you must obtain," Evrard said.

It was not lost on Gray that Evrard had waited until the last moment to have this conversation. Gray did not like it because he didn't like leaving such an important quest up to chance. What if they'd gotten separated from Evrard somehow? It had nearly happened only a week prior, and only Rory's quick thinking and years of study had prevented disaster.

But if Gray had made this point, Evrard would only have replied in that infuriatingly calm tone, "What will be is what is."

"What are we looking for?" Rory asked, sounding nearly as excited to find the object that would take back his kingdom as he was to spend the evening alone with Gray. And that's the way it should be, Gray told himself, even as pain pricked him. Rory would be moving on and evolving into a leader and a man. It was right he should be excited at the prospect.

Gray resolutely ignored any feelings of envy. All you want is your valley.

"It is a ring, a ring of great mystical value and importance, and upon wearing it, gives the owner complete truth."

It sounded like complete idiocy to Gray. Who wanted complete truth? A nice gray version was always so much easier to deal with. But then Gray could see how such an object might be useful in dealing with a perennial liar and manipulator like Sabrina. For one, it would be far easier to expose her lies. And if they could get her to don the ring? The web of lies she'd woven over so many years would completely disintegrate.

"You will find this ring," Evrard continued, "called the Bearer of Truth, in a hidden cave tucked between two of the largest mountains."

"Hidden?" Gray inserted. "How do we find something that's hidden?"

"By searching for it, naturally," Evrard said.

"Not helpful," Gray grumbled.

"It can't be a huge area, between the two largest mountains," Rory reasoned. "How hidden could a hidden cave be?"

"The Bearer of Truth has remained hidden for several centuries," Evrard said, immediately ruining Rory's optimism. "It will not be easy to find it, but it is necessary to defeat the Regent Queen."

"No pressure," Gray interrupted. "Why don't you tell us something more helpful, like how to actually find the stupid cave?"

"Between two mountains of great stature lie veracity, fidelity, and certainty. Tread the peak and scale the valley. Solve the puzzle and gain the ring," Evrard intoned in a serious, ponderous voice.

"Great, a prophecy," Gray complained.

"Do you hate prophecies the same way you hate royalty?" Rory wondered.

"Prophecies, like royalty, can certainly be a waste of time," Gray said carefully, because he didn't want to give Rory the impression he hated him. He hated his title, he hated what his title represented and he sure as hell didn't want Rory's princely status to come between them—but he could never hate Rory.

"It is not a prophecy, only an ancient saying, from a time when the ring was hidden away. I thought it might add clarity to your search," Evrard corrected.

Gray rolled his eyes. Only Evrard would believe that an "ancient saying" would actually be helpful.

"Thank you," Rory said, and actually sounded like he meant it.

A few hours later, the road began to widen, and there were more men to be seen, riding carts pulled by mules or old, shabby-looking horses. The men themselves looked worse than the horses; they either ignored Rory and Gray completely, like they were too worn out from the hand life had dealt them to care, or they shot sly, avaricious looks in their direction. Their clothing was hardly rich, but more than once Gray caught a man eyeing them up and down, seemingly mentally pricing out every visible item of clothing and the saddlebags. Evrard was exempt from these thorough examinations every time, their eyes sliding right over his figure. Just as Gray expected.

Still, this part of the road was much rougher than Gray remembered, and he began to worry what Nargash would be like when they finally reached it. Would they feel comfortable stopping there and renting a room? And if they did not, would they be any safer camping out a distance from the town? Even off the road? Gray did not particularly think so, not if the road continued to be full of such unsavory characters. He transferred his dagger from his calf to his belt, and when they stopped to rest for a minute at a stream, Gray approached Rory.

"We have almost no weapons," Gray began, uncomfortably aware of how inappropriate his request was.

Maybe if he'd truly been Gray the Farmhand, and never raised to be a prince, the question would have felt different, but Prince Graham of Ardglass knew what he was about to ask was completely wrong and in many areas would have been considered both a betrayal of trust and a fighting offense.

"I know," Rory said, and his gaze was anxious as it met Gray's. "You have your dagger, and I have the dagger and the sword."

Gray cleared his throat. "About the sword."

Sometimes Gray still forgot how very different their upbringings were, and so was shocked when Rory unceremoniously unbuckled his sword belt and thrust Lion's Breath, still in its protective sheath, at Gray. "You carry it," he said. "It doesn't make sense for me to have it, I can't even use it."

It was what he'd wanted, specifically what he'd approached Rory for, and still Gray hesitated to take it. "You can use it," Rory added impatiently, pushing it closer. "You used it before."

But that had not been premeditated. They'd been surrounded, and Gray hadn't thought through the action before he'd done it. He'd simply taken the sword because, if he hadn't, he'd believed they would either be captured or killed.

"It's . . ." Gray looked down at Lion's Breath. Another reason why Rory could never learn about his past or his true parentage. A nameless farm boy taking a royal sword because they needed it was one thing; a prince of a neighboring kingdom appropriating a royal sword was entirely another. In some circles they might even consider this an act of aggression or Gray declaring his intention to usurp Rory's throne.

The problem was that Rory's throne wasn't currently Rory's, and it might never be Rory's again if Gray didn't wield this sword.

"I know it's not usually done," Rory said. Of course he knew. He knew all the ancient traditions, and what carrying a sword of Fontaine would mean. "But if you don't take it, I'm not sure we're going to survive the night."

Gray reached out and clasped a hand around the decorative scabbard, encrusted with rubies and topaz. "Thank you," he said, "you're likely not wrong. Nargash will be much rougher than I anticipated when we began this journey."

Rory's eyes glowed as they gazed up at him, and the honesty in them was humbling and terrifying. "I trust you," he murmured. "Maybe I shouldn't, but I do. I know you won't betray me, and I know you'll do everything in your power to help me regain my throne. You won't take Lion's Breath and use it for your own gain."

Gray was speechless. Rory's words meant even more because he wasn't quite the silly, naive princeling that Gray had assumed the first time they'd met. He had strength— albeit a different kind than Gray had always recognized— and intelligence. He'd been manipulated by Sabrina, but then Sabrina was a master manipulator. And now? Gray thought it would be extremely difficult, maybe even impossible, for anyone to manipulate the man in front of him.

"You know a lot of things," Gray said softly.

"I know you," Rory said with earnestness, "even though I don't know as much about you as I'd like."

It was the wrong time and the wrong place to kiss him, even though that was nearly all Gray could think about. Tonight, he thought, if we can survive the journey to an inn and after we bar the door . . .

Still, Gray raised his fingers and brushed them, even as dirty as they likely were, against Rory's cheek. The reddish-blond stubble there was patchy and he'd caught Rory grumbling about it more than once, but Gray loved it for the sole purpose that it helped keep Rory invisible and protected.

Rory smiled as Gray's hand fell to his side. "Maybe someday you'll tell me," Rory said, and while there was nothing more that Gray wanted than to be honest, the truth about who he was had to remain hidden.

"Are you going to stand there and stare raptly into each other's eyes all afternoon?" Evrard interrupted.

Gray turned towards the grumbling unicorn. "You did this, you know," he murmured to Evrard as he mounted him.

"All you needed was the slightest of prompts," Evrard countered back primly. "Barely even a push at all."

As Evrard continued to canter down the road to Nargash, their surroundings edged closer and closer to disreputable. The outskirts of the village were particularly unpleasant, consisting only of broken-down buildings, some with collapsed roofs, some with their windows and doors hanging crookedly open, like teeth knocked out of an ugly man's face. And even worse, as they passed some, there were clear signs that people were still living in what Gray could barely term shacks: small fires in the front yards, clotheslines hanging between two straggly trees, and in one particularly unsightly home, children running around the ramshackle walls of the structure.

"Why is it like this?" Rory wondered aloud after they passed that particular dwelling. "Why does each village we pass look worse?"

Gray did not answer, because he didn't trust himself. They were on the edge of Ardglass now, and the village of Nargash was considered one of the very western borders of the furthest western clan. This responsibility was his father's, and eventually would have fallen to him. As it was, it seemed to be that Gideon had let his kingdom continue to slide into ruin even after Graham's departure. As insidious and evil as Sabrina was, at least Fontaine was not overtly falling to pieces, shabby and ill-used, its inhabitants forced to live in squalor.

Evrard answered instead. "Taxes," he said. "This technically falls under the purview of the kingdom of Ardglass, and its king has let unscrupulous advisors pick his treasury clean. As a result, has raised taxes throughout his kingdom to compensate."

Gray felt the burn of shame rush through him, but what could he do? Raising his head out of obscurity would only likely end in it being chopped off.

"Something must be done," Rory said quietly but with purpose.

Turning his head from the children in their threadbare clothes and dirty faces, Gray said nothing. Maybe, with his own throne recovered, Rory would eventually turn his attention to Ardglass. The thought might have been a comforting one, but the injustice for himself and for every other creature living in Ardglass raged too strongly inside him for Gray to listen to reason.

"Something will be done," Evrard promised. "You will see, Your Highness."

Gray gripped Evrard's mane tighter and nearly lashed out in anger and frustration. How did he know? What did he know? Why did he never share with Gray? Why were they going to all this effort to restore Rory to his throne when it was Ardglass that needed help? Gray had long since learned that Evrard only answered questions he chose, and they were almost never of any importance. Still, it was only by biting his lip until blood welled that he managed to stay silent.

Finally, they came upon the village proper. The marketplace was a sad sight, with wilted vegetables and rotten grain. Gray turned away and wondered how long he could bear to look, only to look away again. "There is an inn," Gray said, pointing to a faded sign. "The Chimera," he read, the irony definitely not lost on him. "I will inquire for lodging and a stable berth."

Rory stayed with Evrard and Gray approached the inn, opened the door and went inside. The inside was somehow worse than the outside—the smell of years of burned meat embedded in the exposed wood of the great room. The beams were dark with smoke and grease, and even though a little dirt never bothered Gray, he flinched when he walked across the floorboards. The innkeeper was wearing a dirty white shirt with an open neck, and a stained leather apron torn in one corner, wiping his hands on a filthy cloth as Gray approached.

"I would like a room for the night," Gray said, "and a meal, as well as lodging and feed for my horse."

The innkeeper looked Gray up and down, and though Gray knew his clothes were poor, they did nothing to conceal his tall, strong frame or his straight back. Greed flashed in the man's eyes and if they'd had any other choice, Gray would have turned back and taken them all far away from this place. But there was a particularly masochistic part of him that stayed put and let the innkeeper look his fill. None of this was Gray's fault, but it had been irrevocably set into motion when he'd left Ardglass all those years ago.

"Two gold pieces, and another if you want hot water," the man said.

It was high above the going rate for shelter, but Gray handed over the gold without arguing. He took a deep breath of semi-clean air when he walked outside, but one glance in Rory and Evrard's direction told him that, even though he'd hurried, he might have tarried too long. Several rough-looking men were eyeing Rory with interest, despite his patchy beard. The problem with Rory was, that even in ugly ill-fitting clothes with that awful facial hair, he was still beautiful, and in the middle of this muddy yard, he shone like the brightest diamond.

As Gray hurried over to them, his face must have reflected his worries, because Rory glanced at him and flinched. He's seen the men looking, Gray thought, and didn't know what to say. Rory had promised him trust, and Gray couldn't fail him, even in this depressingly bleak place. He pushed back his cloak, hoping the sight of his sword would warn away anyone who was considering an attack. He did wish the scabbard of Lion's Breath was slightly less ornate and contained far fewer gemstones. Some idiot might decide the threat wasn't nearly as great as the prize, and would come for it anyway, and the last thing Gray wanted was to fight off robbers.

"You'll be fine in the stables," Gray said to Evrard under his breath. "The hay will no doubt be moldy, but you will have to suffer through it."

"And us?" Rory asked, clearly concerned.

"The door will have a latch," Gray promised. "And if not, I will fashion something that will keep them out." He looked straight into Rory's eyes and, as best he could, told him without words, you put your trust in me, let me prove it to you that it wasn't unfounded.

"It's barely early evening," Rory pointed out. "And we must eat, too."

"It's a crowded public room, and I will not leave your side," Gray promised.

"We will all be careful," Evrard said, "for the coming days will be a test of our strength."

This night will be a test of my strength, Gray thought as he delivered Evrard to the stables.

When they walked into the common room, Rory could not quite contain the disgust in his expression as he took in the stained walls and floors, and the plates of corn mush and burned, fatty meat.

"This is not . . . not quite what I was hoping for," Rory whispered under his breath as they passed down the row of occupied tables to an empty space by the great hearth. Putting the fire at their backs was not ideal, but at least it would be difficult for anyone to approach from that direction.

"We must make the best of it," Gray said, though he was equally disappointed. He'd wanted a respite from the stress of their journey, but instead, what they'd gotten in Nargash was a rude awakening and an increasingly dangerous situation.

They sat and the innkeeper motioned to a sullen serving boy, who brought them warm mugs of ale and two plates of the unappetizing-looking food.

"I cannot believe I am complaining about a hot meal," Rory said, but he shuddered as he pushed the corn slop around his plate with a spoon that was likely none too clean, "but I would rather have some of the dried meat from the saddlebags."

"It's not so bad," Gray said, shoveling a spoonful into his mouth. "It's hot, at least."

"I guess," Rory said, clearly not convinced.

His voice must have carried, because a moment later, a man with a wicked facial scar bisecting his bushy gray eyebrow and then meandering down from cheek to chin, sat down opposite Rory. "This one seems a lot of work," he said to Gray, motioning towards Rory. "Seems haughty. Rich, even. A pain in the ass."

Gray might have felt that way at first, and still occasionally, but he was hardly going to agree with the newcomer, at least not in front of Rory. In Rory's defense, the food was bad and the atmosphere even worse.

"I am not," Rory answered hotly, obviously offended.

Jabbing Rory's side with his elbow under the shadow of the rough-hewn tabletop, Gray gave the scarred man a ferocious smile, baring his teeth. "He's not for sale," he said.

Rory made an affronted noise as Gray's words revealed the man's real purpose in visiting their table.

"I meant it," he said, "he looks damn expensive."

"Too expensive for you," Gray said steadily. He pushed back from the table, and risking it again, exposed the scabbard of Lion's Breath to the man's gaze.

"As are you, my friend, though you take pains to hide it," the scarred man pointed out.

"We are just traveling through and have no interest in deals or discussions," Gray said in a flat voice.

"As you wish," the man said and stood. "But you may find your mind changed."

After he left, Rory turned to Gray and the expression in his eyes was definitely anxious. "Was he really trying to buy me? And what did he mean, you might find your mind changed?"

"He assumed you were my property," Gray said, not wanting to address Rory's second question. He was edgy enough and might lose whatever nerve he had left if Rory knew they'd just been threatened.

"But slavery isn't allowed in Ardglass. Or Fontaine, for that matter," Rory argued.

Gray gave a short, unamused laugh. "Do you really believe that stops anyone with enough money?"

Glancing down at his plate, Rory shook his head. "He threatened you," he stated.

"Us," Gray sighed. "He threatened us. Finish your meal, because I intend to go to our room and bar the door and not leave it until morning."

Rory ate slowly, but he did eat. Gray had long since finished his meal and was savoring the last few drops of the warm ale when Rory finally finished cleaning his plate. Glancing around, Gray realized that the hour had grown late, and the main room had emptied out somewhat. They weren't alone, but as Gray observed each of the groups left, each one looked more villainous than the last. And even worse, they were watching Rory—and to a lesser extent, Gray—intently.

"Do you have your dagger?" Gray asked, leaning closer to Rory so they wouldn't be overheard.

Rory nodded.

"Keep it close," Gray said. "I hope you won't have to use it, but I don't want you undefended while I have to fight off the rest of this crowd."

Rory's eyes grew wide. "Is that really going to be necessary?"

Gray watched as Rory's gaze followed his own, taking stock of each man that was left in the room.

"They think we're rich," Gray said softly. "Rich and easy pickings. Especially you."

Swallowing hard, Rory looked over at Gray. "We can't be. Not tonight."

"Not tonight," Gray agreed, and slowly stood. Rory followed him as he skirted around the tables against the hearth, always keeping it at his back.

Every step they took was observed, and Gray swallowed hard against the nerves that had settled low in his stomach. He'd promised to protect Rory, but he could not hope to take on a dozen men with only a small, sharp dagger and Rory's ancestral sword, no matter how fancy the title. Anyone who approached would need to be dispatched quickly, before the rest decided to join in.

Gray's destination was the staircase at the other end of the room. The key the innkeeper had given them dug into his palm and he slid it further, exposing the rough iron edge. It too could be a weapon if they were pressed. None of the men in the room moved, but there were shadows at the base of the stairs.

A perfect place for several men to lie in wait for their prey.

Gray edged closer, Rory not far behind him, and finally they made it to the corner of the room, right where the concentric circles of candle and firelight ended.

A man stepped out of the gloom. The scarred man, which did not surprise Gray at all, though worry billowed in his chest. He'd warned them, after all. No doubt anyone else who came here with any coin to speak of did so with a whole troop of armed guards.

Gray put his other hand on the hilt of Lion's Breath. "Let us pass," he said in the sternest voice he could muster. He felt Rory tense behind him and pull his own dagger.

He might not have much knowledge of how to defend himself, but he was brave—Gray would give him that much. And unfortunately, unlike with the nomadic tribe, there was no way to talk their way out of this one. It would have to be done with fists and blades.

"I don't think so," the scarred man said, a devilish smile lighting up his face. "Boys, why don't we relieve our good man here of his valuables, including that sweet, pretty boy?"

There was no time to think. Gray lashed out, punching the scarred man in the face, taking a blow back, blinding his vision for a split second. Another two men materialized out of the shadows, and he saw Rory lash out with his dagger out of the corner of his eye as one of the men attempted to grab his arm. Blood spurted, and Gray was too busy fighting off the man with the scar to check if it was Rory's.

He hadn't pulled Lion's Breath yet because he didn't want to give the men any more financial motivation to win, and it was a very small, closed-in space. Perfect, Gray thought grudgingly, for a good fist fight. But not exactly ideal for a swordfight.

Gray's training hadn't been very formal after leaving Tullamore, but he'd picked up what he could, where he could, and he'd never forgotten those first eleven years of lessons and advice. He gripped the key and slashed out at the man's eyes. He defended the blow, landing another in the vicinity of Gray's ribs, the pain and breathlessness winning for a split second, before he countered with his other free hand, a satisfying crack of bone echoing through the room.

Blood started to pour and the man gazed at him incredulously for a second. "You're a tough one, you are," he said with disgust as he snorted blood and then, with a quick, sickening motion, wrenched his nose back into place.

Shit.

These men were tougher than Gray had anticipated, living for years on the rough, lawless edges of Ardglass. You're their rightful prince, a voice inside Gray reminded him, you were born to subdue them, to remind them who sets the rules.

He was bigger, Gray realized, and started putting more of the brute force of his larger body into his blows, landing a few on the ribs and stomach, and then finally cracking one on the man's shin. He took some back, sweat dripping into his eyes, and he just prayed that Rory hadn't been dragged away in the length of time it had taken to subdue the scarred man.

Gray landed one last forceful blow and the man's head lolled back and eventually he fell back against one of the rough-hewn walls, and he finally had a moment to glance behind. There was blood on the floor, and one of the men who'd gone after Rory was holding his arm, from which red flowed freely, and Rory held a dagger at the throat of the other.

"You good?" Rory asked breathlessly. He had a dark bruise forming on his cheek. There were drops of blood on his hands. But he seemed otherwise uninjured.

"I'm good," Gray said. "Let's go before anyone decides to steal you."

They retreated up the stairs, and thankfully, the men didn't follow. Too much effort, Gray thought, we made it too tough for them to follow through. No doubt they'd look and likely find easier men to prey upon, and perhaps Gray should have felt guilty about that, but he was all too aware that they'd barely escaped with their lives. For now, that had to be enough.

Their room was three doors down from the top of the staircase, and Gray shoved the key in the lock, turned it, and they stumbled into the doorway. A single candle flickered in the corner, lighting the corners of the room well enough that Gray was reassured nobody was waiting to ambush them. He slammed the door shut and threw the heavy metal bar across it.

"There," he said, relief pouring through him, "that should hold them until morning, and by then, attacking won't be prudent."

"Do you truly believe that?" Rory asked as he crossed the room and examined the rest of the contents. A simple trunk bed with a mattress of certainly dubious cleanliness and a few blankets folded at the base. A basin of water sitting on a simple wooden stand. Dipping a finger in, Rory turned to Gray. "It's actually warm," he said with surprise.

Gray's knuckles felt sticky with blood. "We should wash," he said, gesturing to the droplets that had fallen on Rory's cheek.

He lifted a rag from next to the basin, but Rory reached over and stopped his hand. "Let me," he said quietly.

Gray watched as Rory took his hand and examined it—the split knuckles, the smears of blood, the bruising already beginning to appear. They didn't look good, but then Gray looked up at the red splotches on Rory's flawlessly pale skin and wished he could scrub them away until they'd never existed.

"You saved me," Rory said, dipping the cloth into the water and wringing it out. Gently he began to clean Gray's hands, carefully dabbing off the blood and cleaning out every wound.

Gray closed his eyes, suddenly exhausted. "You helped," he pointed out.

"It was more accidental than purposeful," Rory admitted. "I swung with the dagger and it was only happenstance it hit somewhere important."

"And the other man?" Gray asked.

"I grabbed the dagger, and I think he was so surprised by all the blood, he didn't move. I held the dagger to his throat before he could take me."

"I think he was so surprised you came out swinging," Gray said dryly. "You don't look like the type."

"They weren't very quick, and I don't think they were very smart either," Rory confided as he continued to clean Gray's hands with soft, careful strokes.

"They're robbing men at the local inn," Gray pointed out.

"Still, things could have turned out far worse." Rory took a deep breath. "This wasn't quite what I'd hoped for when you said we might get a room. Alone."

"Nor me either." Gray's voice was wry.

One hand finished, Rory rinsed the cloth and picked up Gray's other hand. Glancing down, Gray saw how huge and rough his single hand looked in two of Rory's. While he might have once been royalty too, it felt like all that polish had long since been scrubbed away. Still, he remembered how much Gideon had boasted that the men of Ardglass had always been brave and determined fighters. "Ardglass never loses," he had always been fond of saying. And Ardglass, Gray realized, hadn't lost today.

Now that he had a clean hand, Gray reached up and his fingertips gently probed Rory's bruised cheekbone. "I didn't realize someone got a blow in," he said, anger mounting despite his attempts to dismiss it. How could men see someone who looked like Rory and put their rough hands on him? It was a crime to take something so beautiful and attempt to ruin it. Even if they hadn't succeeded, Gray still wanted to go seek them out and break all their noses.

"I ducked at the last minute, I thought it had mostly glanced off me," Rory said, bending over Gray's hand. "But

I suppose it didn't. It doesn't hurt so much now."

"It will in the morning," Gray pointed out. "I wish I could find some ice, take some of the swelling down."

"I'm fine. You've done plenty. I'm alive, and not in the clutches of those men, about to be sold, aren't I?" Rory observed.

"If I'd been quicker . . ." Gray said softly.

Those glorious golden eyes glanced up at him, skewering him with a single, pointed look. "If I thanked you more eloquently for saving my life would you stop lamenting at how poorly you did it?" Rory asked sharply.

The heat of the violence had just about finished leaking out of Gray, but Rory's words brought it roaring back, with teeth and claws and a very specific hunger that Gray didn't quite understand. He'd been with men before—and women too—and none of them had ever made him feel the way that Rory did, a helpless, desperate mess of terror and desire.

Gray didn't answer, but Rory must have seen the look that passed across his face—all that starving desperation—and he let go of Gray's hand. "Take your clothes off," he said, casually, like it was of no great importance. Meanwhile, Gray's insides were trembling and his fingers wouldn't cooperate, pawing helplessly at the strings of his tunic.

Finally, Rory took pity on him, and after prepping another cleaner cloth, reached out and began to untie the laces. His nimble fingers moved efficiently and soon Gray was pulling his tunic off, followed by his boots, and then his breeches. He stood in front of a kneeling Rory in only his smallclothes, his cock pulsing awkwardly between them.

He knew what he wanted, but Rory had so little experience. Almost none, by his own admission. What if he didn't even understand Gray's desires?

You may not be a scholar, worthy of delivering a lecture on sexual satisfaction, Gray told himself, but you can always show him. You're better with actions than with words.

"Let me," Rory said, and Gray was hardly going to stop him as Rory reached up and pulled down the cloth hiding his cock. It bobbed free, hard and red and wet at the tip. Gray took a deep breath.

But Rory didn't take him in his hand or even, as Gray had so wished, into his mouth. Instead, he took the clean, damp cloth and ran it down his chest, to the dark hairs that began at his pubic bone. He cleaned him thoroughly and efficiently, but gently, with careful touches that shouldn't have set Gray on fire but did anyway.

He was beginning to realize that anything Rory did had that effect. Him contradicting Evrard? Definitely arousing. Him shoving a knife into a brigand's shoulder? Unexpectedly arousing. Him giving Gray a bath? The most arousing thing in the whole universe.

Finally, just as Gray thought he was not quite above begging, Rory put down the cloth and looked up at him, his gaze steady as he leaned closer. "Let me," Rory said again, and this time it was his tongue on Gray's cock, Gray's head tipping back against the wall as he gasped in pleasure.

"Do you like that?" Rory asked and Gray's only answer was a moan, much louder than he'd intended. "I guess you do," Rory said, and Gray realized as he glanced down, that yes, that was absolutely a smirk on his face.

While Rory might not have had much practical experience, Gray could guess that he'd likely read about this particular act before because he seemed determined to wring every ounce of bone-melting pleasure out of Gray, and did it shockingly well. After only a few moments, Gray already felt alarmingly close to the edge of orgasm, the pressure building inside of him, even as he wanted to make it last. The problem was that Rory was a vixen, teasing and coaxing and impossibly beautiful as his eyes fluttered closed and he slid Gray's cock inside his mouth. I will remember how this feels forever, Gray thought, and his control splintered as Rory twisted his hand and sucked on the head.

It took a long moment for Gray to recover his bearings. The violence followed by the intense bliss he'd just experienced had left him feeling hollow and suddenly exhausted. Finally he glanced down and his heartbeat accelerated again.

Rory was sitting there, his breeches untied, his cock in his hand, his head thrown back and his teeth biting down on that perfectly plump lower lip as he stroked himself.

"Let me," Gray begged this time and when Rory nodded soundlessly, he reached down, his own much larger, much rougher hand joining Rory's, and that was all it took to push him right over the edge into ecstasy.

They cleaned up, and this time Gray refused to let Rory take the cloth. He cleaned Rory, and their hands, and then after fetching a new cloth, carefully wiped the blood spatters off his cheek and neck.

"I guess we should get some sleep," Rory finally said quietly, rising up and walking over to the bed.

It was not a large bed, and for a second, Gray nearly offered to sleep on the floor. But after what they had just done, sleeping close together felt right. So he followed Rory's lead and climbed in next to him, pulling the blankets over them.

"Sweet dreams," Gray said, the tenderness in his voice surprising him as he brushed away a strand of bright auburn hair from Rory's bruised cheek. "May they be better than this place."

CHAPTER TEN

WHEN RORY WOKE UP the next morning, the inn was blessedly quiet.

Gray was still sleeping next to him, stretched out on his back, one hand carelessly thrown across Rory, and the other partially covering his face, no doubt to shield his eyes from the bright morning sunshine spilling from the dingy window. He looked more peaceful and more relaxed than Rory had seen him before, even under the bruises scattered over his face and torso. Rory didn't want to wake him, but in the next moment, one brilliant blue eye opened.

"We're still alive," Gray croaked groggily.

Not quite the romantic words that Rory had hoped he'd hear this morning upon waking; especially after the night before. What did you expect? he thought A confession of love? And maybe he hadn't expected it necessarily, but he'd wanted it. Nobody had ever loved him in spite of being a prince, and Rory discovered that was something he dearly desired. He wanted to be loved not because he was royal, not because he was beautiful, not because he was rich, and not because he spoke so many languages and was famous throughout the kingdoms for his translations and analyses.

After all that, what's left? that annoying voice inside Rory's head asked.

Rory didn't know, and he knew enough to realize that if he himself was in the dark, he couldn't possibly expect another to discover it. Even someone as clever as Gray.

"We're still alive," Rory finally murmured.

Gray groaned and stretched. "You look like you're thinking too hard for this early in the morning."

Rory might be inexperienced, but he knew he couldn't say, I want you to love me, but I don't know what I want you to love me for.

"I was thinking of the riddle Evrard told us yesterday, about the cave, and what it could mean," Rory lied.

Gray groaned again. "It's definitely too early to think about anything Evrard says."

Rory secretly agreed but admitting so would also mean admitting he'd lied. "We need to find the ring, the Bearer of Truth," he offered instead. "We should get up and get ready to go. Didn't you say the road up to the mountain is rather difficult?" He didn't want to get out of bed. He wanted to stay here and stay naked with Gray, but he remembered the promises he'd made that night in the valley.

If I get out of this, I will make different choices.

The Rory of old would have self-indulgently let the quest for the ring slide, trading the unpleasant realities of their journey for the much more pleasant pastimes to be found in bed. But he'd already acknowledged that he needed to leave that Rory behind, so instead of reaching for Gray, he climbed out of bed, searching for his clothes.

"You really mean it, don't you?" Gray asked, watching him with eyes suddenly and intently awake.

"Find the ring and take back my throne?" Rory pulled on his tunic. It pulled slightly against his bruised cheekbone as it slipped over his head, and he grimaced. "I do mean it."

Gray was quiet for a long moment. "You are not what I thought you were when we first met."

Glancing back at him, Rory smiled. "I believe the feeling is mutual. I didn't know you were familiar with so much territory outside of the valley, and I didn't know you could wield a sword as well as some of my guardswomen."

"That's one thing I'm good at," Gray grumbled, sliding out of bed and also reaching for his clothes. "Fighting for my life."

When they were dressed, Gray slipped the bar off the door and opened it only a fraction, checking both directions to make sure that nobody had lingered overnight, waiting for them to emerge. But the hallway was empty, and as they descended the staircase, the main common room was quiet.

"Any food?" the innkeeper asked as they paused by the door to the outside yard. "It's included with your room."

Gray looked him up and then back down. Rory was startled to see his gaze suddenly blazing with righteous anger. "I wouldn't take another scrap from your table, sir," Gray said, the edge of his voice hard and uncompromising.

He turned and walked out the door, leaving Rory to scramble to follow.

"Do you think he gave those men information about us?" Rory asked as they walked towards the stables to fetch Evrard. "Why didn't you say so last night?"

"Of course he did," Gray said, his voice still hard. "How else would they know? It's not an uncommon practice."

"Oh," Rory said.

"And I didn't say so last night because I was too . . . distracted to think clearly," Gray admitted, and this time this tone was softer. "A good distraction."

They entered the stables and stopping in front of Evrard's stall, received a snooty look from him. There were people milling about, including a stableboy cleaning out a stall, so he could not speak, but words were often unnecessary for Evrard to express his feelings.

Gray led Evrard out to the water trough, let him drink his fill, and then they both mounted, and rode out of town. The outskirts on the other side of Nargash were equally as poor, but Rory still had a smile on his face that he couldn't quite dismiss.

"I see you two had an interesting evening," Evrard said. "Bruises, Gray?"

"Robbers," Gray said between clenched teeth. "Unsuccessful robbers."

"Did you draw Lion's Breath to fight them?" Evrard asked, his deceptively casual tone cluing Rory in that this was actually a rather important question, though he could not figure out why. Evrard knew that Gray was currently wearing Rory's sword on his belt. Why would it matter if he used it?

"I didn't want to and I didn't have to," Gray said dryly. "I had no intention of motivating them any further." He turned his head to glance back at Rory. "Did your ancestors have to be quite so generous with the gold and jewels on the scabbard? It's like you wanted to announce to everyone you're carrying a priceless weapon."

"I think . . ." Rory hesitated. "I actually think they did want to announce that particular fact."

Gray shook his head in disgust and muttered something under his breath that Rory couldn't quite make out.

"Not everyone is hiding," Evrard pointed out primly.

"No," Gray said, his annoyance clearly spiking. "Just me."

Rory thought that he was also in hiding, and that Evrard spent every moment hiding his true existence from anyone who couldn't understand it, but despite waking up in a seemingly good mood, Gray's mood had worsened with every step Evrard took toward the Karloffs. Rory didn't understand it, but he wasn't stupid enough to ask why.

The road grew rougher and steeper the further they rode, and the further from Nargash they got, the less people they saw on the road. By midday, they had not passed a single traveler in some time, and even though Evrard seemed to be in good spirits, Gray insisted they stop to give him a chance to rest.

"The rest of the way is difficult," was all Gray would say, and even though Evrard grumbled at Gray's lack of belief in his strength, eventually he stopped by a small shallow pond, and drank his fill.

While Evrard was refreshing himself, Rory wandered over to where Gray stood, silently staring at the tall, craggy peaks overshadowing the road.

"I've been thinking of the riddle Evrard gave us," Rory began. This time it wasn't even a lie.

Gray glanced over at him. "Have you really? Why?"

They'd been riding for several hours from Nargash, and Rory had had lots of time to consider the riddle, how they should approach the search, and how he should approach Gray about his thoughts. He'd remembered how he had managed to convince Gray to accompany them at all; it had been all logic. Emotional entreaties weren't going to work on Gray. Rory was going to have to stick to basic, solid, irrefutable fact.

"Because it's early fall," Rory said, "and those mountains are large. The area between them won't be small, either, and if we want to have a hope of finding this cave before the snows start and we have to give up or freeze to death, we need to use the riddle to figure out where to look."

Gray was silent for a long moment. Rory decided that in this particular case, silence was acceptance, and continued. "Between two mountains of great stature lie veracity, fidelity, and certainty. Tread the peak and scale the valley. Solve the puzzle and gain the ring."

"And that means?"

"I'm not sure yet," Rory admitted.

Gray crossed his arms over his broad chest. "So, when you figure it out, get back to me."

The last thing anyone would ever have accused Rory of being was stupid, and it seemed to him, with several events as evidence, that each time he and Gray grew closer, he always retreated back behind his walls of cold, icy disdain afterwards. It was undoubtedly annoying, but now that he had more than one incident to analyze, it was easy enough to separate out the emotion and compare the differences and the similarities. No doubt Gray would've been upset if Rory told him his reactions were predictable, but it turned out there were very few differences and many similarities. Once he'd realized it, Rory could set aside his own emotional reaction, firmly telling himself getting mad served no real purpose. It wouldn't change Gray's behavior; the only thing that would do that was continuing to chip away at those formidable walls.

That realization reached, it made perfect sense to find a topic of mutual interest. Finding the ring was easily the best choice.

"I do have a few thoughts, though," Rory added hurriedly, not ready to be dismissed quite yet. Not at least until he'd made some progress on demolishing Gray's boundaries.

Raising an eyebrow, Gray motioned for him to continue.

"We begin by breaking down the riddle into its parts. Three synonyms for truth, when the composer could have simply used truth."

"Maybe it was for annoying embellishment," Gray said, his voice warming just enough that Rory was encouraged to continue.

"Or maybe for a purpose," Rory insisted. "So there may be three of something. On top of that, the riddle asks the recipient to tread the peak and scale the valley."

Gray frowned. "Those are . . . switched? Are you sure you remember it correctly?"

Shooting him a look, Rory shook his head. "I'm not wrong. It's tread the peak and scale the valley."

"And that means?"

Though Rory was considered one of the brilliant modern minds, Gray was certainly no slouch either. He cut through all the extraneous information and always managed to single out the most important fact.

"Again, I'm not sure, but I do have an idea."

Gray snorted. "Do I need to pry it out of you?"

"It's . . . it's a stretch. You probably won't like it."

"You're assuming I like any part of this," Gray said dryly.

It shouldn't have hurt. Rory had come to the conclusion that Gray always pushed him away once Rory grew too close for comfort. It wasn't personal. It didn't mean that Gray didn't like Rory as much as Rory liked Gray. In fact, all evidence pointed to the opposite. But despite all that application of logic, he couldn't quite deny the emotional sting of Gray's words.

"Right, of course." Rory hated how flustered he sounded. How emotional. He remembered when he could approach problems rationally for days—for months—on end. But since meeting Gray, he'd never felt as controlled by his emotions as he did now. They fluctuated all over the place—

good and bad and every shade in between—and still, despite the annoyance of it, Rory wouldn't trade this experience for a coldly clinical one. Gray made him feel alive in a way he never had before.

He cleared his throat and continued. "My theory is that the riddle is telling us to look in the opposite location than it's actually telling us to. Specifically, since the riddle states we need to search between the two mountains, in the valley located in the middle, I think we need to go higher."

"To the top of the mountains," Gray added flatly. "No, I don't particularly like it. It'll be a lot of extra time and effort and energy misspent if you're wrong."

"And then, there's the question of which mountain."

"Do you have any idea which one it might be?" Gray asked with a frown.

Rory internally cringed. There was so much of this he was piecing together with the theory that the author of this riddle had meant their inconsistencies of verbiage to be secret messages to the listener. But maybe Gray was right after all, and they were simply extraneous authorial flourishes. "It's possible that the number three, based on the number of adjectives used for the word, truth, is somehow related to which mountain we would need to climb. You know the geography of the Karloffs, do you remember anything that might help us?"

"Really?" Gray scoffed. "That's what you were hoping for? That I might remember something from a book I read fifteen years ago about a faraway mountain range?"

This time Rory externally cringed. "Yes?"

Gray sighed. "You really are desperate, aren't you?"

"You've met Sabrina," Rory said, raising his chin and trying to remember all the promises he'd made. *If I get out of this, I will make different choices.* "I can't let her continue to rule in my stead. I must find a way to stop her, and this ring is my best chance. So yes, I am desperate."

The incredulity on Gray's face softened. "I do know her, and I wish the best way to stop her were to march to Beaulieu and put Lion's Breath through her heart, but it seems like it isn't, so I guess I need to trust you."

On this? Rory wondered. *Or on everything?* But he wasn't naive enough to ask the question out loud, because he knew Gray was burying himself with denial, and Rory probably wouldn't like his answer.

"You do," Rory said. "The number three. Anything to do with that number or what it might represent, when it comes to a mountain."

Evrard had finished drinking, and while he had slowly trotted over, he had surprisingly elected not to involve himself in the conversation he and Gray were having. Evrard refusing to add his opinion wasn't completely unheard of, but it certainly felt unusual, and Rory tucked the thought away to unpack later, when he was working less intently on the problem at hand.

"What do mountains have?" Gray asked rhetorically. "Rocks? Trees? Cliffs?"

"What about water?" Rory asked. "Mountains have streams and rivers, and they usually feed into larger bodies of water."

Suddenly, Gray flashed Rory a bright grin. "Waterfalls! The Larger Karloff, it has three waterfalls! And the biggest one? It's right at the top."

Rory grinned back. "Tread the peak and scale the valley."

"Exactly what I was thinking."

Gray was still smiling and looking at him like he was a miracle as Evrard cleared his throat. "Are we ready to journey to the Larger Karloff then?"

It was hard to tear his eyes away from Gray's handsome, beaming face, but Rory managed it, barely. "We were right, then?"

Evrard glanced down his nose at Rory. "If I knew, wouldn't I tell you?"

"Not likely," Gray muttered, the edges of his lips still curling into that irresistible smile. Rory wanted to tell him how much he liked it when he smiled, but he was afraid his confession might cause Gray's walls to go back up—and that was the very last thing Rory wanted.

"Of course you'd tell us," Rory soothed, but he shot Gray a commiserating look. The list of things Evrard would share did seem to be considerably shorter than the list of things he wouldn't. But maybe that's why he'd repeated the riddle— he'd hoped Rory would be able to solve it, and he had, with Gray's help.

It wasn't the first time Gray had been essential to this quest, and Rory had a feeling that it definitely wouldn't be the last.

I don't ever want to do this alone, he thought, but pushed it aside, because no matter what they were sharing together now, it was impossible for Rory to imagine Gray giving up a future in his valley. It was why he'd agreed to come on this journey at all.

"The Larger Karloff it is," Gray said and mounted, holding a hand out to help Rory mount Evrard—something he'd never done before. It wasn't like Rory wasn't eminently capable of doing it himself, but it meant something for Gray to keep helping him. It made them feel less like two random people coming together to accomplish something and more like a team committed to each other.

"Of course it had to be the Larger Karloff," Gray grumbled as they continued climbing. They'd been heading higher and higher for hours. A little while ago, Gray had suggested that they dismount and walk alongside Evrard, since the incline of the path had made it impossible for Evrard to even trot.

Rory shaded his eyes from the sun and stared up at the looming peak. "Do you think we'll reach the top by nightfall?" he asked.

He almost regretted the question, because Gray frowned, the lines settling deeply into his face. "We need to. I don't want to be exposed out here on the side of the mountain after it gets dark."

Wordlessly, Evrard increased his pace, and Rory scrambled to keep up. "Do you think it's possible the cave is hidden behind the waterfall?" he asked Gray.

Gray shrugged. "I think it'll be a miracle if we find the cave at all. We've figured out one interpretation of Evrard's riddle, but who knows if it's the right one?"

"It needs to be the right one," Rory vowed. He knew they didn't have the supplies to spend weeks, or even days, on the mountain. And there was so little time to lose. He needed to get back to Fontaine, before Sabrina could plan more unpleasant surprises. He also wanted to travel back to the valley, with the hope that maybe some of his guard had survived.

"What are you going to do after you get this ring?" Gray asked. "Waltz right into Beaulieu and shove the ring onto her finger and demand she answer questions?"

Rory frowned. "I don't know."

He'd hoped that Evrard would be able to shed some light on the plan after finding the Bearer of Truth, but despite the subject of their conversation, Evrard stayed frustratingly silent.

"I could put it on," Rory offered. "I could put it on and be interrogated in front of the court."

"She has not truly exposed herself to you, which was no doubt part of her calculated plan," Evrard inserted. Of course, now that he chose to speak up, it was to prove how Rory's suggestion wouldn't work after all.

"Then what is the point of this ring?" Gray demanded. "We're nearly killing ourselves climbing this mountain to get it, and we don't even know who's going to wear it?"

"The plan will be clear in time," Evrard answered serenely.

Rory definitely did not feel as calm as the unicorn, and Gray seemed especially agitated, even for him.

I swore I'd make different choices, Rory thought. My new choices can't be any worse than the old ones.

But the problem was there wasn't any certainty that was true. They didn't know what they'd be forced to face at the top of the Larger Karloff, they didn't know if they'd find the ring, and even if they did, they had no idea how to use it to its best advantage. It seemed to Rory that everything hinged on a series of unknowns, and the realization dimmed even his natural optimism.

Gray was not naturally optimistic, and it showed as their journey continued up the mountain.

They passed the first, lowest waterfall, a small, steady trickle. "The Wash," Gray called it as they walked past.

"It's impressive that you even remember their names," Rory said. He thought he'd known much about the geography of the area, but Gray kept proving that belief to be false. He was incredibly, intimately familiar with the geography of the roads and paths around here, even though technically none of this territory was part of Ardglass.

"My old tutor, Rhys, he loved geography and was always assigning me maps to study," Gray said, in a rough, low voice.

His tutor? Rory wondered what position his father had occupied in Ardglass that Gray would have had a tutor. And then there was the confident certain way he held a sword, which spoke of extensive—and expensive—training that was not usually available to boys who grew up to work on farms.

Who had Gray been before he'd run away? As much as he disparaged Evrard's closemouthed attitude, Gray had plenty of secrets of his own. Secrets Rory didn't expect him to share even if he asked about them.

"Well, that was lucky," Rory said.

"Something like that," Gray retorted darkly.

The sun was falling lower in the sky when they heard the roar of the second waterfall. Much larger than the Wash, it fell in crashing sheets of white-tipped waves to the rocky pond below. "What is this one called?" Rory asked, as they walked by. He kept his voice low, despite the noise. The path had essentially fallen away, and now Evrard was just picking his way through the forest, always heading up, further and further until Rory felt his lungs burn with the thinner air. A ring of trees surrounded the pool, and it seemed that no human had ever been here before. But it was named, and it had been on maps, and Gray had seen them.

"The Thunder," Gray said, turning away. The frown was now ever-present on his face, and Rory knew he was concerned about the coming darkness and the final climb, which was taxing all their energies. They would reach the final waterfall at the top of the mountain, and despite their exhaustion, would need to conquer whatever stood between them and the ring.

But even though Rory felt the echo of fear in himself, he'd also discovered a deep-seated, intense desire to not only survive this test, but to win.

They pressed on, passing by the Thunder without any further comments.

The third and final waterfall—the waterfall all their hopes rested upon—was silent in comparison to the Thunder. They were nearly on top of it before they actually heard it. The sun was setting, but the water was a shining, rainbow-hued wonder of fog and mist, cascading over the smooth cliff into a peaceful, ethereal turquoise pool below. "The tallest waterfall in the Karloffs," Gray said softly.

Rory didn't speak, but peered closer, hoping to see through the thick cloud of mist to what might lie in the darkness behind it.

"We will rest here," Evrard announced, not even consulting Gray, "and you will swim through the pool to the cave behind in the morning. It's not safe to try it in this growing dusk."

"How do you even know there's a cave behind there?" Gray demanded.

Naturally, Evrard ignored this question.

"I suppose a fire would be too much to ask for," Rory said.

The look Gray shot him was what Rory had expected. There was no point in asking for a fire, because he couldn't have one.

"In the morning," Evrard answered instead. "The water will be very cold. You'll need the warmth a fire provides."

If you make it back, was unspoken between them.

Rory arranged a bed of pine boughs and needles, which felt slightly more comfortable than simply curling up on the forest floor. Evrard tucked in between two trees and nibbled at a bit of ivy poking out. Gray did not bother prepping the ground at all, just tucked his cloak around him and sat, cross-legged against a fallen log.

"I'll keep watch," Gray said when Rory gave him a questioning look.

"No," Evrard interrupted shortly. "I will keep watch. You will need your energy, Gray."

Rory was surprised when Gray didn't argue, but maybe he was more tired than he'd let on, because soon his soft snores were resonating throughout the little campsite.

I made different choices was the last thought Rory had before joining him in a deep, dreamless sleep.

"It's called the Veil," Gray said, as he and Rory gazed at the waterfall, which was even more spectacularly eerie in the morning light.

"Do you know who named these?" Rory asked, but Gray shook his head.

"The maps were old," he said. "Very old."

"As old as Evrard?" Rory asked, teasing. It was so much easier to joke with Gray than to face the intimidatingly deep pond and the hidden cave beyond.

"I did hear that," Evrard said stately, coming up next to them. "You should take your daggers, but leave Lion's Breath here," he added.

"For a unicorn that does next to no fighting, you certainly have a lot of opinions on weapons and arming for battle," Gray retorted.

"The unicorn is merely my chosen form," Evrard said. "I could defend myself if required."

"Hopefully it never comes to that," Rory said. The higher they'd climbed yesterday, the pricklier Gray had become, and the more he poked at Evrard. Rory found himself occupying the mediator position in their group, even though he wasn't sure he was very good at it. But you'll need to be, if you have any hope of being a fair, honest, trustworthy king, he thought.

Gray leaned down and began to unlace his boots. "We'll leave our boots here," he told Rory, "but stay in breeches and tunic. They'll slow us down, but I don't want to fight whatever is back there naked."

If their situation had been less dire, Rory might have impudently responded that he would love to see Gray fight naked. But the concept that they might not win this fight was sobering enough for Rory to keep the thought to himself.

Rory followed Gray's suggestion and left his boots sitting next to Evrard and watched as Gray reluctantly unbuckled the scabbard of Lion's Breath, the gold scabbard shining brilliantly in the sunshine.

Evrard bent his head over the sword as Gray carefully placed the sword next to his boots. It seemed that Gray was far more reluctant to leave the weapon behind than Rory, but then surely that was only because Gray was uncertain which kind of foe they would be facing, and no doubt he wanted every advantage they could find.

This time Rory did not wait for Gray to resurface for him to dive into the pool after him. If the mountain lake had been chilly, but warmed by the sun, the Veil's water was bitterly cold, and it stole Rory's breath.

Still, he forced his legs to churn and his head broke the surface right after Gray's. The frigid water turned Gray's skin pale, and his eyes shone starkly out of his carved white features. "After you," Gray said bitterly, "before we freeze to death."

Swimming helped keep some of the worst of the cold at bay, and luckily the pool itself was not very big. They crossed it in a few minutes, Rory's shorter strokes leaving him slightly behind Gray's longer, stronger ones. When Rory reached the mist, he held his breath, not because of the water, but because of the icy fear clogging his lungs. But as he passed underneath it, nothing happened except air even colder and much darker. A smooth ridge of stone greeted them, and Gray climbed up out of the pool with no difficulty. Rory's hands, shaking with nerves and the temperature, scrabbled helplessly against the smooth stone. He felt his panic rising, making it hard to think—logically or emotionally, or in any way at all. I'm going to die here, freezing and alone, his mind screamed.

But then a hand shot out of the gloom, strong and sure, and Rory would have recognized it anywhere. He grasped it and it hauled him out of the water.

"Thank you," Rory gasped as he shivered in the cool air of the cave.

"It's what I'm here for," Gray said shortly, and then turned away to peer through the gloom.

You're here because I want you to be, because I need you to be, Rory argued inside his own head. But he pushed the stupid thought away because right now it didn't matter why Gray was here, only that he was, and Rory knew he couldn't face any of this alone.

The cave was dark, shielded by the Veil's mist, but even as they crept deeper in, nothing interrupted the smooth stone walls except for a few pebbles Rory stumbled over. "Careful," Gray warned after he'd accidentally sent a few skittering across the floor.

It was all Rory could do to prevent whole-body shivering tremors from overcoming him completely. Putting one foot in front of the other was all he felt capable of.

They'd gone several dozen feet when a voice behind him made everything in Rory freeze.

"I knew I would find you here," a melodious voice exulted. Light shone behind them, and Rory knew what he'd see the moment he turned to face her. Had Evrard known she would appear? If he had, why hadn't he warned them? But of course, what could you possibly bring to fight a cold-hearted, manipulative sorceress?

Rory hesitated, but Gray turned immediately.

"And I you," Gray responded tartly. "You've gotten predictable in your old age."

Rory turned to see the shimmering form of his aunt, golden and perfect, toss her dark hair and smile mysteriously. "Old age? I think not. But you will not live to see it. Or you, my sweet, naive nephew."

"Sweet, but not as naive as you might think," Rory insisted, forcing his teeth not to chatter as he answered her.

She held out her hand. "I assume you are here to fetch this." A shining silver ring shone on her palm. "Truth is so overrated."

"You're wrong," Rory insisted.

Gray fell back into a fighting stance, pulling his dagger from its sheath at his calf. "We will be taking that with us," he answered, his voice cold and deadly.

She laughed, as beautifully as she always had, but now Rory heard a darker, uglier edge to it. Like she was laughing at them, but never with them.

I will make different choices. I have made different choices. I'm not the naive boy you watched ride out of Beaulieu.

Gray was partly responsible for that, but so was the world he'd encountered outside of his tower library's walls.

"I always think the old standards work as well as the flashy tricks," Sabrina said, and to Rory's horror, she closed her fingers tight on the ring, and then began to morph, her human form falling away to reveal the thing that Gray had once admitted to fighting before.

A chimera, that's what she was. Snarling lion head and big bulky body, with the tail of a serpent hissing and spitting as it flicked around her mane.

"A good thing I've had many years to consider how I would have killed you," Gray said roughly and re-gripped his dagger.

Rory knew it had to be bravado talking, because evading a chimera once was luck; they could not hope to defeat it with two small daggers and no other weapons.

She must have known it too, because she roared, crowing her triumph before she'd even achieved it, and it echoed through the cave and must have leaked through the wall of mist. Evrard would have heard it, Rory thought despondently, and he would know they were about to be defeated, if they were not defeated already.

But Gray did not flinch even for a moment, and then, suddenly, the dagger was flying through the air, light flashing along the deadly sharp edge, and landing right in the meat of the creature's broad chest.

Rory's breath caught and he hoped that Gray's impeccably true aim would be enough to defeat her, but the chimera only laughed, the human sound from its lion's jaws eerie and terrible.

The dagger fell from its chest, like it had never even hit her, and Gray gasped, disbelieving.

Rory froze, unsure of what he should do. He could never throw his dagger, not nearly as well as Gray could, and even that, with such perfect aim, had not managed to harm her.

Still, as the chimera began to prowl closer, and Gray still seemed stuck in place, disbelieving that such a flawlessly aimed blow hadn't killed the chimera.

Pulling out his own dagger, Rory stepped in front of Gray and pointed directly at the creature's growling snout. He might be terrified, nearly shaking inside with fear, but he wasn't going to let her touch Gray, not when he'd sacrificed everything he held dear to make sure they made it this far. It wasn't Gray's responsibility to kill his aunt, it was Rory's. She was his flesh and blood, and she had betrayed not only their family, she had betrayed their kingdom.

In the dim light of the cave, Rory's dagger shone less silver, and more bronze. He'd never noticed the particular hue of the blade before, and he wondered, as he tried to hold his ground, what material it was made of, and where Marthe had found it.

"You already know that will not stop me," she announced, her voice rising with exultation. "Finally I will have your blood, and even time will bow to me."

"You will never have his blood," Rory insisted. It was one thing for her to claim dominion over him, but to kill Gray? To hunt him so mercilessly he was forced to escape at a young age and remain in hiding all these years? Anger rose in Rory. How dare she? He swung out and the blow was not particularly skilled or even well-placed, as it only swiped across a single heavily furred leg. It was the kind of blow that likely wouldn't have stopped a human man, never mind a magical creature hell-bent on destroying both of them.

But for some reason the blow didn't glance off the skin, but sank in, bright red blood welling at the cut. She stumbled, clearly surprised, and then glanced down at the blade in Rory's hand.

Her shriek was deafening, and Rory realized very quickly that there was something special about this blade. Something that could actually reach her and could actually cut her. He lunged again and sliced her again, her shrieking tripling in volume.

"Keep going," Gray urged him, "it's hurting her."

But Rory had no intention of stopping now. The serpent kept dodging in and out of the space between them, threatening with its wide, needle-fanged jaws, but then Rory got a particularly lucky blow in and it screeched along with the lion's head as Rory partially cut through its long, sinuous neck.

When Rory had landed five strikes against it, blood gleaming on its fur, on its scales, the chimera took a step back, and then another. And then Gray shouldered him to the side, grabbed Rory's dagger, and right before he stepped up to land a killing blow, the creature disappeared completely, a singed scent to the air as the sound of metal against stone rang through the air.

Rory fell to his knees and with shaking fingers reached for the shining silver ring. He finally closed his hand over it and stood, holding it out to Gray with wonder in his eyes.

"We got it," he said, voice trembling. "We got it."

CHAPTER ELEVEN

WHEN THEY FINALLY CLIMBED back onto the bank on the other side of the pool, dripping wet, Rory couldn't stop shivering. Evrard had made use of their time in the cave and had rolled together a handful of logs and other small sticks, gathering everything together into something resembling a pile. With trembling fingers, Gray pulled matches out of one of the saddlebags. It took three unsuccessful attempts to get a handful of the pine needles lit, and then another few minutes for the fire to spread to the larger pieces of wood.

Rory was still standing on the wet bank of the pool, staring across the water to the cave where they'd just battled and then defeated Sabrina. One of his shaking hands was clasped tightly around the dagger and the other was clenched in a fist around what Gray presumed was the ring they'd gone in search of. He hadn't spoken, and he'd ignored two of Evrard's kinder entreaties to come over and try to get himself warm.

It was freezing; that was undeniable. But Gray wasn't even sure it was the temperature causing Rory to shake. The letdown after violence and confrontation could be a harsh one, and Rory was undoubtedly not used to the feeling. Gray, who'd spent most of his life poised and ready for the sort of encounter they'd just experienced, felt shaken. He could only imagine the physical and emotional exhaustion Rory was dealing with.

It was one thing to know your aunt wanted you dead; it was entirely another to watch her transform into a chimera in order to accomplish her goal.

"Rory," Gray said patiently, standing despite his cold, aching muscles, and walking over to where he stood motionless on the bank. "Come stand by the fire and get warm."

"Gray is right," Evrard said, likely breaking every rule of the universe by admitting that particular sentence out loud. "Come, before you freeze to death in those wet clothes."

But Rory didn't move and didn't speak.

"Your Highness," Evrard said after a long moment, and this time his tone was not nearly so sympathetic. "Come to the fire and tell me about the cave."

Rory did glance over, but he still didn't move. "Did you know she would be there?" he asked in a small, hard voice.

"I thought she would find a way, yes," Evrard answered gravely.

"Did you know my dagger would wound her where Gray's would not?"

Finally, Rory took one step and then another, stopping right before Evrard, and extending the dagger until it was right under Evrard's aristocratic nose.

"Yes," Evrard admitted. "Bronze is not something magical creatures enjoy. Myself included." He gave a delicate shudder and turned away from the warm glow of Rory's blade.

"We got back here alive, and we have the ring, that's all that matters," Gray pointed out. "We got what we wanted, and we didn't let her stop us."

"She tried to kill me, but we still got the ring," Rory said moodily, and now instead of the misty wall of the Veil, he was staring into the now-crackling fire. It wasn't much of an improvement, but at least he was growing warmer now. Gray understood how he was feeling all too well. He'd felt much the same way after he'd escaped Tullamore, but then he'd had months and years to dwell on it. Which, Gray could admit now, perhaps had not been truly all that advantageous.

"The ring?" Evrard questioned.

Rory's eyes snapped to his, suddenly blazing and alive in a way they hadn't been only a moment before. "The ring! The Bearer of Truth. The thing you sent us in there to find, so we could return to Beaulieu and defeat her once and for all. The thing we needed to take back my throne and rescue Fontaine from her evil grasp."

"May I see it?" Evrard asked, and Rory reluctantly opened his palm. He'd been gripping the unadorned silver ring so tightly it had left a circular indentation in his palm.

"Is it what you expected?" Gray asked, because not only was he curious about the ring's significance and ultimate role in achieving their goals, he also intended to distract Rory from agonizing over his aunt.

"I did not know what to expect." And that, at least, felt like an honest answer.

Rory stared at the ring in his hand. "How will we use it to defeat her? Perhaps we should discuss the plan going forward."

"Your Highness, you should put your cloak on, and sit by the fire, continue to warm yourself," Evrard said, and again, his words felt very honest to Gray. A little too honest.

"I think it's time to divulge this great plan," Gray inserted. "How will we use this ring to defeat Sabrina?"

Before he had met Evrard, Gray never would have believed he'd witness an animal blanch, all the blood rushing from its face. But Evrard defied human understanding, and even though Gray had never personally seen him blanch before, he was not as shocked as he could have been when he did it now.

"It's difficult to explain," Evrard hedged.

Rory's hands curled into fists, and Gray had to work to keep the frustration out of his voice. Evrard didn't tend to respond well to threats. "Explain it anyway. We risked our lives going into that cave to fetch it because you said it was important, and now I want to know why it's important."

When Evrard still did not respond, Rory said with suitably dramatic emphasis, "We almost died."

"It was dangerous, but then you knew it would be. You were armed, including with a dagger I knew could seriously injure her if she appeared."

Gray ground his teeth together. "But we did not know that. I wasted precious time and a dagger strike when if I'd used

Rory's, she would have been turned away far quicker with far less danger."

"Some things you should not know, you cannot know," Evrard defended, but there was an undeniable edge of guilt in his voice.

"Does it even work? This ring? What does it even do?" Rory wondered when Evrard stayed silent. He slipped the ring on, and outwardly nothing changed.

"Do you feel any differently?" Gray asked.

"No," Rory said uncertainly. "I don't feel any different and I don't think this ring is going to force me to tell the complete truth. I just think it's . . . a ring." He turned to Gray. "Your eyes are brown," he lied, and anger coalesced into a hard ball inside Gray.

"Why," Gray repeated to Evrard, emphasizing with each crisply uttered word how furious he was, "did we go fetch this ring?"

Evrard sighed. "You went and fetched the ring because I wanted you to. Because you needed to do something before you went to Ardglass and then to Fontaine. When we escaped the valley together, you have to understand, Gray, you didn't even want to assist Rory. You didn't even like him. You distrusted him. And you, Rory, you liked Gray, but you liked him for all the wrong reasons. Because you thought he was attractive and tall and had a nice chest."

Rory made an outraged sound, but there was a swelling inside that chest that Gray couldn't identify and definitely couldn't control.

"You wouldn't work together, and therefore, you wouldn't have survived," Evrard continued. "So I gave you time by telling you that the ring was necessary. You had to work together to get it. I knew it was rumored to be located in rough country and was depending on the fact that you would have to learn to trust each other or fail in the attempt. And you did not fail, you succeeded, far beyond my wildest dreams."

"Wait," Rory said after a long, charged silence. "This isn't . . . this isn't even part of the plan?"

Gray stared at Evrard, incredulous, with fury mounting inside him like a fire roaring out of control, hungrily consuming everything in its path.

"And why do we need to go to Ardglass?" Rory didn't seem particularly angry, just confused.

But Gray? Gray was something else entirely.

"We need to go to Ardglass," Gray said, the words exploding out of him before he could stop them in, "because this . . . this . . . lying creature in front of us has been manipulating us this entire time. My entire life. You think lying about a few weeks of traveling together is bad? Try living with him for fifteen years. Try letting him make every decision, including insisting, when you are eleven years old, that you need to hide who you really are, and keep hiding, even as he insists on helping others regain what they have lost. Namely"—Gray paused—"your throne."

"I don't understand," Rory started to say, but Gray was done listening, he was done hiding, he was done blindly following.

"You lied to me," Gray roared, and Evrard ducked his head under his onslaught. Maybe later he would feel guilty for a lifetime of anger and frustration bursting out of him, but now all Gray felt was vindication. "You lied to him. How do we even know that we can get his throne back? You certainly never wanted me to get mine back. Maybe if you wanted me to like him you shouldn't have given him the one thing I always wanted. The freedom to choose for myself. Instead, you picked my escape. You picked my name. You picked my occupation. I've been used and abused by you since the moment you appeared to me. I couldn't help it then, but," Gray said, his voice dropping as the anger exploded out of him, "I can help it now."

Evrard said nothing.

Instead, Rory spoke up again. "I'm sorry, but I don't understand," he attempted again. "Your throne? Ardglass? You're not . . . you couldn't be . . ."

Gray had sworn to Evrard that he would never tell anyone who he truly was. He'd kept that promise for fifteen long years, pushing everyone away who ever could have helped him bear that burden, and then when Rory had come along, he had been so twisted up inside and angry, that he'd sworn to himself that he would never tell Rory who he was.

It wasn't like those promises didn't mean anything, they just meant less in the wake of Gray seeing Evrard for what he truly was. A manipulative monster who possibly wasn't any better or more honorable than Sabrina herself.

Gray collapsed onto the fallen log next to the fire and stared moodily into the flames. "My name isn't Gray. It's

Graham."

"You're the lost prince," Rory said, awestruck.

"I told you I was lost," Gray said bitterly. "I didn't lie about that."

Rory's eyes flashed, not with anger, but with understanding. "That's why you can wield Lion's Breath, you were trained to fight with a sword. And the tutor! Of course you had a tutor, you were a . . . you're a prince."

"I'm not," Gray said flatly, but that wasn't quite true, and he knew it. He was a prince. Even if he wasn't sure he wanted to be.

But that didn't stop Rory. He kept going. "All your knowledge of the road through the edge of Ardglass. The Karloff geography. And Nargash. You knew all that stuff because you were . . . that was going to be yours, someday." Rory turned to Evrard, and this time it was his expression that was accusatory. "You told him not to tell me?"

Evrard's voice was soft. "I told him not to tell anybody. It wasn't safe. Sabrina wanted him; she still does."

"You couldn't have possibly thought . . ." Rory scoffed. "I never would have . . ."

"You liked him for all the wrong reasons, at least at first. You thought he'd help you understand why all your texts talked about sex in reverent tones," Evrard said, and this time his own voice cut deep. "You wanted something from him, but you didn't really want him. To you, he was just a simple farm boy, one you'd remember fondly when you left the valley. But you still had every intention of leaving."

"I didn't . . .I mean I wouldn't," Rory insisted, but even though Gray didn't want to, he heard the echo of the lie in Rory's voice.

"That is exactly what you thought," Evrard said, relentless. "If I must face up to my own shortcomings, then, at the very least, we must all be honest with each other."

"I . . ." Rory hesitated. "I might have thought that then," he finally admitted. "I did think that, very briefly, while we were still in the valley. But then Gray rescued me and then he kept rescuing me, and when we were taken by the tribe, and I rescued him, he looked at me like . . ."

Rory looked at Gray, and his heart was in his eyes.

"I looked at you like what?" Gray demanded. Except that he already knew what Rory was going to say, because the memory of that moment was bright and vivid in his own mind, refusing to fade away.

"Like you saw more than just Prince Emory, a pretty, useless little prince with all his books and his forgotten, dead languages," Rory said quietly. "And I knew by then that I saw more than just Gray, the man who owned a farm and shoveled manure in squash patches."

"Without this time, you never would have seen each other for who you truly are," Evrard said. "I am sorry I lied. I am not sorry that the methods resulted in you trusting one another. I am sorry that you will no longer trust me," Evrard said, and Gray would grant him this: the apology did sound genuine. It also sounded like Evrard—an apology mixed in with a reminder that he'd made the right choices and all his manipulations had worked out in the end.

"I don't think that's necessarily true," Rory said cautiously, despite the looks Gray kept shooting him. He had no intention of trusting Evrard again. He'd exposed them to the greatest possible danger and for what? To build trust? So he and Rory would like each other? In the overall scheme of things, why did that even matter? After all this was finally over, Gray knew he would return to the farm in the valley, and Rory would go on to become the ruler of Fontaine.

"I think his excuses smell worse than a load of dung," Gray muttered.

Rory came over and plopped down on the log next to Gray. "I know you feel betrayed," he murmured, "but there's something you're missing here. I know I couldn't do any of this without you, and if I'd asked you to come to Fontaine, to help me oust Sabrina, you never would have agreed. You definitely would never have agreed to go to Ardglass."

Gray didn't like it, but he had no choice but to nod. After all, how could he remain angry at Evrard's lies if he himself continued to twist the truth?

"Sometimes, we commit dishonorable actions for the greater good. Like when you told me your name was Gray, not Graham. You thought there was a chance I was an emissary of my aunt and I could betray you. That's why Evrard did this; not because he liked the idea of lying, but because without your help, there would be no chance of defeating my aunt or regaining my throne."

When Gray looked up, Evrard had also approached. Gray frowned.

"Prince Emory is partially correct," Evrard said. "I said I would be honest, going forward, and I shall be. Rory needing your help to regain what he has lost is not the only reason you are here, Gray. You are here because you are not really Gray, you are Prince Graham of the kingdom of Ardglass, and it's time you remembered that."

"You spent the last fifteen years hoping I forgot it," Gray objected.

"I never wanted you to forget who you were. Gray and Prince Graham are not two separate men," Evrard insisted. "They are two parts of one complete whole. You didn't just survive in the valley, you built yourself a miniature kingdom. You prepared for strays, and when they passed through, you took care of them. You continued to build and improve upon the foundation you were given when we first arrived. You never accepted, you always pushed for more, for better, for me and for yourself. Does that sound like an unambitious farmhand to you? Or does that sound like a man who is born to lead a kingdom of people who depend on him?"

Evrard's question was one that both required contemplation and also one that Gray thought he knew the answer to immediately. Of course, he had never thought of his life in the valley in precisely those terms before, but nothing that Evrard said was technically untrue. He had done all those things, he had planned and worked and never settled. That was how Rhys had raised him, and those lessons, instilled at a very young age by someone that Gray worshiped, respected and admired, had persevered, right alongside Gray himself.

"Do you remember," Evrard continued, his voice softening, as his head dipped closer to Gray, just as he'd done when Gray was much younger, "when I told you that you would need to be brave and strong and loyal?"

Gray froze. He remembered those words like they'd been said yesterday, but it hadn't been Evrard who'd said them. It had been Rhys, on that last fateful night, when his warning had helped Gray escape with his life.

"I will need to remember them," Gray said, a thought dawning on him that had never occurred to him before, even though Evrard had given him all the pieces through the years. "Rhys never died, did he? You only hinted that he did. Rhys was never Rhys, he was you."

Evrard's eyes were fond as they gazed at him. "I wondered if you would ever realize it."

"You came to Tullamore to be my tutor knowing what would happen," Gray said slowly, disbelieving that not only had Evrard been the stalwart, somewhat smug companion of his last fifteen years, but the dear, kindly disciplinarian of his first eleven. A man he still remembered with great fondness. "You came to protect me."

"I have only ever wanted to protect you, my prince," Evrard said, his skin beginning to glow, like a lantern, lit from within. It was the first time, Gray realized, that Evrard had called him that in fifteen years. He did not know what to do with it. He had spent so long trying to let that part of himself go, only to discover that not only had he never been able to shake it, it was an unassailable, undeniable part of what made him who he was. "I came to Tullamore to protect you. I helped you escape to protect you. I even lied to you to protect you. I know you felt disparaged and set to the side when I asked you to help Rory. You believed that your throne was a thing of the past, but it is not. The situation in Ardglass is complex, but we must still travel there, and you must still reveal yourself to all of Tullamore. It is time."

After their ordeal, Evrard had insisted they stay another night alongside the Veil. Gray, who was unexpectedly worn out from his earlier anger and the emotional revelations, hadn't argued. Instead, he'd gone off alone with his dagger, throwing it and killing several squirrels, which he cleaned and prepped to roast over the fire.

He'd apologized to Rory, because while he might be used to eating such rough fare, surely the other prince was used to better.

"It's a hot meal," Rory argued, "I don't care."

The hunting trip had also given Gray some space, which he hadn't realized he'd needed after traveling in such close quarters with Rory and Evrard for the last week. He was far more used to being alone, with occasional visitors for company, and even though he found himself enjoying Rory so much more than he'd ever anticipated, some quiet wasn't a bad thing.

After dinner, he'd gone off to sit on the banks of the Veil, hoping the quiet mist would help to silence all the questions that kept bombarding his brain. He wasn't ready to ask them out loud yet, but they swarmed him anyway.

It didn't come as a surprise that a few minutes after he'd left, Rory left the warmth of the fire and plopped down next to him.

"How are you doing?" Rory asked.

Gray wasn't particularly keen to share in the best of circumstances, but after the day he'd had? "Maybe there's a simpler question you could ask," he told Rory wryly.

"It's quite a bit to assimilate," Rory agreed. "I keep getting stuck in the most inconsequential of facts, like you knew exactly who I was when I rode into the valley."

"I hadn't actually ever seen a picture of you," Gray admitted. "But the last time I'd been in the village, they were talking about you, and why you hadn't assumed the throne yet. I usually stayed far away from any sort of political discussion, but I needed the supplies. I do remember wondering why they kept calling you the Autumn Prince. Then you introduced yourself, and I understood instantly."

Rory flushed brightly enough that it was obvious even in the falling dusk. "It's a ridiculous nickname," he said.

"No." Gray lifted a hand and stroked a single curl resting against his cheek. "It's a perfect nickname." He cleared his throat. "It occurred to me that if things had been different, we wouldn't have met in a patch of squash, while I was shoveling dung."

"We'd have met across a banquet table or in a throne room," Rory said quietly. "I thought it too. That was actually my very next thought."

"It would've been easier maybe, but not any different," Gray said after a long silence. "Not for me anyway."

Rory reached over and placed his hand over Gray's much larger one. "Not for me either."

"I guess if I have to go back to Ardglass, I'd rather do it with you by my side."

"I would've thought that you'd be eager to do it, to take back what you lost. I feel like we can't get back to Fontaine quickly enough," Rory admitted.

"Going back to Ardglass means seeing my father again, and I would rather never have seen him again," Gray said. He knew how harsh his tone was, but it felt like it wasn't quite harsh enough.

"I guess you'd come to terms with the fact that you wouldn't be going back." Rory hesitated, but Gray moved his hand, tangling his fingers with Rory's, giving them a reassuring squeeze.

"I was just thinking," Rory finally continued, his voice dropping until Gray could barely hear it, even though they were pressed closely together, "that if I were you, I'd want to talk to someone. Then I remembered that I'd been in a similar position, and I did have people to talk to. I had my guard. Marthe and Anya and Rowen. Diana and Acadia. I miss them. I'll probably never know what happened to them."

"You could," Gray pointed out.

"No," Rory insisted. "We have far more important things to do. And I didn't come over here to complain, not when you've faced far more than I ever have. I don't have a right to whine that I've lost them, not faced with what you've lost."

"It's not a competition," Gray observed.

Rory gave a short laugh. "No, no, of course not. You're right. I just . . . I wish I knew what happened to them. If they were all dead or maybe if they survived, and I could have done something to help them. After everything they did to help me. Marthe gave me this dagger, you know, the day we left Beaulieu. She said she'd had it made especially for me. And I couldn't help but think today that she knew and she hoped that it would be helpful when we came to fight Sabrina."

"She was a good friend to you, then, not just a captain of your guard," Gray stated. He hadn't gotten the impression that Rory had been the kind of prince to spend time training with his guard.

"She was, at the very end. And it made me realize that she was probably a good friend to me the whole time, yet I barely ever acknowledged her existence." Guilt edged Rory's voice. "I took that friendship for granted."

"You don't think I took things for granted? It was so silly, but I wished for years that Rhys hadn't died, that he'd been able to come with me, and now today, I realize he did, and I never knew it." Gray sighed. "Evrard can be hard to get to know, but I never really tried. I lost myself in the work that I was convinced needed to be done, and never reached out to him."

"He could have reached out to you, too," Rory pointed out.

"Yes, he could have. Not exactly his strong suit, reaching out." Gray gave a dry chuckle. "We can't look back. We can't live with guilt and regret, not when we have so much else to face."

"It's hard to let it go," Rory admitted.

"That's why I know it's the right thing to do. The right thing is always harder than anything else," Gray said, and to his surprise, he believed his own words. He hadn't realized that the questions didn't necessarily need to be answered, only that he needed to talk to someone, and if he could ever have a choice of someones, it would always be Rory. Another unsettling revelation.

The next morning, Gray doused the fire with a handful of water from the pool, and then stamped it out as Rory strapped the saddlebags back onto Evrard.

"One thing," Gray said casually as he placed a hand in Evrard's mane, ready to mount and continue their journey, "I think we should stop in the valley first, on our way to Tullamore."

"What? Why?" Evrard sounded genuinely astonished at Gray's request, and when he glanced over at Rory, he saw Rory's eyes had grown huge in his face. He hadn't expected it either.

"Because it wouldn't be a bad idea to fetch more supplies, and I'm nearly certain that some of the members of Rory's guard survived the attack, and it wouldn't be a bad idea at all to ride into Tullamore with some experienced fighters loyal to the Crown Prince of Fontaine at our backs."

Evrard was quiet, clearly considering the suggestion. Before, Gray knew he would have simply shut it down, because the idea hadn't been his, but Gray could tell he was making an effort to be more inclusive in his planning.

"I can see the advantages to the suggestion," he admitted, "and it's not very far out of our way."

"It's not," Gray agreed.

Evrard, because he was Evrard, drew out the suspense for another moment by appearing to still be considering the request, but Gray knew he'd already made up his mind. "Yes," he finally said, "we will stop by the valley first, and see if any of Rory's guard survived, as well as add to our supplies."

Gray gave a sharp nod of agreement, and mounted. Rory paused, placing a hand on Gray's arm. "Thank you," he said quietly, "this means so much to me."

Clearing his throat, Gray stared at the trees ahead. Initially he hadn't really done it for Rory, but now, he realized that maybe he had. And maybe that wasn't something he should be ashamed of. "You're welcome," he said.

Evrard took off at a solid canter, clearly not wanting to lose any more time. "What should I call you?" Rory asked, raising his voice to be heard over Evrard's hooves pounding against the ground. "Should I call you Graham or . . .?"

"I'm Gray," Gray replied. "I've been Gray too long to be anything else."

"Prince Gray it is then," Rory said, the edges of his tone impudent, and Gray couldn't help but smile too. "I like it."

Secretly, Gray liked it too.

CHAPTER TWELVE

ON THEIR RETURN TRIP, they avoided Nargash, riding around the dilapidated village and camping far on the other side. It was much easier for Evrard to ride down the hill than up, and it took significantly less time than it had on the front end.

"I'm not taking that chance a second time," Gray said dryly as he dismounted from Evrard. "I don't have a death wish, unlike some people." He nudged Rory's shoulder, and Rory caught a glimpse of his grin before he turned away to get the fire going for the night.

It was only a day after all the revelations and their agreement to be more straightforward with each other, but Rory swore that with every hour that passed, Gray stood a little straighter and glowered far less. He hadn't hidden his lack of excitement about returning to Ardglass and facing his father, but Rory still believed that slowly dismantling his secrets was already improving his mood.

"I don't have a death wish," Rory shot back.

Gray turned, flashing that quicksilver grin again. "The number of times you've managed to place yourself directly between me and danger tells a different tale." He had his dagger out and was moving further into the woods. In search of more kindling or dinner for the night, Rory wasn't sure.

"I haven't . . ." Rory spluttered. Except that he had. First, with the tribe, and then with Sabrina. The first had been more of a calculated risk—Rory had had time to weigh the hazard and the likelihood of whether there might be another chance of escaping—but the second time, when Gray's dagger had glanced off Sabrina's magical creature? That had been pure instinct, with no time to think, only to react. He'd done it because the idea of living without Gray, without his quiet, steadfast loyalty at his side and watching his back, seemed unthinkable. And despite what Evrard had said, Rory had done it before he had any idea of Gray's royal background, and it hadn't mattered if Gray only had the valley and the farm. He'd loved him and wanted him regardless of what property and prestige he could bring to Rory.

Rory's hands froze on the saddlebags as he was unstrapping them from Evrard's back.

Evrard made an impatient noise and tossed his great silvery mane at Rory's hesitation. "Those do not feel particularly nice, you know," Evrard chastised as Rory still didn't move. "They can chafe most unpleasantly."

But how could Rory perform a task as mundane as unfastening the saddlebags when his brain and his heart were alight with the knowledge that he'd stepped without hesitation between Gray and danger, and it was all because he loved him?

Craning his head, Evrard finally got a look at Rory's face. "For goodness' sake," Evrard said, his words punctuated with an impatient shake of his tail. "Look at you, mooning. I suppose you just realized why you stupidly stepped between him and Sabrina. He's not going to like it that you didn't tell him before you knew who he really is. He's going to think it's because you discovered he's just like you."

Rory glared at the unicorn. "It's not because of that at all. And the only reason he might think that way is because of what you said to him yesterday. A nice chest? Really?" He flushed, thinking of the embarrassment he'd felt. He'd worked hard to be taken seriously, and then Evrard had tried to ruin it by confessing every humiliating thing Rory had ever imagined.

"It helped for him to think you were hiding things too. Even if they were an unnatural appreciation for his pectoral muscles."

Rory's fingers finally resumed their nimble work and he dragged the saddlebags off Evrard's back with an annoyed glare in the unicorn's direction. "It isn't an unnatural appreciation. They are very fine and absolutely worth appreciating."

"Perhaps that isn't the compliment you should be leading with, when you tell Gray how you feel." Evrard looked at him contemplatively. "The question is, which should you lead with?"

Rory dumped the saddlebags next to the area they'd cleared for the evening's camp. "That is something for me to decide. How I tell Gray how I feel is not subject to a discussion."

"But you've never done this before," Evrard pointed out. "You might not realize you were going about it the wrong way."

Wrenching off his cloak, Rory tossed it down and began picking up sticks and moss. "And you have?" he challenged.

When Evrard didn't immediately answer, Rory finally looked up from the pile he was constructing. Evrard's expression was solemn, and somehow horribly gut-wrenching. Gray had barely shared any information about his past, but Evrard had always been even more tight-lipped, to the point of always giving generic information instead of personal anecdotes. It was entirely possible that Evrard had a deeply hidden, secretive past, full of love, loss, and heartbreak.

"I'm sorry, I presumed . . ." Rory stammered.

Evrard tilted his head, accepting the apology. "I believe in the past I have spoken to you of assuming other forms. There were many periods of many years when I did not occupy the form of a unicorn, when I was a man. And yes, during those times, I experienced much."

"Including love," Rory stated softly, and Evrard did not necessarily say, but the stark look in his eyes made it clear that all those love affairs had not ended happily.

When Gray returned, Rory had cobbled together a pile of kindling and moss, waiting for the larger pieces of wood and the matches to light it. He shot Rory an approving look. "I see you've been watching me," he teased, and this new, lighter Gray who teased and whose smiles set Rory's nerves alight, was definitely different and definitely not unwelcome.

"I like watching you," Rory teased right back.

"We're all very aware of that," Evrard inserted, his dry tone nearly matching one that Gray had utilized on many occasions. It occurred suddenly to Rory that maybe that was where he'd initially come by it.

"I brought dinner," Gray added, holding up a nice fat hare that he'd already skinned. "And before you moan about me killing animals to keep our bellies full, this one was already wounded by a fox I scared off."

Rory rolled his eyes. "I never said I had a problem with you feeding us."

"I saw your eyes when I skinned the squirrels the other night," Gray retorted, even though his eyes were still a warm, reassuring blue. "There's nothing wrong with feeling bad about it, but I'm still going to do it. We need to eat."

"Prince Emory is a sweeter, gentler soul," Evrard proclaimed, even though Rory did not necessarily agree with that pronouncement. He just hadn't had a lot of opportunity to see animals being skinned before, because while he might not be sweeter or gentler, he knew he'd grown up far more sheltered than Gray had.

"No, he really isn't," Gray said, rolling his eyes. "And please don't start with that Prince Emory crap. You know his name is Rory. You've called him that plenty of times. I guess I should be grateful you haven't whipped out Prince Graham yet, though I'm sure that's coming any moment now."

"It's important you remember where you came from," Evrard argued. "I'm afraid we've been too informal on this journey."

"Not informal enough," Gray countered, lighting the fire and gently placing the smoking moss inside the pyramid of kindling that Rory had constructed. "We've been fighting for our lives half the time we've been on the road. I'm not worried about bowing or scraping."

"No, you wouldn't be," Evrard said flatly.

Gray didn't respond, just kept tending the fire until a few minutes later, it was blazing warmly. He sat down on a nearby log and began to use his knife to construct a large fork for cooking the hare over the fire. Evrard trotted closer, settling near the log, but Gray ignored him.

"It feels easier, now that you've told one person, especially since it's someone you care about." Gray didn't bat an eyelash at Evrard's terminology, but Rory figured he was also trying very hard to ignore a very persistent unicorn. "But it's going to feel differently when we ride into Tullamore and everyone is staring at you, and yes, everyone will be bowing and scraping. How will you feel then?"

The dagger in Gray's hand stilled. Rory watched as he breathed in and then out again. "Like a fraud," he finally admitted.

"Then you should get used to it now, Your Highness," Evrard insisted.

Gray resumed his whittling, his dagger making short, angry strokes against the soft wood he was shaping. "I don't have to like it," he finally said, his words sharp. "I just have to live with it."

Tentatively, Rory sat down next to Gray—close, but not close enough that he'd be in danger of the sharp edge of the dagger—and reached out and put a reassuring hand on Gray's suddenly tense shoulder. He wasn't thrilled that Evrard had forced the issue now, not when Gray had been so much happier and so much lighter today. Rory shot Evrard a disgruntled look. It was clear Evrard could read some thoughts though he had never explained the extent of his ability. So Rory thought very hard in his direction, *Couldn't you have saved that for another day? Didn't you see how happy he was to tell someone? To tell me?*

Evrard tilted his head sideways and the clear expression on his beautiful face made it clear he'd understood every word and wasn't particularly pleased at Rory's thoughts. *Too bad*, Rory thought again.

"You may be both men—Gray and Prince Graham—but we know which has taken precedence in the intervening years since you were last in Tullamore. Perhaps Prince Emory and I should give you a refresher course on courtly etiquette."

Gray's expression went from slightly frustrated to downright disgruntled.

"Not happening." He grunted as punctuation to the denial, proving, at least in Rory's mind, that maybe a few etiquette lessons might not go amiss.

"In Tullamore, perhaps, rude and crude behavior might not be remarked upon," Evrard retorted, "but in Beaulieu?

The crown jewel of Fontaine, where the Autumn Prince studies in his castle tower with all his intelligence and grace?"

His pronged fork complete, Gray shoved his dagger into the ground blade-side down and grabbed the hare, unceremoniously mounting it and holding it over the fire. "Feel free to tell him off," Gray said, directing his comment towards Rory, but not bothering to look his way. The wall, which Rory had so painstakingly been tearing down, piece by piece, brick by brick, was back up, and it felt pricklier and sturdier than ever. Rory shot Evrard another glare.

"Beaulieu is a gracious place," Rory allowed, "he isn't wrong about that. But he's wrong about me. I've never fit in there. I wasn't intelligence and grace. I was awkward and uncomfortable and much preferred the company of my books."

Gray didn't say anything.

"We are really not that much different. I'm hardly a prince, no matter what pretty names they call me," Rory continued, all too aware of how desperate he sounded. "If I were a true prince of Fontaine, I wouldn't have hidden away from my duties and let Sabrina take my throne in the first place."

"That we can agree on," Evrard murmured.

It seemed like the kind of comment that Gray never would have let go unanswered, but now he merely sat, turning the hare to brown it evenly on all sides. His silence was more infuriating than any of his bitter retorts. See what you've done, Rory thought in Evrard's direction, now he won't talk to either of us.

"When you have finished sulking," Evrard added, "we will be ready to discuss the plan moving forward."

But Gray, who had been all eagerness to hear Evrard's plan after they'd fetched the useless Bearer of Truth, said nothing.

Rory threw up his hands and went to search for a stream to fill their water flasks. The quiet of the forest helped Rory feel less like he'd like to leave Gray and Evrard to seemingly annoy each other to death, and after a few minutes of walking, he began to smell moisture on the air. It was one of the tricks Gray had taught him to figure out if water was near. When Rory bent down to check the earth, it was damp with moisture. When after a few hundred yards, he came upon a bubbling brook, he smiled even though nobody was there to see his success. Still, Gray would enjoy his triumph later when he was thirsty, Rory thought as he filled up the skins with cool, refreshing water.

When he came back to camp, the hare was done roasting, and Gray silently divided up the portions as Evrard stood at the edge of the camp, chewing happily on some tender clover.

Gray poked at the fire as he ate, clearly grumpy and wanting to be left alone. Rory decided he had no intention of disturbing him, and instead curled up in his cloak on the other side of the fire, staring into the flames and picturing each of the texts he was going to study when he finally returned to Beaulieu.

Evrard announced he was going to find the stream, and went flouncing off, mane and tail rippling with what Rory could only identify as annoyance.

"One day and we're already at odds again," Rory said morosely, mostly to himself since he had no expectations of Gray actually answering him.

To his surprise, Gray looked up, his eyes dark in the firelight. "That's all I wanted," he muttered, "a little respite. A day or two not to think about anything, to be happy that I was actually able to tell someone—you—who I was. And instead the stupid unicorn starts in on etiquette and Your Highness." Gray shoved the dirt at his feet with his boot. "Sometimes I don't know how we survived each other."

Rory had also wondered occasionally how that had worked—but then the valley had been fairly good-sized, and he assumed that most days there hadn't been any obligation for Gray or Evrard to actually converse about anything at all. He didn't think it would help Gray's mood to point out that it was likely they'd survived their life together before by never talking about anything of actual importance.

"And then, sometimes," Gray continued, his voice growing softer and less frustrated, "I don't know how I would have survived without him."

"He saved your life," Rory pointed out dumbly, and then flushed. Of course Gray knew that. Gray knew that better than anybody else. Without Evrard's help, he would have died in Sabrina's dungeon, likely drained of his blood, and she would have become invincible. Rory's life too, probably would have been forfeit, along with his parents, because one kingdom wouldn't have sufficed if two were available for the taking.

"He knows me better than anyone else, and that's not always a comfortable thing," Gray admitted. His voice dropped. "I'm not ready to face anyone bowing to me. I'm not ready to be Prince Graham again. Maybe not ever again. I don't know. And a few days isn't going to change anything, but he's annoyingly right. I suppose I should start thinking if I can face it."

"We're going to Ardglass," Rory said, still feeling stupid, which wasn't something he normally faced, but there was something about Gray that brought out the worst—and yet, the best—in him. "How could you possibly avoid it?"

"The whole court believes Prince Graham to be lost or dead. I don't have to be him. I could just be Gray. I'm lost, remember? Nobody's looking for me." Gray chuckled darkly.

Rory tried to reel in his shock and didn't succeed very well. "What about your father? You'd come face to face with him and not acknowledge that you are his son? Surely he knows you live? And surely he would recognize you?"

Gray shrugged, seemingly unconcerned about his father, which Rory couldn't quite believe. If he'd had any opportunity at all to know his parents, he would have taken every chance, suffered any price. Gray's attitude was baffling to him.

But then Rory's parents hadn't forced him to run away as a child.

"I'm not sure he thinks of anything anymore besides his women and his drink," Gray said. "I doubt he even remembers that he once had a son."

Rory thought even if King Gideon was as far gone in his vices as Gray insisted he was, he could not possibly forgotten his son. Even though Evrard's methods could sometimes be a trifle overbearing and absolutely underhanded, Rory could understand some of his frustration with Gray. There was a well of bitterness and anger deep inside him, and Rory had a feeling that it fueled many of his beliefs.

It definitely fueled the wall that kept Rory out.

"I don't think you should return to Tullamore as anyone but yourself," Rory said, a trifle recklessly. Gray would likely not agree with him, and it might push him away even further, but one thing Rory had learned from his years hiding in the great library tower of Beaulieu was that hiding never altered a situation for the better. "Whether you want to be or not, you are a prince, and you are your father's heir. Don't make him hide that part of you away. If anyone should feel shame for what transpired, it is him—not you."

Gray was quiet for so long that Rory worried that he might have done irreparable damage. Maybe Gray would never talk to him again, he thought morosely, but at least Gray might finally decide being lost was overrated. Some good might come of this journey, even if it never resulted in the love Rory felt being returned.

"That's why I want to hide," Gray admitted very quietly, still staring into the fire. "I'm afraid he won't feel any shame."

Rory couldn't imagine what that might feel like; his parents had loved him very much and had never wanted to leave him alone. It was inconceivable that a father would cast a son away, willingly.

"I'm sorry," he said, knowing the words were not enough. His heart was breaking for Gray; even as he'd lived with his father's rejection and betrayal, he'd grown into a fine man and a fine leader. Perhaps Rory could not exactly fault him for the bitterness and anger that overflowed out of him occasionally.

"Why are you sitting over there?" Gray changed the subject and then shot Rory a diminished grin, an echo of what he'd done earlier in the evening. But he'd still tried, despite all the fears and worries weighing heavily on his mind.

Rory raised an eyebrow. "Because I was afraid I might get my head bitten off?"

Hanging his head, Gray laughed, the sound rusty. "I guess I can't fault you for that. I'm sorry for my rotten moods."

"I'm only sorry for the cause of them," Rory pointed out earnestly, picking up his cloak and moving around the fire to where Gray was sitting. "Is this seat taken?"

"No, Your Highness, it's been waiting all night for you," Gray said, and the smile on his face was deep and genuine.

Maybe Gray was not in as much need of an etiquette refresher as Evrard had believed.

Rory sat down, and Gray put a hand on his knee, squeezing it gently. "I really am sorry," he said, and sounded earnest. "And I'm sorry for not telling you, before. I can't even say I wanted to, because I didn't. I was afraid it would change things. I was afraid that it would give everything between us weight."

It was impossible not to feel the sting of his words. Rory had wanted whatever they shared to have weight, but Gray had been hoping the whole time that it wouldn't.

Gray must have seen the hurt flash across Rory's face, because he flushed, and stammered out an explanation. "No, that's not what . . . I mean it was, but not for the reason you think. I remember thinking that you could never know, because you'd think I could leave the valley, maybe even come to Fontaine with you—and at that point, I didn't even consider it a possibility. I was lost and couldn't see beyond staying lost. I'm still not sure I can, even though there's a voice inside telling me that it's time to rejoin the land of the living. It could be Evrard, but I don't think it is. I think that voice is the part of me who wants more, who wants you."

Taking a deep breath, Rory was really proud of how steady his voice stayed. "If you still want to stay lost, you can. I . . . I really care about you." He couldn't quite manage the word love, just yet, but he was trying. "I want you with me, but I won't . . . I can't ask you to abandon the life I promised to help you reclaim. That would be selfish."

Gray smiled, soft and sweet, and reached up to cup Rory's cheek. "God forbid you get selfish," he murmured.

They'd never kissed before when there wasn't violence or undeniable need pounding in their blood. Rory hadn't known that when their lips met tonight, their secrets laid bare, it would make such a difference. It didn't feel anything like that first, charged kiss they'd shared in the forest after Rory had saved them from the nomadic tribe, or in the lake, cold and wet, or even after escaping the bandits who'd hoped to rob them. It felt both new and old, and Rory knew he'd never felt closer to Gray than he did at this moment. As Gray angled his head, kissing him sweetly and then deeply, the fire of desire rising in their blood, Rory realized while Gray might be rebuilding some of his walls, he was doing it with Rory inside. As hard as it was, Gray was opening himself up to him, one confession and one hard-won truth at a time. Evrard might have been with Gray the longest, but Rory was no longer sure that he truly knew him the best, after all.

Their kiss was beginning to turn heated, Rory panting lightly into Gray's mouth as Gray's hands skated across his chest and then lower, briefly stopping at his waist before reaching in and rubbing at the front of his breeches, where Rory was hard and aching.

"I may take to wearing bells," Evrard said wryly, making Rory jump as Gray pulled his hand away from his hard cock.

"Yes," Gray said, and Rory felt inordinately pleased at the rough edge to his tone. All this annoyance was because they'd just been interrupted—not because Evrard kept pushing him. "Some bells or another sort of auditory signal might come in handy, especially if you keep sneaking up on us."

Evrard sniffed. "I had not realized that you two had progressed to the point of nightly romantic rituals," he said.

Gray rolled his eyes. "You're a meddling fool, so I'm going to let that one slide."

"Next time, I will announce my appearance more obviously," Evrard conceded.

"You do that," Gray retorted, but his tone was amused rather than annoyed. Maybe their "romantic ritual" hadn't solved all—or any—of Gray's problems with his past or his future, but it had seemed to lift his dark mood.

Rory started to move a little further away, when Gray leaned down, and caught him by the shoulder with one firm hand. "Evrard always sleeps soundly after clover and a drink. After he falls asleep, we'll head into the woods towards the stream. There's a cluster of trees, in the middle of a clearing."

That much was something Rory had also observed, but he didn't know why they needed to sneak off to indulge in more "romantic rituals." Couldn't they do it here, a respectable distance from Evrard?

"He hears everything," Gray said, and the look in his eyes made it very clear he had no intention of letting Evrard observe any more of their relationship. Since Gray had grown up with Evrard, that did make quite a lot of sense. "Come with me, please," Gray added, and Rory would have to be deaf not to hear the pleading note in his voice— desperation that Rory felt right along with him.

"Yes," Rory said. "After he starts that snoring noise he likes to claim he doesn't make."

It took Evrard an unconscionably long time to make the noise that signaled he was well and truly asleep. Rory, who had restlessly been pretending to sleep, but in actuality waiting for the sound that meant they were in the clear, stood almost immediately after it began. Gray appeared the next moment, reaching out in the darkness and clasping his hand. "Come," Gray said, and even though it was pitch black, began to lead them through the forest, to the clearing he'd described earlier.

Rory's heart was beating quickly, both in anticipation of what might occur once they made it to the clearing, and also at how eagerly Gray kept pulling him along, like he too couldn't wait until they were finally alone.

They reached the clearing and Gray tugged his arm, drawing Rory against him, as his own back settled against one of the trees. "I couldn't wait to do this," Gray said, and he sounded equally as breathless as his mouth descended upon Rory's, passion flaring between them like it had never been extinguished by Evrard's untimely interruption.

Gray's kiss was ravenous, and after only a few blissful moments, he switched their places, pressing Rory gently but inexorably against the trunk of the tree as they continued to kiss. His lips skated down Rory's neck, finding a whole chain of sensitive spots to kiss, until Rory was moaning and squirming under the onslaught. He wanted Gray to return his hand to the front of his breeches and give him the relief he'd so tantalizingly promised earlier. But instead, Gray sank to his knees, and Rory, who could barely make out his face in the dark, gaped.

He'd done this, yes, and he'd thought about it plenty of times, but somehow he had never imagined that powerful, controlled Gray would ever give himself up to it like Rory secretly wanted him to. But he showed no hesitation as he untangled the knot of Rory's breeches and then stroked his hard cock after Gray had pulled it out from the restraining fabric. "Do you want this?" Gray asked.

Rory worried his swollen bottom lip, afraid to say yes, and terrified to say no. "I want you," he said instead. Gray shook his head, his dark hair shining in the even darker night. "Tell me," he insisted. "I want you to say it."

"I want you to," he practically whispered. "Please."

The single word was all the encouragement Gray needed, because he bent down and Rory's head tipped back against the trunk as Gray's lips enveloped his cock.

He'd read about this so many times, imagining being the giver, and being the recipient, but he'd never dreamed that it would feel as good as this. His hands settled uncertainly on Gray's shoulders, and to Rory's surprise, he pushed against them, encouraging him to do more. Rory wasn't exactly certain what it was that Gray wanted, and as he sucked on the head, pleasure blurred out every logical thought process he'd ever claimed to possess. He wanted more of this, and then he would want it again, and then he would want it always.

Finally, Gray decided to help, as he plucked one of Rory's hands off his shoulder and deposited it on his head. Oh, Rory realized, that's what he wants. And he'd seen this done, in a handful of very tasteful erotic etchings, but nothing came close to the visceral joy of it, being able to sink his fingers into the silk of Gray's hair and pull, giving himself exactly what he wanted. Gray made a happy, encouraging noise in the back of his throat, and Rory felt the last of his reservations evaporate as he carefully thrust, pleasure exploding through him.

There was so much they hadn't done, so much time they hadn't been able to steal, and even taking a little now made Rory feel wild and greedy and desperate for so much more. All those etchings raced through his head, and his orgasm, barely held at bay by the tiniest shred of self-control, roared through him at the thought there might not be a finite end to this after all. They could have more, if everything fell their way. They could be, Rory thought dazedly, everlasting.

He sank against the tree, spent and worn out from the day's journey and from his spectacular orgasm. His cock slipped from between Gray's lips and Rory reached down to help him to his feet and to hopefully, return the favor. Except he found Gray's own breeches undone and his cock softening. "I couldn't help it," Gray said, and Rory could see the glimmer of a grin in the darkness. His voice was a little rough, and between that and the evidence that doing that to Rory had been as arousing to Gray as it was to Rory himself —it nearly sent another rush of desire flowing through him.

"I know," Gray added, "but we'll have more time. We'll make more time, if we have to. But for now, we should get some rest. Else Evrard will be insufferable in the morning."

"Alright," Rory said, gazing up at him. "As soon as my muscles can move again."

Gray laughed and leaned down to kiss him again. Rory tasted himself on his tongue, and thought to himself, we can be everlasting.

CHAPTER THIRTEEN

THE REST OF THE journey back to the valley was, thankfully, uneventful, and they made excellent time, stopping only to rest when they were so exhausted they could not keep moving. Gray should have been worn out by the speed of their travel, but he felt buoyant, even as they began to draw closer to their end, and his eventual return to Ardglass. Gray told himself, whenever he could not force the thought from his mind, that if he had Rory beside him, then he could face anything—even the betrayal of his father. If he felt no regret over what he'd done, then at least Gray wouldn't have to figure out how to forgive him.

Because of all the scenarios that Gray envisioned, him being able to stand in front of Gideon, the man who had so callously given him to Sabrina, and offer forgiveness seemed to be the most difficult for him to fathom. Still, he would go, if only because Evrard was right, though Gray was loath to ever mention that out loud. He'd lived his life trying to hide from that giant pit of bitterness that rose up at the most inopportune moments, waiting and hoping for a day when he could be found again. To rid himself of it, he'd come to the conclusion he would not only need to be found, he would need to make whatever peace with his father was possible. If no way forward existed, then at least he could tell himself that he had made the effort. Then, he would help Rory obtain his throne and decide, once and for all, where he belonged. Was it with Rory? Was it in the valley? Or was it where he'd always dreamt during the nights when he was too tired to deny the thought: ruling from the Ardglassian throne?

On the fifth morning, they descended into the valley, the bright purple flowers dotting the waving green grasses a balm to Gray's soul. Had he really only been gone from this place for a few weeks? It felt like so much longer, like he'd been a different man who had lived here, overflowing with resentment, even as he'd tried to pretend that this place fit him. And it had, maybe, before this journey, but now he'd been back in the world and one less soul thought he was lost.

"Does it feel good to be back?" Rory asked.

It did, and it also felt like a slightly uncomfortable reminder that nothing ever stayed the same.

"You were content here," Evrard observed, "but not happy."

It would never feel comfortable for Evrard to know him better than he knew himself, but it helped, understanding that Rory knew him, too. From behind, Rory's hand reached up and grasped his shoulder, squeezing reassuringly. "You will not be the first or the last," he said softly. To settle, Gray thought, that's what Rory meant. And he knew then that while he might return occasionally to this beautiful, peaceful place, he would never again live here. Because that's exactly what it would be—experiencing a glimpse of what a true life, filled with companionship and love and purpose would feel like, and then rejecting it in favor of a smaller, less fulfilling echo.

"It was a good place to grow up," Gray finally said, hoping that his words told Rory what he wanted to say later, in more privacy—that this was no longer his home.

As they rode toward the farm, Gray was surprised to see that no evidence of the battle remained. There was only a lazy, sunshine-filled silence as they approached the first outbuilding.

"Someone has cleared the bodies," Rory said, dismounting from Evrard, a perplexed frown on his face. "Did they take away their comrades?"

Gray sniffed the air. "They certainly did not burn them. You'd still smell it."

"There is another possibility," Evrard spoke up. "Your guard overcame them and then buried them."

Just as his words faded in the air, a figure emerged from the stables, a sword drawn. Rory gave a shout and ran, falling to the ground in front of one of his guardswomen. She wasn't in her armor, Gray could tell as he approached, but was only dressed in a simple pair of breeches and tunic. Her hair was unbound, rippling in the wind, even as she kept a fierce grip on her sword.

"Rowen," Rory breathed out unsteadily. "You survived."

She still did not lower the sword, and Gray took a step closer, and then another, his own hand braced on the pommel of Lion's Breath. It only occurred to him once he was nearly between them that Rory's guard might not look fondly on a man who was not Rory bearing his ancestral sword. But it was too late to hide the distinctive lion heads, the rubies and topaz sparkling in the sunlight.

Rowen pointed her sword directly at Gray. "How am I to know you did not capture and spirit away our prince?" she demanded. "He disappeared, with no trace to be found of him, right in the middle of the enemy's attack."

Rory had stood and was staring at her incredulously. "He saved me, Rowen. I was about to be set upon in the garden, and he rode up and saved me. We could not be sure you could turn the soldiers away, and so we left."

"And did not return?" Rowen questioned, her expression hard and unrelenting. "And left us here to wonder what had become of you?"

Guilt swamped Rory's features. "I assumed you had all perished in the fighting," he murmured, eyes cast down low. "I wanted to return, to check on you and the others, but there were more pressing matters."

"What pressing matters?'" Rowen demanded, and Gray flinched. Rory could not say that the pressing matter had ended up being some sort of pseudo-bonding mission and the one magical artifact they'd managed to get their hands on was actually completely useless and not magical at all. Damn Evrard and his meddling, Gray thought.

Of course, that was the moment Evrard chose to involve himself. He walked up, head erect, mane waving in the breeze, and Gray knew immediately that he had not cloaked himself as he usually did. Rowen, jaw dropped, saw him in all his majestic and true glory.

She fell to one knee, her sword forgotten, and breathed out, "Marthe was right."

"Not entirely a rare occurrence," Rory said with amusement, reaching out with a hand to help her to her feet. "But I can understand your surprise."

"That's a unicorn," Rowen said, "I thought they did not exist."

"We most certainly do, kind lady," Evrard said and to Gray's surprise, he ducked his own head. "You are the lovely creature who cares for the guard's horses."

Rowen's surprise morphed into wide-eyed astonishment. "It speaks?"

"I am Evrard, King of the Unicorns," he said, "at your service. Of course I speak."

Rowen's eyes flitted to Rory and took in his amused expression. "You are not surprised! You knew he was a unicorn? A talking unicorn?"

"Not when we first escaped," Rory admitted, "but he revealed himself very shortly after. Evrard is helping us defeat my aunt."

"And you?" Rowen directed towards Gray. "You knew too?"

Gray took a deep breath and stepped into the unknown. I am found. "Evrard rescued me from Rory's aunt when I was just a boy. He raised me here, in this valley. You might know me under a different name, Graham of Ardglass."

Rowen shook her head, even as the truth dawned across her face. "But Prince Graham is dead."

"I am very much alive," Gray confessed. "I've been in hiding, in this valley."

Rory reached out and took Gray's hand. "We have a very dangerous and important task ahead of us," he said, "we must take back my throne and see if we may restore Gray to his own. Will you help us?"

Falling to her knee again, Rowen said solemnly, "I vowed to protect you with my life, Prince Emory, and that vow remains steadfast. I vow additionally to protect Prince Graham, now that he has finally been found."

Found. It felt to Graham like the word resounded through the valley—a rumble of joyous sound that could not be diminished or hidden again.

"Please rise," Rory said, and shyly glanced in Gray's direction. "Prince Graham and I are very appreciative of your service."

While Gray didn't necessarily like it, he understood the point Rory was making. Maybe he'd always be Gray to Rory —just as Rory was Rory—but he'd need to be Prince Graham to the world. Especially if they were headed into Tullamore, and then Beaulieu. Gray was a lost boy, who'd desperately wanted to stay lost; Graham was a man looking for a place to belong.

"Did any of the others survive?" Rory questioned.

A wide, deep smile bloomed across Rowen's gentle face. "Indeed, my prince. All five of us survived. Acadia sustained a small injury, but she is recovered now." Rowen turned to Gray. "Your stores here are impressive, Your Highness."

Gray held up a hand. "I'm glad to know they were able to serve you well," he said, "and please, call me Gray, or if not Gray, then Graham. I may have been born a prince, but I grew up as a simple farm boy."

Still smiling, Rowen nodded. "I shall go fetch my sisters-at-arms. They will be thrilled to see you back with us, Prince Emory."

She set off towards the fields behind the farmhouse, with Evrard beside her, and when she was out of earshot, Gray turned to Rory. "You have never asked them to call you by your chosen name?"

Rory shrugged.

"But you asked me almost immediately," Gray objected. "I believe in our first conversation, you told me to call you Rory, and you could not have known . . ."

"Known that you were also of royal blood? Of course not. But . . ." Rory hesitated. "I know what Evrard said, about how I thought of you back then. A handsome, pleasant diversion. But he was not being entirely truthful. I knew you were important the first moment I met you. I knew your appearance in my life would change it."

Gray had figured out as much; Evrard's machinations were not as opaque as he usually hoped they were. "Your face revealed as much," he admitted, squeezing Rory's fingers. "I knew you never believed me to be a simple farmhand you could enjoy and then dismiss."

"I did think you were quite rude," Rory said, laughing. "But never simple."

"Tonight," Gray said, lowering his voice even though there was nobody to overhear, "tonight, come to me."

Rory's eyes shone as he looked up at him, the sight more precious than any gold or riches accompanying his resurrected title. "I would like that very much."

"There are some things I would like to show you, and some things I would like to say. And . . ." Gray leaned down and brushed a kiss across Rory's sweet mouth. "Much I would endeavor to enjoy with you."

Rory nodded, but before he could reply, movement out of the corner of his eye must have caught his attention, as it caught Gray's. He turned and saw Evrard cantering towards them, and on his back was Marthe, the leader of Rory's guard, followed by the other four women, running behind the unicorn and his rider.

Evrard stopped in front of them, mane rippling, and face as smug as ever. Marthe dismounted, her face glowing with happiness. "My prince!" she exclaimed and belying her words, reached out to embrace him. Rory did not hesitate for a single moment before embracing her back, tightly. And Gray remembered the bronze dagger had been a present from Marthe, who had so clearly hoped that even if she could not save him, then her gift could.

Here was someone who cared as much about Rory as he did.

Gray dropped to one knee and bent his head. Marthe gazed at him in confusion. "Captain," Gray said, "thank you for all your foresight and care of the Prince. I am most grateful for it."

It was the sort of speech that Gray would have made if he were Rory's betrothed—a formal acknowledgment of the captain's services, before the task could be turned over to his husband. Of course they were not engaged; Gray did not know what he was doing the next day and the day after, or where he would belong, as much as he wanted desperately to belong with Rory. Still, he hoped his words would show Rory a little of how much he'd come to care for him.

Marthe reached down and offered a hand, helping Gray to his feet again. "And you have my gratitude for saving Prince Emory's life outside of this valley. It seems he has been on an important journey, and still has another remaining, before we may return to Fontaine and banish his aunt from the throne."

"It is true," Gray acknowledged.

Acadia, bearing a bandage on her arm, Diana, and Anya arrived, breathless. "Your Highness!" they exclaimed, all exceedingly glad to see him.

Anya, whom Rory had mentioned was originally from Ardglass, quickly switched her gaze from Rory to him. Gray tried not to flinch. Telling Rowen was one thing, confessing his lineage to another of Ardglass? That felt much harder.

"You," she said, directing her words towards Gray, "you are very familiar, sir. Are you from Ardglass?"

Gray bowed his head briefly. "I am, good lady."

"You have the look," Anya said speculatively. "I have not met many of our country outside the borders, though that surprises me still, as difficult as the situation is within Ardglass itself."

"Anya," Rowen hissed, and Gray assumed she wanted to tell her friend that such speculation was entirely unnecessary.

But it wasn't Rowen's place to confess who he truly was.

"I have been living here in this valley for many years," Gray said slowly. The words were still difficult, and he was not entirely comfortable with the truth they contained, but it was time. Evrard had not been wrong about that. "Before I came to live here, I indeed lived in Ardglass, in fact in Tullamore itself. I was also known by another name. Graham."

Anya breathed out in shock and awe. "You cannot be," she said, "but you have his look, very much like King Gideon, and I saw the young prince once, when he was touring the clans with his father. He had your eyes. You must be the lost prince." She knelt, and Gray's heartbeat thudded uncertainly in his chest. Duty, Rhys had told him more times than he could possibly remember, duty is tempered with honesty and loyalty and kindness.

"While I might have been Graham a long time ago," he said, setting a hand on Anya's shoulder, "you must still call me Gray. It has been many years since I was a prince, and I must accustom myself to the title again."

"I pledge my sword to yours," Anya said, "as I am pledged to Prince Emory."

Gray looked over at Rory. It was technically not correct, as Anya had not asked Rory for his permission to resign from his guard, but since Gray had no intention of leaving

Rory's side now or at any time in the near future, there could be no harm in it. In fact, it would be meaningful to him to have a countrywoman at his side as he rode back into Tullamore.

"I am very pleased you have found each other," Rory said softly, the happiness in his gaze making it clear he was not worried at all about precedence.

"As am I," Gray said, discovering that his words were astonishingly accurate.

"We will convene after the evening meal to discuss many important plans," Evrard announced, "but until then I would very much like to retire to my stable."

Gray thought of his large tub and could not help but nod enthusiastically at Evrard's simple request. A bath and a bed. Rory. "I think we could all use some rest," he said.

Steam rose from the surface of the tub, and Gray eyed it appreciatively. On their journey, there'd been cool streams and the even colder lake, but the one time he'd hoped to find a hot bath—in Nargash—the thieves had inconveniently gotten in the way. He'd missed his big tub with its clever pulley system he'd designed, more than he'd even realized. Another bucket dumped into the tub, water sloshing over the side, and Gray's hands hesitated on the ropes.

If he stopped filling the tub now, the water would be a little shallow for just him, but if he added another to the warm water? Like someone . . . Rory-sized? He'd initially intended to spend a quiet hour alone in the tub, trying not to think of what faced him in Ardglass, but what he really wanted wasn't silence. It was that particular wrenching sound of pleasure Rory made when he was close to exploding.

Gray tied the ropes off and was about to reach for his shirt so he could go find what he truly wanted—who he truly wanted—when a knock on his door surprised him.

He was in the middle of slipping his shirt on when he opened it and smiled when he saw who it was standing in front of him.

"You said . . ." Rory said, flushing, and fidgeting with the hem of his tunic. "I wasn't sure when you meant, but I thought if the planning goes late tonight then right now might be . . ."

Gray didn't let him finish his sentence, which was surely that it would be far more advantageous to indulge now. Instead, he reached for Rory and pulled him inside, nudging the door shut with his foot. He bent down and kissed Rory thoroughly, who melted against him like he'd been afraid at how he'd be greeted but wasn't anymore. And the very last thing Gray wanted was for Rory to ever be afraid of him or think that he wouldn't want to see him.

The truth was Gray always wanted to see him, with an all-consuming focus that probably should have scared him more than it did. Instead it just felt . . . good. Like he wasn't alone, for the first time in a very long time.

"I guess you agree," Rory said as Gray lifted his mouth, his voice breathless and edged with anticipation. "Oh!" he exclaimed suddenly, and Gray realized he must have just spotted the full bathtub. "I've interrupted your bath."

"No," Gray said softly, and reached for the hem of his own shirt, pulling it back over his head. "It's our bath."

"Oh," Rory said again, and that breathlessness had tripled, leaving him starry-eyed and flushed. He plucked at the edge of his tunic. "I guess I should . . ."

"Yes," Gray confirmed, smirking impudently "You definitely should."

He was already picking at the laces to his breeches, his socks and boots already sitting next to his bed. Glancing up at Rory, he grinned. "Why does this feel like the lake? Me nearly naked and you hesitating?"

"I'm not hesitating," Rory claimed, though Gray had seen him undress much more quickly than he was doing now. "I'm . . ." His words died as Gray shucked his breeches, and bare as the day he was born, stepped over to the tub. "I'm just appreciating the view," he said in an impressed voice.

"You can look any time you want," Gray said, pleased. "But let me look too, please."

Gray's pleading must have worked because suddenly Rory's fingers were flying, untying his breeches and pulling them off, and suddenly, he was just as naked as Gray.

Their gazes met, and maybe it was the steam or the heat of the water, but Gray's palms grew damp. He wanted to touch, his fingers itching with the need to feel the expanse of Rory's cool, smooth, pale skin. But it wasn't just his skin Gray wanted; he wanted to crawl inside Rory and understand his thoughts and his logical analyses. He wanted to understand how his heart beat, and how he could remain so kind when the world kept conspiring to destroy his life. He wanted so much more than just the fleeting physical pleasure, and that might have scared him, but all his fear was reserved for the possibility that he'd never get the chance to have it.

"Come here," Gray said softly, and Rory fell into him like he'd been waiting for exactly those words. Rory's leg was a long, cool brand against his own, his cock a wet, hot reminder of just how much they both wanted from each other.

Rory kissed him, soft and sweet and trusting at first, but with their bare skin pressed together, his kisses quickly grew hotter and deeper and dirtier, until Gray was drowning in them. There was so much he wanted to show Rory—how good it could be between two people, even though Gray had an inkling that he'd barely touched the real possibilities, at least where Rory was concerned. He'd kissed men and women and taken momentary solace in them before, but he'd never felt like this—a driving, undeniable need to possess this man and let him possess him in return.

"Tub," Gray said, pulling away from Rory's mouth with a desperate gasp. "We should really . . . it's here."

Rory shot him a demure look from under auburn lashes. "Whatever you want."

Chuckling, Gray offered a hand to help Rory into the tub. "If you knew what I've imagined, you wouldn't be so cavalier about it," he teased, and Rory smiled serenely as he settled into the water, his back against one curved side.

"Maybe, maybe not." Rory watched intently as Gray climbed into the tub, facing him. "I seem to like most of your ideas so far."

"And what about you?" Gray murmured, reaching for soap and cloth and Rory's leg, starting at the foot and beginning to cleanse it. "Do you have any suggestions we've neglected?"

The cloth traveled higher, and then higher still, and Gray's hand paused at the top of Rory's thigh. His head had fallen back, his reddish curls shining in the candlelight, his mouth falling open in pleasure.

It was an image that Gray knew he would remember forever—Rory lost to the world, only from Gray washing his leg. "You're killing me," Gray ground out, and let the cloth fall into the water.

This time it was his hands coasting along that sweet, wet skin, until they nudged up against Rory's erection. Rory moaned, his eyelids fluttering in supplication. "Please," he begged, and Gray had never heard anything sweeter in his whole life. Carefully he began to pump him with one hand as the other fished for the cloth and made quick work of Rory's other leg, until he reached the apex of his thighs and the hard cock he was stroking.

Then he shifted lower, fingers brushing up against his balls, and then lower still, until they found Rory's hole, tightly furled against his inquisitive fingertip.

"Oh, oh," Rory moaned, and Gray, fire burning through his veins at even the thought of breaching Rory there, took that as enough encouragement to continue.

"You like that?" Gray asked, hearing the desperation in his own voice.

"I've . . . I've . . ." Rory gasped and his words were lost as Gray slipped just the tip of his finger in and Rory's erection pulsed to completion in his hand.

Rory opened his eyes slowly, the deep amber of them hypnotizing in the low light of the room. He took a deep breath. Slow, Gray reminded himself, he's never done this before, he's never felt this way before—and neither have you —but don't you dare scare him away.

"I've read about that," Rory finally said softly. "I . . . I wondered what it would feel like."

"It feels even better than that," Gray said.

"You've done it?" Rory's voice wasn't judgmental, but inquisitive. Curious.

"There isn't much I haven't done," Gray admitted. Then hesitated. It was a bit like earlier today, when he'd come clean with Anya about his lineage. Being honest wasn't always easy, but there were some watershed moments where if you pushed truth away, you simply couldn't live with yourself after. And this, Gray realized, was another one of them. "But it's different with you. It's . . . I care about you, Rory."

Not entirely what he'd meant to say, but close enough.

Rory stood, water sluicing down his slender, perfect body. "I want to be the one you do it with, I want you to make me feel even better," he said. "Can you do that with me?" He'd taken a very brave stance, but Gray could tell he was slightly nervous, because his voice wavered just the tiniest bit at the end of his question.

"Yes, but . . ." Gray hesitated. It was a big step. He'd be the first, and if he listened to the rumblings of his heart, he'd want to be the last. Would Rory allow that? Would Rory even want that?

"No buts," Rory said and held out a hand. "Take me to bed, Gray."

A stupid man would continue to hesitate, once their greatest desire made their own wishes known, but Gray was definitely not a stupid man. He stood and pulled Rory fiercely against him, his own cock heavy and hard between them. "It would be my honor," he said, picking Rory up and cradling him against his chest as they made their way to the bed. He deposited Rory gently on the bed. Their skin was wet against the rough sheets, but Gray didn't notice as he knelt between Rory's legs and with one hand gently opened them, while the other rummaged in the chest by his bed for the little vial he used when nothing else would satisfy him except being filled.

"This," Gray murmured as he finally pulled it from the depths and began to slick up his fingers, "will make it easier."

"Is it hard?" Rory asked with a giggle, his innuendo seeming to relax him as Gray began to massage the oil into the skin around his hole. Every few rotations he would dip his fingers in, and after the third or fourth movement, Rory was moaning again, his chest flushed against the pale sheets.

"It's very hard," Gray teased back. He wasn't even lying. He didn't think he'd been so engorged in his life, so tightly drawn that it felt like he could pleasure his man all night.

"More, please," Rory finally begged. "You don't have to be so gentle."

But Gray absolutely did. He wasn't small, and the last thing he wanted was to hurt Rory. Not when this was a moment primed to be full of ecstasy. Still, he could do a little more, he reasoned, and slid one of his thinner fingers in, rotating it as Rory grew used to the sensation.

One finger grew to two, and then to three, which had Rory restlessly pushing against Gray's hand, desperate and hard again, leaking profusely at the tip of his cock.

"I'm ready, I'm ready," he insisted. "Please, please."

How could he resist when Rory was begging him, his forehead dotted with sweat, his eyes wild? It was impossible.

Gray slicked himself up with the oil and then carefully positioned himself at Rory's entrance, pushing in as slowly as he dared, even as his blood boiled at the need to go faster, to claim him, once and for all.

His thoughts were a cacophony of nonsense, but the one that stood out the most clearly and the loudest was, you're mine now, as Gray finaliy slid home.

Rory thrashed in his grip, overwhelmed, and it was only a control born of so many years' waiting that Gray was able to hold back. "Is it okay?" Gray whispered. He didn't want to hurt him; he wanted only the opposite.

Golden eyes locked onto his, unbelievably determined and hazy with pleasure. "Move," Rory insisted through bared teeth.

So Gray did as directed and moved, short little strokes at first, stoking the fire higher in both of them, leaving Gray panting and sweat-slicked as he began to let go and go harder, deeper. Rory keened, reaching down to touch himself, only the barest touch of his sending him spiraling into bliss. Rory's body—hot and tight and unbelievable— before this moment, tightened even further, rippling around him, and Gray lost it, thrusting hard and spurting deep inside Rory.

For a breathless moment, neither of them moved, they simply stared at each other.

Gray didn't think he had words for what had just happened. There'd been heat between them before, an inescapable, driving need, but what had just possessed them? It was bigger than that, and not only did it have claws, demanding more, if not now, then very soon, it was somehow also soft and kind and unbearably sweet.

How could a feeling be all those things at the same time? Gray didn't know, and he thought from the wonder in Rory's eyes that he didn't know either. It was something, maybe, that they were both lost in this together.

Slowly, he climbed off the bed and fetched another cloth, cleaning first Rory and then himself.

"They were right," Rory said quietly as Gray climbed into the bed next to him, pulling him against his chest. Rory went pliantly, his face settling against Gray's pectoral muscle like he'd done it a thousand times before—and intended to do it a thousand times after.

"Who was right?"

"The books," Rory said, with an amused giggle that made Gray smile. "They always said it was earth-shattering and all-consuming and I didn't really believe them. But they were right, after all."

"It's . . ." He'd said as much before, but that had been in the heat of the moment, and now it was quieter. Softer. The words, which always held meaning, held more now. "It's not usually like that."

"I assumed as much," Rory said thoughtfully, surprising him. "If it was, nobody would ever leave their beds."

Gray grinned, this time the smile nearly splitting his face. "Unfortunately, I wouldn't be surprised if Evrard has us up at first light tomorrow."

"I know." Rory seemed quite disappointed at this. It warmed Gray's heart. He not only wanted to do it again, he was upset that they couldn't immediately. "And I don't suppose we could on the road."

"With Evrard and your entire guard present? I don't think so," Gray said. He didn't want anyone else to hear Rory's gasps of pleasure. They were his, and his alone.

"I suppose we will just have to defeat my aunt, and then we can do it whenever we like, wherever we like," Rory said, his voice growing sleepy. "One of the perks of being a prince, you know."

It was funny, because Gray had spent the last fifteen years thinking of all the negatives of being royal. Holding on to the reasons why he never wanted to reclaim his lineage. But here was one: Rory.

Rory, everlasting.

It wasn't a particularly honorable reason, and Evrard would have been appalled, but Gray, who had wondered if his doubts over returning to Ardglass would ever cease to trouble him, decided there was at least one reason he didn't need to dread it. And with that thought, curled around the man he loved, Gray fell asleep.

CHAPTER FOURTEEN

LATER THAT NIGHT, GRAY, Rory, Evrard and the five members of Rory's guard gathered around a bonfire outside the farmhouse. Evrard began the planning session by insisting that timeliness was one of the most pressing factors. "We need to rally who we can before Sabrina gets the chance. It is exponentially more difficult for her. You"— Evrard swung his head in Rory's direction—"are the Crown Prince of Fontaine. She cannot outright accuse you of treason, because any treason you would be committing wouldn't be treason at all."

Rory nodded thoughtfully. "Because the throne is already rightfully mine," he said.

"Likely she has already spread the word that you aren't a particularly sound choice to rule, but that won't be enough to turn everyone against you." Evrard hesitated. "There has been talk for the last two years of why she has not encouraged you to take the place that is rightfully yours. That works in our favor."

"Then why do we not ride for Beaulieu?" Gray asked, and he hadn't even tried to hide his eagerness at the possibility they could indefinitely postpone his return to Ardglass. He'd really been hoping they could put off their journey to Tullamore as long as possible.

"We have no army," Evrard said. "How do you propose we find one?"

"You don't mean . . ." Gray faltered. "You don't mean for me to muster the Ardglassian army."

"Unless you have another army at hand that you are willing and able to call to arms," Evrard said pointedly.

This was not at all how Gray had hoped the meeting would go. He'd been hoping that Evrard's plan for returning to Ardglass, back to the castle fortress of Tullamore, would be both slow and steady. Emphasis on the slow. It would have been silly to believe that he'd get more used to the idea with additional time, but Gray had hoped he could put off the inevitable at least a few more days. Give them more time to rest and gather supplies.

But clearly that was not in Evrard's plans.

Instead of continuing to participate, he sat and stewed in his own pointless, annoying thoughts as the meeting continued around him. He barely listened as the rest discussed provisions, weapons, the route, even the formation they would ride into Tullamore in, but it was only at the very end of their summit that Gray chose to open his mouth again.

"What about Gideon?" Gray finally asked flatly. "I very much doubt he will just let me waltz in and confiscate his army."

He met Anya's eyes from across the fire, flashing in the dancing lights. "Your father is in no position to deny a returning prince, wielding his consort's magical sword, the army of his birthright," she said fervently.

Consort? Gray had to force himself not to glance over at Rory to see his reaction. That kind of permanence had never been discussed between them, though Gray had a feeling Rory would not exactly mind it. Still, a commitment of that kind was serious, and should be approached seriously, and not decided by others. Still, Gray didn't address her terminology, because that was a whole other issue, and a voice in his head pointed out, with much of Evrard's inflection that right now is not the right time for that discussion.

"What is the matter with Gideon?" he asked instead, refusing to identify him as Anya had. Gideon might be his sire, but he had not been his father for a very long time.

"I think," Evrard interrupted, "that is a matter you will need to see for yourself, Gray." His voice made it abundantly clear that nobody was to discuss Gideon's state of mind any further.

But, hearing Anya's opinion of Gideon's state had certainly not made him any more eager to return to Tullamore.

Gray slept poorly, tossing and turning in his bed, despite Rory snoring delicately next to him, his dreams full of fire and blood and beautiful women melting into fearsome beasts.

As he'd suspected the evening before, they were on their horses at first light.

The only surprise was that Evrard refused to be ridden. Gray's old horse had returned to the stables, mostly intact, and so he mounted him, and Rory his own horse. Gray did not want to admit it in front of Evrard or any of Rory's guard, but he immediately missed the feeling of Rory's slender frame pressed to his back, reassuring and grounding him.

The truth was, he needed the comfort and encouragement of his touch more than ever, because it had become increasingly clear that Evrard did not only mean for him to reveal himself as the lost prince, but to take his rightful place next to his father like nothing had ever forced him to abandon it. That was a whole other thorny problem that Gray had not even begun to wrestle with—and yet he already felt bruised and battered and stung by its sharp points.

Returning to the place which had once been his home was one thing; returning to command the Ardglassian army was entirely another.

"Are you alright?" Rory asked when they stopped for a meal at midday. "You've been very quiet."

Marthe and Evrard had chatted on and off most of the morning, about various topics such as magical weapons, geographical points of interest, and history. Rory had inserted his opinion several times. Gray had not, and not only because he was not nearly as widely read as the others, but because he'd been sulking.

It was not something Gray was proud of, but the closer they grew to Tullamore, the more out-of-sorts he felt. He knew that he was in no real danger, not with Rory's guard and Lion's Breath at his hip, but the feeling of dread grew in him anyway.

"I'm tired," Gray told Rory shortly, which was not an inaccurate statement. He had slept terribly.

Rory pushed that excuse to the side like it was entirely inconsequential. "Is it because we're growing nearer to Tullamore?"

"Of course not," Gray lied.

Rory shot him a reprimanding look and reached out to take Gray's hand. "It's perfectly understandable if you are nervous or apprehensive."

Nervous? Apprehensive?

Gray was something else entirely. Frightened, perhaps? Fearful? Anxious? He seemed to feel all of the above at the exact same time, the emotions roiling around in his stomach until even the thought of food made him want to lose what little was left in his stomach.

"It's a big step you are taking." Rory tried again, and made a face, scrunching his nose, which normally Gray would have found endearing, but he was not finding much endearing at the moment. "I'm saying all the wrong things, aren't I?"

Gray sighed. "I don't know what the right ones are. If I did, I would tell you so you could say them."

"How about this?" Rory asked and reached for him, pulling Gray into a fiercely protective hug. After a long moment, he leaned back and looked Gray right in the eyes, his golden gaze as fierce as Gray had ever seen it. "I vow to stay by your side, no matter what. You will not have to do this alone."

There was a part of Gray that shrieked loudly that the only way he could do this was alone, but he didn't want to listen to that voice anymore, so he merely nodded his agreement. "I would like that very much," he said. He leaned down and brushed a quick kiss across Rory's lips. "You're a good friend."

Friendship was not entirely all they felt for each other—Gray could hardly deny that his romantic feelings were very strong indeed—but he did not want to unpack another problem by bringing up the particular term Anya had used earlier. Consort.

Rory didn't seem to be upset by Gray's word choice, though, he merely smiled and let him go, drifting over to his horse. "We'll get through this. The worst is always the anticipation."

Gray wasn't sure he quite agreed, but it was undoubtedly not helping. He remounted his horse and tried to clear his mind as they set off again on the road to Tullamore.

During the afternoon's ride, Evrard switched positions from trotting near Marthe and her mount to moving back to where Gray brought up the rear of the procession. Anya had objected to this orientation, claiming that he would not be as well-protected, but Gray had merely laid a hand on the pommel of Lion's Breath and she had stopped arguing.

Gray had also expected to receive some form of protest that he was wielding, at least for now, Rory's ancestral sword, but his guard had accepted it silently. Even Marthe had not argued, which was surprising, considering how many strongly held opinions she seemed to have. He wondered if it was because they'd all accepted him as Rory's consort, and as such, it was his right to hold any weapon he needed to protect the Crown Prince.

"I see you did not correct Anya's use of the word, consort," Evrard said, as if he was reading Gray's mind, which, knowing what he did about Evrard's magic, might be entirely possible.

"Neither of us is eager to place such a label on our friendship," Gray said placidly, refusing to give the unicorn the reaction he was clearly in search of.

"You've only known each other for a few weeks," Evrard pointed with a serious nod of understanding. "But they have been fraught weeks. You are growing very close."

Gray ground his teeth together. "You are clearly aware of what you wish to know, why don't you just pluck it out of my head? You're capable of doing it."

"It would not be nearly so satisfying if you did not admit it freely and out loud," Evrard observed placidly.

"You should just go back to discussing the weather every fifth year with Marthe. You'll get much further in your quest."

Evrard was silent for several minutes as their company made its way down the road, thick forest rising up on either side of the well-kept trail. Whatever state Gideon was in, at least he had not let his kingdom entirely go to rot.

"Yes," he finally said, "that is why they have said nothing about you wielding Lion's Breath. You will be Rory's consort."

Gray stared straight ahead. "Which am I to be?" he questioned darkly, "Rory's consort or the leader of Ardglassian armies? Because I cannot do both. I cannot be both."

"Graham," Evrard said softly, "you are capable of anything you set your mind to. I know you understand that, as I raised you to believe it. And as yet, I do think there may be a different solution to the problem of Ardglass that we have yet to see."

"I was hoping such an enormous problem would solve itself," Gray grunted. Any comfort he'd had from Rory's embrace had evaporated under Evrard's pointed questions, and though he knew he'd regret it, all he wanted was to turn around and ride at breakneck speed back to his valley and never, ever leave. Maybe it would mean losing Rory, which would be difficult, but at least this relentless pressure on his chest might finally lessen.

"I think when we arrive, I will see things differently, and there may be a solution I have not considered," Evrard said, clearly unconcerned. "I do know your love affair with Rory was foretold, and therefore there must be a satisfactory answer to whether you should become Rory's consort and help him rule Fontaine or continue to lead Ardglass and its armies."

Gray rolled his eyes. "The kingdoms could always be united," he pointed out, and then regretted his words instantly. That had likely been Evrard's goal all along in drawing him into this particular conversation. He'd wanted to know if Gray had spent any time considering the problems at hand and had devised any possible solutions.

He would have liked to deny it, but Evrard was right—he'd been raised to be a leader and to face obstacles without flinching. He would have to be an entirely different person than he was to not consider what could be done about his lineage and Rory's birthright.

"Possibly," Evrard said, "though that seems like an inordinate amount of work and statecraft for one royal marriage. Easier, I think, to leave them separate."

"Maybe easier to leave us separate," Gray said morosely.

But Evrard only whinnied in disapproval. "We both know you're lying when you say that would be a simpler solution," he observed. "As I said, your mutual love was written long before either of you were born. You are fooling yourself if you believe your feelings are so weak that you could easily turn away from him and the future he offers."

That was always the problem with Evrard; sometimes he knew Gray's mind better than Gray knew it himself. Because it was not just Rory himself, it was the promise of a future with companionship and love, nothing like the last fifteen years, where he'd been forced to rely entirely on himself. What he had always wanted, much as he tried to deny it, was someone by his side, and now that he had met Rory, there was no other possible person he could ever envision in that place.

"Ah, I thought so," Evrard continued, his knowing tone doing nothing to lessen Gray's annoyance.

They reached the edges of Tullamore midday on the third day of their journey.

The spires of Tullamore stood like solemn gray figures, reaching toward the bright sky. Gray had not seen their unusual spiky shapes in so many years, yet they were so familiar to him it felt like yesterday that he had looked upon them for the last time.

As they rode through the village, Gray noticed many changes from when he had last been here. The houses and huts seemed much worse for the wear, repairs done poorly or not done at all, and a malaise of spirit lay over property and person alike. Everybody they passed gave them a cursory, dead-eyed stare, but nobody inquired who they were or seemed to have any interest past observing they existed. Gray felt himself grow gradually more and more uncomfortable as they rode closer to the gated entry to the keep.

He knew upon the deaths of Rory's parents, Sabrina had returned to Fontaine, and left Ardglass behind. Why then, once Gideon had shaken off the influence of her magic and rotten advice, had Ardglass not returned to its normally thriving state?

The only comfort Gray took was at least the village was not in worse shape than Nargash had been. But with a few more years of neglect, he was not certain anyone would be able to tell the difference.

They approached the gate, the very same one Gray had faced Sabrina's chimera over, but there were no magical creatures present, only a few bored soldiers who barely glanced up at their party before moving for them to pass.

The night before, they had originally planned to approach Tullamore in a diamond formation, surrounding Rory, who would change back into his fine clothes that befit a crown prince, and Gray would take up the rear, next to Evrard— who was, at least for now, remaining in his disguise as a regular horse.

But now, Gray felt his gorge rise at the lack of discipline, and at the appalling lack of security. These men were simply going to let a troop of heavily armed guards ride directly into the heart of Ardglass, and do whatever they wished. Additionally, they were accompanying a man of clearly noble or royal blood. Gray could bear it no longer.

"Halt," Gray called out abruptly and pulled up on the reins of his horse. The rest of the group hesitated, but did not stop immediately, as he had. "I said, halt."

A man with greasy hair and a sullen attitude separated himself from the group of soldiers and approached Gray. Marthe and the others had finally turned around and were trotting back to where Gray had suddenly come to a stop.

"What's the problem?" the man slurred.

Drinking? Gray wondered, a fierce and devastating anger taking hold of him as he observed the rest of the soldiers behind him, one unashamedly taking a long swig from a flask he carried at his hip.

"Are you not on duty?" Gray asked between clenched teeth.

"Aye, yes, we are on duty. Protectin' this gate," he said, expansively waving to the large stone structure on either side of the tall archway.

"Then you are doing a criminally terrible job," Gray said. "Poor enough that I would have you arrested for treason against Ardglass, right here, right now. You are not guarding the gate, you are merely observing the people who move in and out of it, not caring a single bit what their business is or who it is with. An army could come charging through this gate, and I doubt you would even bring yourselves to care."

The man gaped at Gray. "Who are you?" he asked, a little less bored now, but no more concerned about the massive gap in training than he had been before.

Gray heard a horse trot up next to him, and wondered if it would be Rory, there to push home the fact that the guards had just allowed in the Crown Prince of a neighboring kingdom without a single inquiry. When he glanced to the side, he saw it was not Rory at all, but Anya, green eyes flashing, her expression the fiercest he had ever seen it.

"On your knees, soldier," Anya said, drawing her sword, the steel scraping against the scabbard, a sound that nobody in this keep would ever mistake for anything else.

Glaring, the man took a step closer to Anya, which Gray normally wouldn't have recommended. It seemed an especially precarious choice considering Anya's skill with the sword she'd already drawn. All he would have to do was take one look at her, and the quiet, confident way she held it, grip firm but loose, and coupled with her flawless stance, to know he wouldn't want to cross her. But the whole problem was that the guard had clearly stopped thinking.

"I don't know who you think you are. . ."

"Anya, of the Sheahish clan," she retorted calmly. "And you, sir, are too close to His Highness."

The man looked from Gray to Anya and then back to Gray again. He seemed baffled. "His Highness? Who is he?" he finally asked.

It had likely been inevitable from the moment Gray exited this very gate, fifteen years ago. No doubt his return had been foretold in the stars, just as his love for Rory had been. Inevitably, someday he would ride back to Ardglass, back to Tullamore, and reveal himself not to be just Gray, the simple farmhand, but Prince Graham, who had been lost until this moment.

I am not lost. Not anymore.

Gray dismounted and rested his hand on the pommel of Lion's Breath. Rory was behind him, but with his sword in his hand, it felt like he was much nearer. And Gray knew he needed that extra bit of courage for what he was about to say.

"On your knees," he repeated, "I am Prince Graham, come home at last to regain my place in the marble-lined halls of Tullamore."

Incredulous, the man stared at him for a long, drawn-out second. Would he recognize him? Had he ever met Prince Graham before this day? Would it matter? Surely, Gray would be required to provide some proof of his claim, but he could hardly do so now, not in front of this humble soldier.

Then, without a word, the guard fell to his knees. "Your Highness," he mumbled, face practically in the dirt. "Your Highness has finally returned. We are blessed and we are mighty."

The words echoed through him like they'd never been missing from his life for so many long, interminable years. "We are Ardglass," Gray finished.

A hard wind whipped through the courtyard as his words echoed through it.

Evrard stepped up, and as he walked towards the guard, his disguise as a regular horse melted away, revealing his shimmering white body and the single, arresting horn, touched with shades of blue, on his forehead. "We are Ardglass, indeed," he said. "The winds of change come, and nothing shall be the same after."

The man glanced up to see who had spoken and fell back to the ground. "A unicorn," he exhaled in hushed, reverent tones. "Come to Tullamore with our prince."

The other men began to walk over, and seeing the vision of Evrard, also took to their knees.

Gray didn't know whether to be relieved or annoyed that the Ardglassian guard seemed to be much more interested in Evrard than in him. But then, that was exactly the sort of thing Evrard lived for, Gray thought darkly.

But just as the thought crossed his mind, Evrard drew himself up to his full intimidating height and said, "This display is embarrassing. Get to your feet and take us to King Gideon at once."

They scrambled upwards, and that was when Rory and his guard, surrounding him, approached. "All is well?" Rory asked, his concern clearly more for Gray and his chaotic emotions than for their safe passage.

"All is as it should be," Evrard said beatifically.

Gray didn't speak, because he wasn't sure he trusted himself to answer.

As they rode towards the keep itself, the guard walked ahead and cried every minute, "He is returned, your prince has returned."

This time they were not ignored by anyone in the courtyard; every eye was on them—watching their party intently, whispering amongst themselves and pointing, quite obviously, at Gray himself.

Gray found himself wishing that he had heeded Evrard and Rory's advice and had worn something a little less threadbare than his usual shirt and breeches, with his dark, serviceable cloak tossed over his shoulders. No doubt he did not look much like a prince.

But then, he told himself firmly, that was entirely the point. He had not been a prince for the last fifteen years.

Finally, they reached the inner gate, and the steward standing there. Gray did not recognize him, but then that was not so surprising; he had been gone a very long time.

On the other hand, the steward certainly seemed to recognize him. He stared with no shame, so intently and at such length that any other time, he'd no doubt be dismissed for his rude, uncouth behavior. For all they were considered "barbaric," in comparison to the elegant, refined people of

Fontaine, Ardglassians were prickly about the impression they gave others. None more so than Gideon himself.

Or at least he had been, before the lady of Fontaine had come to his court and sucked out every other care he had, except for drink and the pleasures of the flesh.

"Your Highness," the steward said after his long examination. He dropped to a single knee his arm crossed over his chest in a gesture of deep respect. "Your father will be so pleased that you are returned to us."

Gray did not really think so, but he was not going to confess that to the steward. "Please tell His Majesty that I, and Prince Emory of Fontaine, wish for an audience." He paused. "Immediately."

"Will Your Highnesses wish to clean up first?" he asked, rising to his feet.

"No," Gray said at the very same time Rory said, "Yes."

The steward looked between them in confusion.

"Yes," Gray corrected, rolling his eyes. Wiping a damp cloth over his face wasn't going to change his very un-prince-like appearance, or his un-prince-like manners, but he was willing to defer to Rory, because Rory had a much better idea of proper etiquette these days.

The guard dismounted, and their horses were led to the stables to be watered and fed. The guards had hesitated, awed expressions on their faces, as they had stared at Evrard. He was of horse-like stature, but he spoke and was gleaming, flawless white. He did not seem the type of creature to take being banished to a stable very well.

"I will wait here," Evrard said, enunciating his words with dignity. "Then we shall go into King Gideon's throne room together."

Rory and Gray were led to a medium-sized chamber near the main gate, shown warmed, scented clean water, and additional clothing items in a large carved wooden wardrobe. Gray was glad they had not separated them, because he desperately wanted to talk to Rory privately at least once before he was forced to confront Gideon.

"This must seem very strange to you," Rory said, untying his bright blue cloak and carefully pushing up the sleeves on his yellow doublet, so he could dip his hands into the shallow basin of water.

"It is very something," Gray admitted. He supposed, after three days on the road, he could do with a wash. He took his own cloak off, and after a moment of hesitation, also pulled his shirt off. Dipping one of the cloths into the water, he washed quickly and efficiently.

Rory eyed him as he was finishing. "Perhaps you should see the different options available," he pointed out. "Not that your current sartorial choices are not . . . diverting."

Gray sighed. "I'm not a pretty prince. I'll never be like you. It seems foolish to even try."

"You would feel better if you walked into your father's throne room and you weren't wearing the same tunic you wore to shovel manure," Rory pointed out.

He wasn't sure when Rory had started to sound so much like Evrard, but Gray didn't know if he liked it. Still, he walked over to the wardrobe and pulled the large, carved doors open. Rows upon rows of tunics, in a rainbow of colors and sizes, lay before him. Deep drawers with different breeches, and even decorative metal belts greeted him when he gazed down from the racks.

"Here," Rory said, elbowing him out of the way, and plucking a forest green tunic of fairly simple design, but luxuriously soft fabric out of the wardrobe. "You need no belt as you will wear Lion's Breath at your hip."

Gray took the tunic and pulled it over his head. The size was spot-on, and the color flattering. He even felt like he stood a little taller as he gazed in the mirror. Carefully re-buckling his belt with the sword, Gray glanced up at Rory. "Are you certain you wish me to carry it?" he asked. He did not want to necessarily remind Rory that walking into the throne room of Tullamore wielding Rory's sword would give a certain impression, but the last thing he wanted was to fool Rory into doing so without him understanding the full ramifications.

If Gideon saw him bearing Fontaine's sword—and he would certainly recognize its distinctive design—he would assume Gray had pledged not only his defense, but his future, to Rory. That was not entirely a bad thing, but it would be if it wasn't what Rory wanted.

But Rory put his hand out, covering Gray's own as it loosely held the pommel. "The sword is yours," Rory said softly. "And all that it entails."

So he did know, Gray thought, and his world realigned with the idea that Rory not only wanted him by his side, but he wanted him there for the rest of their lives. "I know,"

Rory added, "how big a decision it is, and I am not asking you to make it now, not when so much is uncertain with Ardglass, but it would be my honor for you to bear Lion's Breath today."

Gray swallowed hard. There were words of love on the tip of his tongue, and surely those would need to be spoken before they made any promises to each other, but for right now, Rory was right. This was enough. "And I am honored beyond measure to wield it," he answered, leaning down and brushing a kiss against Rory's mouth. "Nothing would give me greater happiness, in fact."

"Then it is decided," he said, his smile bright and unwavering. So certain that Gray felt his breath catch with all that he could mean.

When Gray and Rory rejoined Evrard, he gave a quick, supportive nod. "I see you have worked your good influence over him," Evrard said towards Rory. "I am impressed."

Gray glared. "I am not so bad as that," he argued.

"No, but very stubborn," Evrard sniffed.

It was hardly like he was the only stubborn creature present. It would be easier to focus on this silly, circular argument with Evrard, but there were far more important matters at hand that required Gray's attention and his concentration, so he kept his mouth shut, and watched as Rory's guard approached. They'd not shed any of their armor, and it shone in the shafts of sunlight that fell into the large entry hall from the enormous skylights above.

"Are you ready, my prince?" Marthe asked, directing the question towards Rory, who nodded. Then, to Gray's surprise, she switched her attention to him. "And you, Prince Graham?" she asked.

Gray did not particularly like that suddenly everything felt so formal between them and that she'd addressed him by his title, but to do anything else, he realized, would undermine his position. And frankly, his position already felt precarious.

"I am, Captain," Gray said.

"Then," Marthe said, gesturing to the steward, "let us proceed."

This hall that led to the main reception and throne room was one Gray remembered all too well. He'd trodden it numerous times over his eleven years residing in Tullamore. Sometimes it was because his father had asked him to meet nobles who had traveled from the clans, and sometimes it was because he'd done something particularly naughty and Rhys had insisted he confess the misdeed directly to his father.

It was very odd to be back here after so much time, and to be walking in the same hall, next to Evrard, who was and also was not, the tutor who had enforced his discipline all those years back.

Finally, they came to a halt at a pair of enormous double doors, worked in silver and studded in iron. "Your Highnesses," the steward said, "I will announce you now."

He pulled the doors open, and Gray dug his fingernails into his palm at the sight. The throne room, with its walls of green marble and intricate silk hangings, was still spotless— every bit as awe-inducing and spectacular as Gray had remembered it being—but the man sitting on the silver throne mounted on the dais was a stranger.

Gideon had always been a broad-shouldered, largely built man, famous for swinging his enormous war hammer from his destrier. But the man sitting on the throne now was bent and weak, his body shrunk and his hair thin and graying. He looked nothing like the man Gray remembered.

"Your Majesty," the steward said, his voice growing louder as he approached the throne. Was he also now hard of hearing? Gray flinched at the thought of his powerful, majestic father brought to this humiliating end, and vowed to do whatever it took to eliminate breath from Sabrina's lungs.

"Who is it?" Gray could barely hear the King's tremulous voice.

"Your son, Your Majesty," the steward said, excitement leaking into his voice. "Your son has returned."

It might have been Gray's desperate imagination, but he thought Gideon sat a bit straighter at the news.

"It cannot be," he said slowly. "Graham is dead. Lost. This must be an impostor, come to torment an old man."

It was no more than Gray had expected, but it still hurt.

"Who else is there?" the King asked, and Rory stepped forward, his guard flanking him.

"I am Prince Emory, Your Majesty," Rory said, bending slightly, as befitted his stature and the man in front of him.

For all his bookishness, Rory clearly knew exactly the etiquette required for a prince to meet a king. Gray had known the same rules once, but he'd banished them from his mind, and now found that they did not return as easily as he'd hoped. Well, he thought, I have no intention of bowing to Gideon anyhow.

"Prince Emory, of Fontaine," Gideon said, rising slightly from the throne, his hands braced on the sides. Upright, the sight of him was even more awful. Gideon looked as if every ounce of health and vitality had been sucked out of him, leaving a decrepit, waning shell.

Gray pushed the despair away because the last thing he wanted was to feel for the man in front of him. He'd brought all this downfall on himself. He'd allowed Sabrina to become an advisor. He'd allowed her to take control. He'd ultimately allowed her to take his only son.

"Your appearance in my kingdom is a surprise," Gideon continued. "What is it you need?"

"I come to present your son to you, returned after many years of absence," Rory said.

Gray flinched again at the denial shadowing the King's features. "You are certainly led astray easily," Gideon said. "My son is dead."

Evrard, who was standing next to Gray still, chose that moment to walk forward towards the dais, and shock replaced the denial on Gideon's face. "Your Majesty, nobody has been led astray. The man before you now is indeed your son, as I am the one who rescued him from your creature. And, I am forced to add, yourself."

Guilt flushed Gideon's features. He said nothing.

Evrard glanced backwards at Gray, whose feet still seemed to be rooted in place, unmoving. He did not want to walk any closer, he did not want to see any more that could not be unseen, and yet this was another thing that he must do. He took one step and then another and then ten more, until he was standing directly next to Rory. Gray reached for his hand and took it, squeezing it tightly.

"I am indeed Graham, and I am no lie," he said, and while he'd hoped to keep his voice neutral, fury leaked into it.

The King took a hesitant step forward and then another, and Gray had to hold himself steady as he came closer and closer, until he was right in front of him. He could see the remnants of who Gideon had been, but they were slight and they were buried under trembling fingers, hazy eyes, and a waning strength that would never again dream of picking up a war hammer and brandishing it.

"Perhaps not," Gideon said slowly, reaching up to tremulously touch the side of Gray's face. "You do look much like him. Much as I'd imagined . . ." His voice trailed off, and Gray had not been mistaken. The guilt and shame in his eyes were unmistakable.

The King knew exactly who he was and he was only attempting to pretend because he did not want to face the enormity of what he had done.

"I am Graham," Gray repeated firmly. "You may either choose to accept me or continue to waste away in your disgrace. That is your choice. But I will not keep Prince Emory and his representatives here, subject to your uncertainty. Nor will I stay. If you have a question you wish to ask of me, then you should ask it. Otherwise"—he paused, remembering finally, some of the rules that Rhys had taught him about oration—"we will be gone from your borders by nightfall."

He started to turn, intending to leave, and a single desperate wail broke the silence. "Wait!" the King shouted. "Wait!"

Gray turned back, and knew his face was hard and unrelenting. This had been the hardest thing he had ever done, and instead of welcoming him home, the King had claimed he was a fraud.

"I was mistaken," the King said in a quiet, despairing voice. "I was wrong to call you a liar. You could be a pretender, but we both know you are not. But mostly I was entirely wrong to give you to her, all those years ago. If you are here, and willing to hear my apology, I would hope to hear your forgiveness." The King looked pitiful and pathetic, tears rolling down his cheeks, and Gray might have been more moved by the sight, but all he felt was righteous and indignant anger.

"You were wrong, yet I have no intention of offering any balm to your conscience," Gray stated. "I was given no quarter and had no choice but to abandon my home and my friends and my father, for fifteen years. There is no forgiveness left in me."

"I understand," Gideon said, his head bowed. "I would expect no less from the Crown Prince of Ardglass."

"Your Majesty," Evrard cut into the uncomfortable silence that followed. "We are also here to discuss the woman who convinced you to condemn your son to death. Certainly you are aware she is attempting to usurp Prince Emory's throne."

Clearly miserable, Gideon nodded. "I had heard of this," he finally acknowledged.

"We are here to formulate a plan to defeat her," Evrard said. "And for that we will need your assistance."

Gideon said nothing for a long, drawn-out moment. As if he almost did not trust himself. "I am willing to give whatever help you need," he said. "But my kingdom has, unfortunately like myself, grown weak. I am not sure we can offer much."

"Ardglass will offer whatever assistance is requested by my party," Gray said. "It is the very least you can do."

Gray collapsed onto the bed in the suite of rooms he'd just been shown to by the steward.

The rooms were not his own, or even the rooms of the Crown Prince, something he knew he was entitled to, but Gray was so exhausted, he couldn't find it in himself to care at the moment. From the moment he'd spotted the spires of Tullamore, he'd been braced for . . . something. Rejection? Acceptance? Apathy? He couldn't have predicted how Gideon would react to his arrival, but what he'd ended up facing had been truly worse than anything his imagination could have conjured.

There'd been a time when all he'd wanted was for his father to regret his actions. Gray had never guessed that regret could be so much more dangerous, so much more upsetting than dismissal. Regret carried claws with it and struck at his most tender, vulnerable spots. Regret brought visions of what could have been, and those hurt so much more fiercely than any memory of what had actually been.

He sighed, lying back and staring at the tapestry hung above the bed. Detailed and finely wrought, it told the story of the first Ardglassian king, the one who had originally united all the clans, and who had become their leader, at the people's insistence. Without him, Gray would never have existed. This castle would never have existed. And yet, he found himself not being particularly grateful this evening.

A knock sounded on the door, and Gray groaned softly, not wishing to rise from the bed. Only the thought that it could be Rory, come to find him, got him up and moving. Except when he opened the door, it was not Rory's slender figure and auburn curls he saw, but a stooped, wizened figure with thinning gray hair.

Gray stared at his father. "What do you want?" he asked. They'd parted—not on good terms, precisely, but at least under the assumption that Gray and Rory could summon the clans and request they lend their swords to defeat Sabrina.

Kill, Gray had corrected firmly, because after all the devastation and destruction she had wrought, he had no intention of letting her breathe past their inevitable confrontation. After all, she would have killed both him and Rory to serve her own purposes, and while his own life did not feel particularly valuable anymore, Rory's was priceless, and that could never be forgiven.

"I wish a word with you," Gideon said stiffly. One of his guards was a good distance away, watching the interaction between father and son intently, but made no move to follow when Gray eventually waved him in. He supposed they were not particularly worried that Gray would decide to perform patricide in retribution for Gideon's betrayal all those years ago.

"What is it?" Gray demanded, awkwardness at finally being alone with him overwhelming any manners he might once have had. He hadn't known that being alone together would make him alternately want to cry and shake his father so hard his teeth vibrated.

"You stated your ultimate purpose is to defeat Sabrina and place Prince Emory on the throne of Fontaine," Gideon said, and Gray would have to be a lot stupider to miss how careful his words were. "And you also stated your intention is not to leave her alive."

"I will kill her if she can be killed," Gray said grimly.

"You may . . ." Gideon cleared his throat. "You may hesitate when you hear what I am about to say. Or maybe you will not. I cannot say. I wrestled with my conscience if I should tell you the legacy Sabrina left me with, but I decided that it is only fair that the decision lie with you."

"What decision?" Gray did not like where this was going. Sabrina's legacy?

"Her magical hold on me was exceedingly strong. Otherwise"—Gideon glanced at the floor, and Gray was astonished and embarrassed to see his eyes were suddenly full of tears—"she never could have controlled me to the extent she did. I wished for many years I was stronger, not only because her hold over me devastated this kingdom, but because it cost me you."

"That is water under the bridge." Gray knew his tone was unrelenting, but only because if he did not stay strong, he too would break down. He'd been eleven when he had been forced to flee this place. A home and a father were supposed to be a bastion of safety and comfort, and it was a cold, hard realization when they were not.

"It is, but it is not," Gideon said regretfully. "Because when she removed herself, she let me know unequivocally that I would return to making my own decisions, but that I was also forever weakened by the void left by her power. The remnants are what keep me alive. Without the weak spark of her magic remaining inside me, I would . . ."

Gray swallowed hard. "You would die. Her death means your death."

Gideon spread his hands. In supplication? In apology? Gray was not sure, and truthfully was not sure he wanted to know. "She has known from the beginning that you could be her doom."

"And this is supposed to be a barrier forcing me to stay my hand?"

"I do not know, though I suspect yes, that is a convenient complication for her." Gideon leaned against the edge of the huge bed. "I know you are very angry with me, and you have every right to be. I simply . . . I did not want you to be ignorant of it when the moment came, even as I urge you with all haste that you must be her undoing."

The anger inside him surged dangerously. Gray's hand clenched into a tight fist. "So it is to be patricide, after all," he said bitterly.

"I do not tell you this to stay your hand against her," Gideon said. "I tell you this because if this is the last time we meet, I would like us to do so at least under honest terms."

CHAPTER FIFTEEN

IT WAS NOT VERY surprising that when he was shown to his chambers for the night, Rory felt unsettled. It had been an eventful day, and even though eventually King Gideon had technically welcomed both him and Gray, Rory knew the King's refusal to believe who Gray truly was had been upsetting for both of them.

Why had he so fiercely insisted it had to be a lie? Rory wasn't sure, but with every second of the King's rejection, his heart had broken for Gray.

Up until those fateful minutes in the throne room, Rory had believed he'd understood Gray's reluctance to return to Ardglass. But the King's reaction had been even more complicated and difficult than Rory could ever have foretold.

He walked over to the window of the tower room he'd been shown to and sighed deeply, wishing they hadn't been forced to come here. Maybe Gray would eventually have wanted to come of his own accord, to settle things with his father. But then, considering how poorly King Gideon looked, Rory thought that time was certainly not on Gray's side.

Rory, lost in his own thoughts, gave a sudden, terrified yelp as a shadowy figure emerged on the other side of the darkened window. Was it another magical creature, come to claim his soul? Rory pulled out his dagger, and though he did not know if he could defeat this monster as he had defeated Sabrina's chimera in the cave, he had to try.

But then the window swung open, and it was only Gray, dangling in front of the window, his hands and feet tangled in a thick rope.

"Gray?" Rory exclaimed. "Why are you here? And like that? Couldn't you have come in through the door?"

Gray simply shrugged, easily climbing over the stone threshold of the wall, and lightly landing on his feet. He pushed the window closed, and after he turned to look at Rory, he finally got a good look at Gray's face.

It was . . . ravaged, nearly.

Rory reached out for him before he even registered what he was doing, taking his arm and leading him to the bed, where he sat him at the edge.

"My father just came to see me," Gray said.

Rory had carefully noted all the names that Gray had used to refer to King Gideon, and most conspicuously, father had been entirely missing from the list. But now, now, he was using it, though it hardly felt like a conscious choice either. Instead it felt to Rory as if Gray had momentarily forgotten why he'd been refusing to call King Gideon his father.

If Gideon had come to see him, alone and apart from everyone else, it must have been serious, and nothing was as convincing an argument as the currently stunned look on Gray's face.

"What did he have to say?" Rory asked.

"Sabrina . . . her magic weakened him, and yet is the only thing keeping him alive." Gray looked up at Rory, who had knelt in front of his lover. "If I kill her, he will also die."

Rory did not know what to say in response to this. One of the things they agreed upon the most—and that was saying something, as they were usually in complete agreement—was that Sabrina could not be allowed to live. But now, how could Rory continue to hold to that line if doing so meant the death of Gray's father?

Pushing suddenly to his feet, Gray began to pace back and forth in the room. "Do you know," he asked, his voice surprisingly conversational, "that this used to be my room? That these are the Crown Prince's chambers?"

"I . . ." Rory was having difficulty keeping up, yet he knew he was considered one of the brightest minds of their age. "I didn't know that."

"I escaped from this room," Gray said, his voice hardening. He turned around in a circle. "The bed was there. I woke up a moment before Rhys warned me, because the noise in the castle was suddenly too loud. I knew something was wrong."

Rory walked up to him and placed a hand on his chest, right over his heart. Felt it beating true and strong. "You are the bravest man I know."

"For escaping when I was a child?" Gray laughed, the sound ringing with bitterness. "I was not brave at all. I was petrified. If not for Rhys and then Evrard, I would have died that day or someday very soon after."

"Not just for that day," Rory corrected softly. "For that day and for all the days after. For this day."

Abruptly, Gray went back to the bed. "I wish he hadn't told me," he finally said, in a devastated murmur.

Rory wished he hadn't told him either. "Was he attempting to sway your opinion?"

"No." Gray was silent for a very long time. "No, he still wants me to kill her."

Frankly, Rory could have wrung Gideon's neck himself, at this point. How dare he place that sort of responsibility on his son's shoulders? After leaving him to the wolves—or one very ruthless chimera?

"It is the right thing to do," Gray added, with grave finality. "I know it is. I know. And yet . . ."

Rory, who had never been lucky enough to know his own father, felt horribly torn. On one hand, he agreed that Gray was right—Sabrina deserved to die and should die, not only for the crimes she had committed, but also to prevent her from committing any in the future. Anyone with her magical power and particular ruthlessness could never be trusted, and prison or exile would mean they were never truly safe from her machinations. But then this was also Gray's father, who had betrayed him, yes, but there was still love between them. Without love, guilt couldn't exist, and Gideon's conscience had seemed very guilty indeed. Added to that fact was the additional wrinkle of Gray's anger—the furthest thing possible from apathy. He would not be so angry if he did not care.

"There is time to consider the choice, and to weigh our options," Rory said.

Gray stared at him starkly. "I usually find very little to argue with when it comes to your logic," he said, "but I'm afraid you are wrong this time. In fact, I believe we have very little time and very little choice."

Wrapping his arms around Gray, Rory held him tightly. He was afraid Gray was all too right.

"She's your aunt," Gray murmured roughly, and Rory squeezed his eyes shut. He had been trying, very hard in fact, not to consider Sabrina in those terms. And he realized, Gray had been doing the exact same thing with his father. Trying to separate himself, trying to pretend he wasn't the only family he had left.

"And he's your father," Rory responded softly. "We will find a way out of this, I promise. And . . ." He hesitated. "If the worst comes to pass, and we have no choice, I will stand beside you, no matter what. You'll not be alone."

The dampness on his shoulder told Rory that at last, he had said the right thing.

After a long, dreamless sleep and a subdued breakfast, Rory and Gray went to meet with Evrard in the stables.

Gideon's stewards had been at a loss as to where to house the noble unicorn, but finally, Evrard had put them out of their uncertainty. "Anywhere that is clean with good, clean hay and water will be perfectly sufficient," he'd snapped at them, annoyed at their own indecision.

"I trust you both slept well, at least better than I," Evrard said after they greeted him. "The horses in this stable are most restless."

Gray said nothing, and Rory hadn't wanted to be the one to speak of King Gideon's confession, so he'd merely nodded. "I was thinking," Evrard continued, "it might be nice to get some fresh air. A ride, perhaps?" He leaned down, nose brushing against Rory's shoulder. "Perhaps someplace with less open ears."

"I know just the place," Gray said shortly, and in no time they were both back on Evrard's back, galloping out of the keep itself to the town beyond, and then further than that.

The place Gray brought them to was awe-inducing. Rory had known the keep of Tullamore was built at the peak of a tall hill but had not realized the keep overlooked a large canyon, with a river below, and at the head of the gorge, a spectacular waterfall. Gray had navigated them around the keep, to a spot further down the canyon, and the thundering water would likely drown out their voices to anyone who had attempted to follow.

"Now," Evrard said, when they both dismounted. "Your father said the messengers would leave early this morning for the clans, to ask them to gather. Do you know if they left?"

Gray nodded. "I asked three separate stewards. They indeed rode out first thing this morning."

"Good, they will be back on the morrow," Evrard said with a satisfied nod. "Prince Emory, you will need to work on composing your plea, as none of the army of Ardglass are required by anything other than honor to come to your aid. Even Prince Graham cannot force them. They must come willingly."

"If they don't?" Rory asked, suddenly apprehensive. He was not a great orator and had never before given a speech designed to lead troops. He'd read plenty of them, but that had hardly prepared him to give one himself.

"They must," Evrard said, and the pressure settled on Rory's shoulders like a heavy cloak.

"If they don't, that is not our only problem," Gray said. Rory found himself holding his breath. Surely after Gray confessed about his conversation with his father, Evrard would come up with a creative, inventive solution. Surely, he must. Gray could not be asked to kill his own father, as he killed Rory's aunt. Every man had his limit, and Rory was terrified that asking Gray to do this would be straining his.

"You spoke to your father, then," Evrard said gravely, and Rory's heart squeezed. Did Evrard know? How had he never said? Gray should have been warned.

"You suspected then," Gray said with a heavy sigh.

"You yourself remember the conversation we had after our first fight against her," Evrard said quietly, all smugness leaking from his voice. As if he knew how hard this would be for Gray, and wished he could be spared it, but knew he couldn't. "She leaves creatures in much worse shape after she departs their forms. Most die, but your father is—was—

strong, and he resisted her for so long that a spark of his own power remained behind to keep him functioning after she left Tullamore. Unfortunately, it will not be enough to keep him alive after she dies."

"Then he was right." Gray stared at the waterfall, expressionless.

"I wish very much that he had not been, but I'm afraid his intuition is correct here."

Gray turned back to stare at Rory and Evrard, his eyes like two unbearably hot fires. "She cannot be left alive."

Evrard nodded again. "I do not believe there is a safe way to hold her that she would not eventually subvert to her own purpose. She is dangerous, but then you know that already. You've experienced it firsthand."

"There is one problem then," Gray continued, his voice relentless. "One you partially foresaw. Without my father alive, there is no ruler in Ardglass. I will have to return and take up the throne."

"Will you?" Evrard questioned softly.

Gray's eyes burned. "There is hardly any other choice. I cannot simply shirk my duties." He swallowed hard, his Adam's apple bobbing with emotion. "At least not because I wish to be somewhere else. With someone else."

That was when Rory, breathlessly, realized the inherent problem. Gray wanted to stay with him, actually wanted to accept the mantle that had been offered to him with Lion's Breath. He was saying he wished to stay with Rory and be his consort and help Rory rule Fontaine. But he could not, at least not when Ardglass was in desperate need of a ruler, and the only one who could take the throne was Gray himself.

"What if there was an alternative?" Evrard asked.

"There isn't one," Gray scoffed. "We already talked about this. The options available to us aren't good."

"What about combining the kingdoms?" Rory offered.

He didn't think it was a horrible thought; it was one he'd considered before, at least peripherally. But Gray made a face.

"I don't think it's fair to ask two kingdoms with very little in common, despite a geographical border, to merge together simply because we want to be together," Gray said. Rory frowned, because he was precisely, completely right. It wouldn't be fair. "And," Gray added, "how would we possibly convince the clans? There'd be a rebellion."

"And maybe there should be a rebellion," Evrard said with great satisfaction.

"Excuse me?" Gray said.

"Maybe there should be a rebellion. Why does Ardglass need to be ruled by a king anyhow? Ardglass began as a loose collection of clans, who fought together occasionally, and held summits once a year," Evrard pointed out. "Your father has grown weak. The clans are already ruling themselves. Let them."

"I . . ." Gray hesitated. "Would that even be a good idea?"

"Thirteen generations ago your ancestor conquered the clans and styled himself King. Back then, there were more inter-clan wars. But the acrimony has faded over time, and I no longer believe that a central figurehead is needed to mediate. Maintain your relationships with the clan chiefs and let them rule themselves."

Gray was silent for a long while, digesting Evrard's point of view.

Rory was afraid to offer his own opinion and accidentally sway the other man unfairly. But he did, desperately, want Gray with him, now and in the future. He wanted to grow old with him, to watch him bear Lion's Breath until they were as gray and withered as King Gideon.

"I suppose we could discuss this with the clan representatives after . . ." Gray hesitated. "After our victory." Because until that was achieved, there was no point in discussing this plan with anyone. Gray could die, Rory could die, they could both die and then there would be no need to change anything about the governance of Ardglass. Though if they were defeated, Rory was sure it would only be a matter of time before Sabrina overcame Ardglass' defenses and took that kingdom for her own, along with Fontaine.

Maybe, in the end, the two kingdoms would end up merging regardless of anything Gray or Rory or Evrard did.

"After the victory," Evrard agreed. "Now, about your speech, Rory."

Rory grimaced. "I suppose there is no point in arguing that a speech won't be necessary."

"It will very much be necessary." This unexpectedly came from Gray, not Evrard.

Rory's expression must have reflected surprise because Gray gave a short, humorless laugh. "I was raised to be the Crown Prince of Ardglass, and the future leader of its armies, until I was eleven years old. Rhys taught me well." Gray's voice took on an ironic tone, because essentially he was praising Evrard at that moment, and not really Rhys at all. "I know the clans. They respond to strength and honor. You may not possess much physically of the first, but you have an abundance of the second. And the throne is yours, not hers, which will sway them further."

"It will not be easy, but there are several key facts on our side that will win at least a few clans to our defense, which is all we need," Evrard added. "Still, we will hear your speech."

Rory had certainly not expected to make the speech now and was unprepared. His first version was halting, and painfully awkward.

The second was a slight improvement.

The third time he went through it, he'd grown more comfortable with the most effective phrases, and delivered it, he thought at least, with more than a little aplomb.

Evrard's and Gray's eyes met. "It will do," Gray said. "I'll stand next to him, Lion's Breath prominently displayed. They'll know what it means. Rory might not have the physical strength, but I can project it for both of us."

"It will have to do," Evrard said. "For we have no other choice."

The sun was high in the sky over Tullamore as representatives of the thirteen clans gathered in the main courtyard. Gray and the stewards had overseen the quick erection of a wooden platform, since Rory was on the shorter side. "And," Gray had added, wiping the sweat from his brow as he'd pounded in nails with the rest of the workers, "it has an added bonus of giving you a slightly more physically imposing appearance, since you'll be up higher."

Rory had glanced at him questioningly. "I'm not sure there's much that can truly improve that," he'd admitted.

"Just trust me," Gray had responded. "I can make this work. All you have to do is give the best speech, the most persuasive, speech you're capable of."

Rory had practiced for several more hours with Evrard the evening before and the morning of, as clan members started to pour through the main gate. The only advantage of practicing with Evrard was he refused to lie and claim Rory was doing better than he truly was. The opposite was true actually. Even when Rory felt like he was improving, his dictation and the soaring rise of his voice capturing all the fervor and excitement of helping him reclaim his throne, Evrard would gaze at him with a bored expression and ask, "But are you really trying, Your Highness?"

He was trying, very hard in fact, and so Evrard's words were galling. But they also helped to push Rory to improve much quicker than he would have otherwise.

"Again," Evrard said, and then, "again."

Finally, just when Rory was about to reach over and see if a unicorn could be strangled, Evrard gave him a thoughtful —and extremely rewarding—nod of approval. "You are not as hopeless as I thought you might be," he said.

Not entirely a compliment, but then Evrard was hardly the complimenting type.

As Rory climbed the platform, Gray behind him, sweat dotted his forehead. Nerves, or the heat of the day, Rory wasn't quite sure. But something he did know was that he'd never felt so determined in his life. Not even when they'd left Beaulieu an age ago, or when he'd escaped from the mercenaries come to kill him in Gray's valley, or when he'd faced down the chimera in the cave behind the Veil. It felt as if all those moments were building to this last, great one. He was going to give his speech, and the clans of Ardglass would listen.

He situated himself on the platform, and felt Gray stop next to him, and out of the corner of his eye, watched as he pushed his cloak back, revealing the distinctive pommel of Lion's Breath. A murmur went through the assembled men, as they recognized the sword.

"Clans of Ardglass," Rory exclaimed after a long, drawn-out moment of silent anticipation, "you have been called here today by your king, because your assistance is needed to right a wrong."

Initially Rory had been determined to lead with the fact that their prince had returned to Tullamore, but both Gray and Evrard had immediately dismissed that idea. "This is about you, not Gray," Evrard had cautioned.

"It's a little about Gray," Rory had argued, fiercely. And had then lost, because Gray had spoken up and refused to be mentioned in the speech. From the glint in his eye, Rory knew he wouldn't be easily forgiven if he broke his promise not to do so.

"You know the woman who has taken my throne in Fontaine," Rory continued, voice growing in strength. He tossed his cloak behind him, the bright blue reflected in the sky high above, and strode confidently over the floor of the platform, even though it squeaked and groaned dubiously. Would it stay intact for long enough for Rory to finish his speech? Rory really wasn't certain, but he couldn't let the doubt show either on his face or in his voice. He needed to look the part, like a true leader, and he couldn't do that while worrying the entire structure would collapse under his weight.

"She is dangerous and conniving. In fact, she manipulated and seduced your own king with foul, dark magic. Without her spells, King Gideon would be healthy and strong and your kingdom would mirror his own well-being. Instead, your kingdom is growing weaker, and is prey to others, including a Fontaine led by my aunt. If we do not defeat her now, the chances of doing so later are slim."

Rumblings grew in the crowd. Rory took that as an encouraging sign and continued speaking, his tone growing increasingly impassioned. "That is why you have been called here today. There is an evil lurking in our lands, and it is our responsibility to root it out, destroy it and salt the earth underneath it so no more can ever grow here again. Tomorrow I march on Beaulieu, with my guard and my sworn shield beside me, determined that she will no longer control us with her malevolence. Who is with me?"

His voice died slowly across the echoing courtyard, and he panted a little. Giving speeches was far more difficult and far more exhausting than he'd ever imagined, but he'd done it, at least as well as he ever had, the moment grabbing him and propelling him along.

The only problem was that dead silence had met his fervent plea for assistance.

Not exactly the conclusion he or Evrard had had in mind.

Rory met the stubborn gazes of the clan representatives and quailed. They did not seem at all interested in participating in a war over the throne of Fontaine. Their clans were weakened by what Sabrina had wrought in Ardglass, and in their own king, and that was obviously less pressing than Rory's immediate problem. And that, as Evrard had worried, was exactly the problem with trying to rally soldiers of another country. They were always more interested in fixing their own problems, than meddling in anybody else's problems.

He knew he needed to do something, but what he knew he needed to do was dangerous—as in Gray might not ever forgive him for it. But without saying it, Rory did not know if they would have any men to march with them to Beaulieu. Without an army, they would have no chance of making it anywhere near Sabrina. Definitely not close enough to kill her.

In the end, Rory's decision was surprisingly easy. He was stuck between one stubborn near-consort, and the rest of the even more stubborn men of Ardglass.

I'm so sorry, he thought fervently in Gray's direction. *I know this is not how you wanted to do it, and I did not want it this way either.*

"I stand here today, not only as a prince of Fontaine, a neighboring country to your own, but also as a man who has found what has been missing from Ardglass for all these many years." Rory heard Gray's intake of breath behind him, sharp and tight, and Rory figured that since he didn't grab him or physically stop his mouth, then that was as good of permission as he was ever going to get. "I present to you," he continued, "the lost prince returned, Prince Graham of Ardglass, here bearing my sword, the Lion's Breath, and sworn to protect me til death."

That got their attention immediately. Murmurs swelled in the audience to shocked gasps and confused exchanges among the different clans.

One of the clansmen stood. "How can we be sure?" he demanded. "Aye, he looks much like Graham did, but His Highness was small when he was killed."

Come help me answer these men, Rory thought, glancing backwards, where Gray was staring at him with a mixture of anger and resignation. *Nobody else is going to convince them who you are except for you.*

Rory held out his hand and urged him with his eyes. *Come, please.* And finally, he did, albeit very reluctantly. Gray stepped forward, and even though he'd clearly accepted the position that Rory had placed him in, he did not look thrilled about it.

"I am indeed Prince Graham, and yes, I was quite small when I was lost. Because that is what I was. Lost, not dead."

A louder rumble echoed through the gathered crowd.

"Prince Emory found me and restored me to you," Gray said, his voice rising perfectly with the rising excitement of the crowd. He didn't even practice, Rory thought glumly. "And with me at your side, it is our duty, our responsibility, to make sure that the woman who forced me to abandon my home does no other harm. To Prince Emory or to any of the clans of Ardglass."

A great yell reverberated through the men—first one and then another and then a hundred resounding confirmations, followed by foot stamps and clapping.

He had won them over when Rory had failed. At least they had been successful, Rory thought, because if this gamble had failed and he'd been left with no army and no Gray, he'd have had no chance of ever retaking his kingdom. He'd probably, Rory contemplated moodily, have died unhappy and alone, with Sabrina's unearthly eyes the last thing he saw. It was not a pleasant vision.

The exclamations coming from the crowd were excessive enough, but then one by one, the men fell to one knee, arms crossed over their breasts, to honor the man who stood on the dais. Not Rory, but Gray.

Rory could see he wasn't outwardly frowning, but the edges of his lips had drawn together so tightly they'd turned white. Gray was clearly displeased, and it was not a stretch to believe that it was Rory he was the most displeased with.

Finally, the painful exercise ended, but the moment he and Gray descended from the platform, they were overtaken by maniacally happy, rejoicing soldiers, who believed that their savior had finally come, all in the guise of a lost prince returned to them. Rory, watching Gray borne away on a tide of goodwill, eventually turned away from the crowd in the courtyard and made his way back into the keep, listlessly meandering through the hallways. He hadn't seen where Evrard had gone to, because he'd tucked himself away, not wanting to overwhelm and distract the clans with his magnificence.

That, Rory thought despondently, was a real irony. Because in the end, all he'd done was to overwhelm and distract with his reveal of Gray's true self.

After a few minutes, he found himself at the huge carved double doors leading to the throne room. He'd overheard one of the stewards mention the King rarely used it, and since all the guests were outside, falling to their knees in front of Gray, surely it would be empty now. At least, this would be a great place for Rory to hide, since he wasn't quite mentally ready to come face to face with Gray just yet.

He pulled open one of the doors and slipped inside.

The candles were not lit, but the skylights still brought impressive light to the enormous space. The throne on the dais was empty, and Rory skirted it, instead choosing to walk near the silk banners lining each side of the hall. Heavily embroidered with gold thread, the overall number must mean they depicted the sigils of each of the Ardglassian clans.

"Hiding? How unprincely of you."

A voice started Rory and he turned to see the King lurking in one of the shadowed alcoves between two of the fluttering emerald green banners. He stepped out, and slowly hobbled over to where Rory stood.

"I'm sorry," Rory stammered, slightly ashamed at being caught in another country's throne room, clearly hiding from the chaos he'd just created outside. Then he realized that the King had been in here too, by himself. Hiding as well? Rory wondered.

"How unkingly of you," Rory added, giving him a sheepish smile. "But it's alright. I won't tell anyone."

"Even my son?" Gideon asked with a heavy sigh.

Rory thought this over for a moment. "I'm not sure he's truly interested in anything I have to say, now," Rory said slowly.

"He is very proud," Gideon pointed out. "But then it's likely you already knew that."

Rory nodded.

"He must have been very surprised that you chose that moment to reveal who he was," Gideon said.

Surprised? Rory wasn't sure that was exactly the right term. He couldn't have been all that surprised. Perhaps disappointed, instead. "He asked me not to and I did it anyway," Rory confessed. "I suppose I'm not a very convincing orator." Of all the shame he felt, this was the strongest. If he'd given a better speech, perhaps it never would have come to revealing Gray.

A glimmer of a smile emerged on King Gideon's face. "You're not as bad as you think. The Ardglassians are bitter, indignant, and excessively stubborn. Graham knows that, even if he's tried to forget it. He'll forgive you."

Rory was not quite so sure. After all, Gray had explicitly asked him not to, he'd agreed, and then he'd done it despite his promise.

"I do know," Gideon continued, "how much my son cares about you, because I do not think he ever would have returned here otherwise." It was impossible to guess how difficult an admission that was for both a king and a father, and the pain in Gideon's voice echoed that fact. "He'll come around."

"Perhaps," Rory said, not feeling particularly optimistic despite the King's words.

That was when Gideon's prediction was put to the test, as that was the moment the doors swung open, and then Gray came stalking through them, a dark glower on his handsome face.

"There you are," he said, only to Rory, ignoring his father completely. "I've been looking for you everywhere. You're missing the summit to plan our attack on Beaulieu."

"I didn't know we were having one," Rory said hesitantly.

Gray frowned. "Of course we are. And you have important information we need." He turned to go, assuming, Rory supposed, that he would simply follow when summoned. For someone who didn't think he was a born leader, he certainly seemed to take naturally to it. Behind Gray's back, Rory glanced over at the King, who was staring sadly at the floor. Rory gave him a shrug and went to follow Gray's long strides out of the throne room.

CHAPTER SIXTEEN

THOUGH HE'D HOPED TO feel differently, Gray wasn't any less furious at Rory the next day. His anger had been building from the moment on the platform when Rory had glanced back at him, shot him an apologetic look, and had proceeded to blow his life apart.

He'd hoped after a few pints of ale with the clansmen and a dreamless night of sleep, he might feel differently about Rory's betrayal, but the self-recriminating look on his face had haunted Gray and he'd not slept a single wink. Rory had known how much revealing Gray's parentage, as publicly as possible, in order to convince the clansmen, would hurt him. And yet, he'd done it anyway.

Gray wasn't stupid; he'd known that enough of Tullamore knew the truth, including the stewards—the biggest gossips in the whole keep—so it would be impossible to hide it forever. But Gray had been counting on being able to slowly reveal who he was. Certainly not blurt it out without any finesse and without any preparation, and all because Rory wanted men to march with them to Beaulieu?

He knew just how much Rory wanted his throne back, because at one point, he'd felt the exact same way. There hadn't only been seeds of uncertainty and doubt that anyone else could do as credible a job as himself but going from prince to farmhand had been a blow to his pride. For the first eleven years of his life, he'd been raised to be one thing. Being the Crown Prince had defined who Gray was. That was no longer true, but he still felt the painful echo of loss. Strangely, he'd felt it less since returning to Tullamore. Seeing his father, incalculably diminished, and the clans hampered rather than helped by his rule over them, had sweetened much of his bitterness. He'd listened to Evrard's suggestion, and then spent the last few days considering the possibilities. If they survived—a very big if—then Gray knew he would do his part to help untangle the monarchy of Ardglass, suggesting to the thirteen clans that they might rule themselves.

Gray also wanted Sabrina dead just as much as Rory. Perhaps more, if he was willing to sacrifice his already-failing father over it, but the point remained. Rory had taken precipitous action yesterday, and he hadn't apologized for it, which Gray could only assume meant he wasn't actually sorry.

Considering how many men were saddling in the courtyard, fires extinguished in the early morning dew, smoke rising from their ashes, Gray thought maybe it might have been worth it. But surely, surely there had been another way.

Evrard trotted over to him, ignoring all the awed expressions in his wake. Gray knew a little how he felt now. Everywhere he went, Gray was treated like a savior, the man who could rescue all of them from ruin.

I rescued myself, Gray thought as Evrard stopped in front of him. You should do the same.

"You aren't riding with Prince Emory," Evrard said, his tone chastising. "You cannot be angry with him for doing what needed to be done."

Evrard had yet to discover that telling Gray he could not do something ever actually prevented him from doing it.

"I can and I am," Gray retorted, swinging his leg over his saddle and placing a calming hand on the twitchy neck of his horse. Like Gray, he was used to solitude, and there were so many people in this courtyard. All willing, Gray thought, to help them kill Sabrina. It was a heady thought, and for a second, he hesitated. Rory's words had given them this chance.

Gray's eyes snapped to Evrard. "Get out of my head," he insisted coldly. "You are not welcome there, and certainly not to change my mind about Rory."

Evrard did not look the slightest bit apologetic. "I hardly had to insert any thoughts at all. There's a part of you that doesn't just want to forgive him, it needs to forgive him." He shook his mane out, his voice growing just as strident at Gray's. "You should think on that during the journey to Beaulieu."

Gray did not think Evrard had much power over his mind. Not enough power anyway to force him to do anything he did not want to do, and certainly not enough power to force him to think on something he did not wish to think on. Yet, for the whole morning of the first day of their journey, it was difficult to think of anything else. It was true, he wanted to forgive Rory, but as Evrard had said it was definitely more than that.

Was this the power of fate driving him towards Rory? Or was it his own feelings? It was so difficult to separate one from the other anymore, and though Gray believed his feelings were true, he couldn't help but wonder if they'd been impacted by his and Rory's intertwined destiny.

Ten of the clans had sent troops, and Gray thought their number was at least five hundred. Easily enough to march upon Beaulieu, especially if they were not expecting an invading force. Beaulieu did not hold a particularly large garrison, Marthe had explained, there were only a few dozen guards stationed there at any given time.

This would hopefully be an easy march, followed by a quick defeat.

Gray tightened his fingers on the reins and refused to let himself contemplate the terrible possibility that he would not be staying on at Beaulieu at all, but that he would end up returning, alone, to the valley.

Only a month ago that was all he'd wanted out of this quest, but now, coming to the end of it, it was impossible to deny how much more he wanted.

A life. A future. Companionship. Love.

Gray shook his head, wishing the physical motion could dislodge the frustrating thoughts from his uncooperative mind, but as they continued to ride down the road, they stuck persistently. And this time, he couldn't even blame Evrard.

When the sun was high in the sky, Marthe, whom he had elected to lead this combined company because of her experience and her knowledge of the Fontaine fortifications and armies, held up a hand to signal they were to stop in this clearing for a midday break.

Supplies of dried meat and bread and cheese were distributed, along with flasks of cooled, refreshing water fetched from a nearby stream.

Gray must have had a thundercloud on his face, because to his surprise, he was left alone, an empty circle around where he sat under a shady evergreen tree.

The abrupt delineation between him and the rest of the soldiers made it very obvious when Rory finally approached him.

Who are you kidding? Gray sneered at himself. You would have spotted him in a crowd of a thousand men. And not just because of that ridiculously bright blue cloak.

He refused to let himself touch the pommel of Lion's Breath as Rory approached, contrite expression on his face. His fingers had wanted to stray to it so many times during the morning, and he'd forced them to remain at his side. He did not need to touch a sword to remind himself of his obligations or his feelings.

"Gray," Rory said, the single word punctuated with a heavy sigh.

It was difficult, but Gray did not look up. Instead, he fixed his eyes on a small pile of evergreen needles to the right of

Rory's boot.

"Gray," he sighed again. "At least look at me."

Rory clearly did not understand that avoiding his gaze was the only thing keeping Gray from immediately getting to his feet and wrapping his arms around him. It was self-preservation, only.

"I understand how upset you are with me," Rory continued, as Gray's fingers dug into his thigh. "I really am very sorry that I said what I did, but you have to understand how little choice I felt like I had in the matter. Something needed to be done. Evrard made it very clear that it was my responsibility to convince the clans, but truthfully, they didn't care about me. What they care about is you."

Worst of all, Rory's apology made plain and indisputable sense. Of course the clans of Ardglass wouldn't care about Rory's plight. They were struggling, after the departure of Sabrina had made Gideon so weak, and it was all they could do to keep their own borders and lands intact. Marching out to defeat an enemy currently entirely occupied with another country? It didn't make sense and it provided them with no tactical advantage whatsoever.

But bringing the lost Crown Prince of Ardglass into the situation? Using him to convince the clans that fighting was necessary? Logic was no longer a part of the discussion; they had volunteered based on emotion alone. He was their savior and even if he was marching them off to free another land, he would return and free their own.

In a manner of speaking, anyway.

Rory had known this, maybe not before his speech began, because he'd wanted to believe he could deliver a rousing enough argument that would convince them anyway. But Evrard? He surely had known Rory's oratorical skills wouldn't be enough.

"That meddling unicorn," Gray spat out under his breath. "Someday . . ."

Rory looked at him in confusion. "What does this have to do with Evrard?"

"Everything has to do with Evrard," Gray said, rolling his eyes. "I'm sure you've realized that by now. You're a very smart man, Rory."

Slowly, Rory nodded. "I do see that . . . but . . . how does Evrard have anything to do with this?"

Gray sighed.

"He wanted to show me that we were much stronger together than we are apart. I knew it already, but . . . I let my bitterness overwhelm me. I'd believed it was fading, over time, that I didn't care anymore, but I guess I do."

Rory, encouraged by this confession, sat down next to Gray, unceremoniously plopping himself on the ground, regardless of his buff-colored breeches. He put a hand on Gray's shoulder, an earnest expression on his face. "Honestly, Gray, how can I blame you for being bitter? We are stronger together than we are apart, though I don't find I understand how Evrard telling me explicitly not to mention your lineage and then me being forced to do so is supposed to convince us of anything." Rory stopped, a suddenly blinding, lopsided smile freezing Gray's heart. He could sit here and watch Rory smile forever. "Unless he was trying to convince us he's a meddling, foolish creature. Because that I understand completely."

"It's a common military technique," Gray said slowly. "Pretend battle. A minor skirmish to prepare your troops for the larger, much more real fight. He wanted us to understand our strengths now, before we approach Beaulieu, where Sabrina will do everything she can to sow doubt between us."

Rory was quiet for a long moment. "I still should have asked you first," he said quietly.

But Gray knew he'd been wrong. Evrard hadn't come out and said it. Rory hadn't even done so, though he'd obliquely referred to it in his apology. But the truth of it was currently blinding him. He reached out and clasped Rory's hands in his own. "You see these men around us? Five hundred of the clans of Ardglass marching with us to a battle that isn't even theirs. We wouldn't have them if you hadn't announced to them who I was. This army wouldn't even exist, and without it, our future wouldn't exist."

Rory's eyes warmed, amber turning to gold. "You truly mean that," he whispered.

"After this is over, and we survive, and you have taken your proper place on the throne of Fontaine," Gray said, more certain of this than anything he'd ever been in his whole life, "I will take my place, which will always be by your side."

After lunch, Gray retook that place, by Rory's side, as they rode towards Beaulieu.

Rowen had shot him an amused glance. "I see that you have returned to us," she said.

"Like he could possibly hope to keep away," Anya said with an affectionate smile for Gray.

"If you're theorizing that I'm irresistible, I won't object," Rory had inserted, with a delighted laugh.

They rode in loose formation for the rest of the day, Gray refusing to leave Rory's side. He wore Lion's Breath proudly, never keeping his fingers from touching the hilt if they wanted to. He might have been born in Ardglass, and raised to be the Crown Prince of that country, but the years in the valley had changed him and now he no longer felt taking over the throne from his father was the right path for either him or for his country. He was meant to protect Rory, to shield him from harm, and help him become the fairest, kindest ruler that Fontaine had ever known. The sword, which wasn't supposed to be his ancestral bequest, had begun to feel like it anyway. As for Ardglass, Evrard's words kept echoing in his head: it had originally been thirteen clans.

Two days passed, much the same, and then on the last night, Marthe announced over the fires that on the morrow, they would be in Beaulieu. The reckoning had arrived.

Rory's tent was bright blue with dangling golden ribbons. Gray glanced at it, fondness in his gaze, and even though he'd set up his own, much plainer tent, he had no intention of letting Rory sleep alone tonight.

He'd kept to his own tent the previous two nights, because Marthe's pace, directed by Evrard, had been intense and exhausting. They needed to reach Beaulieu before Sabrina managed to call up any additional armies to her cause and before she spread any more poisonous lies about Rory's preparedness for the throne. They'd been worn out each night, but tonight, they'd stopped early in preparation for the battle tomorrow. Marthe, who many of the clansmen had initially muttered about following under their breath, had proven to be an adept leader of their forces and Gray felt justified in her appointment with every thoughtful, wise choice she made.

But tonight, he'd not keep to his own tent. Gray could not imagine spending possibly his last night on earth with anyone other than Rory.

Acadia had cornered him before the evening meal was served, and offered the tidbit of information, under her breath, that she had deliberately pitched the guards' tents further away tonight. "Privacy is important," she'd told him quietly. "We understand that."

Gray joined Rory's fire as he had the other nights, the rest of the guard sitting around it, except for Marthe, who was very busy with preparations for tomorrow's final march.

"Are you ready for tomorrow?" Diana asked Rory softly. "You may have to do things you would not normally choose to do. Battle is like that."

It was clear from the shadows in Rory's eyes that he had considered this possibility already, and had come to terms with it, even if he did not necessarily like it. Gray himself had been forced to do so, with his own father's confession. He did not know if his father would die the moment Sabrina perished, but he did not expect to ever see him again.

Their goodbye, brief but fraught, had been additionally on his mind the last few days.

"May your sword swing true," his father had said, offering him a handclasp. Gray had hesitated for a long moment but had finally taken it.

"May my shield guard you," Gray finished, the words an ancient Ardglassian adage for those headed to war.

And that was all they had said to one another. Somehow, it was going to have to be enough, Gray thought as he stared at Rory.

It would have to be, because Gray had no intention of returning to Ardglass without Sabrina's blood on his hands.

"We may all have to do things we would not normally choose," Rory said carefully, and he glanced over at Gray.

"Some things are bigger than us," Anya offered. "I would give my life to ensure the safety of both your kingdoms. And I do not offer it lightly, because in all honesty it's a good one and I wish to keep it, but this quest is more important than a single life."

Gray could not help but think of his father, sitting in Tullamore and waiting to die. Wanting to die, if it meant the woman who had destroyed him preceded him.

"Tomorrow will bring many changes," Rowen said, and her quiet, decisive words left a thoughtful silence.

She did not need to say that some of the people sitting around the fire in a loose semicircle might not be there the next evening.

"Enough," Rory said suddenly, and stood. His eyes glowed in the firelight, intent and purposeful, his gaze settling directly onto Gray. "Yes, we might all die tomorrow. Yes, we might all do terrible things so we can survive, but tonight we're alive still and I'm not going to waste this moment by worrying about what the morning might bring." He held out a hand to Gray.

Gray stared at him, surprised and more than a little aroused. If Rory wanted to spend this night—the last night they might possibly have—proving he was alive with Gray, he certainly was not going to turn him down. Reaching out, he took Rory's hand and rose to his feet.

"Goodnight," he said, and it was hard, following Rory, who was very clearly leading him to his tent, not to flush. There was something about Rory being so overt about his intentions that unmanned Gray. Rory never flaunted his affections, but there was a bluntness to his behavior tonight that Gray discovered he really enjoyed. Everyone who was watching—which was basically everyone in the whole camp, since Gray was their long-lost prince, and Rory was the famous Autumn Prince—knew exactly how it was between them.

The tent was much smaller inside than Gray had anticipated, even though his own was barely any bigger. He tried stooping, but the height of the bright blue fabric eventually defeated him and he sank to his knees, gazing over at Rory, who'd sat down at the edge of the low-slung cot.

"I see you're properly kitted out," Gray teased him. "I don't think I even got one of those."

Rory smiled. "If they'd tried to give you one, you'd have given it back."

That was definitely true, and it made Gray's hands feel warm and clammy to hear Rory knew that about him. Knew it and not only didn't mind but enjoyed it enough to bring that amused little half smile to his beautiful face.

"I won't deny," Gray said, rising up to move over to the cot where he gently sat down next to Rory, "that I'm pleased we won't have to make love on the ground tonight." He picked up one of Rory's hands. They were still smooth-ish, but Gray could feel the beginnings of callouses from the reins, from sword practice, and from the much harder living he'd been doing. He raised it to his mouth and dropped kisses on the tips of each of his fingers.

"Is that what it would be?" Rory asked quietly. "Making love?" His eyes met Gray's, questioning. Unsure, still, which was something Gray couldn't abide any longer.

"I'm ready to dedicate my life to your service. Not only as your guard or your sworn shield, but as the man who stands by your side every single day, through the good and the bad and the worst you can imagine and loves you through all of it." Gray had imagined it would be harder to say those words, since he'd always longed to say them, but had never actually imagined he would meet someone he'd feel comfortable saying them to. But to say them to Rory felt natural, like breathing. Like he was confessing something he'd known was true for a very long time, and his brain was only just now catching up to his heart and soul.

"You truly mean that," Rory exhaled slowly. "You love me."

Gray grinned, and maybe he should've been more nervous that Rory wouldn't return his feelings, but he knew Rory as well as Rory knew him, and it was indisputable, like the sun rising in the east, that Rory loved him too.

"I do. I do love you." He hesitated. "I know you want to celebrate being alive tonight, but I couldn't let you go into Beaulieu tomorrow without you knowing. It would be the biggest regret of my life."

Rory's eyes were luminous as they locked onto his. "Do you have any right now? Regrets?"

"Only that I'm not kissing you right now," Gray said, and Rory laughed.

"I do think I will like having you by my side," Rory said, laugh lines still creasing his face. "I would be honored if you would be with me."

"The honor would be all mine," Gray said, and leaning down, covered his mouth with his own. They kissed and kissed, Gray drawing the kisses out forever. Soft and slow and gentle giving rise to fast and hot and damp, his mouth slanting over Rory's as he memorized every single part of what it meant and what it felt to kiss him this deeply.

He couldn't think that this could be the last time, but the words lay between them anyway, unspoken but very much present in the air.

Gray undressed him slowly, carefully, dotting kisses over every bit of pale skin he exposed, until he finally sank down, bending over Rory's boots to unlace them.

Glowing, Rory reached for him once the rest of his clothes had been disposed of. "I do love you too," he said, the tender look in his eyes something that Gray knew he would take to the grave. Whether that was tomorrow, or in fifty years.

"Lie back, my darling," Gray murmured, and Rory, who usually tried to push or argue in bed, went quietly, like he understood how important this was for Gray to do this.

As he slicked his tongue up Rory's hard length, he remembered the first moment he'd ever seen this prince. He'd been dressed like a peacock, all shining satin and gold thread, and his very presence had been a confusing revelation to Gray—a bright intrusion of a world that he'd long since come to terms with losing. But it had hurt that day, not just because he'd been jealous of Rory's peaceful childhood or his title, but because he'd believed then that there would be no chance to get to know the beautiful boy with the auburn curls any better. They were meant for two different worlds, and Gray knew he shouldn't even bother hoping for better.

But now he had better, he had the very best, and he'd earned it, not because he was Prince Graham, but because he was Gray. He knew it wouldn't have mattered to Rory if he'd claimed his lineage or not. Or if he'd never had any lineage to begin with. Rory bucked and groaned, Gray's tongue wrapping around the head of his cock. It was easy because what lay between transcended the right and wrong of the world.

Fated, Evrard liked to say, and Gray, who'd never particularly believed in fate one way or another, believed in it now.

"Gray," Rory gasped, reaching down to tangle his fingers into Gray's hair as he rolled his hips, searching for the bright hot heat of Gray's mouth. He knew Rory was growing closer, the tension tightening between them, and he slipped a spit-slick finger down between Rory's thighs, teasing his entrance, circling it. That, and a single fierce suck, was all it took for Rory to give a fierce shout, his orgasm pumping into Gray's mouth as he swallowed.

"You are perfect," Rory said drowsily as he recovered, eyes golden and languorous, the most beautiful thing Gray had ever seen. "Let me," he added as Gray loosened his own breeches.

How could Rory say he was perfect, when Rory's small delicate hand moving over his own rampant erection felt like the most spectacular thing in the world? He'd never understood before why men and women killed and died for this fleeting physical pleasure, but when it was with someone you adored, who adored you back, the truth of it undeniable and undiminished? It was only enough to feel that pressure and feel the love spreading through him, and Gray was groaning too, exploding all over that small, surprisingly adept hand.

Rory dug for a handkerchief and wiped Gray's come off his hand. He was unhinged enough, the magic of this night wrapping around them so tightly Gray wasn't sure it would ever let go, that he was almost sad to see it disappear.

"Come," Rory said, and held out his hand again. He'd reclined in the cot, pulling the blankets back to make a spot for Gray. He didn't need any further encouragement, he quickly unlaced his boots and shed the rest of his clothes, lying down next to Rory.

Placing a hand over his heart, Rory cuddled close. "Tomorrow," he said softly, "I'm afraid everything will be different."

It would be. Tomorrow, if they were both very skillful and very lucky, Sabrina would be dead. "This won't be different," Gray promised. "That will have to be enough."

And it was.

CHAPTER SEVENTEEN

VERY EARLY THE NEXT morning, they marched for Beaulieu. Rory hadn't felt much like eating—anxiety and nerves coalesced in a tight, unpleasant ball at the base of his stomach—and even Gray hadn't pushed him.

They'd camped half a day from the tower gates of the castle, and by the time they'd been on the road for a few hours, the advance scouts Marthe had bidden to ride ahead were already beginning to return.

After the third had arrived in a cloud of dust and echoing hoof beats, Marthe ordered a halt.

Gray, Rory, and Evrard rode up to where she stood, with the rest of Rory's guard and several of the clansmen. She glanced up as they approached, a frown on her face. "Somehow, I believe Sabrina has been alerted to our presence," she said. "I suppose it cannot be too surprising. We are a company of nearly five hundred men. She could have had spies alongside the road from Tullamore." They had taken a lesser-known route, trying to avoid any of Sabrina's informants, but clearly she was better prepared than they'd anticipated.

"I would have," Gray volunteered. "And she is far more conniving than I am." Evrard nodded, his own face grim.

"Regardless, she has managed to put a force together, and they are currently encamped in front of the first gate." She shot Rory an apologetic look. "I'm afraid, Your Highness, that our original plan of using the men as an arrow to drive you into the castle proper is not going to work."

"How many men?" Gray asked. It occurred to Rory, after hearing Gray's question, that he had been raised much differently for those first eleven years. He'd truly been educated and trained to be a king, as well as a leader of the Ardglassian armies. And while they might not have been the reasons Rory loved him and wanted him by his side, those were skills that were undeniably helpful now and would continue to be in the years to come.

"Approximately as many as we have mustered, Your Highness," one of the advance scouts said, pushing his hair back, as he addressed this answer to Gray, not to Rory. Who definitely did not feel a tiny twinge of guilt, despite Gray's forgiveness. He'd done this—revealed Gray's lineage to the clans and brought this force together. It was entirely his fault that Gray made a face at the way the soldier addressed him. Maybe it had been a necessary evil, but Rory couldn't pretend he wasn't responsible for it.

"Theoretically, then," Marthe said, "we could engage this force, and perhaps be a distraction to help a much smaller force sneak into the castle proper, in order to confront the Regent Queen. Her men will not continue to fight for her if she is dead. Rory is the heir. Once she is gone, then their loyalty should be easily won."

Rory did not particularly like the idea of anyone fighting and potentially dying for him, but since he'd called this army for exactly that purpose, he could hardly express this thought.

"This plan is . . . risky," Evrard offered. Nothing else. In Rory's experience, Evrard had an opinion about everything. Right now might be the first time Rory had ever heard him demure. But then it occurred to Rory why he was doing it; he was letting Gray, who had been born to be a leader, lead.

"Sabrina is dangerous, but I agree it's best to engage her with a very small force. The distraction will help." Gray shifted in his saddle. "I will take Rory and a handful of his guards. Rory—do you know a different way into the castle?"

"I do," Rory said slowly. "Through the sewer would probably be the best for what you have in mind."

"An excellent choice of route," Anya added. "I will come with you."

"As will I," Diana said.

"I would also be honored to accompany you and Prince Emory," said the scout who had given them the earlier information.

"Thank you . . ." Gray said.

"Kristian," the man said, bowing his head.

"Thank you, Kristian," Gray repeated, with a smile. "Then we are decided. Marthe and the main force will distract and delay with their attack on the army at the gate, while we go through the sewers to reach Sabrina."

Marthe nodded. "Do you have a plan on how to kill her?" she asked.

Gray had a troubled but unsurprisingly resolute look in his eyes. "I intend to kill the bitch any way she can be killed," he said.

The rest of the force's progress crawled nearly to a halt as they crept closer to the army waiting for them at the gate of Beaulieu.

Before separating, Gray and Rory consulted with Evrard, who, to Rory's astonishment, demurred from participating in their small group. "I will stay with the army," Evrard said. "They are vulnerable. You are strong. I must continue with whoever needs my help the most."

If Gray was surprised at Evrard's identification of their five-person group as "strong," and the five hundred soldier force as "vulnerable," he did not look it. Instead, he asked Rory where the best place was to enter the sewers.

"Not at the front of the castle, by the gate," Rory said. "Instead, we should go around the side, where an extension of the drainage system runs down to a creek that's a few thousand feet away from the castle. That's the best place to go in." Admittedly, Rory had never actually seen this part of the sewer system, but he knew it existed because he could picture very clearly in his mind the layout of the castle and the detailed drawing of the sewer system laid over it.

"Then we will head toward this stream. It's also advantageous as Marthe's force will move slower, forestalling a confrontation as long as possible, whereas we will need to move quickly and urgently. It also takes us away from the main force in case there's a trap that Sabrina's laid for them."

"If she's breathing, there will be a trap of some kind," Evrard warned.

And that fact, Rory assumed, was why the main force was so vulnerable. He prayed that Evrard was able to identify the trap and unravel it before it caused any terrible damage.

"If you're right and there is a trap," Gray said grimly as they tightened their saddles, disposed of any superfluous baggage, and armed themselves for the skirmish to come, "we will be their only remaining hope."

Five of them, Rory included, did not feel like a particularly hopeful number, but Gray sounded grimly determined that this plan would work.

It had to work, Rory reminded himself. If they were defeated today, then it would give Sabrina more time to muster additional soldiers, and their own small force could not possibly hope to overcome those odds. They might not be catching her entirely unawares, but they would have to find and kill her nonetheless. Rory gripped the hilt of the bronze dagger he'd hung at his belt, remembering their confrontation in the cave behind the Veil. He'd injured her then, but none of the blows had been mortal. Despite Gray's grim confidence, they did not really know how to kill her.

"Evrard," Rory hissed as Gray gave directions to the rest of their group, "Evrard," he repeated again, when Evrard seemed disinclined to answer him right away. "How can we possibly kill her? Do you know any weaknesses that she might possess?"

The unicorn swung his great head towards Rory. "Between you and Gray, you are capable," Evrard said. "Did he not tell you he asked me?"

Rory frowned. "No, he did not."

"I told him the identical thing. What I know is you are capable of it, but that is all I can share."

That was all Evrard, being exceptionally helpful to the end. But Rory also couldn't be angry with him, not when he was staying behind, and attempting to protect the five hundred men Rory himself had convinced to come on this quest.

"Good luck," Rory said, heart suddenly in his throat. He realized that if anything went wrong, this might be the last time he ever saw Evrard. Impulsively, he dismounted and reached out for the unicorn, wrapping him in a quick, tight hug. "Thank you for saving my life, and for bringing Gray into it."

"I did very little," Evrard insisted, but Rory didn't think he'd imagined the pleased note in his voice.

"Farewell," Rory said, remounting his horse, and turning to join Gray and the rest of the group.

As Gray had planned, they rode hard towards the creek. Rory, who was not used to riding at the point position, was directed there by Gray because he was the only one who knew the way.

Even though he was terrified down to the marrow of his bones at what the rest of the afternoon would bring, Rory discovered that it was easier to be expending energy on a solid plan, working towards a concrete goal. As they continued to ride, Rory discovered that both his hands and his confidence felt steadier.

He did not know how Gray had felt, seeing the spires of Tullamore for the first time in fifteen years, but when the generously round towers of Beaulieu appeared for the first time, Rory abruptly drew up on his reins, slowing his horse, and as a result, the rest of their group.

"What is it?" Gray asked, concern leaking into his voice. Surely, he was afraid that Rory had spotted something untoward that might not bode well for their party, but instead it had just been the towers of his home that had given Rory pause.

It's only been a few weeks for me, even though those days have irrevocably changed my life, Rory reminded himself. It was fifteen long years for Gray. Stop being silly, it's not the same.

But it felt something like what Gray must have experienced; a lesser echo of that same feeling. The joy of seeing home again, crossed with dread at what entering it again might hold. The realization that after this day, he might be solely responsible for its sturdy brick walls and thousands of people living not only within its walls, but scattered throughout the countryside.

"It will be all right," Gray finally said, when Rory said nothing. "I will be right here, by your side."

Rory would never deny that this promise helped him enormously, but he knew now it could not be all his strength.

The rest of it he needed to find inside himself.

He took one deep breath, and then another. A voice inside him said, you were born for this. And he had been, hadn't he? He'd not been raised to it, like Gray had, but the same blood ran in his veins that had run in the veins of his father, whom Evrard had said was a fair and benevolent ruler. He would never get the chance to see what sort of king he would be, if he didn't forcibly eject the woman who had taken his throne.

Purpose coalesced inside Rory, and he looked up at the towers of Beaulieu with a firm, steady gaze. "Yes, you will," he said to Gray. He didn't need to tell him that he'd found a similar well of strength inside himself, because Gray's approving glance told him that he looked it.

Strong. Kind. Honorable. Determined.

He had read so many texts about the great kings of old, and he knew what separated them from the rulers that history didn't remember. Rory vowed that, if given the chance, he would live up to his father's example.

Anya gave a shout, and Rory looked over where she stood, and realized she'd found the creek the sewer system dumped into.

Unfortunately, the diagrams Rory remembered hadn't detailed exactly the state of entrance of the system, and when they approached it, he realized it was covered by a very sturdy-looking grate. The holes between the iron bars were small—far too small for even Rory to fit through.

Gray sighed, and dismounted, walking over to the opening of the sewer. "We must take this off," he said. "Did anyone bring an ax?"

Kristian brought one over from one of his packs. "You never know what you might need in a battle," he said, handing it over to Gray. "D'you need any help?"

Dubiously, Rory eyed the grate. It seemed immensely strong. Impenetrable, in fact. Yet, Gray took the ax and headed towards it anyway. His first strike was slightly higher than the foundation of the iron bars, set into the wide stone entrance of the sewer, but the next were perfectly aimed, and he swung again and again.

Still, when he took a step back to shrug his cloak from his shoulders, it appeared that he hadn't made any progress in even denting the bars.

"Wait," Anya said, approaching. She was carrying a pickaxe. "Let's chip away at the stone, instead. It's got to be softer than those metal bars."

It was a difficult and exhausting process, if everyone's expression was any indication. There were not enough real tools to go around, and Gray had forbidden Rory to use his bronze dagger—truly, that did make sense as the dagger was the only thing they knew of that could cause Sabrina any harm—but the other four spent the next hour taking turns to gradually demolishing the stone around the grate.

When it finally fell away, Rory cheered loudly, but the other four looked too tired to celebrate.

Gray collapsed against a tree and wiped his face with a sleeve of his tunic. "A few minutes of rest," he suggested, "and then we will proceed into the sewers."

Rory sat down next to him, offered him first his waterskin, and then his handkerchief. It had been laundered in Tullamore, but after being on the road for several days, it had grown dusty again. Still, Gray didn't seem to notice as he took it and wiped his face, exhaling slowly.

"Somehow," Gray said, "it doesn't feel right that Evrard isn't with us."

"I think. . ." Rory hesitated. "I do think he stayed to protect the rest of the army, but I also think he wanted us to know we could do this on our own."

"That sounds very much like Evrard," Gray pointed out dryly.

Rory shrugged. "Once you get to know him, he's quite predictable."

"What about you? Do you think we can do this on our own?" Gray, who had sounded so determined and sure only a few hours before, now had an edge of uncertainty in his voice. Maybe it was exhaustion from pulling out the grate, or maybe it was doubts, beginning to creep in. They didn't know how to kill Sabrina. They didn't know how effective the sewer routes would be in finding her. So much in this very important quest was being left up to chance, and if Rory dwelled on their chances for success, he knew he'd be overwhelmed by terror at the incredibly slim possibility they'd actually succeed.

"I think we can't do anything else," Rory said softly. "We were always meant to be here, right here, right now, and I think that has to count for something."

"You're right." Gray shot him a lopsided, incredibly charming smile. "Why do you always have to be right?"

Rory grinned back. "You love it."

"I do, I do. I love you." Gray said it softly, earnestly.

"I love you, too." Rory stood and held out a hand for Gray to take. "Let's go reclaim my throne."

Their journey through the sewers was just about as unpleasant as Rory had been expecting it to be. It was dark, smelly, and extremely tight. At moments, Rory felt like the walls were going to close in and simply swallow him up, but he kept breathing, despite the horrible stench, and continued to plow ahead, following the makeshift torch that Kristian had constructed and then given to Anya.

Anya had insisted on going first through the sewer. When Gray had questioned why, she'd merely fixed him with a single-minded glare. "Because I can," she'd said.

That was enough reason for Rory. He didn't want to ask anyone to put themselves in danger for them, but he also wasn't going to stand in the way and stop anyone either, because as much as he hated it, he and Gray needed Anya and Diana and Kristian. With them the chance of succeeding was incredibly slim; without them, it was nonexistent.

Occasionally, a rat would skitter through the puddles lining the tunnels, and Rory would jerk and then force himself to calm down. He wasn't happy about it, but eventually he stopped being surprised by the random creatures that showed up alongside them in the sewer tunnel. They'd been in the dark, creeping forward, for what felt like an eternity, when finally the light bobbing ahead of them came to a halt.

"Rory," Anya called out. "This tunnel splits ahead."

Luckily, when he thought back to the diagrams he'd seen, he remembered the split. "Left is towards the throne room," he said decisively. "I'm assuming that's where we want to go. That's where she spends most of her time."

Gray's expression in the dull light was thoughtful. "Will she be there? Could she possibly be with the rest of the forces at the gate, instead?"

"She'd never do that," Diana spoke up. "She doesn't believe women should involve themselves publicly in the matter of war."

"Publicly?" Kristian asked, a frown creasing his face. "But she'll do it behind the scenes?"

"There's a general she likes, well," Diana hesitated, "a little too much if you get my meaning. In any case, he's essentially her puppet. She'll have him out with the forces at the front of the gate, while she directs the action from the throne room."

"So the throne room it is," Anya said.

Initially, Rory was surprised by Diana's matter-of-fact answer. He'd never heard his aunt make any comments like that, but ultimately, her words made sense. Sabrina had been enamored of her public visage of beauty and grace. She could fight as dirty as anyone, with skills she gained privately. But her training was always done in secret, like it would somehow diminish her authority if anyone knew how ruthless she truly was.

But somehow, Rory had always known. Perhaps, she'd made sure he knew, in anticipation for this day.

Course decided upon, Anya continued moving, with the four of them behind her. At some point, Rory recognized a particular configuration of turns, and observed that they had moved from below the courtyard into the castle proper. Another two turns, and with Rory's heartbeat pounding in his ears, he announced they should be very close to the throne room.

"I think we're here," Rory whispered. They'd all dropped their voices since entering the main section of the castle, as nobody was sure if the sound would carry.

"I see a grate," Anya said. "It's in the ceiling."

Everyone peered up into the gloom as Anya held up the torch closer to the ceiling. "I hope it's not set into the stone," Gray muttered.

Kristian boosted himself up briefly, using the sewer walls. "It's not set in," he confirmed. "Diana—let's use your spear to pry up a corner of the grate and then push it over."

"It's going to be heavy," Diana warned. "It might take more than one of us." She hefted up her spear and Anya helped her position it in the corner of the grate.

Kristian put his hands on the spear, alongside Diana's, and at the count of three, they pushed upwards with all their combined might. The grate did not move. Rory exhaled slowly, trying not to panic that they might be stuck in these claustrophobic tunnels quite a bit longer.

"We need more force," Diana said reluctantly. "Gray, can you help?"

Gray moved to one wall, and feeling up it carefully, found a good handhold in a stone that had not been placed with the same care as the others. He gripped it and leveraged himself up, gripping the spear at a much higher point than Diana and Kristian. "Now," he barked. Rory couldn't imagine the coordination and balance it took to hover there, nearly suspended in mid-air and then add his strength to the others as they thrust upwards.

This time the grate moved, and with a great screeching groan, it shifted to one side, just far enough for a person to fit through.

"Quickly," Anya said. The grate moving had indeed not been very quiet and if this opened into the throne room itself, the sound would draw any soldiers left to guard the Regent Queen.

She braced her hand on the ground, and Gray, after lightly jumping down from his perch, used her boost to pull himself through the opening.

After a moment, Gray's face reappeared, framed in the opening. "It's all clear," he said. "I'm in a hallway outside the throne room itself. It's empty, at least for now."

Anya then assisted Kristian and Diana, and finally Rory. "What about you?" he asked her. "How will you get up?

Anya just smiled. "Ardglassians are adaptive," she said. "I'll manage."

Then she set her hands out for Rory, who embarrassingly struggled for a moment to get a good handhold on the smooth edges of the stone. Luckily, Gray was there to give him a hand, and pulled him up as Rory pushed.

Once Rory's eyes adjusted from the gloom, he saw they were indeed outside the throne room, just as he'd hoped they would be. This was a lesser-used passageway, and it was indeed empty.

Anya joined them, barely breathing hard at all, and Rory wondered if she'd actually managed to climb the walls like a spider.

"Cautiously," Gray mouthed and this time, he took the lead.

Pulling Lion's Breath from its scabbard, Gray gestured towards a side door. Rory nodded, afraid to speak, lest the sound travel too much and alert Sabrina to their presence. Gray was right; it was a side door into the throne room.

He opened the door a crack, and then at his signal, weapons raised, they ducked through the opening to enter into the throne room of Fontaine.

Sabrina, despite all their attempts at secrecy, sat on the throne, the wrought gold lions' figures on either side of her head shining with the reflected light of the dozen chandeliers above. She might have been expecting them, but at least, Rory thought as they approached, cautiously, she was alone.

Perhaps this meant that she was so certain of her own magical power that she had relegated every member of her army to the front gate, where they would hope to repel Ardglassian force.

"Nephew," Sabrina said in a particularly silky tone, "how pleased I am to discover that you have returned." Her gaze fell upon the rest of the party. "And you," she sneered, voice changing from sickly sweet to dangerously angry, "you are here."

Rory knew Gray wanted to protect and shield him. His positioning made that clear enough, but Rory couldn't let him take the brunt of whatever attack she flung at them first, and instead stepped around him.

"You," Rory said calmly but certainly, "are trespassing."

She erupted in peals of honeyed laugher, tossing her long dark hair, completely unconcerned at his words. "You really think you can remove me?"

Rory was not certain at all, but they had come all this way, and everything was resting on the idea that Rory believed he could.

It was so easy to let that belief show now, to let it radiate out of his expression and hit her, perhaps not where it hurt, because Rory doubted she had anything as primitive as feelings anymore—but right at the heart of all her conviction.

"I do," Rory said, his words echoing his expression. "I intend to remove you, if you will not remove yourself."

Then she stood, her brilliant cerise gown falling around her in graceful folds, and she gestured, absently, like she was swatting a fly. "Then, come and try."

An iron grip took hold of his upper arm, and Rory glanced up to see Gray frowning at him. "No," was all he said.

Rory considered arguing, but instead, decided that what Gray needed the most right now was certainty that he was safe, before he took on this age's greatest sorceress. And, Rory thought, he'll also need a bronze dagger.

He held out the weapon towards Gray who considered it for a long moment, then glanced back at Diana, and it was clear he was ordering her to stay with Rory—no matter what. Rory was fine with that; he truly didn't know anything other than how to perform basic maneuvers to defend himself.

Gray took the dagger, and then began to advance on the throne, with Kristian and Anya flanking him, one hand carrying Lion's Breath and the other Rory's dagger.

It was obvious the moment Sabrina realized that he was bearing her country's ancestral sword into battle against her. Her face grew dark and furious, and suddenly she was no longer the most beautiful woman, she was the most horrifying.

"How dare you bear that sword with your filthy hands and filthy blood," she spat in Gray's direction, her voice rising enough to echo off the great carved wooden beams holding the roof in place.

"They're a hell of a lot cleaner than yours," Gray said calmly. Rory's own blood was roaring at this point, in fear for Gray and in anger at how callously she'd dismissed his importance.

"Go shovel manure," she hissed, and then, as Rory had expected all along, she muttered a sharp phrase and began to shift into a chimera.

Her dress and then her skin fell away in long, tattered, flaming shreds, like it wasn't the woman changing into the chimera, but the chimera emerging from the woman.

Rory didn't want to know what sort of evil spirits Sabrina had promised her soul to in order to wield this sort of power.

But Gray was prepared for this form, as he had been for her other, and taking a step forward, threw Rory's bronze dagger, the metal flipping gracefully end over end until it ended . . . embedded in a giant silver plate that Sabrina had suddenly flung up in front of herself.

She cackled with delight at their confused expressions. "As if I would let you try that again," the chimera roared.

Anya yelled and charged, tossing her spear, tipped with bronze, at the chimera's head, but at the last second, the creature ducked and her snicker was triumphant.

"You cannot hope to defeat me," she announced, reckless and over-confident.

Use it, Rory prayed, use all that certainty against her.

The trio regrouped, and after a quick, whispered consultation, Rory watched as they split, approaching the chimera on three sides. Kristian bore a heavy ax, its blade dully shining, and even though Anya had yet to retrieve her spear, she had pulled out a short but deadly-looking sword from a sheath at her hip. They stepped closer even as the chimera roared, fire beginning to ferment in its mouth, spittle becoming specks of ash and red-hot burning coal.

Rory's heart stuttered. Any moment, as they pushed Sabrina towards the throne, the chimera would lash out and turn someone into ash. He wasn't ready to witness anyone's death—certainly not any of the three in front of him.

But then, shocking Rory and no doubt Gray, she suddenly sprang up, wings extending from either side of her golden-hued body, and she flew over Gray's head.

Gray frantically turned and met Rory's eyes. He looked wild and unhinged, terror leaking out of him as they could only watch as the chimera easily flew over their heads and then settled behind Rory and Diana, its feet landing with a resounding thud.

Gray was strong and fast, but he was not quick enough to forestall a magical creature, and Rory realized, the thought racing through his mind like quicksilver, that it was just him and the chimera now.

Anya tried to step around him, but the viper-tail whipped out and snapped her in the chest, sending her flying back, skidding across the marble floor until she was an impossible distance away. Rory could hear the others yelling and running to his rescue, but there was no time. They couldn't reach him before she turned him into dust.

"Nephew," the chimera said, Sabrina's voice deepening and lengthening. "The time of reckoning comes."

It would be easier if he'd had his dagger—Rory missed the feel of it in his hand—but he knew it wouldn't have done him any good. Gray had already made the best effort they could with the bronze weapon, and they'd gotten nowhere. Still, to face her with no weapon? Rory's heart beat faster in his chest, and it took everything, but he still straightened and looked her dead in the eyes.

"Good," it said. "You face me as a man, not a sniveling boy. As your father did."

Realization sank deep into Rory's bones, with teeth and claws and pain. "You killed my parents," he said tonelessly. "That's why they died. You killed them."

"Just," the chimera echoed gleefully, "as I will kill you now." It took a step and then another and then, with no weapon, Rory could only brace himself for the inevitable impact of the chimera's jaws around his neck.

He had just a single moment to think, as hard as he could in Gray's direction, I'm sorry, and I love you.

Just as it seemed preordained that Rory would die as his parents did—at his aunt's hand—suddenly Gray was there, panting with the effort it had taken to cross the length of the entire throne room. He'd skidded in front of Rory and he was wielding Lion's Breath as if he had been born to it.

"Don't you dare touch him, you traitorous bitch," Gray shouted, and thrust the sword just as the chimera opened its massive, deadly jaws.

If we die, Rory thought hopelessly, at least we will die together.

But instead of death, there was fire.

Sudden, hot flames flung from the tip of Lion's Breath and the chimera reared back, trying to dodge the fire burst, but it was too close, and it was too late.

Gray looked just as astonished as Rory felt, but he held the sword steady, the flames continuing to envelop the chimera, its skin blackening and curling up at the edges.

The chimera shrieked, an unearthly female sound, and then abruptly, it went still. Unmoving. A flaming mess of fur and skin and cerise silk.

The fire finally drew to a close, and after it extinguished, he took one hesitant step forward and then another. When he was close enough, Rory held his breath as Gray poked the shapeless, still smoking heap with the sword. It did not move.

"I think. . ." Gray said, his voice wobbling. "I think she is dead."

Rory flung his arms around his neck and tried very hard not to sob with incredible relief into Gray's shoulder. He failed.

CHAPTER EIGHTEEN

MORE THAN ONCE AFTER Sabrina's defeat, Gray felt the urge to duck away, behind a convenient gold-fringed curtain or into a shadowy alcove, and when he was certain nobody could see, pinch himself. In the month since Sabrina died and her forces had been defeated, there were so many moments when he could scarcely believe that this was truly his life. Before he'd met Rory, he'd come to terms with his jaded loneliness, with seeing only those who needed help as they passed through the valley, and with the final, inescapable thought that there would never be anyone special to wake up next to in the morning.

But now every single morning, he woke up to Rory's auburn curls in his mouth and his slender body pressed insistently against Gray's own.

He'd never again be alone, unless he chose to be.

It was hard to trust his sudden, blinding happiness, but at the same time, impossible not to.

Gray could still remember what the sword felt like, flaming in his hands, and he'd understood then why he'd been the one who needed to wield it. He was Rory's sworn protector, his consort, and even though they'd said no true vows to each other, every moment together since they'd first met had felt like a vow. The sword must have agreed, and as Evrard had said, adopted him as an honorary member of the Fontaine royal house, as it had responded to Gray's extreme need when it had truly meant death for both of them otherwise.

"It was not a revered artifact of many generations of Fontaine royalty for nothing," Evrard had told him dryly after he and Rory had emerged from Beaulieu to find Marthe and the unicorn holding their own with Sabrina's small army. After seeing her charred body, the general had lain down his own sword and surrendered.

It had, as Rory put it afterwards, been surprisingly easy.

The nobles of Fontaine had welcomed the Crown Prince back as if he'd never left, and even accepted his taller, darker shadow as his consort. Of course, knowing that Gray was, in actuality, Prince Graham likely had something to do with their effortless acceptance of him.

Of course, who would have the nerve to deny Gray his place when he'd demonstrated Lion's Breath's rather astonishing hidden talent?

Nobody dared, and as Rory had said, it went easily.

Anya had ridden the fastest horse they could find and had reported back three days later with the news that the King was surprisingly still alive.

"He feels no different," Anya reported, to everyone's shock. Gray hadn't understood and had confronted Evrard about how this could possibly be, when everyone had been in agreement that killing Sabrina would also mean the death of Gideon.

"Magic works in mysterious ways," Evrard simply said, but that didn't mean that Gray ever trusted it. Something so slippery, with so many rules and yet so many exceptions, wasn't something you could ever depend on.

This particular opinion was a source of very minor strife between Rory and Gray. The former wanted to believe in the power of magic in changing the world. The latter wasn't sure they could trust in something they could never see or touch. And Gray's opinion was actually proven correct a month after Sabrina's defeat.

Rory's coronation was planned for the very next day. The rooms of Beaulieu had all been aired out, invitations to all the neighboring kingdoms had been sent. Messengers had been sent to the Mecant tribe, and a handful of representatives had arrived, and would, per Rory's agreement with the tribe leader, begin re-learning their lost language. Even King Gideon had sent back an acceptance, dependent on his ability to travel. The Fontaine crown, with its roaring lions and giant rubies and topazes, had been polished over and over again until it shone like a star in the deepest darkness, all in readiness to be placed upon Rory's head. Gray had been pressed into too many clothing fittings to count, to his excessive complaints, and had finally come to a compromise with the tailor. Less gold braid on his tunic, and he would agree to wear the fancy, bejeweled sword belt that had originally been designed to be worn with Lion's Breath.

Gray was having one last security check with Marthe, when Rory rushed up to him, breathless, with a distraught look on his face.

"What is it?" Gray asked, fear curdling in his stomach. Things had been too good. Too pat. Too easy. Life and love weren't supposed to be simple. The other shoe would inevitably drop. And it seemed, from Rory's expression, that it finally had.

"It's from Tullamore," Rory said grimly, drawing him off to the side of the courtyard. "It's news from your father."

Gray still didn't know how comfortable he felt calling Gideon his father, but he certainly wasn't going to correct Rory right now, especially with that look on his face.

Rory extended a sealed letter toward him. "Anya came ahead from the royal party, with this."

He wasn't proud, but his fingers shook as he took it. It had been too easy, and Evrard's explanation for his father's continued survival too deliberately vague. He'd known this would happen, and Gray didn't know whether to be angry with him that he'd let Gray enjoy this respite of happiness and rest, or grateful.

The one thing Gray had learned in his life was that you always paid the cost of your deeds; even if it was much later, after you'd imagined your slate already cleared.

"Do you . . ." Rory hesitated. "I can stay with you while you read it, if you want."

Gray looked down at the letter, recognizing his father's spidery handwriting, even finer and wobblier in his decline. Did he want Rory to sit with him? Wasn't that why he was so grateful for Rory's existence? Because his presence made it easier to bear the terrible burden life brought sometimes?

But then he glanced up into Rory's troubled amber eyes, and knew he didn't want to share this particular burden.

He'd killed Sabrina knowing it would, in all likelihood, kill his father too. He'd done it, understanding how difficult that particular cost was, and he'd followed through with his intent, because the benefits still had outweighed it. It wasn't a decision that he'd let Rory help him make, and so Rory shouldn't have to take that weight onto his shoulders. It was Gray's to bear.

"No," he said. Rory frowned more deeply. "I'll read it and find you later."

There was an enormous banquet tonight, in celebration of Rory's coronation, and he and Gray were intended to be the guests of honor. Gray had a feeling that after reading this letter, he wouldn't feel much like celebrating.

"If you're certain . . ." Rory said, clearly not agreeing with Gray's decision.

"I'm sure," Gray retorted, more brusquely than he'd intended.

"All right," Rory agreed finally. "As long as you promise to find me later."

"I promise," Gray said—more to himself than to Rory. He'd need the balm of Rory's love and care in the wake of this, even if he didn't want to believe it now.

He took the letter and headed out the main castle gates, passing by the guards with a single, friendly wave of his hand. They knew he liked to wander alone sometimes, when he craved privacy. After so many lonely years in the valley, he wasn't quite used to spending so much time around so many people, but he was trying.

At first Gray wasn't sure where his feet were leading him, but then after a few long minutes of walking, he looked up and realized he'd headed towards the creek where he, Anya, Diana, Kristian, and Rory had first snuck into the castle. There was the grate, still with bits of stone attached, sitting on the ground next to the entrance. He would have to remind Marthe that breach would need to be re-sealed.

But for now, it was as good a place as any to sit and read what were certainly his father's last words to him.

With trembling fingers, Gray fumbled the letter open, breaking the wax seal, bearing the imprint of his father's ring.

It had been shakily embedded into the bloodred wax, and Gray inhaled sharply as the ring tumbled out of the envelope. He gripped it hard, the edges cutting into his palm as he opened the letter and began to read.

DEAR GRAHAM, it said.

I WAS SO HAPPY THAT I WAS ABLE TO TRAVEL TO BEAULIEU TO CELEBRATE YOUR PRINCE'S CORONATION AND YOUR COMMITMENT TO HIM AS HIS CONSORT. I THINK YOU TWO WILL BE VERY HAPPY TOGETHER. IT IS TO MY IMMENSE REGRET THAT AFTER WE CROSSED OVER THE BORDER FROM ARDGLASS TO FONTAINE, I BELIEVE MY BODY BEGAN TO FAIL ME. MY HEART IS ACHING FOR THE TERRIBLE NEWS THAT WILL BE DELIVERED AT THE EVE OF RORY'S CORONATION, BUT THE SILVER LINING IS THAT I HAVE JUST ENOUGH STRENGTH TO

PEN THIS LETTER AND TELL YOU THINGS THAT I WISH I HAD SAID THE LAST TIME WE SPOKE.

SEEING YOU AGAIN WAS SOMETHING I WISHED FOR AND DREADED IN EQUAL MEASURES. WHEN YOU ARRIVED AT TULLAMORE, I KNEW WITHOUT A DOUBT THAT THE FORMER FAR OUTWEIGHED THE LATTER. I HAVE NOT BEEN THE FATHER TO YOU THAT YOU NEEDED, OR THAT YOU DESERVED, BUT IT SEEMS THAT DESPITE MY GRAVE MISTAKES, YOU GREW INTO A STRONG, HONORABLE MAN THAT ANY FATHER WOULD BE PROUD TO CALL SON. I DO NOT EXPECT YOU TO FORGIVE ME FOR THE EVIL THAT I LET INTO MY MIND AND INTO MY HEART, BECAUSE I DO NOT FORGIVE MYSELF. EVEN NOW. ESPECIALLY NOW. BUT I DO HOPE THAT YOU WILL BE ABLE TO MOVE FORWARD, INTO YOUR NEW LIFE WITH RORY, AND AT LEAST BE ABLE TO LET GO OF YOUR BITTERNESS AND ANGER, BECAUSE THE LAST THING YOU DESERVE IS TO CARRY THAT PARTICULAR BURDEN WITH YOU FOREVER. ALL I CAN SAY NOW, EVEN THOUGH I KNOW IT WILL NEVER TRULY BE ENOUGH, IS I AM TRULY, EVERLASTINGLY SORRY.

YOUR FATHER,

GIDEON.

Directly after his father's wobbly signature was an impersonal notation, inscribed in another hand. Gideon, rest his soul, died this day, and has been borne home to Tullamore.

Gray looked up into the canopy of trees, the sun shining so brightly overhead, and the birds chirping happily, as if they had no cares in the world, but he did not see the green of the trees or the blue of the sky or the red of the robins. The colors blurred together with the sheen of tears he could no longer hold back.

Perhaps his hand had not been the one responsible for his father's death, but at least he had avenged Gideon by slaying the one who was. Still, revenge was less reassuring than Gray had always believed it would be, and far colder. He shivered and wiped his eyes, only to have them fill again with tears.

There was perhaps nothing Gideon could ever say that would erase those fifteen years, and all the pain and uncertainty of them, but he had come close in his final letter. If Gray was painfully honest with himself, there was a part of him that did forgive his father, because he'd apologized sincerely, he'd done it with love, and he'd done it not expecting to ever be forgiven. And that, Gray realized, counted for more than he ever would have thought possible.

"I'm sorry," a voice called out, and Gray was so startled to find himself not entirely alone that he nearly dropped the letter and his father's ring into the stream. He looked up and saw it was Rory standing on the other side of the bank, with an ashamed look on his face.

"I'm sorry," he said again. "I meant to leave you alone, I really, truly did, but I saw the way you looked, and I knew how hard it would be to read the letter, and I just . . . I love you and I didn't want you to be alone."

Gray hesitated. He'd truly believed he did want to be alone, but after reading his father's words, especially about his future with Rory, suddenly that seemed not only unimportant, but categorically stupid.

He'd already been alone for so long. It was an ugly habit that he couldn't seem to break, even though he could acknowledge all the benefits of having a consort and friends and thirteen clans who had agreed to come to his aid if he ever had need of them again.

"I'm the one who's sorry," Gray said, extending an arm to help Rory across the creek. "I shouldn't have pushed you away."

Rory settled down next to him and gazed at the ring in Gray's palm. "Your father's ring," he said softly. "Anya told me what happened."

"It seems . . ." Gray's voice choked in his throat, stuck on absolutely nothing at all. "It seems crossing over from Ardglass to Fontaine was the key to his demise."

"Your father was living on borrowed time, and he was so happy he could come see us," Rory said softly. "To see you."

Gray nodded. "He said as much." And because he didn't have the words to express what his father had, he handed the letter to Rory. It was his future too, and he deserved to read it.

Rory did so, carefully holding the parchment in both hands as Gray turned over and over the ring in his own. Finally, Rory lifted his head, and his own eyes were also full of tears.

"I wish . . ." Rory said, his own voice clogging. "I wish he had been able to say this to you in person."

Gray wished that too, but he couldn't be sad or upset or angry, because in the end, his father had still expressed what he'd felt. And while the speaking of the words might have been transformative, the writing of them had been equally as important—maybe even more so, because this was his father's dying wish. His last thought, before he departed this world, had been saved for Gray.

"I think it will be okay," Gray said, and to his own surprise, it was.

It wasn't a sudden transformation; the hurt he'd carried around forever was too big and too broad and too ingrained to just instantaneously disappear, but maybe, just maybe, each day it would fade a little.

Rory reached over and grasped Gray's hand tightly in his own. "It's more than okay," he said. "It's going to be magical."

Gray knew tonight, he'd take Rory's arm and lead him into the banquet thrown in his honor. There'd be tables groaning with every delicacy from Fontaine, and even from Ardglass, and the best of the wine and ale from the Beaulieu cellar house. Tomorrow, Rory would take his throne, and Gray would be standing right next to him, uncomplaining in his new tunic and the splendid jeweled sword belt designed to showcase Lion's Breath, and he'd be the first one to congratulate and greet the new King of Fontaine. That night, there'd be a private, much more personal celebration between just the two of them. And, Gray realized, Rory, who was usually right, was right once again.

Their happily ever after was indeed going to be magical.

PART II

CHAPTER NINETEEN

SIX MONTHS LATER

Gray woke very slowly, his brain rousing in tiny increments. First he was aware only of a warm figure pressed against his back, and then breath tickling his neck, lifting the hairs and causing him to twitch. Then a brightness against his closed eyelids, and the sounds of rustling and hushed whispers.

He'd been waking up next to Rory for months now, and it never felt less miraculous. Each and every morning felt like the first time. Without opening his eyes, Gray turned and drew the soft, sleeping bundle closer to his own body, and his sleepy brain reveled in how perfectly Rory fit next to him. Like they'd been made for each other. Maybe they had —Evrard dropped hints aplenty, because that was Evrard; always hinting and forever evading any direct inquiry—but Gray had decided that whatever the truth was, it didn't matter, because he knew what it felt like when he was at Rory's side. And something so extraordinary, that gave him this much strength of purpose, had to be born of the strongest, brightest kind of magic.

The rustling departed, and for a single moment, Gray thought another kind miracle had just occurred: Rory sleeping through the servants who prepared the fires every morning.

For the last six months, Rory, with an increasing sense of kingly devotion, had risen with the dawn, and worked long past sundown. There was indeed much to learn and much to do, and even more to administer, now that Rory was the ruler of Fontaine, but even though Gray knew how much his responsibilities encompassed, he still selfishly wished, every once in awhile, that he could keep Rory all to himself.

This morning . . . maybe. Gray held his breath, and carefully tightened his grip around Rory's waist. He sighed, still asleep, and snuggled closer. But then, just when Gray was trying to decide if it was better to let Rory continue to sleep, or to wake him for much more pleasurable activities, Rory jerked awake.

"What time is it?' he asked groggily, and Gray, who had long since learned that beginning their morning with an argument was a counterproductive waste of time, moved his arm, releasing Rory. Gray finally opened his eyes and took in Rory's sleep-mussed curly hair as he stretched his arms upwards, his limbs milky white in the dawn sunlight.

It wouldn't have mattered if he'd been unattractive or even ugly, Gray still would have thought him the most beautiful man in the world. So much of his beauty radiated from within: kindness and cleverness and an indomitable strength that nothing could ever dim.

Gray chuckled tiredly, and rolled over onto his back.

"The fire's already going," Rory said, and Gray heard his feet hit the floor. "I'm going to miss my lesson with the Mecant elders." He paused, turning back to Gray. "What's so funny?" he asked, and Gray would have to be a lot sleepier to miss the aching tone in Rory's voice. He didn't want to leave their bed, even though he knew he needed to. Maybe it should have helped, but even that particular fact didn't really make Gray feel any better.

"I was remembering the first time I met you, and how naive and silly I thought you were," Gray confessed.

"And that was amusing because?" Rory arched an eyebrow as he reached for a shirt, pulling it over his head.

Their gazes caught and held. "Because it's very far from how I feel about you now."

Rory smiled, the sight nearly as bright as the sun shining through the windows of their shared bedroom. "Well," he said, bending over and giving Gray a tantalizing little glimpse of his pale, peach-shaped arse, glorious and muscled from all the riding he did, "it's very far from how I feel about you, too."

Laughing in spite of himself, Gray found his grumpy mood dispelled by just how much he loved the man in front of him—all the parts of him, including the annoyingly responsible part who wanted desperately to care for his kingdom and make sure it was ushered into a new age of enlightenment and prosperity. "You are going to be late now," Gray said. "But first, before you leave, come give me a kiss."

Rory did, leaning down over the bed, his mouth moving confidently and passionately against Gray's own. It was a good kiss, because all their kisses were. This one, however, felt anticipatory, like a dry pile of kindling, desperately waiting for a spark. It didn't take more than a second to light, and Gray's fingers were tightening on Rory's hips, and even as he tried to ignore his hardening cock, it seemed to demand a much different response.

"Sorry, sorry," Rory said, hastily breaking away, mouth wet and red, panting a little. He wanted it too—Gray could see the hard line of his own cock in his breeches. Maybe it should have helped Gray feel better that Rory was suffering just as much as he was with how little alone time they had together anymore, but it didn't. Not even a little. "Tonight," Rory promised.

Gray made a face. "Tonight is that banquet that Evrard has been rattling on about for weeks." *And that I've spent the last month of my life planning.*

"After the banquet?" Rory said hopefully, and Gray didn't have the heart to remind him that after the protracted formality of a banquet and a few glasses of wine, he'd absolutely come back to their room and fall asleep the moment his head hit the pillow. His schedule was so brutal and exhausting that Gray couldn't even be angry about it.

Gray wanted to help ease his burden—desperately, in fact—but whenever Gray brought it up, Rory changed the subject or brushed his concerns away. Gray had been trying a more subtle method up until now, but with his frustration and worry mounting, maybe he needed to be more direct.

While I'm planning banquets and deciding on seating arrangements, you're running a country.

"Sure, after the banquet," Gray said with a reassuring smile. Maybe if by some miracle, Rory wasn't completely exhausted, they could even have a conversation about it. But before that, it would almost certainly be worth his while to consult Evrard on how he could demand to help without being too forceful or accidentally offending Rory, because that was the very last thing he wanted.

Gray knew he'd been meant for more than tending the farm in the Valley of Lost Things, and he knew he could absolutely do more than physically protect Rory's back. And not only that, he wanted to do more, if only because that might mean the enormous burden currently resting on Rory's slim shoulders was lessened.

"I love you," Rory said, and while the gaze in his eyes was dimmed from exhaustion, the bright happiness in them hit Gray square in the chest, leaving him breathless for a moment.

He'd never expected to have this, not for the rest of his life, and even though it wasn't perfect right now, it was still so much more than anything Gray could have dreamt, when he'd been so alone in the Valley.

We're going to figure this out, Gray swore to himself as he smiled at his lover. "I love you too," he said.

It was not quite as easy to be that optimistic a few hours later, when Gray, who'd been looking for Evrard, had ended up being cornered by a handful of courtiers instead.

Evrard, in the form of Rhys, had spent the first eleven years of Gray's life attempting to burn courtly manners and formal etiquette into his brain. Evrard had been resigned, but not surprised to discover that they hadn't imprinted quite as well as he'd imagined, as the informal years in the Valley had eradicated most of this knowledge and every single bit of the diplomacy Gray had once learned. Since then, Gray had been trying to regain the lost language, but truthfully, he still found it difficult to bother. If it had been anybody else's kingdom, even his own, he wouldn't have even made an effort, but for Rory he knew he needed to make peace with the nobles. They were understandably rather perturbed by the Autumn Prince's new consort, whose manners seemed more suited to a stable than a throne room.

"It is imperative that you deliver this message to His Majesty," Count Aplin said stiffly. "The rooms assigned to my party for the banquet are hardly acceptable."

Gray, who was having difficulty refraining from rolling his eyes, counted to five—a technique Evrard had suggested to help deal with frustrating situations—and then counted to five again. He desperately wanted to remind Count Aplin, who knew this particular fact, that it had not been Rory who'd assigned the rooms, but Gray himself. And, as there were only so many rooms available in Beaulieu and apparently a multitude of nobles who wanted them, facts were not on Count Aplin's side.

He turned to Anya, who had pledged her sword to him, even as Gray had pledged his to Rory. He did not have much need for a personal guard, a job which Anya was greatly overqualified for anyway, and so she had appointed herself as both a reminder to Gray that he couldn't tell off the nobles, and also the person he turned to when he wanted to work off his frustration in the practice ring.

"Anya," Gray said, his calm voice deceptive, "as the King's consort, do I not have the task of assigning various rooms in Beaulieu?"

Her gray eyes were glimmering with amusement. "You do, my prince."

At first, he had wanted her to stop referring to his lineage —especially since after the death of his father, the kingship of Ardglass had been disbanded entirely—but then Evrard had intervened and claimed that it was good for the Fontaine nobles to remember that while Gray might have very little patience with niceties, he did in fact outrank them.

"Ah," Gray said, still calm, but his gaze now pinning Count Aplin to the floor. He squirmed, visibly. "I thought so."

"But, Prince Graham, the rooms are truly unacceptable. Only four! And so small! And terribly located, very far away from the throne room and the great hall. I served the King's aunt loyally, and that loyalty should not be repaid with such poor lodgings." Count Aplin was clearly not going to give up without a fight.

"The King's aunt?" Gray prowled a step closer to Count Aplin. "The sorceress who sold her soul for dark magic?

Who threatened the King's life? Who threatened my life? Three times?"

Count Aplin stared at Gray. "Three times?"

Gray stared back, hard. Maybe later, much later, he would feel guilty about how harsh he was being with Aplin. It would almost definitely happen when Evrard inevitably cornered and lectured him about diplomacy and using honey instead of vinegar. But right now, playing nice with one of Sabrina's ex-supporters felt impossible.

"Three times," Gray confirmed.

Aplin flushed. "I . . . Just please pass on my complaint to the King."

Nodding sharply, Gray didn't say he would—because he wasn't going to and he definitely wasn't going to lie and pretend like he was going to bother Rory with such a silly request.

Finally, the Count seemed to understand and turned away. Gray let out the unsteady breath he hadn't known he was holding. Anger and frustration were still coursing through him, the indignity making his blood boil. Maybe if Rory finally let him do something important, he wouldn't have the time to listen to the sort of petty complaints Count Aplin and many others had.

Gray was just about to go find Evrard so he could ask for advice on how to convince Rory to help share some of his burden, when a sound stopped him short.

Slow, arrogant clapping.

Turning, Gray saw one of Sabrina's other supporters, the Duke of Rinald, approaching. While Count Aplin was annoying, he was ultimately harmless—like the complaint he'd just made about a bad suite of rooms. But the Duke was an entirely different problem; he was clearly disgruntled and intelligent enough to actually do something dangerous about it. Out of all of Sabrina's old supporters who still lurked in the Fontaine aristocracy, the Duke of Rinald was by far the most worrisome.

Gray felt his anger congeal into ice. He'd stupidly lost his temper with Aplin, and the Duke of Rinald had witnessed the entire exchange—and likely would find a way to use it against him.

"You certainly have no love for Count Aplin," the Duke drawled. He had dark hair, and even darker eyes. Beady, unforgiving eyes that brought to mind dark deeds and even darker purpose. Gray could very well imagine him standing next to Sabrina as she cast her spells, dooming Gray's father, and then Rory's parents. Aplin might have enjoyed Sabrina's influence in the court at Beaulieu, but the Duke of Rinald had run it with her. Had been so influential, in fact, that Evrard initially had been concerned about leaving him free to continue plotting. But Rory had insisted that without any actual proof of his misdeeds, the Duke and any other of Sabrina's supporters, would remain free. It had been a calculated risk, and Gray still wasn't sure it had been the right path to take.

"Sir," Gray said, acknowledging his presence without actually saying anything of substance. Because what else could he say? He certainly had no love lost for the Count and his whining, and he certainly felt even less kindly inclined towards the Duke.

"Highness," the Duke said icily, inclining his head. "You certainly have made your influence felt here at court."

Maybe without that clutch of fear for Rory and his somewhat precarious position, Gray would have been proud of the Duke's statement. He'd tried to do what he could to keep an eye on the men who could hurt the man he loved and the future they'd so miraculously created here. Sometimes all he could do was exercise the little influence he had to inconvenience them, like Count Aplin. Until Rory let him become more involved in the day-to-day running of Fontaine, he'd take every path available to him—even the ones that felt insignificant.

"Thank you," Gray said. "I'm so pleased you've noticed."

"Count Aplin might be satisfied with complaining about accommodations, but others will not be," the Duke said. "I will warn you, not everyone is so pleased that King Emory has taken his aunt's throne or brought a prince of Ardglass to Beaulieu as his consort. We must be vigilant against those who would threaten the King."

The Duke would never be stupid enough to say it was him who was unhappy about these two events, but the message was clear enough. Watch your back. Watch Rory's back.

"I appreciate your concern," Gray offered stiffly.

"Of course you do," the Duke said, his voice oily and ingratiating. "Shall I see you and the King tonight at the banquet?"

"Naturally," Gray said. "Until tonight."

"Tonight," the Duke agreed.

When Gray finally found Evrard, tucked away in one of the brighter corners of the royal stable, his hands had finally stopped trembling.

"What is the matter?" Evrard asked, his tone annoyingly complacent. Gray knew when he heard what had just transpired, he would not be nearly so calm.

"The Duke of Rinald," Gray groaned, leaning against the rough-hewn wood of the stable wall. "I think he just threatened me and Rory." Gray paused. "Mainly Rory."

To Gray's surprise, Evrard's expression remained unconcerned. "We knew that he was going to be unhappy about Rory ascending to the throne," he said.

"Also, Aplin is complaining again," Gray said with a resigned sigh. "This time about the bad rooms I gave him."

"Perhaps if his focus remains on those indignities, he will not be interested in additional conspiracies," Evrard pointed out.

Gray was secretly afraid this wasn't true at all, and that both Evrard and Rory were frighteningly certain of their own invincibility. But Gray, who was the one somehow relegated to actually addressing their complaints, was increasingly concerned. All it took was one or two nobles grumbling, and discontent could spread like wildfire. He remembered when Sabrina had first come to Tullamore, and when her influence on King Gideon had grown by leaps and bounds very quickly, how angry the Ardglassian clan chiefs had been. An interloper, and a beautiful woman at that, suddenly had their King's ear. Gray remembered when he had first awoken that fateful night, how certain that the threat came not from Sabrina, but from the clans themselves. Perhaps that was why she had chosen that night to finally exercise her control over the King, forcing him to relinquish Gray—she'd known she could not continue to hold the clan chiefs off for very much longer. Of course, he would never be able to ask her, because he and Lion's Breath had turned her into a harmless pile of ash.

But now Gray was the interloper at a foreign court, and he had strange, inexplicable magic. The people of Fontaine loved Rory, and would willingly follow him—but it was unspoken that they were not quite as thrilled that along the way, he had discovered the lost prince of Ardglass and insisted on bringing him home.

"I need to be doing something else than listening to Aplin's petty complaints and the Duke's veiled, ambiguous threats," Gray said, squeezing his fists together. He'd felt this way once before, when he'd first come to the Valley, and the only thing that had kept him sane was as much useful work as he could possibly accomplish in a day. Assigning rooms and listening to the nobles' squabbles and being available for whenever Rory had a spare moment for him—that could never be classified as useful and absolutely was not enough to keep him occupied.

Evrard cocked his head, considering. "You have, I would assume, discussed this with the King."

Gray rolled his eyes. "Yes, of course I have."

Evrard's silence prompted him to continue. "And he keeps saying he will find more for me to do, but deep down, I don't think he intends to find me an occupation. He wants to do it all, even if the attempt leaves him bedraggled and exhausted."

"He feels guilty," Evrard supplied, and then hesitated. "Perhaps that is an expected emotion. Rory let his aunt control him and his kingdom for many years, without complaint or interruption."

"But that doesn't mean he needs to take care of every single thing in the kingdom now," Gray argued. "He's made it right by taking responsibility. In fact, he's taken on much more than he could possibly handle. We both know I could help with the burden."

"You pointed this out, and he still refuses?" Evrard asked —even though he already knew the answer. Of course Gray had asked. Rory had never even turned him down. But then he'd never actually made an effort to include Gray either.

"He never outright refuses," Gray explained. "But it's become clear that he's not going to assign me more important tasks until he believes that it's a good idea."

"Perhaps . . ." Evrard paused for dramatic effect, something he'd always enjoyed and now used far more than was necessary, now that he was back at court. "Perhaps your position needs to be more official. Then it would not be a matter of Rory choosing to include you, but a matter of royal protocol."

It took Gray a long moment to realize what Evrard was saying. "You think we should be married?" It was hard to keep that edge of disbelief out of his tone. He and Rory were already committed, already in this together through both the successes and the failures. Their union was even official enough that Lion's Breath had decided he deserved to wield the power it held.

"Did you not intend to be married?" Evrard inquired mildly.

That was an even stupider question. "Of course. Someday," Gray said. Except that, truthfully, there had been much unspoken assumption and no actual conversation about it—except when Rory had asked him if he wanted to continue carrying Lion's Breath. They'd both known what that meant implicitly, and what it meant when Gray said he did. But somehow, in all their time together, they had never discussed having an actual wedding.

"It didn't seem important right now," Gray added ruefully. "Rory being crowned officially seemed much more pressing."

"It was much more pressing, but I do believe having a wedding, in which you both commit yourselves to each other and to the kingdom of Fontaine, will solve both your problems admirably."

"So humble," Gray grumbled.

If Evrard had been in human form, Gray could imagine his insouciant shrug. Both elegant and infuriating, a special skill of Evrard's. "You have come to me for a solution to your problem with Count Aplin and the Duke of Rinard's displeasure and a way to convince Rory to transfer some of his burden of kingship to you. This does in fact solve both problems admirably. It solidifies your position and gives the kingdom a chance to celebrate, thus muffling any discontent and also requiring Rory to share his duties with you as his official consort. A neat, tidy solution, and one, I might add, that you already had planned on performing, someday."

Per usual, Evrard was not wrong. His overconfidence was then not misplaced, and his ego continued unchecked.

Annoyingly unchecked. Gray sighed.

"I do not doubt the solution, only the timing," Gray said.

"Ah, then this hesitation is borne of romance. You wish to get married because of love, not because of matters of state." Evrard sniffed. "You are a prince, and Rory is a king. Your love affair might have been foretold for many years, but that does not mean you are not incredibly blessed to have your soulmate be your chosen mate. Many others are not so lucky."

Gray knew the marriage between his parents—which had eventually become a happy one—had been arranged. It wasn't that he didn't want to marry Rory; indeed, the opposite was true. But he could not, with a clear conscience, suggest marriage now to Rory, without further explaining why the timing was ideal.

"Rory isn't going to agree," Gray finally said. He wasn't lying, but he wasn't being entirely honest either.

"You should still ask." It was framed as a suggestion, but Gray knew better because Evrard's tone had become particularly stern.

I will try one more time to convince him, before this step is necessary, Gray thought to himself as he took leave of Evrard to return to the royal suite and dress for the banquet. Surely I can convince him.

CHAPTER TWENTY

THE BANQUET WAS AS crowded as Gray had worried it might be. He'd gone over the invitation list himself, and then helped undertake the onerous task of assigning seating based on rank. But it was one thing to see hundreds of names in tiny print on a long scroll of parchment, and quite another to see the faces all those names represented, crowded together, even though the reception rooms at Beaulieu were enormous and dwarfed even the throne room in Tullamore.

It was no surprise that since he had spent so much time in the Valley, with only his own thoughts for company, Gray still found such crowds daunting. He put on a good face for Rory, because this couldn't have been easy for him either, as he understood Rory had rarely participated in such gatherings prior to his coronation, but like all things, they were in this together.

"I feel like I cannot even catch my breath," Rory muttered as he and Gray stood at the very end of the receiving line, bowing to every noble and aristocrat that had deigned to attend—which, it seemed to Gray, was all of them.

So far, they had yet to see either Count Aplin or the Duke of Rinard, and for that Gray was extremely grateful. Still, there had been a distinct coolness in the air as they'd greeted some other members of the court—nobles that prior to this evening, Gray might have counted as at least impartial.

Rinard had warned him, Gray thought morosely. They needed to combat this growing discontent quickly and without drawing any additional attention. Maybe Evrard was right, and the best way to fix all their problems would be to make what was currently unofficial, very official.

"I think we are almost at the end," Gray reassured Rory, tightening his fingers on the back of the gold embroidered white silk tunic he wore. "It will be over soon."

Rory glanced up at Gray, his amber eyes wide and filled with exhaustion. "Sometimes it feels like it will never be over."

Straightening, Gray greeted the next guest, and then the next, before he had a chance to respond. "You should let me help," he repeated. It was the kind of entreaty he'd made many times before, and always Rory had kindly but firmly brushed him off. But now, Rory hesitated.

But before he could answer, the Duke and the Count, arm in arm, stopped directly in front of them.

"Highness, Your Majesty," the Duke of Rinard said. He bowed, as befitted both Gray's and Rory's positions, but Gray remembered enough of his own etiquette training to know it was not quite low enough to greet a king. Perhaps not an overt slight that anyone else might notice, but enough that it made Gray uncomfortable. Rory shifted next to him, Gray's hand falling away from his back.

"Duke," Rory greeted Rinard coolly. "And Count Aplin is with you as well. How appropriate."

The Duke leaned over, brushing a quick, possessive kiss over the Count's cheek. "I did not realize you were aware of my consort," he said. His voice slithered across Gray's consciousness, and his anxiety, already heightened, ratcheted higher. Maybe Rory had been aware the Duke and the Count were committed consorts, but Gray hadn't known. Not for the first time, he thought what good he could do by creating a network of informants, even within Beaulieu itself. It would prevent anyone from developing unsavory ideas, and keep Gray informed when they did.

Not only was Rinard developing them, but Aplin clearly was as well. The hair on Gray's neck prickled as Aplin's eyes, usually a mild gray, flashed an odd glowing green.

But as soon as Gray had seen the change, it was gone, leaving him wondering if he had really seen anything at all. Surely, if another member of the court possessed magic, the same kind of magic as Sabrina, someone would know. And since nobody ever kept their mouth shut here, someone knowing typically meant everyone knowing. But he had heard nothing of this phenomenon and it filled Gray with an anxious dread.

"Of course I am aware of Count Aplin," Rory responded smoothly, "I made sure that my own consort supplied him with rooms appropriate to his station for this very banquet."

Aplin frowned, and then his expression smoothed. "Of course, Your Majesty," he said, bowing at precisely the same height as Rinard had.

Watching their backs as they departed, their figures melting into the thousand invited nobles, Gray realized that if Aplin was Rinard's consort, he could not be nearly as harmless and easily dismissed as he'd hoped. There was a conspiracy afoot, and Gray was going to have to untangle it before it suffocated Rory.

"How did you know about the rooms?" Gray asked. Aplin had passed along the message to Gray, but Gray had declined to ever give it to Rory. Had Aplin found another method to deliver it?

Rory shot him a long-suffering glance. Gray looked down the line and saw there were easily another twenty-five aristocrats in the receiving line. Under any other circumstance, he'd have cried off, suggesting that the King was exhausted and would hopefully find time to greet the rest at a later time. But if Rinard and Aplin were conspiring to depose Rory from the throne, then he couldn't afford to alienate any other possible supporters.

"We're almost done," Gray reassured him—unfortunately all too aware of how much of a lie that was. They weren't almost done. In fact, it felt like every day they were only beginning.

"Aplin sent along about twenty messages to my personal steward," Rory explained under his breath. "He said he spoke to you."

Gray ground his teeth together and gave the next noble, Countess What's-Her-Name, an entirely faux smile. "I did speak to him. I declined to pass on his complaints because I believed they were silly."

The look in Rory's eyes was stark. "Silly, yes, but unwise to ignore."

Gray didn't like the feeling he'd been chastised, but then whose fault was it that he was currently on "placate nobles" duty? Especially when he was terrible at it?

They made it through the remaining twenty introductions, and then had at least a few minutes where they could retreat to a small adjoining room before the banquet began in earnest.

Rory looked slightly surprised that Gray led him out of the receiving room, but also seemed resigned as Gray pulled him into the antechamber, and then closed the door firmly behind them.

"I need a minute," he said.

Rory leaned against the wall, still impossibly beautiful in his white and gold silken finery, but when his eyelids drooped, the dark circles underneath them stood out starkly on his pale skin. "We have a minute," he said, and then paused. "Aplin and Rinard aren't harmless, you know."

It was difficult, but Gray restrained his eye roll. "Yes, I'm aware," he said. "They're incredibly dangerous, especially Rinard." Gray took a deep breath, trying to calm his suddenly racing heart. Why had he ever believed that once Sabrina was dead, they would be safe? Safety, after all, was something he could never take for granted.

"Aplin is far more dangerous than Rinard. Rinard postures, and talks a lot, but I believe Aplin's naivety and pettiness hides a deeply calculating mind."

It was a possibility that had never occurred to Gray before this moment. And once he thought about it, his conclusion chilled him. He'd wanted to wait, but waiting wasn't possible. Not now.

"I spoke to Evrard today," Gray said. "There is a possible solution he suggested to help balance out your duties as well as dismiss any insidious talk amongst the court."

Rory's eyes opened and he gazed into Gray's own. "What was his suggestion?"

This was entirely the wrong time to suggest it, and Gray was hardly prepared, but he was not going to ask Rory to marry him without some semblance of romance. He had no ring, but he could at least get down on one knee.

He did so, and Rory blinked in shock once, and then twice. "What are you doing?" he asked, his voice a surprised squeak. Lately, especially, Rory acted older and wiser than his years, but occasionally, his playfulness would return, and Gray would be reminded that he was really a young man, taking on too many burdens at too young an age.

"King Emory," Gray said, praying his voice would remain steady, "Rory, it would give me the greatest happiness and honor to take your hand in marriage, if you would be so willing."

Deafening silence filled the air between them. Rory was still gaping at him, clearly shocked that Gray had chosen this moment to propose—frankly Gray was shocked he had selected this moment too, so he could hardly fault Rory for that—but the automatic agreement that Gray had expected was nowhere to be heard.

Finally, Rory took a step towards him, and then another, reaching out to grasp Gray's hands in his own and lift him to his feet. Rory's expression was full of regret and Gray experienced a sudden burst of anxiety that maybe he had made assumptions all along that could not possibly be justified. "This was Evrard's idea," Rory stated, but didn't ask. He clearly already knew why Gray was proposing. And even though Gray had not gone out of his way to prevent it, he'd hoped that happiness over being together forever would help make the origin of his proposal more palatable.

Unfortunately, that did not seem to be the case.

"It was Evrard's idea," Gray agreed, but tightened his grip on Rory's hands, pulling the man closer to him, pressing him against his own body. "But I love you. I want to spend the rest of my life with you. The idea to get married now might be Evrard's but it was always my intention to be with you, for as long as you would have me, you know that."

Rory did not look quite as convinced as Gray had hoped.

"I do know that." Rory's voice was regretful, and Gray felt the immediate loss of contact as he pulled away. "But I do not want to get married because it would silence my critics. Especially Aplin and Rinard. This is my life, not theirs, and they do not get to control it simply by existing."

"Then marry me because you want to," Gray begged, uncomfortably aware of his own pleading tone, but also painfully aware that he had just been turned down. For fair and just reasons, but they didn't prevent the rejection from stinging.

But Rory didn't say anything, just continued to look pained, like somehow his own heart was cracking, right along with Gray's. "We should go back to the party," he said gently, and this time he did reach for Gray, tucking his hand into Gray's much larger one. "We will be missed."

Gray wanted to tell him that for once, Rory's royal duties shouldn't come before his personal ones, that they should stay here and decide how to move forward, how to eliminate the threats against them while staying committed to one another, but the distance in Rory's eyes—the first Gray had ever seen—kept his mouth shut.

Gray didn't stop the servant from filling his wine glass again with the ruby red liquid in the glass pitcher. Rory shot him a look.

"What?" Gray asked, "I'm enjoying this party."

"You don't usually enjoy parties," Rory pointed out. "And banquets, those you especially dislike."

It was impossible to keep his hurt inside. It felt like it showed on every inch of his body, radiating out of him like the sun and its warm rays. Except that Gray felt like the exact opposite. "This is my first banquet," he pointed out slowly.

"And you seem to be having a much worse time," Rory retorted. At least they were seated at the very head of the gigantic table, separated by enough sparkling glassware, delicate porcelain, and shining silver that nobody could hear them bickering. Or notice that perhaps Gray had imbibed much more than he usually did.

"Perhaps that has nothing to do with the event, and everything to do with the proposal you just rejected," Gray said.

Rory's gaze shuttered close. "I didn't reject you."

"You didn't say yes," Gray pointed out, gesturing with his glass. "I think I would have noticed if you had."

"Can we not do this now?" Rory hissed. "At least save it until we're alone. Please."

It was not fair, but then life felt particularly unfair right now. Maybe it was that he was seeing everything through the haze of the wine, but to Gray, it felt like all he had done since arriving at Beaulieu was to be everything he thought Rory wanted, to be available whenever Rory had a free moment, to take care of every pressing matter that he could, so Rory could be free to rule his country. And in payment, Gray received very little if any personal time, possibly treasonous nobles, and a rejection of his marriage proposal.

If Evrard was here, at this stupid, blasted banquet, then Gray could at least complain to him, but he was in his stable, snug and undisturbed, and likely completely unaware of the chaos he'd created with his simple suggestion.

Gray had resented the unicorn many times in his life, but his resentment had never burned as acutely as it did right now.

He leaned back in his chair and glared at the liquid in his glass. "I think I should go back to the Valley." The words came out without him even thinking about them, and definitely without him considering the effect they could have. For when he'd lived in the Valley of the Lost Things, it was not as if he had felt life was any more fair. In fact, he remembered all those painfully lonely nights, wishing to meet someone he could share his exile with, and never, ever glimpsing even a possibility on the horizon.

Then Rory had arrived, changing everything, but now, somehow, life as Rory's consort was nowhere near like he'd imagined it during those lonely nights. But then, Gray thought, watching as Rory's expression went pale, he had never imagined that his consort might be a prince or a king. He'd only ever wanted some poor shepherd boy or a sweet milkmaid. He'd never dreamt that he would find himself back in a place similar to where he had been born.

Maybe . . . just maybe . . . he had had the right idea all along.

"Do you mean," Rory hesitated, "do you mean to leave? To go back?"

Gray didn't know what he meant. He knew, objectively, that he was still in love with Rory, and that he never wanted to leave him, but there was something about Beaulieu that was driving him slowly insane and was making him say things he'd never have considered under normal circumstances. But then, becoming the consort to a king and wielding a magical weapon was hardly normal, even for someone who'd grown up with a unicorn as a father figure.

Maybe what he needed was a little break. Some space, for both of them. Maybe Rory would miss him more when he was gone, and realize they were meant to be together, regardless of circumstance. "Not forever," he admitted softly, setting down his glass and catching up Rory's hand in his and raising it to his lips. He brushed a kiss, agonizingly slow, over Rory's skin. "Just . . . for a little bit. I could use some time away."

It was impossible to miss the hurt in Rory's eyes. Truthfully if anyone needed a break it was him, but he was the King now, and he felt the obligation so keenly that Gray knew he didn't believe a break was something he deserved.

Another problem, heaped upon the million others on Gray's plate, and he couldn't hope to solve any of them.

"I will put together a small company to escort you in the morning," Rory said, and this time his voice wavered and Gray would have to be blind to miss the sudden sheen in his amber eyes. "But I will miss you."

This time, Gray's kiss landed on Rory's lips, and it crossed the line from polite to something else entirely. He didn't care. "I will miss you too, you know that. I don't want . . . I don't want to end up like this, me drinking too much wine, you working all the time, and us bickering at banquets."

Rory wiped a tear away. "We won't. I swear it."

"I'll forego the company," Gray added. "I'll take Evrard. I have Lion's Breath. I shall be fine."

"You'd best promise you will be," Rory said, a smile threatening to break through the thundercloud on his face. "I will not tolerate anything less, and I hear the King of Fontaine is completely unable to compromise."

Gray smiled back. He felt better already, like he could already feel the hard dirt of the road beneath Evrard's hooves, and the wide-open grasslands of the Valley. "He's still learning," he said, brushing another kiss across Rory's perfectly flawless nose, "but I believe he will get there. Someday."

"Someday," Rory agreed with a sniff.

As predicted, Rory fell asleep nearly the moment his head hit the pillow when they finally returned to their quarters from the banquet. Gray stayed up later, packing a bag, but mostly watching Rory sleep, his auburn curls spilled across the ivory sheets, his face so peaceful.

Even though Gray knew in his gut that going back to the Valley was the right thing to do, his stomach clenched at the inevitable sorrow they'd both feel at being separated. Even a few weeks was far more than they'd been apart since the first time they'd met.

Still, in the end, he wouldn't be leaving if he didn't believe this wouldn't lead to a breakthrough. At the very least he had to try because they couldn't keep going as they were.

When the first rays of early morning sun crept over the castle, Gray gently rolled Rory over and watched as his eyes fluttered open. For a split second, only joy and love were reflected in their depths, and then after a moment passed, and Rory woke further, he remembered why his lover might wake him, and a shadow crept in.

"You're leaving," Rory said, and there was an edge of hurt to his tone.

"I wanted to get on the road early," Gray said softly.

Maybe leaving Rory right now wasn't particularly kind, but at least to Gray's mind, it was necessary. "Of course you did," Rory said. Bitterness joined the hurt. "When should I expect to see you again?"

"I won't be gone very long. Maybe a few weeks. Just to make sure the Valley is secure. Give you time with the Mecant elders."

Rory could hardly argue that while the elders were at Beaulieu, and he was fulfilling his promise, there was very little time for Gray. Still, he'd just begun to frown, before Gray leaned down and kissed the disgruntled expression right off his face. Gray poured everything he felt into that kiss: the hope and happiness he felt whenever he thought of their long, glorious future, the pride in Rory's accomplishments, the deep pervading heat that filled him at just the thought of Rory, panting and aroused, perched above him. They were both breathless when Gray finally lifted his head.

The shadows had disappeared from Rory's eyes completely.

"I love you," he said, and it wasn't that Rory didn't say it often, but this time it sounded fervent—like a vow. And Gray took it as such, holding the words close to his heart and letting the balm of them soothe the wounded hurt he'd felt when Rory had chosen to answer his proposal with silence.

"I love you too," Gray responded, leaning in to brush one more kiss against Rory's glorious curls. "I'll be back home before you know it."

"I thought we had solved this particular set of problems," Evrard said, sounding incredibly put out, "and then I discover, to my utmost shock and horror, that we are going back to the Valley. The Valley! You hated the Valley."

"I didn't hate the Valley." Gray made sure to keep the amusement out of his tone. Evrard wouldn't appreciate Gray finding his outpouring of melodrama funny. "I was lonely there."

"Yet, here we are, going back, and for what reason I am still endeavoring to discover."

"We needed some space. I . . . ." Gray took a deep breath. "I did as you suggested, and it was a disaster. Rory hated the idea."

Evrard stopped trotting down the road so abruptly Gray nearly lost his seat. "He what," he exclaimed.

Gray was even more relieved he'd decided Evrard needed to accompany him back to the Valley, because if he'd discovered the truth with Rory within lecturing distance, he probably would have put Rory so firmly off marriage, a wedding never would have occurred.

"I told you that he wasn't going to want to be married because of Aplin and Rinard's gossiping," Gray said, despite the fact that he was truly afraid what Aplin and Rinard were doing was far worse than a little loose talk.

"Well," Evrard sniffed, "I never suggested you inform him of that particular benefit. That was all on you."

"I wasn't going to lie to him." That was something Gray had vowed never to do.

"Still," Evrard hedged. "There is a method of communication called diplomacy."

"And I'm exercising it by putting some distance between us," Gray insisted.

"You are so sure this will work?" Evrard did not sound particularly convinced.

"It's better than continuing the same thing and continuing to let it separate us further." Gray took a deep breath. "By the time we get back, the Mecant tribe will have departed for the season, and perhaps Rory will have had some time to reflect on what he really wants his rule to be like."

"And some time to miss you?" Evrard chortled. "Perhaps you are more conniving than I had given you credit for."

"It's not . . ."

"Yes it is, and I applaud it," Evrard said, sounding very final about his decision. "After all, you are doing it with every intention of it helping Rory, not hurting him. You mustn't worry. You're not Sabrina. You could never be her."

Gray let out the breath he hadn't known he was holding. It was annoying that occasionally Evrard knew him better than he knew his own mind, but then it could be illuminating too.

He'd never have thought what bothered him about being labeled "conniving" was that he never, ever wanted to resemble the sorceress he had slain.

"A half day and a hard ride and we will be at the Valley," Evrard continued. "That is plenty of time to not only review your plan for Aplin and for Rinard, but to continue your etiquette lessons."

Gray groaned, hard.

Maybe he shouldn't have left Beaulieu after all.

CHAPTER TWENTY-ONE

RORY WISHED FERVENTLY THAT Gray hadn't left. He missed him already, more than he had ever imagined he would—and his imagination, from all the many years of burying his head in books, was extremely well-developed—and it was all quite a bit worse because Rory placed the entirety of the blame for Gray's departure on his own shoulders.

"Your Majesty," Anya asked, breaking her silent position near the doorway to his office, and coming to stand near his desk, "are you alright?"

"No," Rory said miserably. "I'm not."

"I did wonder, because you were making a quite pitiful groaning noise just then," Anya offered, a glimmer of a smile breaking through her solemn expression.

Rory didn't know whether it was better or worse that Gray had left Anya behind, ostensibly to guard him. If he'd wanted Rory to think of him every minute of every day, and never be able to escape his memory, he'd have accomplished that even without Anya. But with his countrywoman right there as an additional constant reminder, Rory's suffering felt particularly acute.

"I miss Gray," Rory said, not that this revelation was particularly new to anyone, especially not to Anya, who had been present for the last two days and had witnessed every ounce of Rory's regret.

"If you miss him so much," Anya said, resting a hip against the edge of Rory's enormous, intricately carved desk, "why did you let him leave in the first place?"

It must have been Rory's somewhat shocked expression— in the six months since he'd ascended the throne of Fontaine, it was rare that anyone, barring Gray and Evrard, actually told him the blunt, unadorned truth. Anya must have realized a moment too late that she was addressing Rory, who was the King, and not Gray, with whom he knew she had a much more informal relationship.

"I . . . uh . . ." It was unusual to witness the Ardglassian warrior feeling anything other than supremely self-possessed and confident. "My apologies, Your Majesty," she added, with an apologetic frown. "I appear to have overstepped my boundaries."

Rory was not jealous, precisely, of Gray's easy way with people, even those who did not like him, but he was beginning to see that his own stiff formality was doing him no favors. Another blame to lay at the gravestone of his aunt, who by allowing him to hide away, had neglected to teach him some vital lessons about social interaction.

"No, no," Rory said, "it is I who should be apologizing. You said nothing wrong. In fact, I . . . I find I need more people who tell me the truth." There was Gray, of course, but it was not the same. "And you are right, absolutely right. If I did not want him to go, I should have asked him to stay."

"Your Majesty," Anya said, absently reaching down to pet one of the enormous carved lions holding up each corner of the massive desk, "you have recently taken your throne. Gray is still coming to terms with his own legacy and his own power in your kingdom. Some . . . growing pains are to be expected, I think."

Rory, who had spent the last two days, and in many ways, the last few months, beating himself up mentally for the problems he and Gray were experiencing, gaped at her.

"You really believe that?" he asked slowly. In all likelihood, it was entirely inappropriate for Rory to be having this conversation with Anya, but he knew she was good friends with Gray, and if he couldn't talk to someone, there was a strong chance he would simply explode.

"Both your lives completely changed when you became King," Anya said simply.

Rory knew Anya was right, and that even as they had both struggled to adjust to their new reality, their feelings for each other had remained steadfast and true. He still loved Gray, he still wanted and needed him in equal parts, and he hoped— no, he believed—that Gray's feelings were similarly unchanged.

"Has Gray ever told you about how he came to terms with his exile in the Valley of Lost Things?" Anya asked.

Gray did not typically like talking about his feelings, especially feelings surrounding him leaving Ardglass. He had mentioned it offhandedly once or twice, but never in any depth, and Rory found himself more disconsolate at the fact Gray was talking to Anya, but not to him. But then, Rory reminded himself, when would you have time to have these deep conversations? You barely have any time to ask each other how your day was.

Rory was forced to shake his head, at least a little embarrassed that they were supposed to be soulmates, but Gray was talking to his countrywoman instead.

"I explain this because I have the impression that your upbringing, at least after the death of your parents, was quite different," Anya said seriously. "But Gray was raised to be a king. He was trained from a very young age to not only be a statesman, but to be a general. Nearly everything he did was in service of helping him become a better, more just ruler to his people. And then, at age eleven, everything changed for him. Every bit of foundation that he had was ripped away, and instead of being a king, he was essentially told that he would be a farmhand the rest of his life."

Of course Rory knew the facts of the situation; that at eleven Gray had fled Ardglass, and then had settled in the Valley of Lost Things. He also knew, from offhand comments Gray had made from almost the very beginning, that such an abrupt change weighed heavily on him then, and now.

"He dealt with this," Anya pointed out, her voice gentling, "by staying so busy he couldn't dwell on the sudden changes that had overtaken his life."

Rory was renowned for being one of the most intelligent men of his age. With Anya's words, he realized just how stupid and blind he had been. Instead of giving Gray something to do to help him adjust to the new circumstances in which he'd found himself, Rory had rebuffed every single attempt Gray had made to find an occupation.

He was silent for a long moment as so many of their conversations were re-framed in his head, taking into account this new angle. And all of them suddenly felt quite different. Gray, not dissatisfied with Rory, or thinking that Rory was not good enough or Rory was not working hard enough, but desperate for something to do because he was struggling and because he was bored. Here Gray was, with half of the education normally given to a king, and no way to use it, because Rory was too stubborn to let anyone else help.

"I'm an idiot," Rory finally pronounced, disgusted with himself. He'd become so self-absorbed, juggling all the new duties he'd taken on, that he'd failed to notice the man he loved was struggling. It wasn't like Gray hadn't said anything; he'd asked more than once if he could help. But Rory, feeling his own heap of guilt from letting his aunt rule unchecked for years, had never made an effort to make a place for his lover.

A smile glimmered at the edges of Anya's mouth. "Not an idiot," she said, "merely a king trying to do right by his people and a man in love, trying to navigate a new relationship."

A new relationship.

Was that why Gray's proposal had bothered him so much? Rory, too, had taken it for granted that they would be married someday, and had been unpleasantly surprised that Gray would decide now, when they barely saw each other, was the perfect time.

Maybe it was the perfect time to use a wedding to silence any treasonous gossip, but it certainly wasn't anything close to the most ideal time for Rory and Gray personally. He'd known they were struggling a little bit, had inevitably seen it, but had been unsure how to solve their problems. Had hoped, somewhat naively, that with time for them both to adjust to their new roles, everything would revert back to how it had been at the very beginning.

But that wasn't right either, Rory realized. That wasn't even something he should want. Their relationship shouldn't march backwards, back to the beginning, but progress and move forward.

"I can see why Gray keeps you around," Rory said to Anya, who only shrugged.

"I think he likes having me around because I'm from Ardglass and I make sure his head stays the same size," she said.

"Maybe we can share your service, and you can assist me similarly," Rory proposed.

Anya regarded him speculatively. "I don't think a huge ego is your problem, Your Majesty," she said.

"Perhaps not, but an application of brutal honesty never goes amiss," Rory said firmly. Too many advisers were treating him like particularly delicate glass, afraid to see how much he could bear. The Rory of six months ago might have been equally concerned about his strength of purpose, but the Rory of today had dug deep and discovered he was much tougher than he'd ever imagined.

Somehow, miraculously, the Valley looked unchanged as Gray and Evrard rode down the slope towards the farm.

"It never changes because I wish it that way," Evrard pointed out, answering Gray's unspoken question.

"Magic," Gray muttered under his breath, even though he was perfectly aware that Evrard would hear it.

"You hardly disparaged magic when you summoned it with Lion's Breath and saved Rory's life as well as your own," Evrard pointed out.

"There's a place for it. That I won't argue with. But to keep this valley green and bright and perfect?" Gray shook his head. "It feels like a waste."

"It's not my magic that keeps this place pristine," Evrard observed. "But a much deeper, much more archaic magic set in place long before I even existed. I could hardly change it, even if I wished to."

The crops Gray had planted in the spring before Rory's arrival with his guard to the Valley were still sitting in the fields, seemingly frozen in time. He'd fully expected to ride in and immediately have to rip rotten crops from the fields, but everything was preserved, like the last six months hadn't passed at all.

"You could have told me that we didn't need to check in on the Valley," Gray grumbled as he dismounted, running his fingers along the tall corn stalks Rory had once hid in.

"And deprive you of an excuse to run off when you and Rory were having problems?" Evrard said, clearly much amused by himself. "I wouldn't dare."

Gray glared at the unicorn next to him. "That isn't why we came. We came . . ."

"Because Rory wouldn't listen to you? Because he won't let you help him? Because he turned down your proposal of marriage?"

Gray stalked over to the farmhouse and yanked the door open. He was already missing Rory and regretting leaving in such a huff, but Evrard was not making this any easier. A common problem with Evrard; he tended to rub your nose in it before you finally admitted he'd been right all along. Gray's hands tightened into fists as he took in the main room of the farmhouse. It was just as he'd left it, like he'd merely stepped outside for a moment. "It wasn't like I thought it would be," he finally admitted in a low, despondent voice. "I thought . . . I don't know what I thought."

Evrard paused in the doorway. "You thought even though Ardglass was lost to you, you could pick up where you left off with Fontaine." He tilted his great head, his bright white mane falling to the side. "You thought you'd found a purpose again."

"I did," Gray said savagely. It annoyed the ever-living hell out of him that Evrard knew him so damn well, but it turned out there was some benefit to discussing his problems with someone who could read Gray's mind. He wasn't used to Evrard being so entirely wrong. "I found a purpose, I did, I had adopted Fontaine as my own, and Rory as my future and . . ." Gray broke off with a muffled oath and stomped over to a chair and slumped down into it.

When he glanced up, Evrard was carefully picking his way across the threshold, despite Gray's longstanding order that animals, even animals who talked, didn't come in the house, they stayed outside or in the stables. "You thought being Rory's consort and protecting him would be enough," Evrard said softly. "But it's not."

"I'm angry with myself for believing that was the case. For thinking that loving Rory would be enough." Gray's head fell into his hands. "I want it to be."

"How could it be? You," Evrard said, his voice growing, and taking on that magical quality of excessive confidence, "you were born to be a king."

How was that supposed to make him feel any better? "And now, thanks to Gideon, I'm not," Gray observed wryly.

Evrard's mane shimmered in the dim light of the farmhouse. "You are not listening," he said, clearly frustrated. "What do you think you would be if you and Rory were married? An assistant? A mere consort? You would be a king, same as him. He is able to bestow the title and powers onto you, same as his own. And you should share the throne. You possess some of the knowledge and the skills needed for ruling Fontaine, and while Rory's learning was different, it's complementary. Together, you are the balance."

"That means asking him to share his birthright," Gray said. He wanted to believe Rory would be willing, but then very few men who obtained power were ever able to give it up. Rory definitely was not most men, but he was still a man, with the same weaknesses, no matter how fiercely his intelligence shone.

"He would do it and more, for you, and for Fontaine," Evrard pointed out softly. "And regardless, he cannot, if you do not ask."

"But I have asked," Gray burst out.

Evrard's gaze seared into him. "Did you truly ask? Or did you hedge, afraid that he'd turn you down?"

Gray stared moodily at the floor. "I did ask him to marry me, and while he didn't outright reject me, he certainly didn't agree either."

"It sounds to me like you both need to talk through your problems." Evrard's voice was unbearably wise. And Gray was fairly certain he was also trying to point out that the last thing he should have done was run away instead of talking through everything they were struggling with. Because that was what he'd done, wasn't it? At the first overt sign of trouble, he'd packed up and left.

"I needed to know this was still here, in case . . ." Gray hesitated; he didn't even want to say it out loud.

"Rory has taken on a huge responsibility, but you've given up your life twice now, without hesitation." Evrard paused. "Looking back to make sure that what you left still exists isn't the worst thing you could have done. And as you can see, the Valley is still here. If you wanted to come back here and live, you could."

Even though Gray didn't respond to Evrard, he already knew what his answer was. He wouldn't be coming back here, not permanently. He belonged in Beaulieu, with Rory. They just needed to figure out his place there, and how to rearrange things so he fit a little better.

After settling Evrard into his stable with fresh straw, Gray collapsed into his old bed, and to his surprise, slept well, and then rose with the dawn, feeling his mind settle on a decision.

He'd cared for this farm for too long to see it stand stagnant, even with the strange preservation magic that had settled over it.

"We made the effort to come," was all Gray said when Evrard questioned their schedule, "and so I'll harvest this crop. We'll leave at the end of the week." His heart was already yearning to return to Rory, but another part of him— the part that had worked so long and so hard to make this farm his home—knew he couldn't leave it like this.

"We talked about this . . ." Evrard began to say, but Gray held up a hand, stopping him.

"I don't care if it stays frozen like this for a hundred years. I'm not leaving these vegetables behind when the people of Fontaine could eat them."

He'd have to be a lot blinder to see Evrard's satisfied expression as he turned away.

The days passed more quickly than Gray anticipated. He worked hard from sunup to sundown, harvesting the crops in the fields, and then packing them away in crates he'd put together during many past winters. Evrard could not be expected to carry such a heavy load, as well as Gray, so he traveled to the village, and with his coin purse full of Fontaine gold, bought a solid work horse and a brand-new cart. It was the first time he appreciated not having to bargain for every piece of dried meat or stick of wood. He'd had the results of his hard labor to barter with before, but never before had he been able to outright purchase anything. He hadn't even wanted to take the gold, but Rory had insisted. Now Gray was glad he had, because, when he returned to Beaulieu, he'd have something to show for his absence. Without the gold, and the transportation it had purchased, the crops never could have left the Valley.

The day before they were planning to leave, Gray was out in the corn field, sweat dripping down his forehead even though it was very late autumn—nearly winter—and the weather had definitely turned cooler. This was the last field he had to harvest and pack onto the already full cart, and he wanted to get done earlier so he might have time to relax in the bath, in anticipation of the journey home.

The noise of hooves pounding the ground startled him out of his rhythm, his knife falling to his side as he glanced up.

Since they'd arrived almost a week ago, he'd seen not a soul except for the quick trip he'd taken to the neighboring village. He was certainly not expecting to see anyone, though he supposed that the rules of the Valley still applied.

If someone was lost and needed shelter, the Valley was accessible to them.

At first, Gray couldn't see anything, even as he shaded his eyes from the weak wintery sunshine.

Then, like a vision from his fantasies—or perhaps from his memories—he made out a group of riders, horses in formation, with a slight, but erect figure crowned with bright auburn hair riding at the forefront.

Gray's first thought was sweet, blessed relief. He'd known he was missing Rory terribly, but he'd pushed the feelings away because they'd hurt, and keeping busy helped numb him, at least a little. His second thought, as Rory and his guard rode closer, was that something terrible had happened to make them flee Beaulieu again. You never should have left him. You weren't there to protect him when he needed it the most.

Gray wiped his face with an already dirty sleeve, and stepped out of the corn patch, waiting for the riders to come closer. When they were finally near enough to make out which of Rory's guard had come with, joy swept through him in a dizzying rush. Marthe was not with him, which hopefully meant that all was well, and Rory had left her behind to maintain Beaulieu's defenses.

Which meant only one thing—Rory had come for him.

Finally, they stopped. Gray met Anya's gaze, and she smiled brightly at him.

Then Rory swung his leg over his horse and Gray couldn't look at anything except his lover as he walked towards him.

Rory was smiling too, so sweetly that Gray could barely stop himself from rushing and throwing himself into his arms, no matter how dirty and sweaty he'd gotten.

"I hear this is an excellent refuge for the lost," Rory said, his hot, possessive gaze making it clear that he didn't care how dirty or sweaty Gray was either.

Rory might be one of the most brilliant minds of this age, but Gray could still keep up. "Are you lost, then?"

Rory didn't say a word, but walked closer, closing the last few feet behind them. He reached up, cupping Gray's cheek, rough with the beginnings of a beard because Gray hadn't been bothered to shave while he was alone in the Valley. "I was lost without you," he admitted softly. "I'm so sorry, more than I can even say."

Gray let out the breath he'd been holding—maybe from the moment the crown had been placed upon Rory's brow, or maybe even earlier than that, from the first moment they'd entered Beaulieu.

"I'm sorry too," he said. "I was coming home. I swear." He gestured towards the loaded cart. "But I couldn't let all this go to waste when our subjects could use it."

The corner of Rory's mouth quirked up. "Our subjects?"

Gray steeled himself—reminding himself that they both wanted the same things, that they were still wildly, madly in love, and that most important fact hadn't changed, even though nearly everything else had. "I hope to call them my subjects too, whether or not you consider my proposal," Gray said quietly. "I want to help you. I want to help them. Please let me."

Rory's expression didn't waver. "I think we can work something out. But first, there is something you should know." He paused, and his gaze grew darker, more determined. "I'm afraid that Sabrina isn't quite as dead as we hoped."

CHAPTER TWENTY-TWO

A WEEK BEFORE

Missing Gray, while slightly more manageable with every passing day, was a feeling that didn't abate merely because Rory had realized how many mistakes he'd made with the man he loved. Still, he couldn't stay in bed, feeling sorry for himself, or stare moodily out the window and not attend to the mountain of paperwork heaped upon his desk. Still, he made time—time he realized he should have been making all along—to summon Marthe to his office.

"Your Majesty," Marthe said dipping into a quick, economical bow.

"I told you that you needn't bother," Rory said, but Marthe's lips compressed into a stubborn line.

"You are my king, and I am your general," Marthe said. "Anything else would be unseemly."

And even though she would continue to resist, Rory knew he would continue to ask, and maybe someday, she might relent. Probably not though, Rory thought with an internal grin.

"You've summoned me?" Marthe asked.

"Please sit," Rory said, indicating a chair opposite his own. "I wish to discuss tradition with someone I trust. Someone who knows the nobility, but isn't a member of the court."

Marthe's gaze sharpened as she sat down. "You are thinking of changing things," she said, and Rory was pleasantly surprised to see that she looked delighted at the possibility.

"I am," Rory admitted. "I . . . perhaps for other men, or other women, ruling a kingdom isn't overwhelming, but I am still learning, and still want to make many of the decisions myself. So I find myself with more work than I know what to do with."

"I know Your Majesty wishes to stay involved," Marthe suggested, "but there are some that would be willing to assist."

"Some?" They both knew exactly who she was referring to, but just like Marthe refused to concede to informality, Rory wasn't going to make this easier on her.

"I know Prince Graham was raised and educated to be the King of Ardglass, and you trust him completely. Perhaps you could share some of the burden with him."

Rory smiled. "I could, unofficially. But what if I wished to make such a division of labor more formal?"

She didn't reply immediately, and Rory knew that now he'd surprised her. "You mean," she asked slowly, "to give him some of the power traditionally held by the throne?"

"I mean to marry him," Rory said simply, "and upon our marriage, elevate him to kingship, alongside myself. Some decisions, those impacting the whole of the kingdom, would be ones we would need to make together, but others . . . I was thinking of splitting the traditional duties in half."

"I . . . I was not expecting this, Your Majesty," Marthe finally admitted.

Rory stood and wandered over to the window overlooking the courtyard. "I haven't found many references to such action in the past. But even more than myself, I know you to be a scholar of history, especially of Fontaine. Is there any precedent?"

"I . . ." Marthe hesitated. "Whether there is precedent or not, this will not be popular with the nobles and with the court."

Rory turned. He knew he was still too pretty, still too young, to have a truly kingly bearing, but he was working on it. He drew up to his full height—wished he had a few more inches—and leveled his most royal look at Marthe. "This throne is my responsibility and my birthright and those who oppose me should take care to remember that."

Marthe had known him since he was a young child, bookish and quiet, and he was pleasantly surprised to see how astonished she looked. "Of course, Your Majesty," she said. "I do not know of any precedent, though if I remember correctly, there were some ancient documents, from the beginning of this kingdom, giving you the permission to do so."

"I have read them too," Rory said, returning to his seat and leaning forward, capturing her gaze. "I was hoping you would say so, and that we could agree on this particular interpretation."

"Your Majesty." Marthe took a deep breath. "Rory. You are the King. You are free to do whatever you wish. Your aunt saw fit to do the same, but while she was clearly corrupt and sold her soul for the use of dark magic, she did so without the kingdom knowing. Plainly speaking, to the majority of your subjects and your court, she was a decent regent. There is no saying once she held full control that she would have maintained fair and just rule. The common people, they do not care who holds the throne as long as they are treated well, and as your aunt treated them well, there is belief that you will do the same. For the nobles, however, it is different. She cultivated many of them, elevated them, spoiled them with power and riches. They are not so easily persuaded to support you, especially when they never knew she was an evil sorceress."

"She was power-mad," Rory said. "It would have shown eventually, but you are right. It was not evident to the country when she was killed, and that hurts my own position."

"The kingdom does not trust Prince Graham yet. Ardglass is not, and has never traditionally been, an enemy of Fontaine, but the court sees him as a prince from another country—one you are very close to, one whose bed you share."

Rory drummed his fingers on the table. "I'm not trusted."

"Perhaps an exaggeration, but there is a current of distrust, and I am sure you know of whom I speak, but there are those who curry that distrust, to their own benefit."

"Count Aplin, and the Duke of Rinard," Rory said bluntly. Marthe nodded.

"It would be a great benefit to me and also to Gray if I could somehow expose my aunt's treachery and dark magic to the court," Rory thought out loud, "but it cannot be as simple as merely saying so."

"There needs to be evidence," Marthe agreed. "Evidence they can see with their own eyes."

"They must make the decision that she would have been a poor ruler themselves. But . . ." Rory smiled. "Perhaps we can lead them there."

"I have yet to do much investigation of the catacombs underneath some of Beaulieu. You knew there was an existing structure, when your great-great-great-grandfather began the construction of the existing castle?"

"I was aware," Rory said, "though I was under the impression those areas had been sealed off."

"They were, but I have long held the belief that Sabrina opened some of the rooms and used them as a secret lair to experiment with her dark magic."

"Why would you think so?"

Marthe held out her hands. "Have you found any evidence of dark magic in the castle proper? I have not, and I have searched. Yet we know unequivocally that she had it. I was hoping to leave the place where it was kept buried, deep in the ground, but perhaps we should expose it—and her, along with it."

"I too would rather leave it buried but . . ." Rory could not help but think of Gray's soft expression on the early morning of his departure, and the desolation in his eyes when Rory had turned down his proposal. He could not lose him, no matter what the cost. And this plan of his, where they married and shared the ruling of the kingdom, was instrumental to their future. "We must find it and we must show it to the court."

To Rory's surprise, Diana came to fetch him, short of breath and with panic in her eyes, the very next morning. "Marthe needs you," she said, giving Rory a quick, perfunctory bow that made Rory's heartbeat accelerate with uncertainty in his chest. The only one of his guard who was more of a stickler for protocol than Marthe was Diana. So the fact that she essentially eschewed it this time in favor of speed did not bode well at all.

"Is everything alright?" Rory asked as he and Diana, with an accompanying Anya, hurried in the direction of the throne room.

Diana's expression was grim. She led them past the throne room and they stopped in the hallway, where they had entered Beaulieu six months ago, trying to surprise Sabrina and defeat her before any of the armies could engage. The grate had been pulled open, and Rory could see the flickering of torches in the dark tunnel below.

"You must see what we discovered," she said, and refused to say anything further as she held out an arm to assist Rory in descending down to the tunnel below. Within moments, Anya and Diana had followed him, and his eyes slowly growing accustomed to the dim light from several torches, posted a few dozen feet apart down the length of the dank sewer.

"Follow me," Diana said, and picking up one of the torches from the makeshift holder, led them in a direction that Rory was fairly sure was opposite of the one they'd taken that fateful day.

"How did you find it?" Anya asked.

"We started here, in the sewer, as that seemed the most obvious method of entry from the castle itself," Diana said as they picked their way down the waterlogged stone. "It did not take us very long to find it." She shuddered, and Rory was sure, with a growing sense of dread, that it wasn't because she was cold, even though there was a distinct chill in the air down below.

Finally, they emerged into a central meeting of several of the large pipes, and there, at the very end of the most forward tunnel, stood Marthe, a bleak look on her face.

"Your Majesty," she said, inclining her head. "I have found what you requested." She gestured, indicating the large metal door that had blocked Sabrina's lair off from the rest of the tunnels.

"Should we not go inside?" Rory asked.

Marthe hesitated. "Your Majesty, we can collapse this tunnel and everything in it, and ensure that the likelihood of it being found and anything inside it ever being used again would be extremely slim."

"But you said earlier, just yesterday in fact, that you thought we should use it to expose Sabrina as the dark witch that she was," Rory objected. He'd been hoping that with the execution of her plan, he could enact his own, and ensure that his and Gray's future was as happy and joyful as he'd always hoped it would be. But now instead Marthe wished to close all the evidence away? Hide it?

"Before you make the decision, you should see inside," Marthe said, her voice as hard as the stone walls surrounding them. "And we should hurry."

Anya placed a hand on the sword hilt on her belt and Rory began to comprehend why Marthe might have changed her mind.

He followed Marthe, pulse thudding dully, into the darkened chamber, secretly (or perhaps not so secretly) terrified of what he would find.

The room itself was fairly basic and non-threatening, with no corpses lying around or blood splashed along the walls. Merely a few old, battered wooden tables, covered in glass jars filled with a creepy assortment of animal parts and some rather more innocuous-looking herbs, and parchments scattered every which way. An enormous deep black cauldron stood in the middle of the room, its interior crusted with burned-on bits that had Rory shuddering.

"This, Your Majesty," Marthe said, pointing to one of the tables, "was what concerned me the most."

Rory stepped over to the table. On it was a vial of some substance, and it was open and clearly fresh, as it had not yet dried out in the container. Next to it was a large stone mortar with a matching stone pestle. Rory put a single fingertip inside, and felt the wetness of whatever mixture had been in process. "You interrupted someone," Rory said softly. "Someone knows about this place and has been using it since Sabrina's demise."

"Or it could be Sabrina, back from the dead," Diana piped in fearfully.

"She's dead, Gray burned her to ash," Anya answered flatly. "But this is clearly one of her sycophants, trying to continue her evil work."

"Unfortunately," Marthe added, "the person fled before we could get a good look, and it was so dark and the terrain so uneven, it was impossible to follow them. However"—she pointed to a scrap of parchment next to the mortar—"they were using one of her recipes. You know it's not her, because look, see the handwriting?" Rory peered closer, and made out his aunt's distinctive handwriting, though he did not recognize the language, and then the very different notations that had been made next to some of the lines.

"Someone is trying to take her place," Rory said in a hard voice. "No, we cannot expose this. We must destroy it. Everything in it. And I must go get Gray, now."

Marthe frowned. "Is it such a good idea to leave the castle at this time of unrest? Surely we could send a messenger to bring Prince Graham back to Beaulieu."

Rory had known she would suggest that; after discovering this lair, she wouldn't want him to leave the relative safety of the castle. But was it truly safe when someone within the walls was attempting to practice Sabrina's particularly warped version of magic?

"We will be quick. I will travel light, with only a small guard. After all, the person who opened this chamber will be here, and not in the Valley." Rory could see Marthe was unsure, but she finally nodded her approval. He hadn't necessarily needed it, because he was the King, after all, but it was certainly easier if she agreed.

"Hopefully we caught whoever was here mid-spell, and they will be unable to complete it," Anya said ominously.

"Hopefully," Rory repeated, but he did not feel particularly hopeful. He felt afraid, and until Gray was back, safely within these walls, and they were again united, he wouldn't sleep easy.

CHAPTER TWENTY-THREE

TELLING GRAY ABOUT MARTHE and Diana's discovery hadn't been the first thing he'd wanted to lead with—there were definitely other subjects he was dying to discuss with Gray—but after Rory's confession, that was all Gray wanted to hear.

"Tell me everything," he said, pulling Rory towards the farmhouse, as Anya directed the guard towards the stables. "What do you mean, she isn't dead? I fried her."

"You did," Rory agreed. "We all saw it. But, Marthe found a room, deep in the catacombs, near where we snuck in using the old sewer tunnels, where Sabrina performed her magic spells. And it seems that someone else is using it."

Gray stared at him, as Rory sank into one of the chairs near the fireplace. Gray's old home might be very simple, but it was comfortable. "Someone else? Who?"

"Unfortunately, they seemed to have run off just before they were discovered. But," Rory sighed, "I do have my guesses."

"Aplin or Rinard," Gray said in a hard voice. "Of course it would be them. It surely has to be Rinard."

"Perhaps not. I have my concerns about both of them."

Gray sighed, and began to pace back and forth. "I won't disagree with you. But why were Marthe and Diana searching in the catacombs in the first place?"

This was less easy for Rory to admit, because so much of the explanation why touched on the other reason he'd been desperate to talk to Gray.

He held out his hands towards Gray, who came nearer and took them in his own, clasping tightly. Rory's heart beat a little faster, and even though he knew this was the right thing to do, he still felt a frisson of nerves. "It was actually Marthe's suggestion. She said many of the nobles didn't fully understand what Sabrina was capable of, and perhaps I should show them what she was truly like. It was good timing, since I was looking to curry favor with the court, because I'm planning to announce a new proposal that might not be popular."

Gray frowned. "Is that really the best idea right now? Even if you can convince them Sabrina was evil, the risk might not be worth the reward."

He couldn't have known it, but his words gave Rory the strength—the certainty—he so desperately needed. "The risk," he told Gray seriously, "would be worth every bit of the reward. At least I hope so."

"What could possibly be worth it?"

Rory stood, and tugged their still connected hands in the direction of Gray's room, where he knew the bath was set up. "Let's take a bath and talk about it, more privately," he said. "I've been thinking about your bathtub since we left Beaulieu."

Gray laughed, his expression was baffled. "You have marble tubs the size of whole rooms in Beaulieu; why on earth would my tub be worth dreaming about?"

"Because you're in it," Rory said, closing the door behind them and wrapping his arms tightly around Gray's neck. He rose on his tiptoes and kissed Gray square on the mouth. From the moment their lips touched, Rory realized that they hadn't been kissing nearly enough. Touching, either. Or really talking, when it came down to it, but tonight, at the very least, other than one important question, he didn't intend to do much talking. Touching and kissing? That was another matter entirely.

Rory's fingers made quick work of the buttons on Gray's stained shirt, and he quickly shoved it aside, resting his palms against Gray's heart, beating hard in his chest. He pulled away, momentarily entranced by Gray's damp red-tinged lips. He didn't believe it, but he was so handsome. Gray was always telling him that he was the beautiful one; the most stunning man he had ever seen. But Rory had been looking at Gray that way from the very first moment they met, and he had no intention of ever stopping.

"Bath," Gray said breathlessly. "I thought you wanted a bath. I know I need a bath. Harvesting corn is no minor job." He hesitated. "I wanted to finish this afternoon so we could leave tomorrow."

"Tomorrow," Rory said firmly. "Bath now. Talk now."

Gray started working the pulley system, bringing water from the cistern to the bathtub. "What is this new plan of yours? You should've talked to Evrard about it."

"I don't think I need to. I think . . . I know now, at least I think I know, what you were trying to do the other night, when you . . ." Rory hesitated.

"When I proposed," Gray said flatly.

"Yes, when you proposed," Rory responded softly. "I didn't know then. I was too overwhelmed and drowning in my own problems to see it, but now I see what you were trying to do. And it would be a good start, but I think we can improve upon it."

Gray shot him a quick, pointed look. "Improve upon it?"

This is it, Rory's subconscious unhelpfully supplied. Now you find out if you waited too long. If you refusing to answer the other night was the nail in the coffin of your relationship. Carefully, he dropped to one knee. His riding breeches were stained and dirty, his tunic had not fared much better, and his hair was mussed from the ride and from Gray's own fingers. But hopefully what his attire lacked, he could make up for with his words. After all, words were his thing.

"I love you," Rory said. "I do want to marry you. It would give me the greatest happiness in the world if you would do me the honor of becoming my husband. But something that would make me even happier—and you too, I hope—would be if you would take the throne of Fontaine with me. Share it. Rule with me, Gray. I don't just want you to be my consort, I want you to be my partner. My equal. My king."

There was no other word for Gray's reaction than complete shock.

"You . . . this is what you want?" he asked, and Rory could only nod in agreement.

"But, every time I asked you, you . . . you put me off!" Gray answered. He sounded frustrated and Rory couldn't say he blamed him. Rory had been blind, and had a lot to apologize for.

"I've not been treating you right, not for awhile now. I wasn't thinking of you, and all the adjustments you've had to make since you came with me to Beaulieu. And when I did, it became so obvious to me that the solution to so many of our problems was to stop trying to handle them alone and share them."

Gray crossed his arms over his bare chest, but didn't say anything. The water continued to fill in the tub, and Rory, feeling awkward that he was still kneeling with no answer in sight, finally stood and walked over to the vessel, dipping his fingers in to test the temperature of the water. Rory supposed he couldn't really blame Gray for being angry, for wanting to make sure Rory wasn't merely trying to placate him with empty promises. And perhaps Rory did deserve a little payback for his own non-answer to Gray's proposal.

Finally, he spoke up. "This will not be a popular choice for you, as King," he said softly. "You are taking an enormous risk here. We could do this more slowly. First, an engagement. Then marriage. Then gradually involving me more in sharing your duties until you finally appoint me as your equal. We don't have to do this . . . I'm not going to leave you just because I'm frustrated."

Rory couldn't deny he'd considered a plan very similar to Gray's suggestion. It was slightly terrifying, trusting to chance and his very newly won ability to govern his people, that they wouldn't become frustrated and find a new ruler to take his place. "Gray," he said, reaching out to him again, and pulling him close, pressing their bodies together. "You were born to be a king, and more importantly, you were trained to be a king. What kind of husband would I be if I chose to diminish that part of you? Not a very good one. I would not have the first choices of our committed life together be half-hearted compromises."

"You do mean to do this, then, fully. No turning back."

It might have felt more difficult than it was, except that Rory knew how much they could accomplish if only they worked together, if only they married Rory's knowledge with Gray's strength. "I am as fully committed to this as I am committed to you," Rory vowed.

Gray stared at him for a long, measured moment. "I love you," he finally said, and leaning down, kissed him soundly, passionately. Lifted his mouth briefly and smiled. "And yes, of course I will marry you."

Relief and happiness cascaded through Rory. He reached up and cupped Gray's bristled cheeks, kissing him again, and then again. "You won't regret this," he vowed. "I swear that you won't."

Gray was smiling now, as widely and as brightly as Rory had ever seen. "I haven't yet," he confessed. "Even all those times we ended up fighting because men lose their heads around you."

"They do not," Rory scoffed. But Gray's gentle teasing, after a week apart, and what felt like months where they barely saw each other, was a balm.

"They absolutely do," Gray said, and he was definitely grinning now. "But then so did I, so I can hardly blame them."

"You did?" Gray had always seemed so sure, so confident, so purposeful, that it felt strange for Rory to consider that it was him, and not circumstances out of Gray's control, that had been enough to change his path.

Gray bent down, his dark blue eyes growing serious, as he swept a hand through Rory's hair, pushing it back gently. "I thought you were everything I hated, condensed into one person, but then I discovered who you really were, the man underneath the Autumn Prince, and it wouldn't have mattered if you were an emperor or a beggar, I was yours. Heart, soul, and body."

Rory couldn't help the glimmer of a smile that escaped him. "Body?" he inquired hopefully.

Laughing, Gray scooped him up and, depositing him on the edge of the tub, made quick work of his clothes and boots. Rory slid into the tub and watched expectantly, with his blood racing and heat building in his stomach, as Gray shed his own pants and boots.

He was every inch the warrior that Rory always fantasized about: all that smooth golden skin covering muscle that bunched and flexed as he leaned over to untie a stubborn lace. When Gray raised his head again, his gaze had darkened. "I like you watching me," he said softly, but with clear erotic purpose. His cock was growing harder, and Rory watched with rapt attention as Gray's hand gripped it, stroking from root to tip and back again. "But I think I like you touching me even more," he admitted.

"Then come here," Rory pleaded, and Gray did as requested, stepping into the tub and positioning himself opposite Rory.

Reaching out, Rory was surprised when the other man batted his hands away. "But . . ." Rory pouted. Hadn't Gray just said he liked Rory touching him?

"Wash first," Gray insisted, and he was already scooping out the soap, suds trailing across his broad chest. Rory shut his mouth and followed suit, washing up quickly and efficiently. The moment the soap returned to the dish, Rory was pushing off from one side of the tub, floating over to where Gray sat, waiting, his eyes gleaming with so many possibilities that Rory felt breathless.

When Rory finally settled on his lap, knees on either side of Gray's thighs, they both let out a sigh. "Better," Gray said, and that was the last word he said for awhile, as Rory leaned down and kissed him thoroughly, tongue slipping inside his mouth and exploring every inch that he'd missed over the last few weeks. His fingers, trying to grip Gray's damp shoulders, slipped, and their heads nearly knocked together. Gray gasped and then suddenly, without warning, picked Rory up, his powerful muscles straining as Rory wrapped his legs, water streaming off them, around Gray's waist.

"Bed," Rory agreed, answering Gray's unspoken question.

It had always been hot and perfect between them, even when they'd been in a half-frozen lake, and it was just as perfect now, but now, as Gray lay down on the bed and Rory crawled up his chest to continue kissing him, it wasn't just unrestrained lust. There was tenderness and care between them. Every time Gray touched him, fingers sure on his skin, Rory experienced an echo of every bit of love Gray felt. And hovering behind every kiss, every touch, every gasp and every moan was the knowledge that they would be doing this for a long time, and every moment of that forever, they would be together.

"Please," Rory begged as Gray's touch fleetingly brushed against his own hard, leaking cock. "Please touch me."

"As my king commands," Gray teased, but this time his fingertips didn't just graze his skin, but settled with purpose against the cradle of his hips. "How did you want me to touch you?"

Rory, panting and half-crazed with want, opened his legs, spreading them wide in an open invitation.

Invitation received, Gray slicked his fingers up from the bottle by the bed, and when he slid the first finger inside Rory, he threw his head back and moaned. No matter how much they did this, it always felt so good, somehow even better than it had the first heart-stopping time they'd indulged.

"You feel so goddamned perfect," Gray ground out, his voice growing low and intense, gritty around the edges.

Another finger joined the first one, and as they delved deep, touching that electric part inside him, Rory gasped.

Typically this was the extent of the preparation Rory needed, usually both of them were so incredibly eager to have Gray inside him, but this time, Gray kept fingering him, alternating his deep thrusts with shallower teasing brushes, until Rory was panting, sweat beading on his brow, his cock painfully hard as it tapped his stomach wetly.

"Please, please, please," Rory pleaded, feeling at the very edge of his self-control, driven there by Gray's own. He was clearly as ready as Rory was, but still he held off, apparently content to drive Rory mad with pleasure.

He only relented after Rory felt like he might explode from the tension wracking his body, and at the very least, orgasm before Gray could even slide his cock inside him. Gray carefully withdrew his fingers and slicking his cock up, positioned himself between Rory's legs.

"I love you," he said, his intense gaze boring straight into Rory's own as he finally slid home.

Rory trembled with the effort it took not to give himself over to the overwhelming bliss. When Gray's cock slipped in those last few inches, Rory's head fell back against the pillow, and he groaned, "So good, so full."

"I'm gonna make you feel even better," Gray promised, and began to thrust, his rhythm overwhelming Rory almost immediately. "See, I promised you," he grunted, as Rory found himself hurtling right over the edge without even a single touch on his own cock, spurting all over his own stomach and Gray's too.

Gray followed him only a moment later, letting out a loud, incredibly sexy groan that might have made Rory hard again if he hadn't just finished coming as hard as he ever had in his life.

"That was," Gray said, pulling out and then collapsing next to a completely worn-out Rory. "That was something else."

"You're a closet sadist, as well as the sexiest man in the world," Rory said, pulling together the energy to roll over and gaze at the man he loved. The man he was going to marry.

"It's part of my charm," Gray said with a rough chuckle.

"You're perfect," Rory said as his eyes began to droop. "You're perfect, and I love you."

It was clear; Rory did not think Gray was perfect the next morning. "Come on," he said, half-dragging Rory out of the warm cocoon of the blankets. During the last six months, it was always Rory pushing to get up earlier and earlier, and somehow get more done in a day than was physically, humanly possible, but maybe that was finally catching up with him, because he was resisting Gray's efforts to coax him out of bed so they could finish the harvest.

"Your guard is already out, they're in the fields right now," Gray grumbled, pulling Rory's leg out, only to have him retract it rather forcibly.

"Then they should keep it up," Rory mumbled into the pillow. "I'm tired. So tired."

"You've been pushing yourself too hard," Gray said, sitting down with a hard thump on the side of the bed. "I told you that you were, and you wouldn't listen."

"No need to say 'I told you so,'" Rory complained. "I already figured out how to fix it, didn't I?"

"But we can't really fix it if we don't harvest this corn and travel back to Beaulieu."

Rory's head tilted to the side, as if he was considering this. "And we can't plan our wedding either," he pointed thoughtfully.

"Exactly," Gray said. Six months ago, he might have asked why a wedding would take a lot of planning—but then he'd entered the rank-fixated and event-obsessed court at Beaulieu, and he'd discovered that everything he knew about events was wrong. At Tullamore, they'd prided themselves on keeping state occasions simple. As long as there were plenty of roaring fires, enormous roasts over them and plenty of ale and whiskey to go around, the clansmen had not been particularly hard to please.

At Beaulieu, a court event was an event. And a royal wedding was likely a whole other level of obsessive planning that Gray wasn't sure he was prepared for. Yes, he desperately wanted to marry Rory, but he also didn't want to worry about who was going to sit sixteen seats down from the royal table.

"Why don't we just . . . get married," Gray said.

Rory stared at him blankly. "I thought that was what we were going to do."

"I mean, without all the pomp and circumstance." Gray sighed. "The banquet to honor the Mecant tribe took a whole month of planning! I don't want to wait that long."

Reaching out and stroking his arm, Rory smiled up at him sweetly. "I want to get married now too, but unfortunately, part of what will help distract the court from stewing about your future kingship is plenty of pomp and circumstance."

Gray sighed. "So we can't avoid it?"

"I'm afraid avoiding it will likely be impossible."

"Then," Gray said, suddenly rising to his feet and wrapping his arms around a squirming bundle of blanket-swaddled Rory, and lifting him up, "we'd better get started." Rory grumbled, but finally he discarded his blankets and began to get dressed.

It took the rest of the day to get the corn harvested and packed into the cart. When Gray went to visit Evrard and prepare him for the next day's journey, the unicorn merely stared at him.

"Go with you? Why would I go with you?" Evrard asked, clearly uncomprehending what Gray was asking.

"We're going back to Beaulieu," Gray said slowly, enunciating every word, knowing it would likely annoy Evrard, but doing it anyway. "Rory and I are getting married. He came here with nearly the same plan you had."

"Imagine that," Evrard said smugly.

"Don't you want to be at the wedding?" Gray asked, trying to prepare himself if Evrard claimed that he didn't. Or if he maintained this charade that he wouldn't be coming back to Beaulieu at all.

"The wedding is merely a formality, and mark my words, it will indeed be a formality. I will miss seeing you stuffed and glittered and wrapped in enough gold-embroidered thread to decorate a regiment."

Gray couldn't understand. "Why will you not be there?"

Evrard's gaze finally turned towards him, and to Gray's shock, it was soft and empathetic. "I know you wish me to be there for you, but the last thing the royal court will need at your wedding is a reminder of Rory taking the throne. I am associated most strongly with that event. You need to present a front of unassailable strength."

"Wouldn't us standing with a royal unicorn help present that strength?" Gray asked slyly.

But Evrard's expression never wavered. "I wish I could return with you, I do. But it cannot be helped. Your life is situated. Rory's life is situated."

Gray had told himself that he would not let his feelings be hurt if Evrard refused to come. But it was inevitable. Evrard, while hardly the most appropriate father figure for a child, had been the only one he had known. And now that his own, real father was dead, Evrard was all that he had remaining.

"You have your family," Evrard said, reading his mind yet again, even though he knew it annoyed Gray, "and they will be there, and on that day, I will be thinking of you and Rory and sending you all my good wishes and happiness for the future. But as you well know, I have served my purpose here. I saved you. I saved Prince Emory, and saw him to his kingship, and now I have seen you to yours, and also to marriage with your soulmate. There is little to keep me here. I am like the Valley; I come as needed, and now that we have both outlived our usefulness, we will fade into the ether."

"I'm sorry to hear that but I understand," Gray said, but truthfully, he couldn't feel anything but hurt and bewildered. Part of him desperately wanted to say that Evrard should stay for him, and for all the good, measured advice that he would surely need in the future. But he also had his pride, and his pride stopped his tongue. "Then this is goodbye." He placed a hand on Evrard's neck, and Evrard bowed, his mane flowing to the straw below their feet.

When Gray came out of Evrard's stable, Rory immediately knew something was wrong, and came up to him, a concerned expression on his face. "What has happened?" he asked.

"Evrard will not be returning with us. Not for the wedding. Not ever again, possibly." Gray took a deep breath. "If you wish to say goodbye to him, now would be the best time."

"I shall say something, certainly," Rory said, and marched off to the stable. No doubt to inform Evrard that he was being an idiot and that he would be coming back to Beaulieu with them in the morning.

But Rory returned from the stables with a defeated look in his eyes and they did not speak of it again.

In the early morning light of their departure, Evrard did come out of the stables one last time, white coat shining and glimmering in the dawn, and if Gray had to turn his head away to prevent anyone from seeing a tear fall, then it was between him and his horse.

When they departed the Valley of Lost Things, Gray took everything of value to him, as he knew, instinctively, that it would not remain any longer. This was the last of its magic, and with Evrard gone, it too would dissipate after their departure.

CHAPTER TWENTY-FOUR

RORY HAD BEEN CERTAIN that they could not possibly organize a royal wedding in under a month, but three weeks and six days later, he was standing in the enormous throne room at Beaulieu, watching as Gray went toe-to-toe with Rowen, who had appointed herself as the wedding planner. Normally, the steward would have done the job, but after Rory had announced his intention to crown Gray to conclude the ceremony, the grumbles had increased exponentially, leaving some, like the curmudgeonly steward who had spent nearly his entire career in service to Sabrina, to either accept the changes or leave. At first, Rory hadn't been certain they could even pull off such an intricate and complex event without someone who had any experience, but Rowen had scoffed at Rory's concerns.

"I've spent my whole life at court," Rowen said. "I know how to plan an event."

And it turned out she did, at least when Gray allowed her to do her job properly.

"I've discovered the problem here," Anya told Rory under her breath. "You didn't give the Prince enough to do, thus he had enough time and energy to interfere with Rowen."

Rory shot her a look. "I gave him plenty to do."

"The Prince used to run an entire farm with practically no help. I don't think either of us is good at estimating what he's capable of handling."

It was difficult to argue with that, or with the fact that Gray was here, and despite ten council meetings this week, and shadowing Marthe in her role as General of Fontaine's armies and Rory keeping him occupied for hours each evening in bed, he apparently had plenty of energy to argue over floral arrangement placement with Rowen.

"If only the Prince had been able to apply himself so successfully to finding the person who used Sabrina's lair," Anya said, and Rory had to nod his agreement. No matter how they'd searched, it was hard to find someone who clearly did not want to be found. The room, buried deep in the catacombs, had been guarded night and day, and nobody had even attempted to approach. They were no closer to finding the culprit and they were about to lose their best tool —the day after the wedding and Gray's coronation, the room was to be demolished entirely.

"The biggest one should go in the front, right over the dais," Gray argued. Rowen didn't say a word, only nodded. Rory already knew that she was going to put the floral arrangements wherever she wanted, no matter what Gray said. Rory had agreed with putting her in charge for a reason; she knew what was needed and how to accomplish it.

Which was why this was an enormous waste of time when they could actually be going over the complicated ceremony

—the entire reason why they were in the throne room today.

"Darling," Rory said, approaching the pair, "why don't we leave these minor arrangements to Rowen, and go over the ceremony itself. The etiquette is rather complex, and well . . ." Rory gave him a look that was both fond and exasperated. "Well, we know formal etiquette is not your strongest skill."

Gray glanced over at him, eyes warm—quite possibly just as warm as Rory's own. "No? I'm hurt, sweetcheeks."

Rory blushed. It was one thing for Gray to try this new nickname out in private, in their bed, but to do so in front of Rowen, Anya, and the handful of nobles who had chosen to witness the rehearsal? Entirely another.

"Darling," Rory repeated between clenched teeth, still amused and still fond, despite the nickname and despite a hundred other things that should drive him crazy but somehow, never did, "we are wasting time."

Gray smiled broadly, like wasting time was his favorite thing and not at all the opposite. "Well, then, lead the way, Your Majesty."

A slight improvement over sweetcheeks.

Truthfully, in less than twenty-four hours, Gray wouldn't be required to use that particular honorific for Rory any longer. Not that he had ever been particularly diligent about its use. But after his own coronation, there would be no need, because he and Rory would be equals, both Kings in their own right.

It hadn't quite caused any outright riots just yet, but it wouldn't matter if it had. Rory was adamant and completely sure that this was both the best choice for him personally, and for the kingdom he ruled over. He'd given a speech to the court, which was something he was finally getting the hang of doing, detailing why it was a necessary step. It must have been fairly convincing because afterwards, the grumblings had mostly died down. Along with the steward, the Duke of Rinard had left Beaulieu, followed very shortly after by Count Aplin, and Rory knew he wasn't alone in hoping that was the last they'd seen of those two—and that the reason they'd been unable to catch the magical practitioner was because they'd already departed and would hopefully never return.

Rowen led them through the lengthy ceremony, and thankfully, Gray had only a few questions and remarks for her until they reached nearly the end of the marriage rite. "And now," Rowen said, pulling a length of cloth from behind the podium they stood in front of, "Prince Graham will bestow upon King Emory a length of valuable tapestry from his kingdom of Ardglass, as a symbol of his commitment to this union."

Gray blanched and stared at the cloth like it was a coiled serpent, poised to strike. "What is this?" he demanded.

Rory barely held back a resigned sigh. It had been his idea to add this particular flourish to the ceremony, and he'd known that Gray wouldn't like it—at least on the surface. Gray still held a lot of complicated feelings towards the country of his birth. "This is a part of the Ardglassian commitment ceremony," Rory began to explain, hoping that the bored, informative tone he adopted would calm Gray down and not inflame him further.

"I know what it is," Gray said, gesturing to the cloth. "I meant, why is it being included as part of our ceremony? We are being married in Fontaine, and approximately ten minutes after this, I will be crowned a king of Fontaine. Do you think we should further remind everyone that I was born to be a king of a neighboring country?"

Rory had struggled with whether they should include it for exactly those reasons—but then he'd realized that those concerns could be reframed, and therefore seen in an entirely different way. Gray's lineage should be seen not as a detriment, but as an advantage. The court was concerned that Rory had no experience, and had never been trained to be a king. Well, here was someone who had been trained to be a king. It was one of many reasons why Rory had become convinced that Gray needed to share his throne.

"I think we should, yes. We can hardly make everyone forget it, and why should you not celebrate your country on the day of your wedding?" Rory said, but the glower on Gray's face only grew.

"I need to talk to you," Gray said, and the edge to his voice made it abundantly clear that it was not optional. "Privately."

"One moment," Rory said, and followed Gray over to the edge of the throne room. The massive room, with its enormous vaulted ceilings, was a feat of engineering and virtually guaranteed that even a hushed whisper could be heard, but Rory wasn't going to remind his betrothed of that particular fact.

"Are you insane?" Gray demanded.

"The last time I checked, no," Rory responded quietly.

"Then why do you insist on possibly jeopardizing your throne with these stunts? We've just barely got the court calmed down over me sharing your throne. And now, you're going to stir up all this talk all over again by adding this to the ceremony." Gray crossed his arms over his chest and Rory was reminded of how Rowen must have felt, feeling absolutely sure the flower arrangements were in the right place, but having Gray argue with her anyway—for no real purpose except to argue.

"Are we doing this or not?" Rory finally asked. "Because when I suggested this plan to you and then I proposed, I meant to commit to it, without flinching, no matter how difficult the path got. You are from Ardglass, that's something you could not possibly change, even if you wanted to, and you shouldn't want to—even if the reminders can be painful. You are who you are because of what happened, and I love you for that strength. It brought us together and it should be celebrated, especially on our wedding day."

Gray stared at him, expression inscrutable. "You really believe that."

"I do. I believe in it," Rory said firmly, "and I believe in you."

"I don't want to bring you to ruin," Gray admitted softly, brokenly, his eyes haunted. "I love you too much to do that."

Rory reached out and took his hands, squeezing them tightly in his own. "You could not possibly. And I prefer to see that we bring each other strength, not ruin. I could not do this without you, and I like to believe you could not do this without me. So let us do this without flinching, without hiding away those parts of ourselves that might make others talk."

Gray did not say anything for a long, drawn-out moment. His expression went from sad to resigned to finally one that Rory at least wanted to believe was hopeful. "And," Rory added, "Anya has spent many evenings embroidering this cloth that came from Ardglass. It has great significance to her, and I believe she hopes it will hold the same for you. It is a gift, from the remnants of a kingdom that you gave the best chance to succeed, and they wish to thank you for it."

Tears glimmered at the edges of Gray's eyes then. "It's from the clans?"

Rory reached up and pressed a firm, loving kiss on his cheek. "In another life, you would have been their king. In this one, you're mine."

Gray couldn't say exactly why he had been arguing with Rowen over floral arrangement placement. He could say why he'd argued with Rory over including the Ardglassian custom in their marriage ceremony. Evrard would have told him that both definitely boiled down to one thing, and one thing alone: fear. Fear that he wouldn't be a good husband or a good king. Fear that taking this step would hurt Rory more than it would help him. He wished he could be as confident as Rory was, but the truth was, Fontaine felt balanced on a knife-edge these days, and the smallest thing could send it toppling over into chaos.

Evrard would also have told him he was being overdramatic; something he enjoyed accusing Gray of on a regular basis.

Gray stared moodily at the pile of documents on his desk, in his brand-new office opposite Rory's own, and tried to ignore the pulse of pain at every thought of Evrard. Of course Evrard could not hang around forever, just in case Gray or Rory got into trouble, but still the thought of never hearing another of his sarcastic and smug retorts filled him with a strange kind of anguish. He'd never thought he would miss those things; in fact, he'd hoped many times to never hear them ever again. But that particular wish coming true had ended up being far thornier than Gray ever could have imagined.

A knock on the door shook him out of his reverie. The night before his wedding, and he was pouting. Gray walked to the door and opened it with a smile. It was Anya, and she smiled back. "And here I thought I would find you worried about all the ways this could go wrong," she said, slipping inside Gray's office.

"I was," Gray confessed. Anya shot him a reproachful look.

"You thought I could be Rory," she finally deduced. "And you didn't want him to know that you were pouting."

"I was not pouting. I was merely . . ."

"Contemplating every which way this could go wrong?" Anya finished helpfully.

"Essentially," Gray admitted.

Anya sighed. "Well, regardless of how fatalistic you're being, I thought you might want this." She held out the package in her hands, wrapped in plain brown cloth, and tied with string.

Gray took it and turned it over in his hands. "Is this the fabric you embroidered for the ceremony?"

Nodding, Anya gestured for him to open it, and carefully, Gray did so. To his surprise, the embroidery was pristine and intricate. "I had no idea you could do work like this," he said, his eyes meeting Anya's with surprise.

"Why? Just because I can wield a sword better than you?"

"Well . . ." Gray had to admit that had been part of his assumption.

"You're not entirely wrong," Anya continued, shrugging in a slightly embarrassed fashion. "I'm not usually interested in needlework, but this was important, and I wanted it to be right."

Gently, Gray unwound the cloth and was shocked to see an abbreviated version of both his escape of Tullamore at age eleven, and then his and Rory's triumphant return to Fontaine fifteen years later. And then, finally, on the last panel of the tapestry, the last council meeting of the clans that he had presided over himself, after the death of Gideon. The meeting where the clans had, with Gray's support, voted to officially disband the monarchy of Ardglass.

"It might have been the most convenient choice," Anya said, still self-consciously refusing to meet Gray's gaze, "but it was a noble one, too. And we of Ardglass appreciate it more than you can know."

"Anya," Gray said slowly, "thank you. Thank you for all the time and care you put into this, and for wanting me to have something of Ardglass when I marry Rory."

Her eyes were bright and fierce as they finally met his. "Even though you will be Fontaine's king now, you were ours first. And you shouldn't forget that."

"I won't, I swear I won't," Gray said, and to his own complete surprise—and definitely Anya's—he pulled her into a tight hug. "Thank you, again. For everything."

Her gaze was slightly damp when he finally released her, and his own was definitely not any dryer. "I said someday that I would serve the King. It's not as I imagined it, not exactly, but I'm honored to be in your service, Your Majesty."

Gray cracked a smile. "Not quite yet."

"But soon. You need to get used to it."

Gray didn't think he ever quite would, and maybe that was what would make him a good king. Never entirely believing he deserved a part of the throne, or the entirety of Rory's heart. It would keep him working hard and giving his all, even when the road felt smooth and easy.

If that ever happened. With the way things were going now, that future seemed both very far off and also right around the corner—if only he could reach out and grasp it.

"I'll do my best," Gray promised.

Rory had promised himself that when some of the kingly responsibilities shifted to Gray—tomorrow, it's actually tomorrow, he thought, triumph mixing with a little bit of panic—that he would do so with a mostly clean desk.

Which explained why, the night before his wedding, he was working late in his office, sorting through the last of the parchments he'd been asked to read.

A quiet knock interrupted his concentration and he glanced up, sure it was Gray, insisting he not work quite so late tonight, but then, Gray would not bother knocking.

"Come in," he said, and to his surprise, Shaheen, the leader of the Mecant tribe, entered his office.

"Your Majesty," she said, bowing low, nearly as low as she had long ago, when Rory had begged for their lives in the middle of the Mecant camp. "I wondered if I might have a word with you."

Rory stood, and gestured to one of the comfortable chairs opposite his desk. "Of course you may," he said. "You know you never need ask. My office is always open to you."

Shaheen's glance was swift and cut him to the quick. "You are the King of Fontaine," she said, her tone remaining kind, "and I am the leader of a dying tribe. Of course I must ask. We continue to survive only due to your graciousness."

Rory sat, somewhat humbled. Whenever he met with Shaheen, which had been frequently since their arrival at Beaulieu two months earlier, he often felt the breath punched from his lungs with painful realizations.

"My apologies," he said. "I did not think."

"You are young, very young," Shaheen said, settling in the chair, her multicolored robes flaring around her, "I was much more foolish when I became the leader. You must give yourself room to breathe, to grow. And also a little credit, as you are not nearly as poor as you think you are."

Rory was touched. Being a leader was much tougher than he'd ever anticipated, his decisions having far-reaching effects he did not always foresee. As much as Shaheen's tribe was learning from him at their daily lessons, he enjoyed talking with their leader and gleaning as much knowledge of leadership from her as he could.

"Thank you," Rory said. "What is it I can help you with today?"

"It is Merleen," Shaheen said with a heavy sigh. "I think . . . I think I would like for him to stay behind, when we leave next week."

Rory liked Merleen very much—he was blunt and amusing and very good with a weapon, from the sparring he'd seen out his office window—but also had the impression Merleen was anxious to return to the forest and to the rest of his tribe. It was understandable, considering the ultra-civilization of Beaulieu and its many high walls might certainly be stifling to someone who had grown up in the forest, living in a tent, always on the move, never being settled.

"Have you spoken to him about this?" Rory asked.

Shaheen nodded. "He is willing to remain behind. I intend him to be a bridge, between Fontaine and the Mecant, if that is acceptable to you."

"Of course it is acceptable, and an excellent idea." Rory mentally kicked himself for not thinking of it first. The Mecant, their ways slowly being lost, would need to adapt or die out. And Shaheen, like every good ruler, was doing her utmost to assist in that transformation.

"Then it is settled," Shaheen said, a small, mysterious smile blooming on her face. "I think he will discover that his place here will do him much good."

Rory was not quite as certain, but envied Shaheen's confidence.

"How do you know?" he asked, leaning forward and setting his elbows on the desk. "How do you know what is the right thing and what is the wrong path to take? I find myself constantly questioning whether I am making the best choices for Fontaine, and in a lesser sense, for myself."

Shaheen was quiet for a long moment, contemplating his question. "I believe that your very doubt is what will make you a good leader, Your Majesty," she finally said. "You worry about your people. You place them above your own happiness and comfort, much of the time. You may not always know the right path immediately, but you search for it, and it is that quest that will bring peace and prosperity to Fontaine."

"Sometimes I am not always selfless," Rory admitted.

"You are a man, not a figurehead. You matter, too." Shaheen's voice was firm, and brokered no arguments.

"A man," Rory thought out loud, pondering her words.

"And tomorrow, you will also be a husband." Shaheen smiled.

The morning of the wedding and coronation dawned clear and cold, the bells in the very highest tower of Beaulieu ringing so brightly and so loudly that Gray thought, as he lay in his bath, that if Evrard was still in the Valley, he might have heard them.

To his surprise, it felt like the day passed very quickly. First, his bath, then being dressed—as of course, a future king of Fontaine could not possibly dress himself, even though he'd told everyone who would listen more than once that if he couldn't dress himself, he certainly wouldn't make a very competent king. But nobody wanted to listen to him, and they sent the valet in anyway. Gray, who had finally decided that it was worthless to argue when it felt like the entire court, including Rory, was against him, let the man dress him.

"You look very handsome, Your Majesty," the valet said, voice worshipful as they both took in Gray's very fine reflection in the floor-to-ceiling mirror dragged into their bedchamber just for this occasion.

Gray's first inclination was to make a face at all the glittering silver and gold embroidery on his forest green tunic, but he could hear Evrard's voice in his head, asking, is that what a king would do? Gray knew the answer to that particular question—and this time, decided that he should be embracing this new change, instead of constantly fighting it. He'd have to send Rowen one of the biggest floral arrangements as an apology for being difficult.

It was different; thinking of others first, instead of himself, but he'd already had some practice, because from nearly the first moment he'd met Rory, he'd been putting him first.

He straightened and without any silly or gross expressions, looked at himself seriously.

He'd turned out as tall and broad as Gideon had always hoped. As he looked, Gray realized the evergreen of the tunic, trimmed with all that silver and gold thread, as well as the broad red epaulets—distinguishing him as royalty and not merely a high-born noble—actually suited him. His breeches were supple and butter-smooth leather, fitting to his legs like they had been tailored just for him, and to Gray's embarrassment, they actually had been. His dark hair shone under the candlelight of the chandelier overhead, and though his head was bare now, a brand-new crown that Rory had commissioned especially for him was waiting in the throne room, for the moment of his crowning. It combined the fiercely sparkling amber of the traditional crowns of Fontaine with the deep green emeralds of Ardglass. A special piece that Gray knew Rory hoped would help establish his blending of both heritages.

He reached for the final touch; his leather and gold sword belt, from which always hung Lion's Breath.

"Wait," the valet said, reaching out to stop him, "the King left especial instructions that you should wear this instead." He indicated an even more ornate belt made of gold links and more amber and emeralds.

"But I can't wear a sword with that," Gray objected.

The valet frowned. "A sword would completely ruin the line of your ceremonial tunic," he said.

It felt wrong leaving Lion's Breath behind, like he was only half-dressed. For the last eight months, the sword had been always at his side or in his hand. But then, Gray reasoned with himself, practically all of Marthe's army would be guarding the outside of Beaulieu, as well as inside the castle and even the throne room itself, for the ceremony. Of all days, he shouldn't need to carry Lion's Breath. He was being crowned a king, not a general. Certainly anyone of importance or with any influence already knew he bore Lion's Breath. It was hardly a secret. He did not need to have the extra reminder today, of all days. Not when Rory was about to place a crown on his head.

Gray reached for the jeweled belt, and told himself the weird voice in his head, begging him to reconsider, wasn't the remnant of Evrard's influence, but merely what remained of his nerves.

"Excellent, sir," the valet said and helped to position the jeweled belt around his middle. "I believe you are ready, Your Majesty."

"I'm something," Gray said under his breath, looking one last time in the mirror. The next time he saw himself, he would be a king, and perhaps even more life-changing, Rory's husband.

"Shall we meet the King's party?" the valet inquired and Gray nodded.

A few minutes found them outside the hallway of the throne room. Ironically right where it felt like his entire journey to the throne began; when they'd sneeked into Beaulieu in an attempt to remove Sabrina from both life and power. Anya was already there, her armor shining and her eyes sparkling. She was carrying his length of embroidered cloth that she had labored over. Gray had decided that she needed to be the one to present it to him at the appropriate moment, so he could bestow it upon Rory.

Rory approached with several of his guard surrounding him. He was dressed in finery typical of the Autumn Prince —golds and burnt oranges with a bright turquoise silk cape falling from one shoulder. A delicately wrought gold crown with carnelians, amber, and topaz adorned his head. He looked stunning, a fairy tale brought to life, and somehow all Gray's own.

"We would like a minute," Rory finally said, staring at his betrothed. The guards around them moved away, but Gray noticed that they did not leave entirely. Smart, considering he was not wearing Lion's Breath and the trespasser had yet to be caught.

"You look . . ." Gray reached out and took Rory's hands, laughing self-consciously. "I'm afraid words fail me."

Rory's eyes shone just as brightly as the jewels crowning his brow. "From the first moment, I have never looked away from you. Whether you are as beautiful as you are this day, or are stooped and worn and aged, I will love you all the same," Rory vowed. "One kiss before all the dull ceremonial processes?" he asked hopefully.

"Just one?" Gray teased.

"I'm not sure we have time for much else," Rory said earnestly, "and if we are off-schedule, Rowen may cry and that would be a catastrophe."

"Marthe wouldn't be very happy with us," Gray agreed. "One kiss, then."

"And make it a good one," Rory suggested, with a twinkle in his eye that promised that he knew Gray would apply himself properly whether he reminded him to or not.

Gray did as asked, his hand sliding to the small of Rory's back as he bent them both back, and captured Rory's perfect mouth with his own. He kissed him deeply, feeling Rory's fingers come to clutch at his shoulders, and then smooth back his hair as he pulled back just enough to see the shine of his beloved's eyes.

"Promise me something," Rory said softly.

"Anything," Gray vowed.

"Kiss me like that at least once each day, for the rest of our lives?"

Gray chuckled. "Like what?"

"Like you love me more than you imagined you could, and you're surprised by it every single moment."

"I think that can be arranged," Gray said, and reaching down, tucked Rory's hand into his own. "Are you ready to get married?"

"I've never been more ready," Rory said, his smile luminous and happier than Gray had ever seen it.

They walked down the central aisle hand in hand, their progress slow but stately, and even though Gray knew he was supposed to be staring ahead, expression solemn, he couldn't help sneaking a look every foot or so, smile breaking through his serious demeanor. He'd been so afraid that at the last moment, he'd be nervous and terrified and sure they had made all the wrong decisions, but instead, all he felt was the unimpeachable rightness of this moment.

Marthe, in her golden armor with a stern countenance, was to hear their vows between themselves, and then Gray's vows to Fontaine.

"I'm but a general of an army," she had protested, because she never wanted to make more of her position than she should, but Rory had held up a hand, quieting her argument.

"You are the most right person I know for us to make our vows to," he'd insisted. "You saved my life, you made it possible for us to regain the throne of Fontaine. You hold the armies, while we hold the support of the people of Fontaine. Who else should we make such vows to?"

Finally, Marthe had conceded the point, and as they stood in front of her, Gray could think of only one additional person—or one additional unicorn—who would have been more appropriate for Rory and him to swear their fealty in front of. But Evrard wasn't here, and he wasn't going to be here. Gray needed to let that go, no matter how much it stung. He refocused on Marthe, who was giving the short welcome.

"Ladies and gentlemen of Fontaine, of this royal court, we are here today to see our king pledge his faith and his hand to Prince Graham, his consort and his protector, and for Prince Graham to return his own promises, both to our king and to the kingdom. Will you hear their pledges?"

A rush of sound met Gray's ears. He'd been most concerned about this section of the ceremony, as there was a definite possibility that the court would not want to hear their pledges. But it seemed that was hardly a problem at all. All Gray saw was smiles and encouragement reflected back at them from the crowd.

Everyone loves a wedding, Evrard echoed in his head. Gray supposed he'd been right the whole time. It was only too bad he wasn't here so Gray could tell him so and Evrard could gloat properly.

"I, King Emory of Fontaine, take you, Prince Graham of Ardglass, to be no other than yourself. Loving what I know of you, trusting what I do not yet know, I will respect your integrity and have faith in your abiding love for me, through all our years, and in all that life may bring us." Rory's fingers tightened on Gray's own, like he was trying to calm their trembling, and Gray understood. His own heart was thumping irregularly, excited and a tiny bit terrified.

"I, Prince Graham of Ardglass, take you, King Emory of Fontaine, to be no other than yourself. I take your faults and your strengths, as I offer myself to you with my own failings and successes. I will do everything in my power to help you when you need help, and vow to turn to you when I need assistance. I choose you as the person with whom I wish to spend the rest of my life." Gray took a deep breath as Anya took a step forward and extended the embroidered cloth, which he took. He ignored the rustle that went through the crowd; they were surprised, but it remained to see if it was a good or bad surprise. "And now I will pledge my past, and my present, and my future to you, and your kingdom. My promise is represented by this tapestry, illustrated with the story of my birth, and of the most important journey of my life—my journey to finding you."

Rory reached up and wiped a single, crystalline tear from his cheek. "Nothing would honor me more," he said, letting Gray wind the cloth around his neck and cinch it down by his turquoise sash. The golden threads echoed his eyes and as Gray caught a glimpse of Evrard, immortalized in silver thread, he realized that Anya had made sure that he was present for this most important day.

"Now that you have made your pledges to one another . . ."

A snarl rose from the crowd, and Marthe hesitated, Gray's gaze immediately dropping from Rory, to scanning the crowd.

It parted, and stalking towards the dais where he and Rory stood was Count Aplin, looking worse for the wear. Mud smeared up one side of his silvery tunic, his hair looked as if he had just ridden for hours, and his eyes were wild and unfocused.

Panic lanced through Gray in a sickening rush as the guards stepped in front of the Count, who with a single wave of his hand, sent them toppling backwards in a frightening rush of power.

"Guards," Marthe called out, and Anya stepped in front of Gray and Rory, pulling her sword from its sheath.

But Gray knew it wouldn't do anything, not when the Count was clearly the magic user who had utilized Sabrina's lair in the catacombs, and who had tried to enact a dangerous spell, before he'd been interrupted.

Or had he been interrupted? Gray wasn't sure if he had or not, but his deepest fear was that the only one who could stop Aplin was him and the magic of Lion's Breath. Gray reached for the sword, and only realized, after his fingers closed around dead air, that he had stupidly allowed himself to be dressed without it today. Today, of all days, he was unprotected, and Aplin was possibly going to murder both him and his almost-husband before Marthe could even complete the wedding vows.

"Ah," Aplin cackled, "missing something, Your Majesty?" His snide tone made it horrifically clear that he had interfered with the valet, and made sure that when Gray dressed this morning, he would be without the one weapon that could possibly defeat the kind of magic that the Count wielded now.

"You will not get away with this!" Rory shouted, his tone deadly angry.

"Oh really?" Aplin questioned, brushing aside more fully armed guards like they were children's toys as he made his way even closer to the dais. Gray's heart constricted. "It seems as if I am. And very easily, too."

Gray clenched his fists. How could he have been so stupid? Maybe he was a king, but he was also protector of this kingdom, and of its ping, and he was failing utterly.

Marthe let out an appalled gasp as pieces of Aplin's face began peeling away to reveal an enormous silver serpent in his place.

"This is . . . really not good," Rory muttered between clenched teeth as Marthe drew her own sword and joined Anya in front of them. But Gray knew the two women, despite their experience and skill, would be no match for Aplin's magic. The only way he could be defeated would be with the purifying and cleansing fire of Lion's Breath, and without the sword, Gray could not hope to summon it.

He reached out and gripped Rory's hand. At least if they fell, they would fall together, and at least it would be in front of the entire court. Unlike Sabrina, who had carefully worked behind the scenes and concealed all evidence of her dark magic, Aplin was doing it front and center, stroking his ego with every slithering movement he made towards the group huddled at the back of the dais.

"I want you to run. You and Rory both," Marthe ordered under her breath. "Perhaps you can escape him, lose him in the halls of the castle."

"And expose more people to his dark treachery?" Rory shook his head. "This will end now. What he wants is me."

"You and that usurper," the serpent rasped out. "That foul-mouthed Ardglassian that you permitted to touch you, to protect you, to marry you. And then you were going to allow him to destroy the throne? I could not let him or you take that step."

The crowd gasped as the snake approached the group. Anya's grip tightened on her spear and she threw it with deadly accuracy—perhaps one of the best throws of her life. The serpent ducked at the last moment, its huge head wavering on its neck, sharp teeth shiny with venom in its great mouth. The spear glanced off its neck, but green blood flowed from the injury.

"He's not as strong as Sabrina was," Rory hissed. "He can be hurt."

"If one could get close enough," Marthe retorted testily.

It was a split-second decision that later, Gray wasn't sure he'd truly thought through at all. But the truth was, after the age of eleven, he'd never expected to be anything at all. He'd believed, without a single doubt, that a great life, a meaningful life had passed him by, and that any opportunity to truly change the world was gone. Rory's love had given him a glimpse of a different future, and it evolved even further with his new plan of crowning Gray King. But what else could give the most meaning to a life? Sacrificing his own for a greater purpose.

Gray reached out and grabbed the dagger from Anya's belt, and darting forward, moved past the protection of the two best warriors in Fontaine, so he could face the deadly serpent alone.

"Gray!" Rory cried out, but Gray blocked out the voice, because it already hurt that the beautiful future that he'd hoped for with Rory was going up in flames. But he could do this.

He ducked as the great head swung, its jaw snapping shut and just missing his arm. Rolling closer, he eyed the exposed underbelly of the snake, hoping that it was as vulnerable as its real-world counterparts. He poised, hoping to strike with the dagger, praying it would be deadly enough to stop the Count from continuing his attack, but before he could swing with it, flames suddenly erupted out of the pointed end.

The serpent reared back, screeching as flames engulfed him. Gray, as surprised as the first time Lion's Breath had summoned its deadly magic, couldn't believe that this little dagger, of no ancestry whatsoever, was summoning the same flames the ancient sword had.

Abruptly, it was over, the remains of Aplin smoking on the marble floor, a horrified hush spreading through the enormous chamber.

"Gray!" Rory yelled, running towards him, after finally loosening Marthe's grip. He fell to his knees next to Gray, who dropped the dagger like it had scorched him, even though the metal was as cool as the first moment he'd held it. "Oh god, what happened?"

Gray stared at his almost-husband. "I don't know . . . I didn't have the sword. I just thought I could hurt it, hurt him. Enough to maybe stall him, maybe give Anya another shot, enough to save you."

Rory was crying, tears dripping down his cheeks as he clutched at Gray's shoulders. "You insane idiot, you saved me, you saved us all." He put his head in the crook of Gray's shoulder and hugged him fiercely.

"I think . . ." Marthe approached now, her voice as uncertain as Gray had ever heard it. He supposed that it wasn't every day a gigantic serpent was burned to ash in front of her. "I think it is my utmost honor to pronounce you committed partners and Kings of this realm." She extended her hand and Gray realized that she carried in it his new crown. Rory glanced back, and smiled, taking it in his own two hands. Gray, who had knelt down to be closer to Rory, found he did not have to move at all. So it came to be that in front of the smoldering ruins of their second-worst foe, Prince Graham of Ardglass became King Graham of Fontaine, and to his own shock and his husband's, the entire court erupted into wild applause.

CHAPTER TWENTY-FIVE

A WEEK LATER, IT was as if a magical fight had never happened in the throne room. The ash from Aplin's body had been cleared away, and the floor cleaned. A second throne had been moved to join the first, and today, in their first audience as Kings, Gray and Rory sat side by side, holding hands across the space between their respective seats.

"Your Majesties," Anya said, approaching the platform they were sitting on, "one last report, this is a message from the unit you sent to track Rinard. He has not been found, and no trace of him exists."

Gray sighed. He had not expected Rinard to be found, not after what had happened to his consort in this very room, but the effort had been the very least Gray could do, now that he was nominally in charge of the defense of Fontaine. Still, it did appear from Anya's reports, mostly given in her guise as the head of the new informant network, that the nobles had mostly, if not entirely, pledged their support to the new Kings.

"And," Anya continued, "I believe that is everyone who has submitted a proposal to be heard before you."

Gray let out a breath he hadn't known he was holding. He knew he'd been trained, at least until age eleven, to be a king, but he'd discovered that king-ing was not as simple as he'd believed it was when he'd been a child. It was complicated and difficult and mostly involved making a lot of compromises and then couching those in such attractive terms that everyone believed they'd gotten their own way, when in fact nobody had. And it turned out, he did have a surprising affinity for it. Or maybe that was the man at his side, who had believed in him, and who he believed in, to the very last breath in his body.

"See?" Rory said with a bright grin. "It was not so bad, was it?"

"Well," Gray grumbled, because it had still been slightly stressful. He hadn't been entirely sure he was going to convince John the farrier to accept only three cows for his daughter's hand in marriage, and not five. But love had prevailed, as love had only a week ago, and now the farrier's daughter was going to marry the farmer.

Gray decided it had a pleasant symmetry.

"You did great," Rory said, leaning in to give him a quick kiss.

"You were . . . tolerable," Gray teased, and then turned to get up to lead Rory away from the throne room and hopefully to more pleasurable pursuits, but then out of the corner of his eye, he saw a sight he had never expected to see again.

Gray dropped Rory's hand and stood up slowly with shock racing through every vein in his body.

"You . . ." Gray whispered as a man approached the dais. His face was as familiar to Gray as his own face, his own body, his own mind. He'd been sure a month ago, when they had left the Valley, that he would never again hear that voice, or that smug, certain tone ever again.

And like so many other countless times, Evrard had made sure that Gray was wrong.

"Your Majesty," the man said, bowing, "I would like to offer my stewardship services to the throne of Fontaine."

"You would?" Gray knew his own voice was strangled, but he wasn't as young as he once had been, when he'd been equally as shocked.

"I have heard," the man continued, as if Gray hadn't spoken, "that you had a bit of excitement at your wedding, only last week."

Gray would have rolled his eyes but that was almost certainly not kingly, and likely he would never get away with anything un-kingly ever again. Especially not with the man currently standing in front of them around. "We did," Rory said, a puzzled expression on his face, as he approached where Gray and the man stood.

"I like to think that if I were on the job, nothing of that sort would ever happen again," the man said confidently.

"You would be able to prevent . . . a disgruntled member of the court from unearthing his predecessor's magical lair and turning into an enormous poisonous serpent, hell-bent on interrupting a royal wedding?" Rory asked archly. "That is quite a promise, indeed."

"Indeed," Gray echoed.

"I have much experience in negotiations, and on councils of various kingdoms. And . . ." The man flashed a knowing smile at Gray. "And much experience in educating future princes to be kings. I assume you do not have a child as of yet, but there is still time . . ."

"I would say so," Gray muttered. "We were just married."

"Regardless," the man said, "I offer you my services, such as they are."

"I think . . ." Rory hesitated. "I think we could find a place for you, good sir. And your name?"

The man flashed Gray's husband an incorrigible smile. "My name is Rhys, Your Majesty. And it is excellent to finally meet you."

Evrard will return in *Yours, Everlasting,* releasing in Spring 2022.

BETH'S BOOKS

FOOD TRUCK WARRIORS

Drive Me Crazy - Lucas is just looking for some summer fun while Tony wants it all. But when their undeniable chemistry heats up the food truck kitchen, all bets are off.

Kiss & Tell - a New Year's Eve novella set in the Food Truck Warriors universe. Jackson lives to work, but what happens when he runs into Greek food truck owner, Alexis? When midnight strikes, sparks fly, and two lives change forever.

Hit the Brakes - Tate has had a crush on famous football player Chase since high school. But what happens when Chase suggests they fake a relationship to give Tate's food truck a much-needed boost?

On a Roll - Sean and Gabriel accidentally named their food truck the exact same thing. Can they stop arguing about it long enough to fall in love?

Full Speed Ahead - Lennox isn't the only one keeping secrets. A stalker has discovered one about Ash, and when

Lennox intervenes, the electric chemistry between him and Ash erupts into something very much like love.

Wheels Down - Shaw isn't Ross' friend—Ross isn't sure he has friends, anyway—until he discovers that Shaw is actually so much more than just his friend. He's his lover, and his partner, and his salvation.

Ride or Die - Ren & Seth's story and the final Food Truck Warriors novel. Can Seth woo and win Ren's bad boy heart once and for all?

KITCHEN GODS - Available on audio

Complete Box Set - including all four novels, and additional bonus content.

Bite Me - Miles' and Evan's story. They were sure they were enemies . . . until they were sure they weren't.

Catch Me - Wyatt and Ryan's story. Their relationship is completely fake . . . until it isn't.

Worship Me - a short story about Matt and Alex from Catch Me.

Savor Me - Xander and Damon's story. They're partners in a new restaurant . . . until they're so much more.

Indulge Me - Kian and Bastian's story. Working together is a necessity, but their mutual love? It's every bit an unnecessary indulgence.

LOS ANGELES RIPTIDE

The Rivalry - Rival. Enemy. Teammate. Friend. Lover. Two very different quarterbacks end up playing for the same team, fighting for the same starting spot - and end up fighting for each other, too. *Available on audio.*

Rough Contact - Their romance is forbidden. Their love is a secret. Neal and Jamie are the Romeo and Juliet of football - with all the feels, and much less tragedy.

The Red Zone - With Alec's help, Spencer can change everything about his life he's come to hate. An extraordinary future—and an undeniably extraordinary man—are waiting for him.

STAR SHADOW

Complete Box Set - including all four novels, and an exclusive short story.

Terrible Things - a little grittier, a little darker, a little more terrible. A rock star romance. Available on audio.

Impossible Things - Benji & Diego's story, and the sequel to Terrible Things. Available on audio.

Hazardous Things - Felix's had a crush on Max forever. But he's straight. Ish. Right?

Extraordinary Things - The final book of the Star Shadow series. Revisits Leo & Caleb's love story.

STANDALONES

Merry Elf-ing Christmas - a North Pole elf who doesn't belong, and an engineer who doesn't realize what he's missing in his life is Christmas magic. Coming November 18.

The Rainbow Clause - Shy NFL quarterback meets immovable object AKA the journalist assigned to write his coming out profile. Sparks are definitely gonna fly. Available on audio.

All Screwed Up - David is Griffin's annoying contractor. So why does Griffin want David to nail him? An enemies to lovers romantic comedy co-authored with Brittany Cournoyer.

Snow Job - Micah & Jake have always been enemies. They used to be stepbrothers. But they could be so much more.

Taste on my Tongue - Kitchen Wars is the hottest new reality show on TV, but pop star Landon can't even turn an oven on. Will baker Quentin be able to give him a culinary education so they can win?

Wrapped with Love - Losing Jordan is the biggest regret of Reed's life. Will Secret Santa and a little holiday magic be able to repair what was broken?

Fairytale of LaGuardia - Once upon a holiday season, a hockey player and a baseball player walked into a bar . . .and the rest is history. A Christmas story co-authored with A.E. Wasp.

Musical Notes - Two teachers with nothing in common, except a high school musical that's only three weeks away from Opening Night.

ENCHANTED FOLKLORE

Yours, Forever After - a lost Prince, a lonely bookworm and a surprisingly chatty unicorn go on the quest of a lifetime to save their kingdoms from an evil sorceress. Now available in the Complete Edition, featuring an epilogue novella.

Yours, Everlasting - Evrard . . .Rhys . . .Evander . . . Evander has gone by many names in his thousands of years alive. He's also lived many lives. But while he may have left his past as the Guardian of Secrets behind, it refuses to stay buried.

ABOUT BETH

A lifelong Pacific Northwester, **Beth Bolden** has just recently moved to North Carolina with her supportive husband. Beth still believes in Keeping Portland Weird, and intends to be just as weird in Raleigh.

Beth has been writing practically since she learned the alphabet. Unfortunately, her first foray into novel writing, titled *Big Bear with Sparkly Earrings*, wasn't a bestseller, but hope springs eternal. She's published twenty-eight novels and seven novellas.

Join Beth's Boldest, her Reader's Group
Subscribe to Beth's Newsletter
Follow Beth on BookBub
Facebook / Instagram / Twitter
www.bethbolden.com

Made in the USA
Coppell, TX
03 June 2023

17633773R10271